WILLOW FALLS

(MATT BANNISTER WESTERN 1)

KEN PRATT

Willow Falls
Ken Pratt

CKN Christian Publishing
An Imprint of Wolfpack Publishing
6032 Wheat Penny Avenue
Las Vegas, NV 89122

Paperback Edition

Paperback ISBN 978-1-64119-543-0

Library of Congress Control Number: 2018966732

*This book is dedicated to my friend, Phyllis Fread,
who from the beginning took an interest in Willow Falls. Well,
Mrs. Fread, it's finally done. I hope you enjoy it more than ever
before. Thank you, Mrs. Fread, for everything.*

ACKNOWLEDGMENTS

This book would not have been completed without the help of a number of wonderful individuals. First I must thank my wife, Cathy, for her support and endurance. It has been a long road to get this story completed and I couldn't have done it without you.

I must thank Shannon Trunde, who was the first to read Willow Falls and whose insight led to the prologue being written.

I must thank Allyssa Engberg, for taking the time out of her busy schedule to read this story. I appreciate your integrity and suggested changes. I have made those changes by the way.

I must thank Wanda McAlister for taking the time to edit this story. I appreciate your honesty and the way you take the time to teach, rather than simply fix. You have made me a better writer.

And to my friend, Dr. Dewey Bertolini, whose Bible teachings and books have been heavily borrowed from for this story.

You are all appreciated!

WILLOW FALLS

PROLOGUE

Cheyenne, Wyoming
September 1882

Reverend Peter Ramsey looked with pride and wonder at his youngest daughter, Hannah, while she stared lovingly into the eyes of Mike Tolleth, her husband to be. She wore a white wedding dress and veil that covered her youthful face as her father finished the wedding ceremony in front of the guests.

Reverend Ramsey hesitated while he looked at his daughter with tears brimming his eyes. The years of her youth passed by too quickly; it didn't seem so long ago when she was learning how to walk and then quickly how to run. He recalled wiping dirt off of her scraped knees with every fall and wiping away her precious tears as the hurts were kissed away. He recalled summer nights laying outside in the cool grass talking under the stars. Each year of her twenty years was its own treasure and the memories of her growing up flooded by quickly. She was the youngest of his eight children and perhaps his most cherished. Hannah had

1

become a beautiful young woman with a heart as pure and fine as her mother's. In a few moments, she would no longer be Hannah Ramsey, the Reverend's daughter; she would become Mrs. Michael Tolleth. She would move out and the Reverend's large home would be empty after all these years. How a child can grow up so quickly right before his very eyes, he didn't understand. A twenty-year prison sentence was considered a lifetime, but twenty years to raise a child didn't seem nearly long enough.

Hannah stared into Michael's eyes, while she held his hands and waited for her father to finish the ceremony. She turned her head slightly towards the Reverend. "Father!" she whispered barely audible out of the corner of her mouth.

Reverend Ramsey smiled tightly. "Ladies and Gentle-men, I give you Mr. and Mrs. Michael Tolleth. Michael, you may kiss your bride." His eyes were thick with tears as Michael gently lifted Hannah's veil and kissed her lovingly. He watched proudly as the guests applauded appropriately within the church walls. The newlyweds quickly joined hands and walked down the center aisle outside where the reception was to be held. They were followed promptly by the guests.

Peter's wife of thirty-eight years met him in front of the pews and lovingly embraced him. "You made it through the ceremony," she remarked of the moisture that filled his eyes.

"Yeah, but barely," he answered with a smile. He held her close.

"Our child rearing is actually over, Peter. I never dreamed it'd come so quickly," came her muffled voice from his shoulder.

The Reverend nodded. "Come on, love," he said quietly, "let's go eat with our family." He walked his wife through the church holding her arm, like he had many years before when he married his bride.

The Reverend smiled at a lone man in his early thirties who was leaning against the back wall. The man wore dark pants with well-worn boots and a brand new white shirt with the sleeves buttoned at his wrists. He was a tall man with broad shoulders and appeared to be quite muscular. His face was tanned by the summer sun, with a neatly trimmed dark beard and mustache covering the lower features of his strong square-shaped handsome face. His long dark hair was pulled into a tight ponytail that fell just below his shoulders. In his left hand was a rolled up gun belt filled with cartridges and holstered Colt.45 peacemaker.

Peter shook his head with a smile. "You sure can clean up well, Matt. Thanks for coming." He shook Matt's hand firmly.

"It was a beautiful wedding. Congratulations, Reverend, Mrs. Ramsey," he nodded to her. His voice was soft and sincere.

"Well," the Reverend replied, "someday, we'll do your wedding here and it'll be beautiful, too," he said with a twinkle in his eye.

Matt smirked slightly. "Oh, we'll see."

Joan Ramsey asked, "Are you staying for the reception, Matt?"

"For a bit," he answered.

"Well, let's go eat. We raised half of that crowd out there and I'll tell you, Matt, if you want to eat; you'd better hurry and get into that chow line," Peter offered with a smile.

"Oh, there's plenty of food," Joan stated with an affectionate slap to his arm.

Matt smiled a touch. "I grew up in a big family too."

"Oh, you did?" the Reverend asked with interest. "How

many siblings do you have?" He had known Matt for a number of years, but he hardly knew anything about Matt's family. He wasn't an easy man to get to know beyond the Sunday morning common courtesies before and after church.

"Five," Matt answered without any other explanation. A subtle sadness came over his face. So subtle it was that the Reverend wondered if anyone else would've even noticed it.

"Brothers or sisters?"

"Both. I have four brothers and one sister. She's the youngest," Matt said without offering more.

The Reverend Peter Ramsey smiled. "Is your little sister married?"

Matt nodded. "Yeah."

"I'll bet he's a perfect gentleman having you as a brother-in-law, isn't he? I can't imagine he'd want to step too far out of line with your sister. She's probably a little tough herself after growing up with five brothers. Especially, if all of your brothers are like you." Peter laughed and then asked, "Are they?"

Matt shook his head sadly and answered softly, "No, I don't think so."

Twenty minutes later, Matt sat comfortably on the church's front steps enjoying a piece of chicken with a group of men. They talked about the weather and preparing their homesteads for the winter's bitter bite. Like everyone in Wyoming, the year's work was tested ultimately by how prepared they were for the long months of winter. It was mid-September and that meant time was short to harvest, can and preserve every bit of the goods that they could. Fill their barns with hay and grain, and winterize both their homes and outbuildings. No one knew what winter would bring or for how long, so every household, if it was to survive, needed to be prepared.

Grant Wilson was an older man who happened to be the biggest hay grower in the Cheyenne area. He was tanned darkly with short gray hair and a clean-shaven face. He leaned against one of the stair rails and asked, "How's your winter stock, Matt? You've been pretty quiet."

"I bought a couple cords of wood from Cleavis and his sons. They've got it ricked up behind my house. I bought a new blanket," he offered with a shrug. He looked up to eye Grant with a slight smile. "As far as food goes, I'm at the mercy of the butcher shop and restaurants."

"You and many others, I'm afraid," Grant replied. "Ten years ago a guy could shoot a couple of buffalo and it would keep through the winter well into spring, all for the price of the bullet and salt. They're getting harder to come by now days. Same with venison though, now we're all kind of forced into eating beef through the winter. Unless, you go a half-days ride to hunt wild game."

The bride, Hannah Tolleth, shouted out loudly, "Matt." She was sitting at one of the three long tables packed with family and friends. They all seemed to be looking at Matt with a grin. She continued, once she got his attention, "My new grandmother-in-law came out here from Philadelphia for our wedding. And she wants to know why you brought your gun to my wedding?"

Matt answered seriously, "Your father paid me to make sure Michael stayed at the altar!"

Hannah's laughter was a joyful sound. Many others, including the visiting grandmother, joined the laughter.

Reverend Peter Ramsey, with his usual large smile, got up from his table and walked over to where Matt and the other men were talking. "That was funny," he said with a laugh.

"Now, we'll just pray that Matt will meet his perfect mate. We'll all have to bring our guns to keep him and her at the altar!" the Reverend emphasized with a laugh.

Matt smiled, but it was young Paul Wilson, Grant's seventeen-year-old son who answered quickly, "Matt's gonna wear his own gun to his wedding, so she doesn't run out on him!" he joked.

Matt glanced at Paul with an appreciative smile. Peter and the others laughed.

Wally Simpson spoke as soon as the initial laugh ended. "My cousin, Joy, is single, you know. She isn't as pretty as she once was, but she's as sweet and caring as can be," he offered to Matt.

Paul replied disdainfully, "She's a wh... I mean a prostitute," he corrected himself. He knew how much Reverend Ramsey hated the word, "whore."

"No!" Wally corrected quickly. "She was, but she gave all that up."

"She still was," Paul stressed with a hint of indignation.

Reverend Ramsey replied softy to Paul, "So was Mary Magdalene, Paul. When she met Jesus he didn't condemn her, nor did any of his disciples. The only ones that wanted to condemn her were the Pharisees. In some ways, I think we Christians become like the Pharisees when we look at non-believers. Joy gave her life to the Lord and repented from prostitution. The Bible says she became a new creation in Christ, and her old ways are passed away. Forgiven and forgotten. The question I have is why do we still hold it against her? That's what the Pharisees did." He posed the question to the youthful Paul Wilson.

He continued, "We need to remember the Lord gives

second chances in life. It is a tragedy when the Lord's own people won't accept a new creation in Christ, because we are ashamed to be acquainted with them. It is truly a shame! Jesus was never ashamed of Mary Magdalene, never once! So why are we?" he questioned to the listening men. He didn't expect an answer. It was a question for the men to think about on their own.

Matt had been listening to the Reverend talk when his attention went to a young girl in a pretty yellow dress, playing with some other children in the grass behind Reverend Ramsey. The young girl was about nine or ten with long dark curly hair that fell down her back. She was arguing with an older boy about who was going to be the teacher over a group of younger children. She playfully pointed her finger at the boy while she lightheartedly laid down the final say without a thought of backing down.

Melancholy filled Matt as he recognized a similarity to his little sister as she smiled gleefully at winning the bid to be the teacher. She had a group of five or six younger children sitting on the grass as she began to teach her class with overly animated hand gestures and lectured on the fundamentals of spelling. It was uncanny how her voice sounded so similar to the way Annie's did all those years ago. Matt's chest tightened and a deep well of emptiness began to grow within him. Unexpected emotions from long ago were resurrected and cut deeply into his soul.

"Is something wrong, Matt?" the Reverend asked. Matt seemed lost in his thoughts. "Matt," he stated a touch louder, getting Matt's attention. The Reverend was taken back slightly by how suddenly a man's demeanor can change; a moment ago Matt seemed joyful and even smiling a little. Now he was near tears for no apparent reason. "Are you all right, Matt? You seem troubled."

"No, I'm fine," Matt answered without enthusiasm and faked a small smile before allowing his eyes to go back to the group of children. He couldn't keep his eyes off of the little girl that looked like Annie. She literally took his breath away with every facial expression and word she'd say. Time travel was an impossibility, but if it wasn't, he'd swear he had traveled back fifteen years ago before he ever left home.

Reverend Ramsey said, "I probably need to get back over to my family. Thank you all for coming."

"I wouldn't miss it, Peter," Grant remarked. "I've watched Hannah grow since she was knee high. We're all family here."

The Reverend smiled appreciatively. "Yes, we are."

"Well, Paul," Grant spoke to his son, "we might wanna get your mother and sister and get back home." A sudden scream of a terrified girl got his attention on the corner of the street. He began to move towards the corner as he asked, "You guys wanna come help me settle these men down?"

At the corner, two cowboys, probably just off the trail, were pushing around a young Negro boy, who was about fourteen or so. His younger sister, who was about eight, stood with her hands over her face crying. Her voice pleaded with a high-pitch, "He didn't do anything, sirs! Please don't!"

She screamed again as one of the cowboys hit her brother in the face. The force of the blow caused the boy to fall to the ground quickly. He curled into a ball to protect himself from the kicks to his ribs and face that followed. The cowboy that kicked him appeared to be exhilarated by the sound of the boy's cries. The little girl ran forward to help her brother, but was scooped up and contained within his arms of the other cowboy. She screamed loudly and fought helplessly to free herself.

8

"Good heavens!" the Reverend exclaimed.

Matt grabbed his gun belt and briskly walked towards the two cowboys.

"Matt, wait up," Grant called. He and the other men couldn't keep up with Matt's determined pace, though they slowed to a near stop when they saw Matt pull his revolver out of its holster as he approached the cowboys. The boy was curled up in a fetal position trying his best to protect himself when the cowboy delivered another kick into the boy's ribs.

Matt raised his gun quickly at the man that kicked the boy. In a loud and threatening voice, he ordered dangerously, "Touch that boy again and I'll put a hole through your head!"

Both cowboys were surprised to see a gun pointed at them. "Whoa!" the more aggressive cowboy yelped, automatically raising his hands and stepped back. "There's no reason to point your gun, fella. This ain't your concern, I'm sure," he stated with his hands raised defensively.

Matt stepped closer without a word and quickly lifted his revolver and forcefully slammed the butt of the Colt's grip into the cowboy's nose. The force of the blow broke his nose and sent the man down to the ground suddenly with a blood-covered face.

The other cowboy tossed the girl aside and quickly went for his sidearm; he froze as Matt quickly turned his gun onto him. Matt's voice was cold as steel, "Finger that gun and you're dead!" he warned. "Drop the gun belt."

"You son of a..." the aggressive cowboy hollered from the ground. He looked at the blood on his hands through his watering eyes. "You jest started a fight you can't finish!" he yelled and looked up at Matt with rage on his face. "Don't drop your gun, Everett! He can't kill us both at the same time!" He began to stand.

"But I will kill you!" Matt's voice stated simply. His gun was still leveled at Everett. He pulled the hammer back until it clicked.

The sound of the Colt.45 being cocked brought time to a standstill. Even the bloody cowboy rising from the ground froze mid-stride in disbelief. He was unsure of what the stranger would do if he stood straight up or made a move for his gun. Only an experienced killer stayed so calm when his gun was cocked and aimed at another man. The well-dressed man was obviously a professional gunfighter and Everett's life was really in danger. The bleeding cowboy no longer felt the need to revenge his blood being spilt to save his pride. At the moment, he just wanted to walk away with his friend, Everett, still alive. He was relieved when an older man in a suit stepped between the experienced gunman and Everett.

The Reverend, Peter Ramsey spoke with great concern in his voice. Like everyone, he was afraid of what could happen. He spoke quickly, "Gentlemen, this is Matt Bannister. I would put your guns down. There is no reason for anyone to get shot over this. So please, lay your gun belts down," he repeated softly. He then turned to Matt and spoke just as softly, "Put your gun away, Matt."

"You're Matt Bannister?" Everett asked in surprise.

"Get out of my sight!" Matt warned severely, neither lowering his weapon an inch nor requiring the two men to drop theirs. His eyes were hard and didn't leave the eyes of either man for long.

"Come on, Harold, let's just walk away," Everett said. He then offered to Matt, "We didn't want any trouble, Mr. Bannister."

Harold, with blood running down his face, eyed Matt in awe. He was stunned to learn the name of the man who had broken his nose. As tough as Harold was, he knew right then how lucky he was to be walking away alive. Matt Bannister was a name known far and wide with a reputation for killing. He was a man to fear, and getting a good look at him, Harold did!

Matt asked before either Harold or Everett could speak. "Is beating an innocent boy fun to you?" he asked harshly. Anger burned in his eyes as he glared at the men.

Harold explained quickly as best he could, "He bumped into me. The nigger was trying to steal my money!"

From the ground the boy replied painfully through his tears, "That ain't true, sir. He ran into me on purpose."

"Ah, shut up!" Harold looked like he wanted to kick the boy again.

Matt leveled his gaze towards Harold. "Get out of my sight. Men like you make me sick!"

"Sorry, Mister Bannister," Everett apologized meekly. He backed up slowly and carefully turned and moved on down the street with his friend, Harold.

Matt looked at the boy who was slowly standing up with the help of his little sister and Wally. The Reverend stared at Matt wordlessly. He was wondering why Matt's eyes suddenly grew so soft and moist when they fell upon the boy and his sister after such dangerous fury a moment before.

"Are you all right, Joseph?" Matt asked with great caring in his voice.

"My name's not Joseph. It's Charlie," the boy said wiping a little blood off his lip and the tears off his cheek. He was dressed poorly like his younger sister.

"What?" Matt asked almost incoherently. His eyes grew

thick with tears and his breathing grew heavy enough that he seemed to choke over the word.

"My name's Charlie. I didn't do nothing. They just hit me for no reason," the boy explained.

"Well, you're fine now young fella," Wally Simpson offered.

Matt's expression contorted painfully as he focused deeply on the young man's face. "Go home," he barely said with a quivering voice. He then abruptly walked away wordlessly down the street slipping his gun back in its holster and wrapping his gun belt around his waist as he walked.

"I wonder what's wrong with him," Grant Wilson asked perplexed. He had never witnessed Matt act that way before, nor of course, had any of the others.

The Reverend shook his head. "I have no idea."

"Do you think we should go after him?" Grant asked with concern in his voice.

The Reverend shook his head slowly as he watched Matt walking away. "No. No, let's let him be."

A SINGLE LANTERN lit the inside of Matt's two-room home. It was nothing more than a simple clapboard shack with a cook stove, along a city block of many others. A square table with two wooden chairs, a ripped up padded bed and gun rack were about it for furnishings. The home was dark, empty, and bare of any decorations of any kind. Matt sat at the table with a full bottle of whisky, a shot glass and his Single Action Colt.45 revolver with Cherry wood grips laying in front of him. He poured a shot of the whiskey and drank it quickly then poured another.

He never drank whiskey, but at the moment it was the only answer he could find to numb the hopelessness that filled him. He had been all over Wyoming and the surrounding states from the Mexican border clear to Canada's. He'd spent years out under the stars on horseback and entered towns of all sizes and dealt with people of all colors, but he had never in all that time experienced anything like what he had today. The little girl in yellow looked so much like Annie that it was hauntingly uncanny. All too suddenly he was reminded of a time fifteen years ago when he belonged to a family and close to his siblings. Annie would be twenty-seven now and if he saw her on the street, he doubted that he'd recognize her. He had run away from home for reasons that had nothing to do with his family. Seeing the little girl at the wedding reminded him of the family and the closeness he used to have before he left home. But seeing the young Negro, named Charlie, being beaten brought his deep-buried rage to the surface like a long dormant volcano exploding to life unexpectedly. It was a rage he'd tried to forget over the years, but it was only buried deeper with time. It would haunt him for as long as he lived.

Matt wiped the tears from his eyes. He stared bitterly at the empty shot glass with a scowl on his face. Life was supposed to be meaningful. It was supposed to have a purpose. He lived a day-to-day life of sorrow that never changed with each passing day. He hadn't smiled in years and couldn't remember the last time he had actually laughed.

"I'm sorry, Lord," he spoke softly as he looked up at the ceiling, "I can't do this anymore. I don't know what else to do," he wiped the tears from his eyes. "I wish they would've killed me, instead of Joseph. It's not fair, Lord. I give up, I don't have anything to live for, anyway. I just...don't! I'm empty, Lord, extremely empty. There's nobody who really cares about me. Sometimes, I wonder if you care about me. It sure doesn't seem like it."

He eyed his revolver lying on the table and picked it up slowly. "Jesus," he cried softly, "I ask for your forgiveness. Please forgive me, but I am done; I can't go on like this anymore. Please forgive me and accept me." He raised the revolver to his head and pulled the hammer back until it clicked. A tear rolled down his cheek as he closed his eyes.

His eyes opened slowly as a rare and loud knocking on his door caused him to lower his Colt. He closed the hammer as he did and set it on the table. Matt wiped his eyes before walking over to unlatch the lock on his door. He opened it carelessly. If it had been someone with a shotgun they could have killed him easily, however, he no longer cared.

It was Reverend Ramsey on the other side of the door. His smile faded the moment he saw Matt's sorrowful face. "May I come in, Matt?" he asked softly.

Matt nodded.

The Reverend saw the bottle of whiskey, shot glass and revolver all sitting on the table. He sat down on the extra wooden chair at the table across from Matt. For a moment neither said a word, leaving a striking awkwardness that became overbearing.

Peter spoke softly, "Do you want to talk about it?"

A tear fell down Matt's face as he stared at the tabletop.

The Reverend assured him, "It will go no further than this table. What you say will go no further than me. I believe you know that you can trust me."

Matt eyed the Reverend with wet and painfilled bloodshot eyes. "Peter, you're a good man. If I told you everything, you'd lose all respect for me."

The Reverend smiled slightly. "If I told you how human I was, you'd lose great respect for me, as well."

"It's different in my case, Peter."

"Tell me about it, Matt. By the appearance of it, you have nothing to lose by trusting me." He nodded at the whiskey bottle and the gun.

Matt smiled sadly. "How much time do you have?"

"I have all night. The only obligation I have is church at nine tomorrow morning. If I'm tired, so be it. Right now, you're my only concern."

It took over two hours for Matt to pour his heart out to Reverend Ramsey. He talked openly for the first time about the day his friend Joseph was murdered. He clarified the misconceptions about the day he'd killed all five members of the Dobson Gang. He talked about being in love with a girl and how her father, a Reverend himself, had ostracized and undermined him. He talked about the day when the girl he loved married his best friend unexpectedly. And for the first time he told the story of how one day fifteen years before, he left without saying goodbye to his family. Tears came and went as he spoke to the Reverend.

When Matt had finished, it was then that Reverend Ramsey said, "It sounds to me like you need to go back home."

Matt looked at him. "I can't."

"Why not?"

"I don't want to see Elizabeth, Peter. I don't want to see Tom. I don't know what my family will say to me, or if they'll want to see me. My brothers and sister are all close to each other... I'm the outcast. I could be forgotten by now."

"Matt, you'll never know until you go home. If you're not wanted, at least you'll know it. I have no doubt that you'll find your family's still there for you." He paused effectively.

"You need to go home, Matt. You won't be free until you do. You just need to pray and ask the Lord when you should go home." Peter shrugged and then added, "But you need to go home."

Matt looked at Reverend Ramsey sincerely. "I'm afraid to go home."

Peter smiled compassionately. "The Bible tells us three hundred and sixty-five times to 'fear not'. Once for every day of the year. With a God so intimate to plan that, he must mean it. Go home, Matt. You have nothing to lose and a family to gain."

1

December 1882

BRANSON WASN'T the first town in Oregon to meet the dreary settlers as they came west on the wagon trains. However, Branson was the first real city that offered anything and everything that the Eastern cities offered, or so it seemed after months on the trail. Branson had become a city of four thousand permanent residents and every wagon train brought a few new citizens. Some couldn't imagine a more beautiful place south of heaven and to others Branson's strong economy was the appeal. Employment was readily available in the timber industry or the silver mine which were the city staples. However, a growing epidemic of gold fever had also struck Branson since it had been discovered on the Modoc River and surrounding creeks. The community was growing quickly as men and women flocked to Branson to carve out a future with the riches of the West.

At the forefront of the expansion of Branson was Lee Bannister. He owned three saloons that financed the

Branson Home and Land Broker's Office. Lee bought and sold land, making him one of the largest multi-property owners in the county. Most of his properties were in or around Branson, including many rental homes and commercial buildings in prime locations to lease to businesses. Lee turned his profits around into buying new properties, lots to build on and investing in the stock of the timber and mining companies. His most treasured investment was the new "Monarch Hotel." It was Branson's only high cost elegant hotel with a fine dining restaurant and private gentlemen's lounge where the higher class patrons were able to socialize, gamble, drink the finest liquor, and have access to some to the most beautiful and costly women in the West.

Lee had started out with nothing, except a few dollars and an unyielding desire to succeed. Hard work, the courage to take risks, and bit of common sense had made Lee one of the wealthiest men in Branson. However, wealth wasn't enough for Lee; He wanted power and was determined to have it. He was already on the Branson Planning Commission, one of the three Jessup County Commissioners.

Lee stood at the bar in his expensively decorated parlor, pouring two drinks into elegant crystal glasses. "In two years, I plan on running for the State Senate, like Grandpa did. City and county politics are great stepping stones and they've helped build my business, but it's time to move up the ladder. Once my name's known around the state, I'll run for Congress and spend my time in Washington D.C. where the real power is. That's my goal, anyway. Here you go." Lee handed his brother a drink with a slight smile. The contrast between the two was vast. Lee was forty years old and dressed in clean black pants and a gleaming white shirt with a black bow tie hanging freely on his neck. He had short dark hair, combed neatly and a thick well maintained mustache on a clean-shaven face.

Matt Bannister was thirty-four and wore stained buckskin pants with fringed legs and matching moccasins on his feet. He had removed his buckskin shirt and now sat comfortably in a dirty blue shirt with the sleeves rolled up. He had long dark hair that fell carelessly onto his shoulders and he had an unkempt full-faced beard that hid his youth. Matt sipped his drink. "I've heard that you had become pretty prominent here in Branson."

"I've done alright," Lee stated as he sat on a red velvet davenport across from two matching chairs where Matt sat. "So is it odd to come home after all these years?" Lee asked.

Matt gave a small, but sad smile. "I don't know; I'm not home yet." He continued, "When I left, Annie was just a little girl. Now she's grown up, married and has kids of her own that are almost the same age she was when I left."

"Not quite," Lee said simply. "Ivan's her oldest, he's seven."

"Annie was twelve. It's going to be like meeting strangers. Chances are, I will hardly recognize Steven or Annie; they were so young when I left. Gosh, when I left, you were young, rowdy, and buying your first saloon. Now you're living...here." He raised his hands to encompass the parlor, "You're married to a beautiful woman and have two daughters that I've never met until a few hours ago. Tomorrow, I'll meet more nephews and nieces I didn't know I had."

"Well," Lee tried to sound comforting, "they all know about you."

"Hmm, I'm just a mysterious name to them. I hope when I leave I'm more of an uncle. You know, like the way our uncles were to us."

"I hope so," Lee agreed and left it at that. He eyed Matt

carefully noticing how tired and worn down he looked, not just physically, but emotionally as well. His eyes seemed to lack the joy of happiness or any other emotion for that matter, except perhaps sadness. It had been fifteen years since he had seen his younger brother or heard the sound of his voice. For all those years he had heard stories about Matt from time to time. Frequently over the years Lee had wished he could talk to Matt just one more time and now he finally had the opportunity to do so, but he wondered if he should. There was so much to ask, so much to say, but the one question that he and others had been asking for fifteen years was: *Why did he leave?* Rumors had started, and everyone back home in Willow Falls seemed to have their own answer, but the only answer Lee would believe was Matt's own.

"Can I ask you something, Matt?" Lee asked quietly.

"Sure."

"You left here without saying goodbye and once in a while you'd write a letter that let us know you were still alive. But my question is... why did you leave? It wasn't anything I did, was it?" He could never think of anything he'd done or said that would cause Matt to run away, but the nagging question still haunted him.

Matt smiled uncomfortably. "No, it had nothing to do with you." He shrugged uneasily and offered no more.

Lee's wife, Regina, walked into the parlor wearing a white cotton robe over her nightdress and sat down comfortably next to Lee. She was a beautiful woman in her late twenties with curly long black hair and large seductive brown eyes in a soft and pleasant face. She seemed to be a joyful woman, except when she looked at Matt. She eyed him now with great suspicion. Lee put a protective arm around her affectionately.

She turned her head towards Lee's ear and spoke softly, but loud enough to be overheard, "Did you tell him?" Lee shook his head in answer.

"Tell me what?" Matt asked with a growing anxiety.

"Remember your old girlfriend? The Reverend's daughter?" Lee asked.

"Yeah."

"Well, she married your old buddy, Tom. He's the sheriff now of Willow Falls."

Matt nodded knowingly. "They were married before I left."

"They were?" Regina asked sounding surprised.

"Yeah," Matt nodded, and sipped the last of his brandy.

"Oh," Lee said in thought, and then laughed lightly. "I don't know how to say this or even if I should, but Annie and Aunt Mary are going to tell you all about it. They swear by it, although, I can't possibly say..."

"I can." Regina offered with fact in her voice.

Lee continued, "Tom and his wife have a son, the oldest boy, who's about fourteen or fifteen. Anyway, Annie and Aunt Mary swear he looks like you. They say he's a Bannister. I've never seen him, but I know his name is Gabriel."

"I've seen him," Regina offered to Matt. "And now that I've seen you, even with your beard, I can say he does look like you."

"Really?" Matt asked quietly. "Fifteen you say?"

"I believe so," Lee answered.

"Is there a chance he's yours?" Regina asked curiously.

Matt tried to swirl the last drop of brandy in his glass. His eyes seemed to get lost in a deep thought of sadness as he stared at the empty glass.

Lee read the silence correctly. "I thought you said they were married?"

"They were," he replied softly. The expression on Matt's face, one of deep sorrow and emptiness didn't go unnoticed. It answered the question Lee and Regina couldn't come out and ask. It was possible that young Gabriel Smith was Matt's son. A son he had known nothing about.

"And that's why you left?" Lee asked carefully.

Matt nodded slowly. "Yes. Elizabeth's father wouldn't let us talk, let alone marry." Matt paused, "She married Tom, but she loved me, so she said anyway. She wouldn't leave him though, not even after we..." he trailed off and then added as he looked up for the first time, "So I left."

"I never knew that," Lee offered.

Matt nodded sadly. "No one did. Now, if you wouldn't mind, I'd like to get some sleep if I could. It's been a long day."

"Sure. Matt we don't know that this Gabriel's your kid. All I know is Annie and Aunt Mary think so. So... don't take our word for it, okay?" Lee clarified.

"I won't," Matt agreed as he stood up. He appeared quite worn down and tired.

"Oh, yeah," Lee offered as he and Regina both stood up as well. "Just so you know, we have a bathtub, so in the morning you can take a good long bath."

Matt laughed lightly. "I'd love to."

"And Mattie, our maid, can wash your clothes. She can even shave off that beard if you'd like," Lee hinted as gently as he could.

REGINA HADN'T SLEPT WELL. She was unnerved by the presence of a stranger with a murderous reputation sleeping in a room across the hall from her and her daughter's rooms. Lee had tried to reassure her that she could relax and sleep comfortably knowing Matt was family and certainly meant no harm. She reminded him that after fifteen years he didn't know his brother any better than she did.

For years she'd heard about Matt Bannister. The famous brother-in-law she had never met. The only time she'd hear something new about him was when the newspaper said he had killed someone else. *The Branson Gazette* kept the community updated about their local legendary gunfighter from Willow Falls. The local boy who had become famous throughout America for his fearless ability with his guns, and that was something that many people were proud of in Jessup County.

It was those same guns that he had carried into her home the night before. He had looked like the refuse of the buffalo hunters dressed in a long thick buffalo coat over his filthy buckskins and moccasins. He carried a Parker shotgun in his right hand, a Winchester rifle in his left, and his name-making Colt.45 on a gun belt around his waist. Cartridges filled the girth of the belt, except for four 12-gauge shells and a hunting knife in its sheath on the left side. With a well-used and ugly brown hat on his head and a pair of large saddlebags strung over his left shoulder, Matt had left a repulsive taste in Regina's mouth when she had first seen him. When she realized who he was and considered all she had heard about him, she felt sick to her stomach. It did not sit well with her to have such a man in her home, in her bathtub or sitting at her table for breakfast as she waited with Lee for Matt to come downstairs.

"Are you sure he's leaving today?" Regina asked Lee as he skimmed through the *Branson Gazette* from the day before.

"I think so," Lee answered.

"Well, will you find out when he's leaving and maybe,"

she lowered her voice carefully, "you could encourage him to go on to Willow Falls today."

Lee lowered his paper purposely and eyed her seriously. "I haven't seen my little brother in fifteen years, Regina. I'm not going to ask him to leave the morning after he arrives!"

"No, I didn't mean for you to. I just..." she hesitated.

"What?" Lee asked.

Regina took a deep breath. She chose her words carefully, "We don't know that we can trust him. He's your brother I know, but well..." she stopped as she heard footsteps coming down the staircase. Momentarily, Matt walked into the dining room wearing an old tan suit that belonged to Lee and a pair of Lee's boots. His long hair, was washed and pulled back into a tight ponytail that fell down over the back of his neck. His beard had been neatly trimmed and his upper cheeks and lower neck were shaven. Regina had to catch her breath Matt had cleaned up well.

He smiled as he pulled out a chair to sit at the table. "Thank you for the bed and bath. I feel a lot better," he replied cheerfully.

"You look better," Lee said approvingly. "Last night you looked like your dad."

"I wouldn't know," Matt chuckled lightly. "I haven't seen him in what seventeen, eighteen years?"

"I thought he came out to see you a few years back?" Lee questioned.

Matt shrugged. "I guess he did, at least that's what I heard. He even stayed at my place for a week or so. I was out of town the whole time he was there," he explained. "Do you see him?"

Lee nodded. "About once a year he'll come to town to visit. Dad's living in Portland and managing a saloon on the waterfront. He's got himself a woman and a small apartment above the saloon. It's quite a fall from what he used to have."

Matt sighed. "Well, luckily, I've never had to talk to him."

Regina spoke softly, "I think that's very sad."

"What? My father?" Matt asked as he looked at Regina fondly. She wore a dark green dress with black lace decorating the front. Her dark hair was pinned up exposing her elegant neck and her large brown eyes glimmered in the sunlight that shone through the dining-room windows. She looked absolutely beautiful.

"Yeah," Lee answered for her. "She thinks we're too hard on dad. She doesn't think we give him enough credit for the good things he did, like teaching you how to ride a horse and how to shoot your gun."

Matt scoffed with disgust. "The only thing I learned from my father is what *not* to do! I can't think of anything good he did for me, except leave us, possibly."

Regina spoke quickly in her own defense, "I never said that! All I've ever said is that you boys should forgive him. That's all he's ever asked for. That's why he went clear to Wyoming to see you. He just wanted to ask you to forgive him." She then suggested to Lee, "Maybe you should tell him about Mr. Swindall's book."

Lee smiled to himself. "Across town, there's a trading post that's selling a book called, '*The Biography of Matt Bannister*'. It was written by the owner, Markus Swindall."

"Fitting name," Matt remarked quietly. "What's it about?"

Lee grew serious as he watched his brother carefully. "You. It's a collection of your gunfights. It tells the story about you growing up under dad's eye and gives a rather bold fictional account of the happenings at Pearl Creek for starters."

"For starters, huh?" Matt asked sounding troubled.

Lee explained, "He's taken quite a liberty with his story telling. I don't know about the other stories, but what he wrote about Pearl Creek and the Dobson Gang is insulting. I won't tell you what it says; you'll have to read it yourself before you leave. I bet you won't read far until you throw it down."

Matt nodded slowly still in his own thoughts. "Well, I might have to pay a visit to Mr. Markus Swindall and put his book-writing out of business before I leave."

"I tried, but there's nothing I could do short of hiring some thugs to break his writing hand," Lee joked with a smile.

Matt smiled as he looked at Lee. "I'll bet you twenty dollars, I can." The look in his eyes sent a chill down Regina's spine.

"No," Lee chuckled, "I don't want to bet. Markus wrote his first book about Uncle Charlie in his bounty hunting days. Of course, when Uncle Charlie found out about it he beat Markus half to death with his rifle butt and burnt every copy of the book that Markus had." Lee paused with a short chuckle and then added, "Markus never wrote another word about Uncle Charlie, that's why dad's the father figure in your biography."

Matt smirked. "It sounds like Uncle Charlie likes writers about as much as I do. I wish I could shoot a few of the writers that I've read, but the cowards never carry a gun. The first one I see that does is going to be my exclamation mark to the whole printing community!"

Lee smiled. "Markus doesn't carry one either."

"Of course not! He's a lying writer!" Matt laughed with disgust in his voice.

"Shall we go see Albert? I know you wanted to see him

today. I wouldn't miss the look on Albert's face when he sees you for a million dollars."

"Yeah," Matt answered. He was surprised by the sudden change of venue. He was somewhat expecting to have some breakfast, they were sitting at the table, after all.

Lee explained as he stood up from the table. "The girls are helping my driver hitch up the buggy. They should be pulling up front any second. We'll go pick up Albert and go to the Monarch Hotel's lounge to eat breakfast. How's that sound?"

"Fine," Matt said standing from the table and followed Lee to the coat closet beside the front door. He reached in and pulled down his gun belt from the top shelf and strapped it around his waist. He was taken off guard to see Regina standing in the main foyer staring at him with a fearful expression on her face. It wasn't necessarily worry, but a form of anxiety mixed with detest that made him ask, "Is something wrong, Regina?" Lee stood beside him placing his derby hat on his head, before putting on his coat. He paused to listen with interest.

She answered slowly, "I'm not comfortable with guns," she admitted. "Do you think taking your gun is necessary? After all, you'll be with Lee."

Matt smiled a little as he pulled on his heavy buffalo hide coat. It was tanned, except for the thick fur left on the shoulders and the large hood that could be pulled over his head. The coat was long and had a slit up the back to make horse riding more comfortable. He answered as he buttoned up the coat, "I never know when I'll need my gun, Regina. If I left my gun here this might be the day I'd need it. And chances are I wouldn't make it back here to get it in time to defend myself." He looked directly into her eyes and added, "My lifestyle's a bit different than yours."

"I realize that," Regina quickly replied. "I'm afraid that guns bring trouble and I don't want my husband anywhere near it." Her words sounded gentle enough; however, neither Matt nor Lee missed the meaning. It was a personal statement to Matt himself, only slightly covered for courtesy reasons. Her gaze at Matt was filled with contempt.

Lee opened the front door. "Regina, we'll be fine. We're just going to eat breakfast, for crying out loud," he said with finality in his voice.

Matt didn't miss the tone in Lee's voice or the touch of anger that burned in Regina's eyes. He pulled on his old ugly brown hat and looked at Regina thoughtfully as he moved to the door to leave. "I'm not here to cause any trouble, Regina. I just wanted to come home for Christmas. Thank you for your hospitality. I'll be moving on this afternoon towards Willow Falls, I'd like to be there before dark," he said and stepped outside and closed the door behind him.

Regina watched from a window as Matt and Lee stepped into the buggy. The differences between the two brothers were as visual as the buggy's black paint against the white snow that covered the ground. Lee had a loving family, a prosperous business, and the respect of a whole community and beyond. Lee didn't need a gun to be intimidating in his corner of the world; he held a natural confidence that made others believe he could achieve almost anything, and a toughness that brought second thoughts about crossing him. Lee was a formidable man to deal with, and had great perception when it came to people's motives and actions. He was seldom on the losing end of a deal. Lee knew what success was, and he knew how to get it.

All Regina knew of Matt Bannister was his reputation and that reputation was fearful. While in her home she had not witnessed anything like his reputation made him out to be. He had been soft-spoken, polite and appreciative. The famous brother-in-law she'd heard so much about was now back, and despite his lofty and tough reputation, Matt Bannister seemed to be the saddest man she'd ever seen.

2

Bannister Blacksmith & Wagon Repair was written in bold black lettering across the top of the high false front of the single story white building that Lee's driver James stopped the buggy in front of. Lee raised his eyebrows at Matt as they sat in the buggy. "You know how they say, you can take a boy off the farm, but you can't take the farm out of the boy? Well, Albert's the perfect example of that. He has a beautiful contract with the Slater Mining Company and the Seven Timber Harvester Company, not to mention everyone else around here. You'd think Albert would smell like roses as he collected his receipts. You'd think, as one of the more successful entrepreneurs of Branson, you'd see him in a suit once in a while. I'll bet you Albert's dressed in rags, smells like a horse and is working himself into a sweat while beating on a piece of iron. Let's go in and see if I'm right." Lee opened his door and stepped out of the buggy. He explained, "You can always find Albert here. He'd rather shoe horses than sit in an office and do his billings." Lee paused at the large front doors of the shop. "Are you ready to see your brother?" Lee asked and opened the door.

Matt felt the same nervous sensation he had the night before when he knocked on Lee's door. He followed Lee into the dirty and darkened shop. It smelled of burnt iron mixed with the scents of human sweat and horse. The forge burned brightly in the center of the shop and there were workbenches spread out from one another along the walls with anvils and other metal working necessities. At one workstation a thin old man wearing a leather apron worked intently on a silver teapot that had a broken handle. He looked up and said, "Morning, Lee."

"Good morning," Lee answered. His eyes went to a big man that was bent over a small vise at a clean and organized workbench next to what would be the office door. "What are you doing, Albert?" Lee asked.

Matt's attention went from the old man he had nodded to, to the back of the big man who was bent over the small vise with intent focus. He was filing the tiny tip of something Matt couldn't see.

"Oh, good morning, Lee. What are you doing here? I thought you said you wouldn't step your foot in here again?" Albert's deep voice asked with a touch of sarcasm. He glanced up at Lee with a smile. The sound of Albert's voice was like a ghost from Matt's past.

"Normally I wouldn't, but I brought you a surprise."

"Oh, yeah, what's that?" Albert asked as he took a final look at the small object in his vise and chuckled lightly. He loosened the vise and pulled out a small chisel that was barely three inches long and at the broadest width barely a quarter of an inch. "Uncle Luther asked if I could make him a fine quality chisel," he explained with a smile and turned to show it to Lee. "So what's my surprise?" he asked and then noticed the man behind Lee. Albert's smile faded, as his eyes slowly grew wider with recognition.

"Him." Lee offered with a smile.

"Hello, Albert," Matt said softly.

"Good Lord!" Albert declared and stepped past Lee with a wide smile and quickly hugged his long lost little brother. "Good Heavens! Matthew, how are you?" he asked loudly.

"All right," Matt answered.

"I can't believe it! When did you get here?"

Lee answered before Matt could, "We're going to the Monarch Hotel for breakfast. We came to see if you wanted to join us."

"Yeah, I'd love to," Albert said and turned to the old gray-haired man working on the teapot, who was watching the brothers with interest. "John, this is my little brother, Matthew. Matt, this is John Peat. John's forgotten more than I'll ever know about metal working. He's an artisan in our trade." Albert praised his employee.

Matt shook John's hand firmly. "Nice to meet you, sir."

"No, the honor's mine," John replied. He shook Matt's hand in awe. "Welcome home, Matt."

THE MONARCH HOTEL was a four story granite block building in the center of Branson with decorative red brick arches around all the windows and doorways. Inside, the Monarch Hotel spared no expense as the walls, support posts and the grand staircase were all paneled with fine mahogany. It was lit brightly by beautiful crystal chandeliers with five decorative oil lamps each suspended from the white ceilings that reflected the light down to the oak floor that was shined to a glimmer. The hotel had twenty-four rooms on the the upper three floors to rent. The main floor consisted of an entry where a stylish thick rug imported from overseas collected a majority of the dust, dirt or mud from the city's dirt streets. Beyond the entry, a second set of doors with large windows, brass handles and kick-plates opened up into the large entrance hall that led to the reception desk. Behind the curved desk a middle aged man dressed in a suit, stood like a guard in front of the grand stairway leading to the rooms upstairs. To the right side of the reception desk were a series of large windows that looked into the formal dining room of the Monarch Restaurant where guests and the public could order fine food and dine in style with quality food, wines and classical music with dinner.

To the left side of the reception desk across from the dining room was a private door that read simply, "Lounge". The Monarch Lounge had a long bar filled with bottles of liquor of every kind and cold beer. There were gaming tables of various kinds and regular square tables like the one the three brothers sat undisturbed while they ate their breakfast. The lounge was closed and wouldn't open until the work day was through, later in the afternoon. The lounge was reserved for hotel guests and members who paid a membership fee to be able to enter and enjoy the privileges that only the Monarch Lounge could provide; such as a first class gentlemen only club where safety and privacy went hand in hand. Hidden through the lounge was a hallway with eight luxurious rooms where the Monarch Lounge's ladies lived and hosted their guests in complete secrecy. The women were all young, beautiful and cost more than most average men could afford. The women weren't the only privilege though. To drink, gamble, smoke and talk among in a safe and private environment of the higher class was worth the price of the membership.

Albert spoke of their younger brother after eating their breakfast of eggs, potatoes and warm biscuits and gravy.

"Willow Falls has never changed. It's exactly the same as when you left. It hasn't grown at all and I don't think it ever will. Steven will always work harder than he needs to get by. I know, I started out in Willow Falls." Their younger brother Steven bought Albert's blacksmith shop in Willow Falls when Albert moved to Branson. He continued, "Twice, I've offered Steven a job, but he refused it."

"Steven's henpecked!" Lee remarked sharply. "His wife, Nora, rules the roost. Her parents bought the mercantile in Willow Falls after you left and now she won't move away from her parents. Albert could double that salary he offered Steven, and Nora would still refuse to move away from her parents," Lee finished with disgust in his voice.

Albert shrugged. "I sweat a lot for very little in Willow Falls. I do pretty well for my family here, and Steven knows I have a job for him anytime he wants it. But he'll never come here; Nora won't let him."

Lee added, "Branson's booming. We're becoming a genuine metropolis that has tripled in size the last ten years and I suspect it'll double in size again. People are coming here from all over to find gold. They pan gold, dredge gold, work all day, day after day, and maybe, just maybe, find a decent flash of gold. Even if they found a nugget of good size all they end up doing is selling it to the bank and spending their rewards in one of my saloons." Lee paused for emphasis. "There's a gold rush going on right now, but Branson is not a gold rush town. We have a solid economy with all the other industry here. Jobs are easy to find and with more people, comes a better economy. You see, the real gold around here isn't in the streams, it's the ground itself and I happen to own a lot of it." Lee lowered his voice to a mock whisper even though he didn't need to in the empty lounge, "I'm also on the city planning commission, and a County

Commissioner, so I have a say on where new housing should go." He finished with a smile.

Albert explained, "Lee's got his corner of Branson and I have mine. Uncle Solomon now owns the undertaking business and furniture store. He's left the quarry to start his own business. If you want to make money, you have to go where the money is, and it's not in Willow Falls. It's here in Branson." Albert was a big man with broad strong shoulders and arms. He had dark bushy hair that was uncombed and fell mid way over his ears. He had a neatly trimmed beard on a square face that had aged a lot since Matt had last seen him. True to Lee's words back in the buggy, Albert was dressed in baggy brown trousers with black suspenders and a gray cotton shirt that had been worn so much that it had patches from old rips and a few new holes in it.

Lee suggested, "You know, Matt, you should think about moving here and getting into some kind of business. With Albert and myself backing you, and a few of our more influential friends, there isn't anything we couldn't get you set up with."

"I wouldn't make a very good store clerk," Matt replied, not interested in Lee's suggestion.

"Store clerk?" Lee almost choked in exasperation. "I was thinking of something a little more professional, like being elected as the county sheriff." Lee paused, "Did I tell you that your old friend Tom's the sheriff of Willow Falls?"

"I've heard," is all Matt said. He sipped some of the brandy that was in front of him. Lee had gotten up after they ate and grabbed three shot glasses and a bottle of brandy.

"It seems to me that he carries some brass. Our present sheriff here in Branson is a bit of a coward, I think at heart. I think a sheriff should at least have the brass to do his job. Your name alone would keep the peace," Lee emphasized.

Albert spoke as Matt took another sip of brandy, "It wouldn't be as exciting as Cheyenne, I'm sure. But we're getting rowdier as we get bigger. As we said before, Branson's growing fast and there's some bad elements moving in."

A beautiful young oriental girl seemed to float into the empty lounge wearing a long green kimono made of silk with embroidered flowers of various colors across the shoulders and down the front. Her black hair was tied up into a tight bun. She floated to their table, refilled their glasses with brandy, and collected their used plates with such a quiet perfection. Every action and movement she made was unquestionably noticeable and erotic to the point of being near hypnotic to watch. Her perfume was sweet and inviting as it enveloped the table. Matt couldn't take his eyes off of her. She was incredibly beautiful and intoxicating as she eyed Matt with hint of a smile and her seductive eyes. With a quiet bow she silently carried the plates away floating on air it seemed.

Lee had noticed Matt had not taken his eyes off her. "Do you like her?" he asked.

"She's beautiful." he replied quite taken by her beauty.

"Her name's Yuko, she's Japanese. For a hundred dollars you can have her for the night," Lee offered. He quickly added, "But since you're my brother, I'll let you have her for no cost if you want? Call it a welcome home gift."

Matt frowned. "She's a prostitute?"

"Prostitute?" Lee scoffed with disgust. "No! She's not a prostitute, she's a geisha! Here at the Monarch, we have classy ladies, not prostitutes. Prostitutes are for the miners and lumberjacks down on Rose Street," Lee sounded offended by the statement.

"I don't know what a geisha is, but if she sells herself for sex, she's a prostitute," Matt maintained.

"Matt, you don't understand," Lee began as he leaned over the table slightly. "Whores, prostitutes, whatever you call them, are on Rose Street. Here, we have first class lady entertainers that come with a steep price. Now, I offered to give you Yuko for free. She's not a prostitute! She's a geisha; which is an ancient Japanese art form. She's the prize of the entire West. I'm giving you a night with for free, which is a dream come true to most men." Lee said sarcastically with a slight laugh.

Matt shook his head. "No thanks. I don't do that."

"Do what?" Lee asked perplexed, as he lost his smile.

"Go to a prostitutes."

"She's not a prostitute!" Lee laughed. "You said she was beautiful. Obviously, you're attracted to her, so why not? It won't cost you anything and no one's going to know if that's what you're worried about."

"No," Matt said uneasily. "I'll pass."

Lee frowned. "Well, if that's your choice. But if you don't mind, I'll leave the offer open in case you change your mind."

Albert looked at Matt oddly. "Are you married, Matt? Is there something we don't know about?"

Matt smiled and shook his head. "No, I'm not married," he said simply and then explained, "I just believe in the Bible." He paused as he noticed the perplexed expression appear on Lee's face. He explained quickly, "The Bible says that all sin is sin against the body, except for sexual immorality. That's a sin against the spirit. It's a much more serious sin. In fact, the only other sin against the spirit is blasphemy of the Holy Spirit. Which the Bible says there is no forgiveness for. So I stay away from prostitutes, even if they are beautiful," he finished.

"Matt...?" Lee questioned. He stopped himself from speaking as he shook his head with a puzzled expression. "So... you're telling me, you never have been with a prostitute since you left here? Because I'd find that hard to believe, Matt, I really would. After all, you were pretty young when you left."

Matt looked at Lee with a slight smile. "I lost my virginity to a girl I loved very much and wanted to spend the rest of my life with. That moment meant more to me than I can ever explain. Paying for a stranger's body is just empty satisfaction. It doesn't mean anything and I don't want it."

"And that was the Reverend's daughter?" Lee asked.

Albert's eyes shifted to Matt. "Elizabeth? You and her?"

Matt nodded. "Yeah," is all he offered, suddenly regretting that he had mentioned it.

"Oh," Albert said thoughtfully and added no more.

"Matt, one thing I don't understand," Lee spoke thoughtfully. "You seem very devout in your belief on sex, no matter how natural it is. But they say you've killed twenty-five people," Lee stated carefully as he watched Matt. "Don't take this the wrong way, but how can you call sex sin, and yet shoot twenty-five people? The Bible does say 'do not kill' doesn't it?"

Matt took a deep breath and spoke slowly. "No. It says '*do not murder*'. I've never murdered anyone. Every one of the men I killed would've killed me, so I don't consider myself a killer. Unfortunately, I do have that reputation. I suppose that brings up the question, how can I serve the Lord with a reputation like mine? It's pretty simple really. I'm a lawman, and when someone pulls a gun on me, I use mine. I have absolutely no trouble reconciling my faith with protecting myself."

3

The road from Branson to Willow Falls was a long sixteen miles under a blanket of fresh-fallen snow. The Blue Mountains rose sharply from the valley floor. They were covered with snow, but the low gray clouds hid most of the mountain range. The valley was still and silent in the late afternoon as Matt's horse walked steadily, tossing the powder with her feet. It was cold, but Matt was warm enough in his long buffalo coat and his fur-lined leather gloves that protected his hands.

It had been fifteen years since Matt had ridden through this valley. He had left quickly, a heart-shattered, naïve kid who had no idea where he was going. Branson hadn't stopped him, but Cheyenne, Wyoming did. Now he was coming home a man who had built a reputation as a gunfighter and killer.

In those same years, Lee had become a virtual millionaire. Albert was set up just as well, Adam, the oldest of the brothers, had a good-sized ranch and Steven, the youngest of the brothers, owned his own business in Willow Falls. The youngest Bannister, Annie, was now grown and married. Albert had commented that Willow Falls was exactly the same, but the changes, even without being seen, seemed too much to bear. Matt realized that he was more afraid now as a man with a tough reputation coming home than he had been as a boy running away. He was tempted to turn around and ride back to Cheyenne, but he couldn't now that Lee and Albert were both bringing their families to the Big Z Ranch for Christmas. The whole family would be together and Matt knew he'd be the only one that would feel like a stranger. He was afraid to see his family after all these years. There were many questions that ran through his mind that brought more anxiety. Would Steven and Annie understand why their older brother abandoned them? Would Uncle Charlie and Aunt Mary welcome him into their home like they had so many years ago? Or would they shun him for disappearing without any explanation? What about what Regina said, did he have a son? Was Gabriel Smith his son? Did it really matter? He would never meet him. What would he do if he saw Gabriel's mother? Could he stomach the moment or the pain it would cause? Would he stand like a man or run for another fifteen years with the same hurt inside?

For the first time he was facing the past and it was racing up on him quicker with every step towards Willow Falls. He hadn't made the wisest choices before he left, and now he was realizing what they had cost him. He had written a few letters over the years to his family, but he never explained to anyone why he left. None of his letters ever revealed the hurt that surged through him with every beat of his heart.

Matt rode along the top of a hill where he could look down over the snow-covered valley and the main road heading east to west through Jessup County. He had intentionally left the road to ride up the hill to get a better view of a large home and barn off the road a ways. It used to be the Bannister Ranch before his father sold it many years ago. His grandfather, Fredrick Bannister had built the ranch in the early 1840s when he settled in the fertile valley. Being an early settler Fredrick was one of the forefathers of Jessup County, Branson and Willow Falls. He was a man of integrity and purpose, a well-respected man, who had almost built a cattle empire and eventually served in the Oregon Senate. He handed the ranch over to his only son, Floyd, while he pursued his further political aspirations in Salem. While Fredrick was campaigning for the gubernatorial election he slipped on an icy Portland street and fell and broke his back. Fredrick Bannister passed away soon after.

Floyd Bannister, Matt's father, had a natural gift for the cattle business. However, Floyd's interests changed when saloons and gambling tables became more accessible. Floyd took to whisky and the saloons like a frog to a pond. He was inept at gambling and it cost him a lot more debt than his money alone could pay. If ever there was a foolish time in a man's life, it was those years when Floyd Bannister lost much of what his father had made.

The original ranch was once the biggest ranch in the territory, but soon the ranch was less than one hundred acres and in financial ruin. Floyd Bannister's growing reputation as a drunk had blemished the once prominent Bannister name.

Floyd had married the beautiful Ruth Fasana, and she had given birth to five healthy boys. When Ruth realized she was pregnant for the sixth time she prayed earnestly that she and Floyd would be blessed with a girl. Matt was seven-years-old the night his mother went into labor with Annie. Floyd and the three older boys were in Branson at the time. Ruth's two sisters were staying at the house because they knew the time for her to give birth was near. The labor and birth of Annie went as well as anyone could hope for, until it quickly became apparent that Ruth was hemorrhaging. Ruth's sisters, Arletta and Mary, tried to stop the bleeding, but there was nothing anyone could do to save her life except pray, while she slowly bled to death.

Ruth laid on her bed and lovingly held her long awaited daughter in her arms. With tears streaming down her face she named her daughter, "Annie." The two boys, Matt and four-year-old Steven, both knew something was terribly wrong when their Aunt Mary burst into tears and could not control her loud sobbing. Matt stepped into the bedroom where his mother held his newborn, sister. Steven ran to her bedside wailing loudly for her to pick him up. Ruth tried to hug him with one arm, but she was too weak to do so and hold the crying baby as well. Matt had paused just inside of the door and stared at the blood-soaked bed that dripped steadily onto the floor. It startled him. He made eye contact with his mother that seemed to last much longer than it really was. He would never forget the moment of chaos that followed as Aunt Arletta struggled to take Steven from his Ruth's bedside. Steven dropped to the floor screaming for his mother to hold him. The newborn Annie screamed for nourishment adding to the loud chaotic scene and Ruth cried out heartbrokenly as Arletta picked Steven up and carried him out of the room. At the same time, Aunt Arletta began to push Matt out of the room as well. It was then that Matt saw the agony on his mother's face as they locked eyes. In her eyes was a heartbrokenness and desperate pleading to stay and raise her children. It was the last time she'd see her boys. "I love you," was the last he heard his mother say before his aunt pushed him through the door and closed it. Aunt Mary was given Steven and she struggled to keep him in her arms. Matt sat beside her quietly as the tears of fear slid down his cheek. Aunt Arletta had gone back in to be with Ruth, and it wasn't long until she stepped out of the bedroom carrying Annie and closed the door behind her. When she looked at Mary and the two boys, she too began to cry. Ruth was dead.

Two hours later, Floyd came home. He was drunk and when the three older boys learned of their mother's death, they were devastated. The home became a chaotic scene and Floyd Bannister choking in guilt from being at the saloon ran out of the house a broken man.

Two days later, Floyd asked Ruth's sister Mary and her husband, Charlie to raise his six children. Floyd then sold all that he owned and moved to Portland where he had remained ever since.

Matt's attention was drawn from his memories of the old ranch to the sound of approaching horses coming from the direction of Willow Falls. Anxiety tightened his chest as he waited. He was in his old home territory and the men riding the horses could be someone he knew, including family members.

A group of about ten horses were being herded by four horsemen; they seemed to be in a hurry as they galloped along the road. One rider leading the way, slowed a bit as he caught sight of Matt sitting on the top of the hill looking down at him. The man waved and kept riding towards Branson. Matt waved back, not recognizing any of the riders that were a couple of hundred yards away. Relieved, Matt moved his horse on towards Willow Falls. The sun was getting close to setting and night would come quickly. He had five more miles to reach Willow Falls and then another mile to reach the Big Z. Instead of riding down to the road, he decided to remain on the hill as it came to an end not far outside of

Willow Falls. The view was better, and it was one of his favorite things to do as a boy, ride on that hill overlooking the road.

"Lord, Jesus," he prayed aloud as he kicked his horse start moving again. "Be with me as I come home. Give me the strength to face my family and I pray that they'll accept me. Help me to enjoy this Christmas with them. It's been a long time since I've been here. I'm asking you to calm my fears and bless this day. Jesus...I don't want to see Elizabeth or Tom. I ask that you'll keep our paths far apart from one another. It's tough enough to just face my family, I don't want to see them too. I'm coming home a man, so give me the courage to be one. In Your name, Lord, Amen."

Two miles outside of Willow Falls, Matt saw five riders on the road. It was nearing sundown, and they were warmly dressed. As they approached, the short stocky leader, wearing a long tan colored coat and hat, veered off the road and up the hill towards Matt. Matt's heart beat faster as he recognized the rider and some of the others. As they drew closer, Matt removed his right glove and unbuttoned the bottom two buttons of his heavy coat and casually pulled the right side back behind his revolver, he removed the leather thong from the Colt's hammer, which held it in place. With his gun exposed, he waited for the leading rider. Matt eyed him squarely and from the outside appeared as calm as a summer lake. Inside though, he was anxious. With his hood pulled over his head, the approaching rider didn't see Matt's face until he was close, but it was Matt who first initiated the meeting.

"Hello, Tom. It's been a long time," Matt said calmly. He pulled the buffalo coat's hood back to reveal his face.

"Matthew!" Tom said surprised. "What are you doing here?"

"Here for Christmas," Matt answered. His eyes quickly scanned the faces of the other four riders. "Hello Clyde, how are you?" he asked Clyde Waltz, an old gray-haired man, almost skeleton thin. Clyde had been the Willow Falls deputy since Matt and Tom were children.

Clyde pulled his scarf off his face, a smile full of bad teeth greeted Matt. "Doing well. It's good to see you, Matthew," Clyde said with excitement. "It's been a long time."

"Yeah, it has," Matt agreed and was interrupted by another rider who pulled his scarf down.

"Remember me?" a dark-haired man asked. "I'm Johnny Barso. I'm Steven's friend."

Matt smiled slightly and cocked his head questionably. "Yes, Johnny! You were just a kid the last time I saw you."

"Well, it's been a while!" Johnny laughed. It sent a stab of guilt through Matt. Matt nodded at the other two riders.

"Cliff Jorgensen," a rough-looking man, of good size in his thirties said. "I know your brother, Steve. He's a good man." Cliff then spit on the ground.

"And who are you?" Matt asked the fifth rider who appeared to be much younger than the others. He pulled his scarf down revealing a young handsome face with high cheekbones, brown eyes, and dark wavy brown hair. Matt recognized him immediately without hearing his name.

Tom Smith spoke gruffly, "That's my son, Gabriel. Gabriel, this is Matt Bannister, the famous U.S. Deputy Marshal. He's coming home for Christmas and hopefully leaving soon," he finished with a glaring sneer at Matt.

Matt ignored the comment and turned his mount towards Gabriel. "It's nice to meet you." He shook the young man's hand.

"We're after horse thieves!" Tom spoke quickly, "We haven't got time to chit chat. Have you seen them?"

"Yeah," Matt answered, "out at the old ranch. Four riders with about a dozen horses, well-armed and cold. They won't make it to Branson tonight; you'll probably find them at the old Anderson farm." He paused momentarily in thought and then added, "I would go with you, but I've waited a long time to come home."

"I don't want you to go with us! I want those men brought back alive, not dead!" Tom spat out irritably. "They aren't Clay Dobson and his gang."

"How's Elizabeth?" Matt asked calmly. If Tom wanted to throw salt, then Matt had some too.

"Great," Tom said evenly. "We've been married for almost sixteen years and have four kids, Gabriel, James, Rachael and Alexis. Life's great! Come on, boys!" Tom continued, as he gave Matt a look of pure resentment. "We've got some horse thieves to catch," he stated and turned away from Matt.

Gabriel Smith hesitated while the other riders followed Tom. "Mr. Bannister," Gabriel said, "it was an honor to meet you. I've read everything I could find about you."

Matt smiled slightly. "You probably know more about me than I do then. I don't read about myself too much."

"Gabe, let's go!" Tom yelled harshly, waiting for Gabriel.

"Hey, Tom," Matt called out, "those men are armed. If gunplay breaks out, keep the boy out of it." He paused, "You know where to find me if you need me."

"I won't need you!" Tom yelled irate. "I may not be a fancy U. S. Marshal, but I am the sheriff and I've done fine without you being here. Remember that!" He warned bitterly and turned his horse to ride away.

Matt watched the five riders; Gabriel rode well. He was a

handsome lad and Matt had seen for himself that Gabriel Smith was a Bannister. He had no doubt that Gabriel was his son. He and Elizabeth had a son that he never knew about. Unfortunately, he had a son that he would never get to know.

4

Willow Falls itself hadn't grown much since he'd left, but it had changed. A few new houses outside of town, a few new houses in town, but the town itself was still small and still silent at night. A few barking dogs were all that noticed Matt as he rode on the outside edge of town. He hoped he wouldn't be noticed, let alone be recognized. He feared running into other people that he knew, Elizabeth Smith to be precise. Which house with faintly lit windows was hers? He didn't even know which one was Steven's. Aside from a few new homesteads and a few new businesses on the main street Willow Falls looked very much the same as it did when he left. The white Church of Christ with its tall bell steeple hadn't changed, except that it seemed smaller than he remembered.

The Reverend Abraham Ash had been the preacher, perhaps he still was. Matt sat on his horse staring at the large white house next to the church that the Reverend and his family had lived in. There were candles flickering in the windows and it looked the same as it always had. It was as though time stood still and he could go knock on the

Reverend's door and be welcomed inside like when he was a kid. He wouldn't be welcomed inside now though. The Reverend had made his thoughts plainly known long before Matt ever left Willow Falls.

Matt kicked his horse gently and rode towards the Big Z Ranch a mile north of Willow Falls. It was five thousand acres of some of the most beautiful and profitable land in the valley. The ranch house and barns were in a wide ravine with a creek running through it. The old white two-story Ziegler home was well-lit with smoke rising from the stone chimney. There was a new house built next to the Zeigler's, it would be Annie's house, which she and her husband had built. There was the old barn and a new one as well, with some cattle in the corrals along with a few horses. The fragrance of home filled Matt's lungs and a nervous smile spread across his face. He paused for a long moment while his eyes simply wandered across the snow-covered ranch. His arrival was unexpected, and it took a few minutes to gather his courage to ride down the hill. "Well, Lord, give me the strength to go home." He took a deep breath and rode forward.

MARY ZEIGLER WAS A ROBUST WOMAN. Her long black hair was in a bun as she and Annie Lenning rolled out dough for the pies they would bake all through the day tomorrow. It would be a busy day as the Zeigler home would be full of family. Most of the Bannister boys would be coming and Mary's brothers. It would be a house full of hungry appetites as all the Fasana and Bannisters were big men with large appetites. Christmas meant more than food though, it was a time to celebrate the birth of Jesus, and a time to celebrate family.

"I swear we'll never get this all done in time," Annie Lenning remarked. She was a beautiful dark-haired woman who was twenty-seven-years old. She wore a plain blue dress with a gray apron covered with flour. "We all should plan to go to Lee's next Christmas. Then we could sit with the men and talk while Lee's maids do all the work."

Mary laughed lightly. "Oh, Annie, I thought that's what we were planning to do last year when we were doing this. Maybe that's why Lee is staying home for Christmas this year. so the maids can cook him up some Chinese duck or something fancy."

"Well, it's too late now," Annie complained. "Uncle Charlie already killed the turkey; otherwise, I'd say we all show up at Lee's tomorrow night. He'd have to put us up in his hotel for the night and we could order a few bottles of wine, put it on his tab and leave!" Annie offered with mocked sincerity.

Mary smiled. "It has to be the same wine he gave me last year for Christmas. I wish he was coming here for Christmas. I'd make him some China-man duck if he brought some of that wine again."

Annie frowned. "It would take a lot of Chinese duck to feed our herd. Lee doesn't like to share his duck." She laughed, and then continued, "Personally, I don't know why he thinks Chinese duck is better than ordinary duck. Maybe we should hire a Chinaman to cook us up a duck."

"And pour our water and ask if we'd like more gravy," Mary added sarcastically.

"The more I think about it, the more I like the idea of going to Lee's tomorrow. Do you think he'd mind?" Annie asked and then answered her own question, "Regina might though. A house full of uninvited guests could anger her, I think. If not her, the maid definitely."

Mary scoffed. "Who cares about the maid? If we can feed this family, so can she. Right?"

Annie laughed. "You just want a bottle of wine!"

"No..." Mary admitted with a smile. "It's just too bad they aren't coming this year. Maybe we should make Chinese turkey. That would show him, huh?"

The silence outside was broken by the sudden barking of Charlie's dog, a black and white shepherd mix that was still quite young. The dog barked continuously as she did when a stranger arrived. She had a different kind of bark for people she knew and still another for coyotes or other types of wildlife. The barking caught everyone's attention as no one usually showed up after dark, especially after dark.

"Charlie is someone here?" Mary asked as she kneaded the dough.

Charlie sighed. He was warming his feet by the fire and reading his newest *Branson Gazette* paper. "Sounds like it," he answered from his chair. He got up and looked out the window to see a man stepping down off of his horse by the door. The man was wearing a long buffalo hide coat with a bushy hood that covered his face. Charlie casually pulled his Schofield revolver out of its holster where it hung by the door. Revolver in hand, he stepped outside into the cold to greet the unknown man. He closed the door intentionally behind him. "Can I help you?" Charlie asked curiously ready to level his revolver quickly if need be.

Matt faced Charlie and pulled his hood back, revealing his face.

"Well I'll be," Charlie said quietly and then smiled pleasantly. "I'll be a son of a gun. Come here!" Charlie stepped forward to meet Matt at the edge of the porch and hugged him affectionately. "How are you? My gosh, it's good to see you!"

Matt laughed with relief; he'd been afraid of this moment.

"Come on in, your Aunt Mary and Annie are in the kitchen. They're not going to believe this!" Charlie put his arm around Matt and led him through the door. "Mary, Annie, look who's come home!" Charlie called out loudly.

The moment seemed to last forever as Matt's eyes connected with Mary's and then Annie's. Mary Zeigler immediately smiled a piercing smile and her eyes filled with thick tears.

Annie screamed, "Matthew!" and ran out of the kitchen, across the dining room and straight into the arms of Matt. She was crying through her laughter; Mary followed until all three had their arms were around each other.

"Thank you, Lord. Thank you!" Mary cried over and over again.

Charlie smiled. Matthew was home!

5

———

"I sure want to thank you for your kindness, Ma'am," Donovan Moskin said. "To take us in and feed us like you did, and tasty, too. Why, I'd say we were pretty near blessed to have the sun go down on us right here at your place. I just can't thank you enough. I don't know what we'd do if we were stuck out in the weather all night." He paused to glance out the window into the darkness. It was fairly light out due to the snow on the ground.

"It's my pleasure," Gladys Anderson replied, with a friendly smile on her kind face. Her husband, Arthur, sat tiredly in his chair. Both were elderly and their farm wasn't what it once was, but they had plenty of room in their corral for the stranger's horses and some hay to feed them. "I couldn't turn two young boys away to the cold outside. It wouldn't be Christian," she explained.

"No, it certainly wouldn't," Donovan agreed. "Like I said, Ma'am, we didn't expect to get caught up in the weather this morning. We hoped to be in Branson tonight. Maybe stay at that new hotel they got," he laughed lightly. "But we have to get these horses over to Fort Boise before Christmas, so we're running late. I just can't, in good conscience, keep those boys working all night in the cold. It ain't right."

"No," Gladys agreed, "it certainly ain't. We enjoy the company; we don't get too much anymore. A lot of folks just don't come this far to visit. It's good to make an extra bit of food to feed hungry men. We don't have a lot anymore, but we always have something we can cut up."

"That's good to know, Ma'am," Donovan said. "We'll be glad to stop back by. Hopefully, we'll be signing a contract with the cavalry to sell them more horses. So we'll be passing through back and forth quite a bit, hopefully, that is. Like I said, me and the missus set up over by Thorton and we're hoping to get into the horse market." Donovan paused, "That's a good business, you know, if you can sell your horses. That's the trick to it," he laughed.

Arthur Anderson opened his eyes. It was bedtime, and he had been falling asleep. "Where you from?" he asked tiredly. His sixty-seven years of age was catching up with him.

"Thorton. The missus and me just acquired a place," Donovan answered clearly.

"I mean originally?" Arthur asked curtly. His eyes watched as the two young men, both still in their teens, fidgeted nervously and appeared to be troubled. The other man, named John, looked to be stern and bitter, in fact he looked like trouble to Arthur. John constantly looked outside through the window like a child expecting a beating when his father got home. Donovan did all the talking and a lot of it. He was unlike the others, he seemed perfectly content to sit and talk. To Arthur, in his life experience, it seemed like Donovan was trying to convince them of his profession rather than telling them. Another thing that Arthur found suspicious was how close the two men stayed to their guns. All horse traders and cattlemen carried guns. Renegades, thieves, highwaymen and wild animals could all be a potential threat to anyone with livestock. But these men refused to be three steps away from their guns even in the safety of a warm home.

"Missouri," Donovan began answering Arthur's question, "then, I went to California searching for a career and found a lady instead," he laughed easily. "Now I'm a horseman just trying to make a living," Donovan finished with a smile. The smile faded quickly as his eyes widened at the medium height stocky man that stepped silently out from the corner behind Arthur's chair. He held a double-barrel shotgun to his shoulder and pointed it directly at Donovan.

The man wore thick wool socks on his feet and a badge on his heavy tan coat. "I'd find another way of doing that," the sheriff spoke tensely.

Gladys screamed and then jumped up quickly. "Tom, what are you doing here?" she was startled by his unexpected presence. She looked at Tom and then at Cliff Jorgensen, who followed the sheriff in. He also pointed a shotgun at the four men.

The two boys were terrified; John appeared to grow angrier than scared, while Donovan was simply stunned. He slowly lost his smile and stared at the sheriff in disbelief.

"Catching some horse thieves, Gladys. Now you and Mister Anderson step over here, please." Then he spoke to Donovan and the others, "You're all under arrest for stealing horses. Stand up slow. One quick move and I'll pull the trigger!"

"There must be some mistake, Sheriff," Donovan replied casually. "My name is Donovan Moskin, out of Thorton. I'm a legitimate horse trader and these are my hired hands.

We're taking some of my horses over to Fort Boise. You must be after someone else," Donovan's voice reflected great sincerity.

Tom wasn't fooled. "If that was true, I would apologize, but it's not. Now get up!" Tom ordered forcefully.

Slowly Donovan stood. "You're making a big mistake. You have no idea who I am."

"I know what you're not and I know what you are. Who you are, I don't care!" Tom answered with finality. His deputy, Clyde Waltz, went to shackle the hands of the two men with metal locking wrist shackles. The two boys appeared to be frightened enough that they could possibly begin to cry. The other accomplice named John, was glaring at the sheriff with pure hatred in his eyes while Clyde shackled his hands. Donovan peered callously at the sheriff for just a moment and then laughed. "Sheriff, Major Jack Johnson over at Fort Boise is waiting for these horses. If I don't show up and lose my sale because of this mistaken identity, I swear, you're going to be buying my stock!" Donovan tried to sound angrier than he was scared.

"Let's go," Tom said impatiently.

"What about our coats?" Donovan asked. "It's cold out there. It's not right that these boys might freeze to death just because you can't find your horse thieves."

Tom paused with his back to Donovan. "Clyde, get their coats, put them on one person at a time. You boys," he spoke to his legalized posse, "keep your barrels pointed at these guys. One quick move, shoot them. Mister Anderson, will you show me their horses and I'll get them saddled? We've got a long trip home," Tom Smith stated, sounding hard and mean. He quickly walked out the back door to retrieve his boots.

Outside in the night's freezing cold, Tom had the two

men in shackles and the two boys had their hands bound by rope sitting on their horses while the posse led them by the reins. Donovan, with his loud voice questioned the harshness of his hands being shackled so tightly. He was outraged by the ludicrous accusation of being a horse thief, as well as being forced to ride like a common criminal back to, well... he didn't know where.

Once on the trail back to Willow Falls, Donovan turned to Cliff Jorgensen, who led the horse of the teenage boy named Rodney. "Where are we heading to?" Donovan asked. He still sounded dumbfounded by being arrested.

"Willow Falls."

"Never heard of it. Is there a judge in the town?"

"Nope, we don't have one. The judge comes to town when he's needed."

"How long's that take?" Donovan asked sounding irate.

"I don't know. It depends on how urgent it is, I guess," Cliff answered as he shuddered in the cold. He personally had no interest in talking to the man they had ventured out into the cold to find. Donovan was obviously the leader of the four. If it wasn't for the fact that Cliff recognized the horses as those of his neighbor, he might believe Donovan Moskin as an honest horse trader. He lied continuously well.

"Well, how urgent is this? Is there a chance we can see him before Christmas?" Donovan asked sounding angry about being arrested. "After all, I'd like to get these horses to Fort Boise, and get back home to my missus before New Year's. For crying out loud, I'm already missing Christmas with her. Now because of you idiots, I'll probably miss New Year's, too!"

Cliff sighed heavily. "I don't know if the sheriff told you or not, but those horses belong to my neighbor, Jeb Stuart.

So don't try to lie, especially to me." Cliff kicked his horse to get ahead of Donovan.

For the first time Donovan looked as though the seriousness of his crime had finally caught up with him. He wasn't going to lie his way out of this one.

The two teenage boys, Rodney and Evan Gray, were visibly frightened and shivering. Their teeth chattered slightly and Donovan couldn't tell if it was fear or the cold that chattered their teeth more. Both of the boys looked back at Donovan desperately for a sense of comfort. He smiled bravely at Evan, the younger of the two brothers. This seemed to bring a touch of some comfort to him. Donovan's friend and business partner, John Birch, was too proud to shiver and too mean to talk as his face was a timeless picture of stern focus and pending danger. John hadn't said a word to anyone, but he watched every move each one of his captors made.

Donovan kicked his horse to move up beside the man leading him. It was the long-time deputy, Clyde Waltz. "So are you a lawman or a farmer?" Donovan asked, making conversation in a friendlier manner.

"I'm the deputy," Clyde offered. He was a thin elderly man who appeared quite fragile and worthless as a lawman.

Donovan laughed. "Well, Deputy, heck what's your name?"

"Clyde, Clyde Waltz."

"Well, Clyde, my boys and I have got ourselves in a bit of a jam. Haven't we?"

"I'd say so," Clyde agreed.

"The judge, how long until we see him do you think?"

"Don't know," Clyde said simply, "depends on him."

"Is he a fair judge?"

"Yep, pretty fair."

"Has he hung anyone?"

"A few. Murderers everyone."

Donovan laughed lightly. "Well, I won't die. We took some horses so now we gotta face the black-robed-reaper. Does he have a soft bone for down on their luck drifters, whose only crime was trying to feed a couple of young lads? It's freezing!" Donovan laughed slightly and then continued, "Certainly he'll take into account the desperate need we had; not much money, no food, and no decent clothes for the cold."

Clyde offered nothing. He simply followed the sheriff who led Evan's horse by the reins about twenty yards ahead.

"The sheriff," Donovan said, "seems pretty tough. Taking his boots off to walk across them people's floor so quietly, that was tricky. I never would've thought of that. What's his name, anyway?"

"Tom Smith. Taking the boots off is an old Indian trick. Indians are so quiet because they don't wear boots," Clyde explained.

"Well, I didn't hear a thing until he had a shotgun on me. He seems like a pretty tough kind. Is he pretty rough?" Donovan asked specifically.

Clyde thought a moment. "As tough as need be, I suppose."

"Sure," Donovan said, "but your town, what's it called again?"

"Willow Falls."

"Never heard of it. Is it small?"

"Pretty small."

"Well," Donovan laughed; it was a deep loud laugh. "That's great. A no-name sheriff, of a no-name town has finally caught me. That's great! I never would've thought."

"Thought what?" Clyde asked curiously.

"You've never heard of me, have you, Clyde?" Donovan asked, not completely surprised.

The question to Clyde seemed a trick question in part. If he hadn't heard of someone even half famous, then it would appear as though he wasn't on top of his profession. If Donovan were famous for anything, Clyde wouldn't know. The fact was he never did keep up with the wanted posters, not that many came through Willow Falls, anyway. Clyde knew mostly the gossip of Willow Falls. "What's your name again?" he asked.

"Clyde, I'm Donovan Moskin, out of Missouri. Sometimes, I'm called Rusty Moskin." He waited for Clyde's response, none came. He continued, "I rode with the Doyle Gang. I'm the guy that shot Mark Chesney." Donovan tried to get his name recognition, but none came. He continued after a disappointed sigh, "That's what I meant. A no-name sheriff, in a no-name town has finally caught me and you guys don't even know who I am. I always expected to get caught by someone who knew who I was, not Tom Smith from nowhere, no how!"

"Maybe he'll become someone now. Just because you never heard of him doesn't mean he can't do his job."

Donovan laughed. "Perhaps! Perhaps you're right. I like you, Clyde, you speak the truth. So tell me, who's the kid with the sheriff? What's your town like? Tell me about yourself."

"What do you want to know about?" Clyde asked. He was cold and conversation always helped to take one's mind off of the chill in their bones.

6

"Mom! Mom! Guess who we saw?" Gabriel Smith asked excitedly as he came quickly into the warmth of their two-story home. It was near ten o'clock when they entered Willow Falls with the four prisoners. Tom sent Gabriel home while he remained in town to lock up the prisoners and get them settled in for the night. He also wanted to get a little of their story. He'd be home in a couple of hours.

Elizabeth Smith looked up relieved to see Gabriel come home; she had been getting nervous. Horse thieves were common elsewhere, but in Willow Falls it was very rare. "Who?" she asked with a soft voice.

"Matt Bannister, the U. S. Marshal! He was coming here to Willow Falls! I shook his hand, Mom! His gun hand! I saw his gun too. His coat was pulled back behind it," Gabriel explained excitedly. He slipped his boots off and walked quickly into the open room and sat down across from his mother. She was holding a quilt she was sewing. He continued, "I don't think Dad likes him! But it was Matt Bannister, Mom! Can you believe it?"

"Really? Well..." Elizabeth replied quietly. His words had

sent a chill down her spine; it felt colder than the snow outside. Matthew was home.

"Do you think he'll be staying at the Big Z, Mom? Do you think we could go see him?" Gabriel asked with excitement.

"Um, I... I don't think so," Elizabeth answered slowly. She was suddenly feeling overwhelmed. "He's been away a very long time. I'm sure he just wants to see his family."

"Well, Steven will introduce me to him. That's his brother, you know."

"Yes," Elizabeth replied uneasily, "I know. But Gabriel, I don't think that's..."

"Maybe," Gabriel continued, "I could have him inscribe my books about him. I can't believe he shook my hand!" he expressed again with an excited smile.

"Of course he would," Elizabeth said as a sinking feeling plunged down to her stomach. She was troubled. "So Gabriel, tell me what happened and how you saw Matthew."

"His name's Matt, Mom," Gabriel corrected his mother. He began to tell her about all that happened. "And we caught the horse thieves at the Anderson's, exactly where Matt Bannister said they'd be!"

"Wow," Elizabeth said. She had listened intently and found herself feeling an uneasiness that she hadn't felt in many years. Matt Bannister meant more in Willow Falls than just a famous deputy marshal with a fast gun. He represented the darkest secret Elizabeth had. Matthew's name could still bring an anxiety that filled her chest. Every time she heard his name mentioned or saw his name in the local paper she feared one of two things; she feared that he was either dead or coming back to Willow Falls.

Now there was a reason for the anxiety that tightened in

her chest. One that she never imagined in her worst possible scenario, her son had actually met the famed marshal. Gabriel tried to learn all that he could about Matt. He read everything he could find about him and talked to Steven Bannister quite a bit, but in Steven's own words he didn't know Matt. Elizabeth had never expected Gabriel to ever idolize, let alone meet, his real father. Tom had to know, Gabriel looked exactly like Matt did at his age. He was tall and had the Bannister broad shoulders. He had Matt's brown eyes, dark hair and handsome square facial features. He looked so much like Matthew did that it was nearly impossible for Tom not to see it. He even had the same strong hands like Matt did. All the other Smith children had Tom's shorter height and round faces, his large blue eyes and Elizabeth's curly blonde hair. Gabriel was obviously not Tom's son, and it showed. Gabriel didn't look like any of his younger brother and sisters; he looked like his father, Matt Bannister.

Now, nearly sixteen years later the guilt of her actions was gnawing at her conscience. Not only was Gabriel a visual reminder of her unfaithfulness, but his fascination with Matt was a sword of shame that stabbed at her heart. She knew Tom had to know by now, but she could never admit it. Not to anyone.

"Do you think," Gabriel asked, "Matt would have killed those men like Dad said?"

"I don't know."

"Dad didn't need to kill them. He just outsmarted them; he took his boots off before he snuck in through the back door and surprised them," Gabriel explained proudly.

"He learned that from Charlie Ziegler," Elizabeth offered simply.

"Charlie Ziegler! There's a scary man," Gabriel

exclaimed. He, like so many others, was afraid of the stern-looking ex-bounty hunter, who had an intensity in his green eyes that even today could intimidate many a grown man, including Tom Smith.

Elizabeth frowned sadly. "Charlie is not scary, Gabriel. He just looks mean," she offered. She'd known Charlie and his wife, Mary, since she was a little girl. Charlie had always been one of the most respectful and caring men she'd ever known. It was too bad Gabriel wouldn't know Charlie the way that she once had. It was a shame that Gabriel would never know that those great people were his family.

"Mom, Mister Ziegler always looks at me as though he doesn't like me. Every time I see him, he just stares at me. It's weird."

"Maybe you should say, hello."

"No, I don't want to get shot!" he laughed.

Elizabeth smiled lightly. "He raised Matthew, I mean Matt. Was Matt scary? You said he stared at you, too."

"Yeah, but he doesn't shoot people for looking at him."

Elizabeth smiled. "Charlie doesn't either, Gabriel. Don't believe everything you hear, he's no more frightening than your father is."

"Right, Mom! Dad's never shot anyone."

"And hopefully he never does," Elizabeth said quietly, "but if he was the sheriff someplace else, he might have to."

"True," Gabriel agreed. "Is there anything to eat? I'm starving!"

AFTER GABRIEL HAD GONE to bed, Elizabeth stayed up waiting for Tom. Elizabeth read the Bible for the comfort it brought. She was feeling unsettled. A sad smile crossed her lips as her thoughts went back to when she was thirteen-years-old. Matthew was fourteen and boldly asked her father for his blessing to marry Elizabeth. The Reverend had laughed at the time and agreed to it when "they were of age." Matthew had always been Elizabeth's best friend and her only true love. As they grew older and came closer to marrying age they dreamed a lot about their future and where they would like to live when Matthew began his ministry career as a Reverend. They discussed moving to the town of Astoria to be near the Pacific Ocean, which neither of them had ever seen. They discussed children names and the type of house they would build overlooking the sea. They had wonderful dreams of a future time together. Those were the most treasured days of Elizabeth's life, as even now the innocence and nostalgia of those days touched her heart.

What would become known as the Massacre on Pearl Creek changed the lives of everyone, but no one's more than Matthew's. Her father labeled Matthew a "murderer" and banished him from the church. The Reverend forbid Elizabeth to associate with Matthew from that day on. Matt was rejected overnight by his own church family and friends. The only people who stuck by him were his family and disobediently... Elizabeth. Even Tom abandoned his best friend after that day.

Elizabeth was seventeen-years-old then and determined to see Matthew. She would sneak out of her house at night and quite often disappear during the day to be with him for a while. When her father caught onto their sneaking around, he gave Elizabeth a severe beating with his lash and demanded that she stop. For the first time in her life, Elizabeth stood up to her father despite the welts from his lash and declared her independence as a young woman of age to marry. In reply, her father threatened to excommunicate her from the church and disown her as his daughter, if she persisted to see him. She was given the choice of being ostracized from everything she knew and loved including her parents, or a life with Matthew. She hated her father for demanding an ultimatum and would have gladly gone to Matthew, but Elizabeth's mother was her truest bond. She dared not to place a separation, even a small one between her mother and her. The threat of being disowned by her parents and forbidden to ever come home again, she was forced to make the decision to no longer see Matthew. Her life had never been darker.

Unexpectedly, Tom came to her house one afternoon and asked her to marry him. She was taken off guard and had no interest in marrying Tom. However, with her father's strong-armed encouragement, she reluctantly accepted. Only later did she find out that her father had effectively persuaded Tom to ask her to marry him.

Matt remained isolated on the Big Z Ranch working with the cattle. When he heard about Elizabeth and Tom's impending wedding he went to confront her about the rumors. All Elizabeth could do was cry with shame and apologize. Matt begged and pleaded with her to marry him. He begged her to run away with him to Branson where they could get married and start a life together, the way it was supposed to be. She was too afraid of her father's ultimatum to say "yes" to Matthew. A day later Elizabeth and Tom were married.

She hadn't been married a week when she walked to the Big Z to see Matthew. It wasn't hard for her to kiss him since Matthew was the man she was in love with and he was the one she had been saving herself until marriage for. That day never came the way she dreamed it would. Her husband took her virginity, but in the hay loft of a barn, Elizabeth held the one man she loved. Instead of the awkward disgust and obligation to her husband on their wedding night, it felt beautiful to experience love the way it was supposed to be discovered for the first time. They were made for each other and the moment seemed more righteous than being with her own husband. However, it was still adultery. It was a sin, despite how perfect and loving it seemed.

Matthew asked Elizabeth to leave Willow Falls with him while they were still naked on the blanket. He didn't know where they'd go exactly, just some place where they could get married and live together without ever worrying about her father. Matt pleaded persistently with her to run away with him. It was all she could do to refuse him, but somehow she did. Matt walked her back to town and told her that he was leaving and wouldn't be coming back. Elizabeth didn't take him seriously at that moment, but she hadn't seen him since that very day. She might've forgotten his facial features, except for the fact that nine months later Gabriel was born.

Tom stepped tiredly into the house and stood by the door to hang up his coat and hat.

"I've saved a plate for you."

Tom smiled tiredly. "Thank you. It's been a long cold night."

"So I hear."

He looked at her. "Gabe told you?" he stated rather than asked.

"Yes. He was pretty impressed with you arresting four horse thieves without firing a shot."

Tom shook his head. "Two of them are just boys, Gabe's age, about. The other two are men. One of whom says nothing, the other talks too much. But it could be that he rode with the Doyle Gang. He claims he shot someone named Mark Chesney, who's apparently rather famous, I don't know. But Donovan, the guy who talks too much, couldn't believe we'd never heard of him." Tom yawned and sat beside his wife on the davenport.

"I'll get your dinner," she said, getting up.

"No, I'll get it when I'm ready." Tom took Elizabeth's hand. "Matt's back," he said simply, "He's here for Christmas he said, and then he's leaving again. He's got long hair now and a beard. I almost didn't recognize him," he finished quietly.

"Gabe told me."

Tom nodded slowly. "I figured he would. As much as Gabe reads about Matt, I'm surprised he didn't drop down off his horse and worship him."

"Now that's nonsense! I remember you being just as interested in Charlie as Gabe is Matthew. There's no difference. Besides, Gabriel was very impressed with you tonight. He's very proud of his father for capturing those thieves," Elizabeth expressed with a pride-filled smile.

Tom smiled. "Oh, I hope so. I don't like him being so interested in a killer."

"Isn't that what they used to say about Charlie? But he's not. Matthew's not a killer, Tom, he's a marshal. You know that," Elizabeth tried to argue gently.

Tom shook his head. "Lizzie, everybody knows that Matt has killed more people than any other marshal or sheriff in the nation, probably. He's killed more people than most outlaws and gunfighters even. He's not the kid we were friends with anymore. He's a killer now and it wouldn't surprise me if he shot innocent people for money," Tom suggested while raising his voice.

"No, I couldn't imagine that," Elizabeth replied intentionally soft. "You know as well as I do what he was like, Tom."

"Yeah, but time changes people. It's changed me, it's changed you, and it has changed Matt. The sooner he's out of this town," he hesitated, "no, the entire valley, the better off we'll be. He's trash, Lizzie, and that's all he is."

"I hope you're wrong," she stated, "but it has been a long time."

"I'm right. If we're lucky, he'll stay on the Big Z the whole time he's here and we'll never even see him. The whole town is going to be talking tomorrow, the whole darn town." Tom knew it would be about Matt Bannister and overshadowing his catching the four horse thieves. He hoped Donovan Moskin was as famous as he claimed. That might bring him the notoriety that he coveted. He hoped that Donovan or his alias, "Rusty Moskin," was a name of some stature. Then he'd get the credit due him.

Tom shook his head slowly. "He's trouble. If he causes any trouble, Lizzie, I'm afraid I won't have any choice..."

"Choice to what?" she asked.

"Lizzie, I'm afraid he's going to cause some trouble with you. If he does, I'll have to end it somehow, whether that means arresting him or..." He paused to consider his words carefully. The fact was that he had never been as handy with his fists or gun as Matt.

"Or what?" Elizabeth questioned with a growing sense of anxiety. Was this the moment she had dreaded for fifteen years? Now that Matt was back in town, everyone would notice the resemblance between him and Tom's first-born son. Maybe even Matt would see the resemblance for himself. What if Matt wanted to know if Gabriel was his son? Could she lie to him? No, she couldn't. Then how could she lie to Tom? Tom was her husband, not Matt.

"Oh, that all depends on him. I'm not welcoming him back to town and I don't expect you to either. I don't expect him to come around here, but if he does, he's not welcome," Tom finished with authority.

Elizabeth said nothing. She couldn't argue with her husband when she agreed with him. Matt couldn't come to their house. What would Matt do if he found out that Gabriel was his son? He would be surprised no doubt, but afterwards she wondered if he would want to get to know Gabriel or simply go back to Wyoming. How horribly would it tear her family apart? There was no way to judge how damaging such a thing could be. She had committed adultery and had conceived a child. Now she could only pray that her secret would stay a secret and that the Lord might bless her prayer.

"What's wrong with you?" Tom asked suspiciously. "Don't tell me you want him here for dinner," he sounded angry at the notion.

"No," she exclaimed. "I'm just surprised that he's back. It's been so long." She smiled and leaned her head on Tom's chest. "I'm glad you're home safely. Congratulations, by the way, maybe you'll become famous now."

He smiled contentedly. "I doubt it."

"Well," Elizabeth added, "you're pretty famous in our house."

"That's all I care about," he said contentedly. He loved his family.

7

Like Tom Smith feared, the news of Matt's return spread like a fire through Willow Falls. William McDermott, the owner of McDermott's Mercantile, the only dry goods store in town, had heard the news late the night before.

William usually opened the doors at seven in the morning, but he'd be opening a bit later this morning. He rode outside of town to be the first to tell his son-in-law, Steven Bannister that his brother Matt was back in town. It was possible that Steven already knew, or perhaps the famous marshal was at Steven and Nora's place. William had been waiting to meet the famous marshal since his daughter married into the Bannister family.

Steven Bannister was a hardworking family man. He was a great husband to Nora and a loving father to William's grandchildren. Steven was a man who took life as simply as he could. He enjoyed laughter and never spoke a false word against anyone. He lived the Biblical principle of *"do unto others as you'd have them do unto you."*

He was the town blacksmith and was known for doing quality work at fair prices. He'd had two offers to move his family to Branson and work for his brother, but Steven always turned it down. He was quite content with his family, small ten acre farm and blacksmith shop. Happiness wasn't about having more money, it was about being content with what you have.

William tied his horse to the hitching post and knocked on the door. His oldest granddaughter, Larea, opened the door curiously.

Her seven-year-old eyes widened. "Grandpa! Did you bring us any candy?" she asked. The announcement of his arrival brought a brief wave of excitement. Her two younger sisters, Melissa, age five, and Mary, age four, ran to the door in a hurry expecting a candy from their grandfather. All three girls had long brown hair and blue eyes, like their mother.

"Oh, let me see," William teased lightly, putting his hand into his pocket. "Well, would you look at that? I've got three extra pieces of candy!" He handed a piece of candy to each of his excited granddaughters.

"What are you doing here this morning, Daddy?" Nora Bannister asked. She was cooking breakfast and the smell of bacon and eggs filled the air. Nora was an attractive light brown-haired lady with blue eyes and on an oval-shaped face. She had a serious demeanor and seldom smiled; it went hand in hand with her belief in strict parental etiquette. Normally, she would never allow her daughters to have candy before breakfast, but she learned long ago that Grandpa didn't listen to her when it came to his granddaughters.

"Is Steven here?" William asked.

"Out in the barn milking," she answered. "Why?" she asked curiously, "is something wrong?" Her father's excitement seemed the opposite of bad news.

"No. So tell me, does Steven know his brother Matt's back in town?"

"Matt? No... Is he?" she asked, bewildered. Matt was the only brother she had never met and never expected to.

"Yes! He rode in last night. Cliff Jorgensen came by late last night and said he and the sheriff's posse ran into Matt. He was coming home for Christmas! I came over to let Steven know."

"Oh, well he's in the barn," Nora replied. "He'll be happy to hear that."

"I thought he might. I know how much Steve misses him. I couldn't wait to tell him. Start his day off right!" William smiled excitedly.

Nora shrugged her shoulders with a slight smile. "He's getting bacon and eggs for breakfast, fresh milk, and his brother back here for Christmas." Her smile widened. "Praise the Lord; I believe Steven will be thrilled." She laughed, growing excited like her father.

Within minutes, Steven Bannister walked through the back door wearing a heavy coat and carrying a bucket of fresh cow's milk. He was about five feet ten inches tall, with a square youthful face. He had short dark brown hair and was built like an ox, muscular and extremely powerful. "Hey, Pa! Stop by for breakfast, did ya?" Steven asked cheerfully, as he set the bucket on the counter.

"No," William replied, "your brother showed up in town last night and he's at the Big Z as we speak."

"Adam? I heard he was coming and Albert should be coming too. The last I heard, he was coming for Christmas, anyway."

"Not Adam, Matt. Matt's back!" William announced with a smile.

Steven froze. "Matt? Matthew! Are you sure?" he asked with great excitement growing on his face.

"I am sure," William said and explained what Cliff had told him.

Steven sat down on a kitchen chair, overwhelmed. "Well, I'll be," he said quietly. "Matthew's home. Honey, I'm going to the Big Z. I'm going to see my brother!"

8

Matt lay on the bottom bunk and stared sorrowfully at the name "ELIZABETH", which he had carved into the cross board of the top bunk above him many years before. He remembered laying there carving it with his knife when he and Elizabeth were young. Those were the happiest days of Matt's life and he wished he could wake up and be fifteen again, even if for just one day. He longed to feel the excitement of being in love again, without the pain of watching the girl he loved marry another man. Seeing her name carved above his bed brought his youth back to life again. She was the only girl he had ever loved or wanted to love. He had forgotten he had carved her name in the bed board above his bed until he had opened his eyes a few moments before. It cut like a knife right through his heart.

The smell of breakfast lingered in the air and he listened for the sound of anyone downstairs. It was past sunup and undoubtedly, Uncle Charlie was out on the ranch doing his chores and Aunt Mary was obviously making breakfast. They must've figured he needed his rest, because he couldn't remember them ever allowing anyone to sleep in past sunup for very long. He looked at the empty bunk bed across from his and looked around the empty room with fond memories of sharing the room with his brothers. Slowly and awkwardly, Matt got out of bed and put on his moccasins before he walked down the steep and narrow stairs and into the living room. The house was empty, except for Mary Ziegler, who was cleaning up after cooking his breakfast. She smiled at Matt. "I thought some home cooking might get you out of bed," she offered with a smile.

"It smells delicious," Matt said and washed his hands in the bowl of wash water on the counter before eating.

"Well, you eat. Then I'd like to talk to you before everyone shows up."

Mary Ziegler sat in her comfortable cushioned chair and waited for Matt to finish eating and then invited him to sit in his uncle Charlie's cushioned chair next to her. He sat down feeling a bit uncomfortable. For some people, conversation came easily, but for Matt it was a task he wasn't accustomed to.

"So Matthew, how are you, really?" Mary spoke softly and sincerely.

"I'm all right," he said awkwardly.

"Forgive my bluntness, but do you like what you do, Matthew? I mean, the stories I hear. I just can't imagine you would." Her expression was empathetic.

Matt nodded his head slightly. "It's what I do, Aunt Mary. I've been doing it for a long time."

"I know," she said simply. "Do you enjoy it?"

Matt paused before speaking. "Enjoy? Well, I believe in what I do. If that's enjoying it, then I guess I do."

Mary smiled slightly. "You know, Uncle Charlie hunted men for a while."

"I know that," he said with a hint of sarcasm in his voice.

"Sure," she added more seriously, "but he hated it. He hated being away from home and his family." She watched Matt carefully. He had never been able to hide his emotions although he'd always tried. Not everyone could see through his mask, but she had always been able to. Even when he was leaving she had seen the brokenness that he hid relatively well from the others. "Charlie hated everything about it. To him, life was more important than chasing someone down who might just end his life, or him having to take theirs." Mary paused, "You aren't such a young man anymore, Matthew. Don't you think perhaps it's time to take a wife, raise some kids, and settle down? Someday, someone's going to get the better of you and your life will be over. Matthew, please put the badge down while you still can. You've done your civil duty for long enough. You have too much to live for to throw it away for a foolish profession that you don't even need."

"Aunt Mary," Matt answered simply, "that sounds good and everything, but I don't have a wife and I don't know anyone that I want to be my wife. Besides, I don't know anything else, except for being a marshal. It's what I am, Aunt Mary."

"There are other things you could do if you wanted to," she remarked quickly. She bit her lip with a serious expression on her face. "You left because of Elizabeth and Tom getting married, didn't you?"

"Yes," Matt answered painfully. Uncomfortable, he shifted in the chair, avoiding Mary's eyes.

"And," Mary continued, "you've been running from that ever since?"

Matt smiled sadly. "I guess," he offered no more.

"Matthew," Mary said affectionately, "you can't run away

from the hurts of life. Elizabeth and Tom are married and have been since you left. They have four children and live day to day just like the rest of us. You're running away hasn't changed anything; it's only kept you away from here for fifteen years. Those years have slipped away from you and you're the only one missing out. Matthew," she paused as she eyed him caringly. "You had an affair with Elizabeth before you left, didn't you?"

He nodded slowly. He stared at the floor with a sorrowful expression that she recognized from the days before Matt left.

"You have a son," she continued softly, but pointedly. "His name is Gabriel. If you had stuck around, things might have been different. Maybe Tom would have divorced Elizabeth and you would've married her." She saw the sorrow on Matt's face grow even deeper as her words sank in. "Running away, has hurt you and us more than it hurt Tom or Elizabeth. Who knows what would have happened for sure, but I do know you'd be happier now if you had stayed here. Maybe you never would have married Elizabeth, but you would have been happier."

Matt replied in a slow, soft tone that came from deep within. "I asked her to leave with me, but she wouldn't. I couldn't stay here knowing Tom was..." He paused and then continued, "It might've been the wrong thing to do Aunt Mary, but I had to leave," he finished. He looked at her with apologetic and moist eyes.

Mary remained silent for a moment while they both listened to the sound of the wood stove. "You met your son last night. Gabriel is your son, Matthew," she stated as a matter-of-fact.

"Lee told me about Gabriel, but when I saw him, I knew it."

"I can imagine how that feels."

"I don't know how it feels, Aunt Mary. I'm overwhelmed just being home. Just seeing my family is overwhelming, but to have a son is... I don't know. I'm numb."

Mary nodded, understanding. "In a few days you will be able to sort out some of those feelings. You're right though, you have a lot of catching up to do. I do want you to know something, Matthew; we've never forgotten you. You're still a part of this family and we are just glad you're home. I hope you'll consider what I said and stay here. You've been gone way too long, and it's not too late to start a new life. You don't have to go back to Cheyenne, your family is here. Your son is here."

"I don't know about that."

"What do you mean you don't know about that?" Mary asked quietly. Her dark brown eyes penetrating deep within her nephew, trying to get a glimpse of what he wasn't willing to admit.

"Gabriel doesn't know I'm his father."

"Of course not! Elizabeth has denied that since the day he was born, but he is," Mary declared pointedly. "That boy is a Bannister and whether Tom likes it or not, you need to get to know your son. He needs to know you're his father and you need to know the only son you may ever have, if you don't hang up your gun like your uncle Charlie did," Mary Ziegler said with conviction.

"Aunt Mary, I don't know if that's such a good idea. Who am I to step into his life after all these years? I didn't even know he existed until two days ago. I think that should be up to his mother, not me," Matt sounded unsure of himself. "Besides, all it would do is cause trouble in their home and perhaps increase Tom and Elizabeth's resentment towards me."

"Matthew, you can stay here, help out on the ranch, and gradually get to know your son. You'd be a good dad, all of you boys are, but you can't just ride back off to Wyoming knowing you have a son, can you? Maybe Gabriel doesn't mean anything to you, but we've watched him grow up year after year knowing he's your son. Gabriel Smith is your mother's grandson! Fasana blood runs through his veins as surely as it does mine. The boy is our family, Matthew! He needs to know his heritage because he is not that Tom Smith's son. He is yours!" Mary expressed angrily. "That boy needs to know who we are! He's a Fasana and I'm tired of seeing my nephew growing up not knowing who he is or who his family is!" she finished strongly.

Matt frowned sadly as he spoke, "Aunt Mary, I..." he paused as heavy footsteps sounded on the large covered porch. The door opened and Steven Bannister stepped into the house. Steven, Matt saw, had grown as big and solid as any man he'd seen. Steven's face was square and handsome with short hair under the brim of his brown hat. He had a slight mustache and was clean-shaven. Matt's first impression of Steven was that he looked happy.

"Matt, you son of a gun, stand up!" Steven yelled with excitement. He wrapped his mammoth arms around his older brother. "I don't think you're so big anymore. I could probably take you now," Steven laughed as he looked at his older brother fondly.

"You'd beat me in arm wrestling," Matt admitted openly, "but, I could still take you. You aren't that big yet," Matt said playfully, glad to see his younger brother.

"Look at that hair!" Steven gasped. "You need to cut those girly locks. Grab your scissors Aunt Mary; we've got a woman to shear up and make look like a Bannister," he teased. His laugh and smile were warm, friendly, and inviting.

Mary smiled. It was good to see the two brothers teasing each other like they had many years before. Steven and Matt acted as if no time had separated them. They were brothers.

9

The Willow Falls Sheriff's Office was a small single story white building with a covered front porch with a small hanging sign that read, "Sheriff's Office". Inside there were two desks with chairs, a file cabinet, gun cabinet and a small pot-bellied woodstove in a corner near the larger desk with a padded office chair. Beyond the two desks was a private bedroom where the deputy Clyde lived. Beside the bedroom there was a three-foot isle between the wall and the two jail cell doors where the prisoners were led to and from the cells. The jail, like most Donovan had been in offered no windows, nor any privacy, as he was surrounded by strong iron bars and a securely locked iron-barred door. The two cells were small and exactly the same with just enough room for a horizontal bunk bed and a single wooden chair in front of each. The cells were side by side with the doors facing the wall of Clyde's room. What irritated Donovan the most was the jail was too darn cold! A guy would think even a small stove could warm a small building, but it definitely did not heat up the jail cells.

Sheriff Tom Smith looked different in the daylight, or

maybe it was the lack of surprise and fright that had caught Donovan Moskin off guard the night before. Tom sat backwards on a wooden chair next to the jail cell with his arms crossed on its back looking at Donovan. Tom was of medium height with a broad chest and a noticeable belly. He wore a heavy gray flannel shirt with his badge on his left breast. Tom looked at Donovan with a serious, but not particularly unfriendly round face with a thick brown mustache and stubble beard from not shaving for a few days. His brown hair was short, oily and receding giving him an older appearance than his actual mid-thirties. His hat and gun belt hung on a series of wooden peg wall-hangers next to his heavy coat just inside the main entry door, which Donovan found odd, since most lawmen kept their side arms closer at hand.

Tom spoke, "Your breakfast will be here soon. My wife is making you a hot breakfast, lunch, and dinner. Don't ask for seconds, one plate's all you get," Tom paused, speaking evenly. "Breakfast is at about eight-thirty, lunch at noon and dinner's around six-thirty. You'll eat after my family's fed."

"That's mighty fine of you," Donovan said sarcastically. He was quite irritated by the lack of heat. "Maybe you could throw some bigger pieces of oak into that stove at night and open the damper up a bit. Or are you guys having a wood shortage around here? I don't think any of us got any sleep, it's too cold in here!"

"Well," Tom sighed. "I'm sure it's not as comfortable as the Anderson's warm household, but you reap what you sow. Stealing horses is what got you here."

"I know," Donovan spoke loudly, "what got us here! But we're people, not cattle. These thin wool blankets don't keep out the cold. Can't you get us some more blankets?"

"Possibly," Tom agreed to try, "I'll see what I can do. But, business first, I need to write down all your names, personal facts and where you're from. Get your side of the story and make a paper report." He paused, "Then I'll inquire about the Justice of the Peace and get a date for your trial. It may take a few days though."

"How many days?" Donovan asked gruffly.

Tom shrugged. "I don't know; it depends on the judge. It's Christmas, so it won't be in the next few days anyway and it's possible that it won't be until after New Year's."

"Who's the judge around here, anyway?" Donovan asked.

"Meryl P. Jacoby, out of Branson."

"What's he like?"

Tom shrugged. "Fair enough."

"Is he a hanging judge?"

"He hasn't hung anyone around here, but we're not used to much trouble."

"Well Tom," Donovan stood up impatiently, grabbing a hold on the bars while glaring down at Tom. "Can you answer me this? Is horse theft a hanging offense in this little town? What is this place called again?" He withdrew from the bars and turned around to face his quiet partner, John Birch, who was sitting on the bottom bunk. Donovan's back was to the sheriff as he continued, "I can't believe we're in this jail." He spun quickly kicking the provided chair into the bars. "Tell the judge to come quick! Okay?" Donovan yelled.

Tom nodded calmly. "I'll add that to my report. You a..." he paused and then continued, "seem eager to be convict-ed," he asked more than stated.

"Convicted!" Donovan almost spit, "I don't expect to be convicted. There wasn't any harm done, and we didn't hurt anyone. We made a bad choice at an inopportune time. We were caught and rightly so. No," he stopped and looked at the sheriff. "I don't expect to be convicted."

"Last night," Tom began, "you implied that you ran with a certain outlaw gang and killed someone of some notoriety. My question is; is there a reward for your arrest?"

Donovan laughed lightly. "No, there's not. If there was, I wouldn't tell you who I was."

Tom smiled. "The judge will find all that out before he comes. So you're really nothing, but a horse thief?"

The smile left Donovan's face and a cold mask of hostility took its place. "I am not a horse thief! I ain't exactly an angel, but I'm not a horse thief. Yeah, we took the horses, but no damage was done and you wait, I'll ride out of this town a free man."

"Maybe, that depends on the judge. Now, let's get all of your names," Tom said as he went to his desk and pulled out a piece of paper and a pencil.

"I'm Donovan Moskin from Missouri. That's John Birch from Texas and those two over there, are Rodney and Evan Gray. We found them in The Dalles. We went through this last night," Donovan said scornfully.

"The Dalles?" Tom questioned ignoring Donovan. He looked over at the two teenage boys. Both boys had blond hair, pale white skin, and greenish-blue eyes. They were both frightened and cold. "How old are you boys?" Tom asked.

"I'm seventeen and he's fifteen," Rodney Gray answered in a nervous and cracking voice.

"Where are your parents?" Tom asked.

"Dead, sir. It's just my brother and me," Rodney answered again.

"So, how'd you fall into stealing horses? Where'd you meet these guys?" Tom asked Rodney.

"Um…" Rodney uttered nervously. His face was turning red and his eyes filled with moisture. "Mister Moskin said he could use a couple of guys to help him."

"Rodney…" Donovan warned gently, but his tone was threatening.

"Don't worry about him," Tom responded. "If you've got more to say, say it. He can't hurt you."

"There's really nothing to say. He just offered us a place to be, we didn't have anywhere to go," Rodney answered with a fearful glance at Donovan.

"And you are?"

"Rodney Gray, sir."

"Evan Gray!" Tom called out sharply.

Evan Gray's eyes widened in fear and he sat up straight suddenly on the top bunk. His face turned red and his eyes watered immediately as panic gripped him. "Yes, sir," he replied meekly, staring at Tom like a beaten and afraid dog.

"Do you have anything to add, anything at all?" Tom asked gently. He felt a sudden wave of guilt for frightening the boy to such a degree.

"No, sir," Evan answered. His eyes were thick with tears as they remained locked on the sheriff.

"John Birch," Tom looked away from the two boys to the quiet rough looking man, who eyed Tom evenly. "Are you a wanted man?"

"Nope," he answered.

"Huh!" Tom huffed shaking his head. "And I thought I'd captured someone important. You were lying last night weren't you, Mister Moskin?"

Donovan smiled slightly. "Sheriff, I rode with the Doyle's; I knew them well. I've done a lot of things in different places, if you go east to Kansas or Missouri people know who I am. I'm not wanted, but they know who I am.

But they'll never know who *you* are, Tom, because we're all walking out of here."

Tom smiled. "You sound so confident. I'd like to know why you think you'll walk out of here so easily, I really would. I mean, you were caught red-handed with stolen horses. We may not be Kansas or Missouri, so we're not *infatuated* with you, but we still have the law here. I don't see how you think you'll be found not guilty."

"Simple," Donovan explained, "we're on our way to Coffee Canyon. You've heard of that I suppose?"

Tom frowned. "Isn't that a rumored camp for outlaws?"

Donovan shook his head. "No, it's a secret hideout on the Idaho Nevada border where people go when the law is after them. There's only one way in and two ways out, very remote and very well protected. I've been there a time or two. Now, don't you think the judge would be interested in a map with the secret landmarks to get there, for my release?"

Tom thought about it carefully. "If..." Tom began and then turned as the front door opened. Elizabeth Smith walked in bundled from the cold in her heavy dark coat and brown scarf tied around her face. Their three-year-old daughter, Alexis, was with her. Elizabeth carried a basket covered by a blanket.

"Oh, come inside dear," Elizabeth said to Alexis as she closed the door to keep the warmth inside of the sheriff's office.

"Hello, my ladies," Tom said while standing. "Hello Sweetheart," he said to Alexis. She smiled widely at her father as he bent down to kiss her forehead then playfully flicked the scarf tied around her bonnet. He smiled at Elizabeth, whose face was reddened from the cold. "Thank you, Lizzie. I'll be picking up the meals from now on, but I appreciate you bringing these into town." He hesitated a minute to look carefully at his wife. "Lizzie, you look very pretty today."

"You're welcome and thank you," she responded with a radiant smile. Perhaps it was a subconscious act to get extra pretty because Matt was in town. If she did happen to see him, she wanted to look her best.

"Well, come meet our guests," he said and led her to his desk not far from the two cells. The two men stared at her and John stood slowly to step near the bars to get a closer look. The two boys eyed her with desperation in their eyes. "This is my wife, Elizabeth. She'll be making your meals."

"Ma'am," Donovan spoke gently, "it's nice to make your acquaintance. I can smell the bacon from here and it smells delicious. I sure want to thank you, Ma'am, for the grub. I haven't tried it yet, but I know it's going to be delicious."

"Well, thank you, Mister..?" she hesitated.

"Moskin, Donovan Moskin."

"Well, Mister Moskin, thank you. I hope it's as good as you're expecting."

"Why, thank you, ma'am."

Tom spoke as he grabbed a double-barrel shotgun out of the gun cabinet. He loaded two shells into the chambers and stepped over to his desk for the cell keys. He then turned to Elizabeth. "Lizzie, I'm going to unlock the cell doors after I have them back up against the wall. I'll hold the gun on them while you set their plates on the floor and lock the doors for me, okay? And you gents," he spoke to Moskin and Birch, "take one step towards my wife and I'll scatter you back against the wall. Got it?"

"Sure Tom," Moskin said as he and John Birch both stepped back against the wall. As promised, Tom held the shotgun at eye level on the two men while Elizabeth slipped two plates of food inside the door on the floor. Only after she had locked the door and tested it, did Tom lower his gun, allowing both men to step hungrily to the plates.

At the next cell both of the Gray brothers were waiting patiently against the wall. They were thin, poorly dressed and the moment Elizabeth saw them, her heart was stirred. "Why, these are just boys' no older than Gabriel," she stated to Tom with concern on her face. She unlocked the door, walked back to the desk to get the other two plates of food and immediately went inside of the cell and handed the two plates to the boys personally. She stood and looked at the two boys with a tenderness they hadn't seen in a long time. "How old are you boys?" she asked, still within the cell.

"I'm seventeen, he's fifteen," Rodney answered, "and thank you for the food, ma'am."

"You're welcome. What are your names?"

"I'm Rodney Gray. This is my brother, Evan."

"Well, I'm Elizabeth. If I can get you two boys anything, please let me know. It looks like you could use some new clothes and warmer blankets?"

Donovan interrupted through a mouthful of food, "That's what we need all right, that and a few pieces of oak on the fire at night."

Tom grew weary. "Come out of there, Lizzy. You can talk to them through the bars." She obeyed.

The boys sat on the bottom bunk and ate as Tom locked the cell door behind Elizabeth.

The hopelessness in the two brothers' eyes broke Elizabeth's heart. "Tom, I'm going home to find those boys' something warmer to wear and warmer blankets. Can you bring them back here for me at noon?"

"Yeah," he replied slightly annoyed.

"Good. Come on Alexis, let's go home, honey."

"Thank you, ma'am," the boys said in near unison as they were finishing their breakfast already.

"Ma'am," Donovan called to Elizabeth, "I was asking your fine husband to hurry the judge to town, so we could get out of jail and go on our way. But now, after tasting your cooking, I might propose the judge waits till spring," he finished with a friendly smile.

Elizabeth laughed nervously at the compliment. "I have never had such a compliment! Thank you," she answered as she picked up Alexis to walk outside.

"No, thank you!" Donovan replied sincerely. "And your daughter has the beauty of her mother. I bet old Tom here doesn't know how lucky he is, does he?"

Elizabeth smiled uncomfortably. "I think he does," she said and stepped out into the cold shutting the door shut behind her.

"Sheriff, you have to be the luckiest man I've ever met, to have a wife that pretty and can cook like this. Heaven can't get much better than that," he stated as he took another bite of bacon.

"Thank you, Mister Moskin," Tom said while he put the shotgun away. He emptied the two rounds back into the drawer below the cabinet. He turned to face the cells. "I am blessed," Tom admitted.

"If I had what you have, Sheriff, I'd call it heaven," Donovan offered.

Tom sat on his desk and shook his head. "Mister Moskin, being a Christian I have to say heaven's a lot greater than that."

Donovan stared awkwardly at Tom for a moment and then laughed. "We definitely have different views, Sheriff. A pretty lady, good food and a bottle of good whiskey is heaven to me."

"Your idea of heaven, Mister Moskin, is a short lived moment with everlasting consequences. Enjoy the cold while you can because if you don't change your thinking, you'll never be cold again," Tom stated simply.

"Well that sounds good to me, Reverend," Moskin said mockingly with a chuckle. "But what about my offer to the judge, think he'll take it?"

The sheriff shrugged. "You don't have any proof."

10

Charlie Ziegler wasn't a big man. His build was quite average although he carried himself as a much bigger man than he was. He was a tough and hardened man who could stand toe to toe with any other without showing a glimpse of fear. Despite his age, he was just as driven to get out of bed on a cold morning, as he was in his thirties. Charlie had short gray hair that was thinning on top and his lean and strong-featured face was clean-shaven most of the time. He had a rough exterior that naturally looked as mean and murderous as any man could with penetrating green eyes and a harsh glare that could unnerve a grown man from across a room. Charlie may have appeared menacing and certainly he could become as mean as he needed to be. Lee had explained to Matt how Charlie gave Markus Swindall a beating with the butt of his rifle for peddling his "*Charlie Ziegler; Man Hunter of the West*" dime novel.

"I didn't see it fit for him to make money by adding lies to my name," Charlie explained when Matt asked him about it. Charlie, Matt, Annie and Steven were all keeping warm by a small wood stove in the makeshift shop where Charlie did his own blacksmithing out in the barn. He continued, "I told him if he ever printed my name again, I'd shoot him. So now he's got one about you. My name's not in it," Charlie pointed out with a half-smile.

"Hmm," is all Matt said.

"I didn't want to buy it myself," Charlie added, "but your brother-in-law did. He let me read it."

Annie spoke pointedly to Matt. "You might want to stop in there and pay your respects to his penmanship."

Matt sighed with a slight smile. "I'd have to decide which rifle butt to use, then I'd get all flustered and end up drawing my pistol and shooting him. Not that it's much of a crime in my opinion, but as civilized as Branson's getting, I might be accused of a crime."

The others laughed lightly. "No," Steven said through his smile, "they wouldn't charge you, but even if they did, we'd just have Lee go get you out. They'd drop all the charges as soon as they realized your Lee and Albert's brother. The sheriff and his deputies do as they're told over there."

Charlie shook his head with disgust. "It's all politics anymore. These soft-handed politicians want to be in power so much that they take any open elected position. They fill that position until a higher one comes along, and then they want that position, in the meantime it lines their pockets with money and makes them feel powerful. That sheriff over there in Branson's the same way." He paused, disgust becoming evident in his voice, "He walks around town tipping his hat to the ladies, exposing his shiny badge on his clean suit, while his deputies do all the work. Of course he gets the credit and paycheck. It's like a few skunks wanting to run a city of prairie dogs. However, there are a few old badgers like me around still who aren't intimidated by their smell. If they try to push me, I'll bite their heads off!"

"Uncle Charlie's giving up the cattle business to run for mayor," Annie quipped.

Charlie smiled slightly as he looked at Annie.

"Lee," Matt announced, "was telling me that he planned to run for the senate, and then maybe even governor."

"Lee will be president someday," Annie offered with certainty.

"Lee could find a way to be the King of England if he wanted to," Steven added.

"You know," Charlie said seriously, "Lee's like a chess player in city politics, he really is. Not only has he placed himself in vital positions in city and county politics that help his business, ironically enough. But according to your cousin, William, Lee has enough dirt on all the elected officials who go to his private lounge to run the city and the county as he wants to. In other words, he's got his fingers on everything, including the elected officials. And that makes him one of the most influential and powerful men in Jessup County. The kid amazes me!"

Steven scoffed. "His teacher must have been better than mine. I went to the same school he did, but I'm just a... blacksmith. Lee grows up and owns a whole city!"

Annie added, "That's okay. I finished school and my husband never finished the fifth grade, but I'm the one that cleans the stalls and cooks' dinner. Plus, I still live at home. I guess school never got me very far either," she added with a shrug.

There were two large houses on the Big Z. The original Ziegler home was a two-story farmhouse, which had a few new rooms built on for the expanded family. The home faced west and was painted white though it was now faded and peeling. It was a sturdy home with a nice covered front porch to sit on and watch the sun go down.

Annie and Kyle's house was next door. It had two stories and was made in the same style of Charlie's, although it faced north. Annie's house was painted yellow with green trim. It was a colorful and pleasant home to look at, but Annie's life wasn't about her house. Annie had spent her whole life on the Big Z Ranch and when she married Kyle Lenning, she refused to move off it. Kyle had to move into the Ziegler home and build their own house next door if he wanted to marry Annie.

Of all six kids that grew up in the Ziegler home and worked on the Big Z Ranch, Annie was the only one who came to love the ranch and chose not to leave it. She wore boots and jeans to clean the stalls, feed cattle, milk and even herd cattle. She rode a horse as well as any man and she could rope, tie, and brand as well. She could break a spirited horse on her own under Charlie's confident eye, and she wasn't afraid to confront hired men on what was expected on the Big Z Ranch. She worked as hard as Charlie and cared about it as much as he did. For that reason, Annie would be the sole owner of the Big Z Ranch when Charlie and Mary retired.

The Ranch would be in Annie's name only; Kyle Lenning reminded Charlie of Floyd Bannister just a little too much. He had absolutely no use for Floyd and sometimes wondered if he had any for Kyle. He was Annie's husband and the father of her children, but his work ethic wasn't the kind to run a ranch. Charlie personally thought Kyle would be better suited for a store clerk.

"Where is your mysterious husband, Annie?" Matt asked.

"He's due back from Branson today. He took the wagon in a few days ago to stock up on some supplies and do a little

Christmas shopping." She quickly added to Charlie, "Maybe he'll bring me home a new saddle for King."

Charlie eyed her affectionately and scoffed, saying nothing.

Matt held a tin cup of hot black coffee he had poured from the pot on the wood stove. He said softly, "I didn't bring any gifts for anyone."

Annie stated. "Your being here is the greatest gift I've ever had. Thanks for coming," she said and gave Matt a quick hug. "It's so good to have you home!"

"It's good to be home. I'd forgotten how good it is." His aunt Mary was right. He had only hurt himself and his family by staying away for so long.

11

"Well, boys," Tom Smith said, pulling himself out of his book, "I'm going to go home and get a bite to eat, then I'll bring you boys back some grub." He stood to put on his gun belt and coat by the door. "If Clyde gets here before I'm back, tell him where I'm at."

Donovan Moskin was lying tiredly on the bottom bunk while the other three horse thieves slept soundly. He looked up and spoke tiredly, "Where's Clyde anyway, Sheriff? He's a bit more talkative than you."

Tom smiled slightly as he buttoned his long brown coat. "He's collecting the horses you tried to steal. He should be back soon enough."

"Aren't you afraid if you leave us alone, we'll bust out of here?" Donovan asked through a yawn.

Tom laughed lightly. "No. I have the keys and the jail is solid. You'll be here when I get back."

"I think you're right," Donovan agreed. "Besides," he yawned again, "we're all a little too tired to try to escape. As long as the food is good and you keep wood on the fire, we'll be content until the judge arrives. After he lets us go, we might decide to stay here until spring, depending on the food, of course," Donovan finished and he rolled from his back to his side to sleep.

"I can vouch for the food, but I don't know about the judge."

"Mmm," Donovan moaned as he went to sleep.

Tom stepped outside of the sheriff's office and looked around the empty street. The store, saloon and every other little shop and business were open as usual, except for the blacksmith shop. No doubt, Steven was out at the Big Z welcoming his brother home.

The noon hour was bright, sunny, and as beautiful as any sunny day can be with the ground covered with bright white snow and a few billowy white clouds to dot the blue sky. It was December Twenty Third and despite the clear sky and sunshine, it was quite cold. The snow wouldn't be melting today, nor would it for a while.

He stepped off the office porch onto the packed snow of the dirt street and walked a short distance to the livery stable. He saddled up his horse and rode out of town.

The Smith homestead was neither big nor impressive, but it had all the room he needed for his family. It was a warm house despite its simple bare walls, floors, and cedar-shingled roof. It was a basic two-story clap-board home on five acres of cleared land with a small, simple barn. The land provided a garden of good size and fields to feed his few cows and horses. Tom was content with his home and with his life. He had a beautiful wife and four beautiful children that they both adored. Life could not get any better than it was. It was Christmas, a time to praise and give thanks to the Lord who had blessed him so richly. Donovan Moskin might have juvenile ideas of what heaven is, but

Tom had to agree with Donovan about his family. Tom knew just how blessed he was.

Tom tethered the horse in his barn and went into the house. The wood stove gave off plenty of heat and he took off his heavy coat beside the door. His youngest ran to his legs wanting to be picked up. "Hello Sweetie! How's my girl today?" Tom asked joyfully as he picked up his daughter.

"Daddy, James said we were eating Bear for Christmas," Alexis Smith said with great concern on her face. 'Bear' was their black dog of various pedigrees that was as gentle and lovable as could be.

"We wouldn't eat Bear, would we?" Tom laughed as he walked across the floor with her. Elizabeth smiled at him from the kitchen.

"I don't know," Alexis responded.

"Well, we won't. Bear's a part of our family, he's not a hog!" Tom emphasized with a kiss. He put her down, giving her a playful swat on her bottom. "Lunch smells great as usual, Lizzie. Where are the boys?" he asked, looking around.

"The neighbors. This will be ready in a minute," Elizabeth said while she stirred the stew. Her voice was as sweet as always.

"No hurry. Our four guests are all sleeping."

"Is Clyde back from the Andersons?"

"Not yet. I expect him anytime," Tom said sitting down at the dinner table. "You know that Donovan is pretty confident that he'll be let go by Judge Jacoby. He says he knows something about an outlaw hideout called Coffee Canyon over on the Idaho border somewhere. He thinks he can make a deal."

"Could he?" Elizabeth asked with her attention on Tom.

He shrugged. "I don't know anything about that kind of stuff."

Elizabeth pressed, "Do you know what he's talking about? Is he lying? He could be, you know." She turned to him and spoke seriously, "Something about him frightens me. Him and that other guy, the quiet one, what's his name?"

"John Birch, he's apparently from Texas. Have you heard of him?" Tom joked with a smile.

"No, of course not," Elizabeth said softly. "Tom, do you think they're dangerous?"

Tom shrugged. "I don't know and I don't expect to find out. They'll be behind bars until the judge arrives, then they are the judge's problem."

Elizabeth turned back to stirring her stew. "Well, I don't trust either of them, they looked at me like wolves. I got a very strange feeling in my stomach when I went in there today. I didn't like it."

"Well dear..." he began, but Elizabeth cut him off.

"Tom, if they were part of the Doyle Gang and know where that hide-out is, then they're outlaws and that makes them dangerous men. They could be wanted men."

"They say not, but they also said they were horse traders." Tom explained simply, "Elizabeth, I'm not a big city sheriff that deals with men like them. I don't know anything about those men, except one talks too much and the other not enough. I don't even have any real proof that those are their real names. This could all be a lie, I don't know. All I do know is that they attempted to steal horses and they'll stand trial for it, and that's all I need to know."

"What about the boys?" Elizabeth asked softly.

"They'll stand trial too," Tom replied. Elizabeth set

down a bowl of thick hot stew in front of him. "Mmm, that looks good!"

Elizabeth sat down at the table. "I feel for those boys. They're innocent, I can see it in their eyes and they're so scared," she added empathically.

Tom eyed her with a knowing glance. He knew what was coming next. Elizabeth always cared too much about down on their luck people.

"I gathered some clothes for them in a bag, that should help to keep them warm. It's too bad they have to stay in jail. I'd almost bet they'd be gracious guests if they had somewhere else to stay," she hinted to Tom. Her pleading eyes held on Tom while he ate.

He smiled and shook his head. "You know I can't do that. Those boys broke the law, they have to stay where they are," he said softly, but firmly, leaving no room to argue.

"They're so young, Tom. Evan's the same age as Gabriel. It just breaks my heart to see those boys in jail. They don't have anyone to love them, that's why they're there. They just fell in with the wrong men, anyone can see that. Those kids need a family just like Gabriel, they need to be loved."

"Uh huh, and I suppose you want to be their mother too," Tom interjected with a taste of sarcasm.

"No, Tom," she said sweetly, "but we could certainly find them homes, couldn't we?"

Tom sighed. "Lizzie, you talk to the judge when he comes to town, alright? The judge will decide what happens to those boys, not me. Until then, they have to stay in jail."

12

Reverend Abraham Ash was a tall and thin man with a full head of gray hair and long gray sideburns. His wrinkled face showed his sixty-five years of age, usually in an authoritative scowl. He always dressed in black suits with a white shirt and black tie. To his credit, he never missed a Sunday's preaching in his thirty-four years at the Willow Falls Christian Church. Life had always been good, but now in his graying years, life was a glorious gift from God. After forty years of marriage he finally understood what *'loving his wife like Christ loves the church'* really meant. He and his wife, Darla, had fallen in love with Willow Falls the moment they arrived all those years ago. It was here in Willow Falls a year after their arrival from Pennsylvania that the Lord had seen fit to bless them with a daughter after six years of marriage. They named her Elizabeth, and she was the only child they would ever conceive. Now Tom and Elizabeth had given them four beautiful grandchildren to love and adore as they watched them growing older. These were the things the Reverend praised the Lord for, the true blessings in his life.

More than ever before, he realized how good God had been to him.

He sat behind his office desk working on his Christmas message. He looked out of his office window at the white church with its sharp angled roof and tall steeple. He had looked out the same window for thirty-four years now at the church next door to his house. The honor of preaching the Lord's word was the greatest honor any man could have. To be called into the ministry of Jesus Christ was the ultimate of all callings, one that Abraham Ash had answered long before he brought his bride West. After all these years, he still loved to teach the Lord's word, like the sermon he was writing for the day after Christmas about the faithfulness of God. Abraham could say without exception that the sun rose in the East every morning and disappeared over the West every afternoon of his life. When his daughter was little, he'd throw her up into the air and catch her when she came back down. He never worried about her flying away when he tossed her up into the air because gravity is a constant law. So is faithfulness to Jesus Christ. Jesus is always faithful to provide for His own people.

It was easier now to look back over his life's journey and see how blessed his life had been by the Lord without ever realizing it. Elizabeth's childhood was one of those blessings that he didn't appreciate at the time. He recalled clearly the many times she was a nuisance, and he had no patience with her when he was trying to work. He had been strict with Elizabeth, stricter than he should have been. The Bible encourages spankings to correct the disobedient paths of a child, but the Bible says to do it in love. Ministers of the Gospel are simple human beings just like anyone else; they make mistakes and have some regrets in life too. Abraham's regret wasn't simply spanking his daughter; it was beating his daughter with his leather strap. Not just once or twice, but more often than he wanted to remember.

He was the town Reverend and Abraham knew the standards of his home needed to be much higher than anyone else's. He was the shepherd and no one would follow a shepherd who couldn't manage his own family. Abraham had worried so much about his reputation and being blameless before the congregation that he wasn't the father that he should have been.

There was a simple gray river rock that set on his desk. It had a smooth water worn surface and was vaguely shaped like a heart. He picked it up and smiled slightly as he turned it around with his fingers. Elizabeth had given it to him when she was a little girl. The memories were bittersweet. It was many years ago on a mid-July Sunday service along Pearl Creek. The entire congregation had shown up for an outdoor service and potluck with an afternoon schedule of games and family fun. It had been a great day, but as the day wore on, it became frighteningly apparent that some of the children were missing, four of them to be exact; Matthew Bannister, Thomas Smith, Joseph Jackson, and Elizabeth Ash. All of their parents and many others had called for the children and then sent out search parties up and down the small river that could be deep and dangerous in places. Panic began to settle into every parent when they couldn't find any sign of the children, who were all between the ages of six and seven-years-old. After an hour of searching and much frantic prayer, Floyd Bannister and his older boys found the four children more than a mile downstream catching crawdads. Floyd laughed as he brought them out of the woods, "Boys will be boys!" he called. The other parents hugged their children tightly and scolded them mildly if at all. All three of the children were wet and covered with mud. Elizabeth's white church dress was ruined. The grass and mud stains would never come out, which infuriated Abraham.

"Well," Ruth Bannister spoke in her gentle way, "it seems my little explorer, Matthew, took all of your kids on one of his wild adventures." She paused to laugh while holding him close in front of her large pregnant belly. "With a little scrubbing the boys will come clean, but I don't know about Elizabeth's dress, Darla."

"Oh that's all right," Darla Ash said gently, while trying to hide her disappointment.

Abraham wasn't as capable of sounding so at ease. He scolded her with his loud baritone voice, "Look at your dress young lady! You've ruined it. Get on the wagon!" He grabbed her arm and quickly led her to their wagon.

"Daddy, I didn't..."

"Don't speak! We'll deal with this at home in the wood-shed! I don't want to hear a word until then," he warned sternly. "Darla, we've got to go," he added in a kinder voice.

Ruth Bannister touched Darla's arm. "Darla, we'll gladly replace her dress. She was with Matthew and he's quite the mud-dauber."

"No, no, that's not necessary," Darla replied.

"I will replace the dress. I feel it's my son's fault, and the Lord knows that if I had a daughter I'd want her in a clean dress on Sundays." Ruth said feeling badly for Elizabeth. "The other six days she'd be in jeans with her five brothers I'm sure!"

Abraham could not react naturally, he had to choose his reaction in front of his flock. Though angered, he spoke with his normal tone, "Well, whether girl or boy," he glanced at Matthew, "discipline is a biblical necessity that teaches obedience. Come love," he said gently to Darla.

Elizabeth had cried all the way home knowing she was in trouble. Once at home, Abraham took her to her bedroom and stripped her dress off of her and gave into his fury with his two-foot long, by one-inch wide, leather strap. He beat her furiously. Her every scream of pain and cry for mercy was ignored as a deep rage climbed up and out of him with every wild swing of his strap. Darla, finally outraged and screaming to stop Abraham's torrent of abuse stepped in between the two. Abraham stood over his withering and wailing daughter trying to catch his breath. Darla glared at Abraham insolently while she held Elizabeth close to comfort her while she screamed in pain. Without apologizing Abraham picked up her muddy dress and tossed it onto her welted body.

Late that night, Abraham was in his study reading his Bible. Unexpectedly, Elizabeth meekly peeked into his office from the opened door.

"What?" he asked sternly. He was still quite angry. Elizabeth sheepishly walked to his desk and laid the rock in front of him.

"What's that?" he asked, as she turned to leave wordlessly.

She turned to face him. Large tears welled up in her eyes, but she refused to let them fall. "I found this heart-rock in the river. I'm sorry I got my dress dirty, Daddy, but I got it for you. Because I love you," she uttered carefully. Her small body quivered as she eyed her father longing to be held. Her tears grew heavily. Her every emotion of fear, sorrow, and wanting forgiveness showed clearly in her innocent gaze. She needed to say nothing more. Her anguished expression revealed her inner turmoil.

Abraham laid his Bible down. No longer was the flame of anger burning, Elizabeth's words and tears had extinguished it. He smiled slightly as he picked up the rock to look at it. It could have been used as a skipping stone; it was worn so smooth and flat. He could not make out a distinct heart shape necessarily, but it was shaped vaguely like a child's idea of a heart. He nodded and pushed his chair back. "Come here, sweetie," he said softly.

Immediately she ran around the big desk and into the arms of her father and began sobbing. She held him tightly, much tighter than he had expected. "I'm sorry about my dress, Daddy. I won't do it again," she sobbed heavily on his shoulder.

"Good," he replied simply and put her down before she was ready to let go. "I'll keep the rock. Now you get to bed." He watched her leave his office and she stopped at the door to look back and wave. After she left, he picked up the rock. It was a symbol of her love and he would keep it on his desk from that day forward.

The memory of that day had always haunted him. For as hard as he was compelled to say the words, he could not say, "I love you". For all these years, he had kept the rock on his desk to remind him of that day. Abraham wished he could say he had changed from that day forward, but he hadn't. He continued to use his strap when he was angered.

It became frequent in her mid-teen years when she and Matt were becoming much too serious. After Matt murdered five unarmed men on Pearl Creek, he became the thorn in Abraham's side. He was consistently sneaking around the Ash home to see Elizabeth and she was more than willing to sneak out to be with him. It came to a head one night when she openly defied the Reverend's authority and proclaimed her intention to marry Matt when she came of age, which was only a month away. She was seventeen and time was running out, it only seemed reasonable for the Reverend to persuade Tom to ask Elizabeth to marry him. It was his responsibility to see to his daughter's future, the best way he knew how. Using his parental control over her decision to marry Tom was his God given right, and he was glad he did it the way that he had. They sure were a happy and loving family now.

Abraham knew Elizabeth would deny it, but his first-born grandson was the seed of Matt Bannister. He couldn't bear to say the words that were so shameful that the very thought of it embittered him. The Reverend disdained Matt with the same compassion that a shepherd has for a wolf pup. Abraham had done all that he knew how to do, short of shooting the wretched young man, to distance his daughter from him.

Matt's leaving Willow Falls was a blessing; it ceased all his worries until Gabriel was born. For fifteen years, life in Willow Falls had been peaceful, but now Matt had come back a more mature killer than when he'd left. It was bad news for Abraham and he had only one prayer, he prayed that Gabriel wouldn't learn who his real father was. The thorn in Abraham's side was back and even more dangerous than ever before to the security of his daughter's family.

The Reverend, for the first time in a very long time, went to the Lord in anxious prayer and his prayer was filled with fear. Matt Bannister himself, probably had no idea of the damage he could permanently cause in the sleepy town of Willow Falls. Abraham had always prayed that Matt would never return, but he had! Abraham went to the Lord for protection as he had done countless times during his life. He knew as surely as the sun rises in the East and falls to the West that the Lord would be faithful to deliver his family from the threat of Matt Bannister.

13

Evan Gray looked very much like his older brother, Rodney. He had a slim build with straight dirty blond hair that fell over their ears and sensitive blue eyes on a thin oval face. The two brothers were often referred to as handsome boys, but neither had an ounce of luck so far. They thought meeting up with Donovan and John was an opportunity at a new life. But now, sitting in the semi-warm jail charged with horse theft, it didn't seem like much luck at all.

The Gray family came West from New York with high expectations of a new beginning in Oregon's Willamette Valley. The Grey's dreams of moving to Oregon were suddenly derailed when their family contracted diphtheria. Their parents buried their two youngest children in the Kansas soil. Their mother was weakened by the disease and badly shaken by the loss of her two youngest. She never regained her strength and became susceptible to every illness that showed itself along the journey. She passed away from pneumonia not long after crossing the Oregon border. Two days later, they entered Branson where a doctor could have possibly saved her life had she survived. They rested for a few days in Branson and then moved on to the mighty Columbia River and ferried to The Dalles. For no apparent reason, other than defeat their father decided to stop and call The Dalles home. Their father, Teddy Gray, found work in the stockyard and rented shack to live in. The two brothers watched their once respected father dwindle into a drunk. Their father's dreams of a new beginning in Oregon had cost him the lives of half his family and left him a broken man. Two months ago, he was beaten to death outside of a saloon of bad repute beside the river. The assailant or assailants, were never caught, found, or named as there were no witnesses or answers; only a lifeless beaten body. The only known fact was that Teddy Gray, the drunk, was dead.

The two brothers were left on their own and worked at the stockyard occasionally, stole some, and even begged a little to survive. Then on a cold November night, a candle caught the rented shack on fire. It burned quickly, and they lost everything their family ever owned, except the clothes on their backs.

The town folks came to the boy's rescue and found them another place to live with a decent church family so they thought. But the brothers weren't treated well and it certainly didn't feel like home. The two brothers wanted out of their new foster home and go back to New York to live with their aunt and uncle. Their aunt and uncle were poor and couldn't afford to help the boys get home. Wanting to earn enough money to buy stage and train tickets, the two brothers took to begging.

Donovan saw the boys panhandling outside in the wind and snow for pennies. He offered the boys fifty cents to take his and John's horses to the stable while they caroused in the saloon. Learning later that the boys were orphans and taking a liking to them, Donovan promised to outfit the two brothers with horses and supplies if they accepted an offer to work for him. They were being given an opportunity to leave The Dalles once and for all and any job that offered benefits like that, was an opportunity of a lifetime! Rodney and Evan quickly accepted the offer. True to his word, Donovan bought the two boys horses and saddles; he supplied them with gun belts and warm clothes to wear while on the trail. It was December, and the Columbia River Gorge was white with snow, with a constant wind that could blow the warmth out of a man far too quickly if he wasn't suitably covered. Donovan spent a lot of money in The Dalles on women, booze, and of course the two boys. He then bought tickets on a sternwheeler up the Columbia River to Walla Walla, Washington. From there they rode to the town of Pendleton where Donovan and John rented rooms in separate hotels. Donovan kept the two boys with him under false names pretending to be a father with his two sons. He stayed for two days studying the town and one particular house, a colonial that was set off by itself on top of a hill. It belonged to the local bank president and city councilman. Donovan waited until late at night after most people were asleep and forced himself into the home. He took what he and John wanted from the terrified homeowners, money, jewels, and any other valuables that they could sell for some quick cash.

Donovan and John didn't rob banks or trains, they robbed empty stores or as they did in Pendleton, a prominent man's home. All robberies were done at night and the unsuspecting victims were tied up with rope. Donovan stressed that the victims had to believe that they were lucky to be left alive. They had to fear that the bandits would return if the sheriff was notified, therefore; the victims had to believe that it was someone local who robbed them. They would have little to tell the sheriff as the robbers wore burlap hoods over their faces. No one in town could place Donovan with John and for all practical purposes, they were strangers. Donovan had spoken of robbing rich homes and empty stores all through the state of California and up through the Willamette Valley of Oregon. "Stay on the move," Donovan explained. "People can't identify someone they don't know and won't ever see again."

They had no plan when they came across the farmhouse outside of Willow Falls. It was just a decent sized home with a corral of horses and no smoke from the fireplace. The house was empty and contained no money or jewelry, the only valuable commodity was the horses. Donovan decided with two extra hands joining them they could herd the horses to Branson at night and sell them in the morning before anyone could track them down. He thought they could make a decent amount of money and then disappear into Idaho somewhere before they did it all over again. Donovan Moskin was a planner and a quick thinker and he thought things through pretty well, except he hadn't realized how far away Branson was from where they stole the horses.

Holding up at the Anderson's home for the night was never part of the plan, but it got too cold to go any further on empty stomachs. The elderly couple offered to warm and feed them if they wished to stay the night. Donovan complied heartedly, despite John Birch's argument to keep pushing the herd through the night. Donovan reasoned that it was past dark, cold and snowing, it was doubtful that any lawman would press through the night for a herd of horses. Donovan also hoped the fresh falling snow would cover their tracks, but even if it didn't, they would be in a good position inside of a warm home with food and two hostages if need be. At dawn they would push fast for Branson and sell the horses to the first offer.

Evan Gray opened his eyes and looked at the ceiling of the jail. The room was silent, except for the crackling of the wood stove. Rodney slept below him on the bottom bunk while John Birch slept on the top bunk in the next cell. Donovan lay on his bed with his hands clasped behind his head with his eyes open. He was deep in thought.

Evan never imagined that they would get arrested. He thought Donovan and John were too smart to get caught, as they had authorities from Arizona, California and all the way across Oregon looking for a pair of strangers that they would never see again. If the law knew of all the crimes committed just since the Gray brothers had joined up; they'd all be hung! Evan had wanted out of The Dalles bad enough to fall in with a pair of friendly strangers who turned out to be vicious outlaws. Now Evan wished he was back in The Dalles begging for change, rather than in the Willow Falls jail waiting for a trial. He turned onto his side resting his head on his arm. "Mister Moskin?"

"Mmm," Donovan grunted without looking at him.

"Do you think we'll be let go?"

"Yep, one way or another," Donovan said matter-of-factly.

"So you don't think we'll be hung?" Evan asked.

"No. We won't hang," he answered turning his head. "Don't worry about that. I got you in here, I'll get you out."

"I've never been in jail before," Evan stated nervously. "My father used to say jails were for fools and criminals. Stealing is wrong, Mister Moskin. But hurting people is worse. If we are let out of jail, I don't want to go with you anymore. We have some relatives back home in New York and I'm going back there," he finished sheepishly.

"How are you getting there, Evan? You don't have a penny to your name," Donovan said bluntly. "I'll make you a deal. Do what I say and keep your mouth *shut*," he emphasized, "and I'll buy you and your brother a ticket back to New York as soon as we get to a railroad. But you have to keep quiet! That's all I'm asking," Donovan sounded sincere.

"I don't know. I mean, I don't want to steal anymore and it's wrong, what we do."

"We..?" Donovan almost shouted. He glared up from his bed to Evan, unintentionally waking up John and Rodney with his deep voice. "You haven't done a damn thing, except hold our horses!" he stopped, realizing he was talking too loudly. He took a deep breath and continued in a milder manner, "Evan, I told you both in The Dalles what we were doing. You and your brother decided to join up. I bought the horses for you boys to ride and bought you guns and your clothes. You owe me that much, don't you?" Donovan asked expectedly. "I'm the only one who gave a damn about you two when you were begging on the street. I may not be much, but I went out of my way to get you out of that place. And it costed me a lot of money. You owe me that much, right?"

Evan was quiet. "Yes," he finally agreed. In their desperation to leave they foolishly indebted themselves to Donovan for getting him out of The Dalles and into the Willow Falls jail. "But it doesn't make it right, Mr. Moskin," Evan finished with a hint of helplessness in his voice.

"There is no right or wrong," Donovan stated matter-of-factly, "there's only survival. And we're surviving, aren't we? We have money and we'll be out of here soon enough. In a couple of weeks, you'll both be on a train to New York. Then you can go back to school and tell all your school chums that you rode with Rusty Moskin."

"How do you know we're getting out of here?" Evan asked troubled by his increasing anxiety. "They hang people for stealing horses and I don't want to die! We should have stayed in The Dalles, at least there I wasn't going to be hung!"

Rodney Gray quickly got out of his bed to stand and look at his little brother on the top bunk at eye level. "Evan, we're not going to hang! The sheriff said the judge wasn't a hanging judge and Mister Moskin knows what to do, don't you?" Rodney questioned Donovan.

"Sure," Donovan spoke with confidence. He stood up and held onto the bars that separated the cells to look at the brothers. "Listen guys, you too, John, don't worry about this," he motioned to the jail bars. "I'll get us out of here, I promise. The judge can't know about anything, and I mean anything, except for the horses. That's why I want you boys to keep your mouths shut tight. If they find out about the robberies or anything else we've done, we're all going to hang, including you two!" he paused for effect. "So keep your mouths shut! I've got a plan, but keep in mind that we're dealing with simple people, who haven't spent much time anywhere, except for here! I know where Coffee Canyon is." He paused for effect as he lowered his voice, "Every lawman in the country would like to find it and the one who does will be quite famous. I'm going to dangle that information in front of the judge like a worm to a Missouri catfish. He'll bite at the opportunity and we'll ride out of here free men!"

John Birch questioned Donovan, "That sounds great and all, but how are you going to prove it? Like the sheriff said, you can't just draw a map and expect him to let you go."

"Nope," Donovan agreed. "I expect them to let you guys go, and I'll take them there. After I'm exonerated we'll all meet up in Boise. Don't you worry, ole Rusty's got it all figured out. I'm offering the judge the chance of his lifetime. It's a chance he'll never get again, but I have to get the sheriff to understand what I'm offering first. I don't think he's the brightest pup of the litter, so I'd like to get him excited about it. What do you think, John?"

"Well," John Birch said calmly, "as long as it gets us out of here and someplace warmer. I'll never come this far north again, I can tell you that. Not ever!"

14

In many ways Matt was still the same quiet, soft-spoken boy he had always been. He kept eye contact when he spoke or listened, but behind his eyes he seemed to be analyzing the very words he was hearing, comparing them to the speaker's body language to see if it weighed up to the truth. He had always been slow to trust and quick to pick up on the tiniest detail that didn't add up. Matt and his brother, Lee, could look into the eyes of another man and somehow know the character of that man. From the character they could guess the person's actions almost exactly. Lee had used that extra sense to build his fortune in Branson, while Matt had used it to track down murderers, thieves, and other outlaw vermin. Matt had become a household name with a reputation that was relentless, harsh, cold, and deadly. He was a nightmare for anyone running from the law.

Charlie Ziegler considered that momentarily as he and Matt drove an empty wagon back from feeding the cattle. The Big Z wasn't the biggest nor the most successful ranch in the state by any means, but it suited Charlie's needs just fine. There were things more important in business than just money, and to Charlie the most important was enjoying the means of earning what money was made, followed secondly by the integrity of the means. There were two keys to living a life of contentment and the first was enjoying one's wife. The second key was enjoying the labor of their work. A bitter man enjoyed neither and despised his life, but a joyful man loved his wife and his labor. Charlie considered that as he looked over at his nephew.

"So tell me, Matt," Charlie spoke as he turned the now wagon westward. "Do you like what you're doing?"

"The Chinese took all the hammering jobs on the railroad, so I had to do something," Matt mused with a slight smile.

Charlie smiled slightly. "You've sure made a heck of a name for yourself," he said seriously. "How much longer you expect it to last?"

Matt sighed uncomfortably. "Your meaning?"

"I got out of the business years ago when I could. Because sooner or later everyone's luck runs out, including yours," he emphasized.

Matt nodded. "Sooner or later," he agreed quietly.

"But you're not giving it up?"

"I don't have anything to give it up for."

"Oh bull!" Charlie scoffed. "You've got a family that loves you, but you've got to decide if that matters enough. You've been gone a long time, way too long. You've been a marshal longer than most ever are. Maybe it's time to give that badge back and come home, before you wind up dead."

"I can't, Uncle Charlie," Matt said with finality.

"Well, Matt," Charlie sounded disappointed, "I won't keep talking about it. If you don't want to come home, I will respect your decision. I won't mention it again. The choice is yours." A moment later he said, "I missed you in Montana by one day,"

"What?" Matt asked.

"About six years ago we took a herd to Missoula. You'd just left town the day before, I heard. I thought about tracking you down, but figured if you wanted to see me, you knew where we lived."

"Six years ago, huh?" Matt questioned himself while thinking back. "You should have tracked me down, Uncle Charlie."

"It wouldn't have done any good," Charlie stated simply. He turned the wagon in a sudden northern direction. "You wouldn't have come back with me, anyway."

"No, but it would have been good to see you."

"Likewise," Charlie agreed. "I read that you killed B.J. Ramsey. You know that he was once a friend of mine. We rode together when I bounty hunted."

"I know," he sounded troubled. "I used to talk to him quite a bit. He was always interested in coming out here for a visit."

Charlie frowned curiously. "You sound as if you were friends with him?"

"We were," he answered without any other explanation.

"What changed?"

Matt frowned. "One night in the See-Saw Saloon, there in Cheyenne, he was drunk and waving his gun around. It turns out he had a love affair going on with a young prostitute that convinced him she was his one and only. Of course, she was only pacifying him. When he discovered she was open to anyone that had a dollar, he hurt her pretty bad. Then he went downstairs waving his gun around looking for the other man; or men to be precise that had been with her. Nobody was safe. The deputy came and got me because he knew BJ and I were friends. BJ had a certain affection for me, that came from being your nephew, I think. He always talked about you, Uncle Charlie," Matt said softly. "Anyway, I went to the See-Saw Saloon and tried to talk some sense into him. I tried..." the sadness in Matt's voice was evident. He took a deep breath. "He was in a rage. I had no other choice."

"Well," Charlie spoke slowly, "BJ always could have a temper when he drank. He was the one guy I could trust to watch my back." He paused and then added, "It goes to show you though that when a moral man gives his heart to an immoral woman, she'll throw it away and break his heart every time. Women like that have been the ruin of many good men. And BJ was a good man." Charlie glanced at Matt and nodded. "I know that has to be tough on you, but I'm glad you're a marshal rather than an outlaw."

"I believe in the law," Matt said simply. "That's why I can't leave it behind. I believe in what I do. Besides, you had all of this to come home to when you stopped hunting men," he said with a wave over the ranch.

"So do you. I'm getting too old to work this place alone. All you boys have run off to do your own things and Annie's got a pretty good head on her shoulders, but she needs men to work it. Kyle is a fair hand when he wants to be, but he's inconsistent and a bit like your father, I'm afraid. Darius, like me, is getting too old to work so hard. So Annie will need some help to keep this place running when your aunt and I hand the reins over. There's plenty of room for you to come back here," Charlie finished making his point clear.

"How are Mr. and Mrs. Jackson?" Matt asked about the

black couple that lived in a house to the north end of the ranch. They had been with Charlie and Mary for over twenty-five years. Darius Jackson was a tough old cowboy who was as dedicated to Charlie as Mary was. Their son Joseph was Matt's best friend.

"Olivia died three years ago," Charlie explained simply. "Darius is doing okay though. Rory still lives with him and takes care of him. She's become a pretty young lady too, by the way." Charlie nudged Matt's shoulder playfully. He added seriously, "Darius hurt his knee about a week ago, so we're heading over to check in. They might need something."

"When I was little," Matt began, "right after meeting Joseph, we'd get together every day and play. One day, Lee introduced me to a new word, 'Nigger'. He had asked me why I was playing with a nigger. I didn't know what a nigger was, so he explained to me that it was a black person, like Joseph. The next day, Mrs. Jackson brought Joseph over to play, while she visited with Aunt Mary. We were out back in the grove playing guns, he had his stick gun, and I had mine. I said to him very sincerely, 'do you know what you are?' He shook his head, no, and I said 'you're a nigger.'" Matt smiled to himself as he continued, "He must've known what that word meant because he hit me in the head with that stick! I started crying and ran towards the house to get Aunt Mary, but Albert stopped me and asked why I was crying. I told him Joseph hit me in the head with a stick. So Albert gave me a bigger stick, a board in fact, to go hit Joseph back with. I ran back up that hill and chased Joseph back down it to the house trying to hit him with my board. Aunt Mary and Mrs. Jackson heard Joseph yelling and met us outside. I thought perhaps Joseph would get a good licking for hitting me, but when he explained why he hit me, I was the one in trouble. Aunt Mary was madder than all get out and was getting a switch when Mrs. Jackson asked her if she could handle it. Mrs. Jackson sat Joseph and me down on the porch step and explained that 'nigger' wasn't a word that should ever be used, especially between friends." He thought back reflectively. "It may not sound too impressive. But it's one of those profound moments in my life that I never forgot. I never heard that word again until that day on Pearl Creek. I've hated that word ever since."

Charlie looked at Matt softly. "Yeah, it's just as simple as the color of a man's skin that gets him killed sometimes. Joseph was just a child, of course, but it can happen anywhere. Darius is the greatest man I've ever known, but if he went to town today no one would care about that. All they'd see is he's black; not the great man. Rory too, it just isn't safe for them around certain people. There is a lot of bigots out there."

"I've met some," Matt agreed, and then changed the subject back to Rory. "How old is she now twenty-four, twenty-five?"

"Twenty-five. She's become quite a beautiful young lady by the way. Your cousin, William, has been trying to court her for a while now, but she's got higher expectations for a husband than most white women I think."

Charlie drove the wagon to the rim of a hill, over-looking the Jackson homestead. It was in a small valley clustered with some oak and fruit trees next to a small pond with a stream running through it. Not far from the pond was a solidly built one-story house with a big covered front porch and a stone chimney releasing smoke. The first thing Matt noticed was the house was painted white with red trim. It had never been painted when he was growing up, and it never looked better than it did now. Not far away was the overly large weathered barn for storing hay and livestock for the Big Z Ranch. Though, Charlie owned the property on paper, the homestead had always belonged to Darius and his family and it always would as long as Charlie owned the land.

15

Rory Jackson stood in the kitchen cooking a large pot of her spicy chili beans for their Christmas dinner. Her chili recipe had been passed down from generation to generation and was an expected part of the Ziegler Christmas. Olivia had made it every year and now it was Rory's turn to make it. She didn't mind though because it wasn't just expected; it was greatly appreciated. As her chili cooked, she kneaded dough for the bread later that evening. She took pride in her bread and every Christmas dinner turned into a competition between Aunt Mary, Annie and herself to see whose bread was best. Rory was determined to make such a delicious bread on Christmas morning that Annie couldn't declare herself the winner like she always did.

Rory was dressed in blue jeans with an apron over her flannel shirt. She normally didn't dress in pants and flannel shirts, but with her father's knee injury she was doing the daily chores out in the barn which she could do easier in jeans. Her long black hair was tied back in a loose ponytail that reached her mid-back. Her face was thin and oval shaped with large brown eyes and a beautiful smile. Her dark skin was soft and smooth and only her hands showed any evidence of being a rancher's daughter. She was a lady through and through.

Rory looked out the window when their dog barked. She recognized Charlie Ziegler immediately as the wagon slowly lumbered down the hill. She didn't recognize the other rider. "Daddy, Charlie's here. I don't know who's with him though," she said as she wiped her hands on her apron.

"Oh?" Darius replied curiously. He carefully stood from his chair with the help of a crutch. His knee had given out on him a week ago when he jumped down off a wagon. He could walk, but it still ached quite a bit and at his age, it was best to just let it heal before going back to work. Darius grabbed his coat that hung by the door and stepped outside into the cold sunny day to meet Charlie. Rory followed him out buttoning her coat.

"Whoa," Charlie called as he pulled the team of horses to a stop. "Darius, I brought you a visitor. You might remember him, but I don't know," he said while he stepped carefully down from the wagon.

Matt had already climbed down and walked around the horses to greet Darius. "Hello, Mr. Jackson," Matt offered, holding out his ungloved hand. Darius had gotten older and his hair had grayed, but his smile was still bright and lively, even though he hobbled on a crutch.

Darius laughed. "Well, I'll be! Matthew, get yourself over here!" He hugged Matt tightly. "It's about time you pulled yourself back here, boy! You look good! Matthew, my gosh, it's good to see you!" Darius held Matt by the shoulders eyeing him happily. "You remember Rory?" Darius asked turning his attention to Rory. She was standing behind him close to the house. She appeared to be as shy as a mouse.

"This is Matthew! You were young when he left, but you remember him don't you?"

"I remember you," she said quietly without so much as a small smile. She stared at him without any sign of emotion.

Matt spoke to Rory, "You've grown up. The last time I saw you; you were just a little girl."

Rory nodded her head slightly. "It's been a long time."

"Too long," Matt agreed with an awkward smile. He turned his attention back to Darius. "I just heard that Mrs. Jackson had passed on. I'm sorry," he said sincerely.

"No need to be sorry, Matthew. She lived a life worthy of salvation and right now she's up in heaven singing praises to the Lord. That was the one thing she loved to do the most, and Joseph's right there with her. So don't be sorry!"

Matt nodded sadly.

"Matthew," Darius continued with a fatherly tone in his voice, "You still carry eyes of sadness, boy. Before you leave, you and I are having a talk, okay?"

"Anytime," he said to Darius.

Darius looked at Charlie and smiled. "Well, come on in out of the cold. Since you did my work today, the least I could do is fill you up with some hot coffee!"

"That and a week's wages," Charlie replied.

"That's pert near my life's savings," Darius laughed. "Oh Matthew, if I'd known how tight your old uncle was going to hold onto his money purse in his old age, I would have run off with you a long time ago. You're rich by now, aren't you?" he asked playfully as he put his arm around Matt to escort him into his home.

16

"Mom," Gabriel Smith called as he came into the house with his younger brother and sisters. "Do you mind if I go to town?"

"What for?" Elizabeth asked curiously. She was busy putting the final touches on her daughter's dress for the Christmas service on Sunday.

"I want to see if Steven's at his shop," Gabriel explained over the chattering of his younger siblings.

"Steven? Why, Gabriel?" Elizabeth asked over the non-stop noise of the other children wanting their mother's attention.

"So he can introduce me to Matt!" Gabriel answered simply.

"You met him last night," Elizabeth said looking at Gabriel with a concerned expression coming over on her face. Like every other young boy in Willow Falls Gabriel grew up under the shadow of the famous lawman. He owned every book he could find about Matt and asked nearly everyone in town if they had known him. Learning that Steven was Matt's brother; Gabriel then spent more time in Steven's blacksmith shop than Elizabeth was comfortable with. She couldn't very well forbid him from going there without having a reason and she couldn't think of one. Steven was one of the town's most upstanding citizens. What she did find unbelievable was Steven nor anyone else seemed to notice that Gabriel looked like Matthew. Which seemed kind of odd because Elizabeth saw Matt's face every time she looked at their son.

Charlie Ziegler was the only person that Elizabeth suspected could see the truth. There was something in his eyes the last time she had seen him that told her he knew Matt was Gabriel's father. It was on Clyde's birthday and Charlie had brought a homemade pie from Mary to the sheriff's office. Gabriel had bumped into Charlie when he was entering the door and bounced off of the older man in horror. He had been conditioned to fear Charlie Ziegler by his grandfather. Charlie looked at Gabriel with his hard chiseled face and penetrating eyes carefully, slowly his stern expression melted into an affectionate grin. He nodded silently to Gabriel and then moved his eyes to Elizabeth's, where she promptly looked away and hurried Gabriel into the office. She looked back at Charlie after stepping through the door. He had turned and held her gaze momentarily with a disappointed expression on his face. A long forgotten layer of guilt layered over her heart like a soft blanket. She had always had a special affection for Charlie and Mary, even after all these years she still had a great fondness for them. Unfortunately, she hadn't spoken to them in years. Elizabeth could fool many people, but she highly doubted she could fool Charlie and Mary. They were two people she could not lie to. So she avoided them.

She once dreamed of living on the Big Z Ranch, but her dream was shattered the day after Joseph Jackson was killed. Matt Bannister, as the world would come to know him, was born that day and the carefree youthful Matthew was never the same again. The account of what happened on Pearl Creek was published in every one of the books Gabriel owned, every version was different than the next. Gabriel had read every version of the story, but still didn't know the truth. Maybe he never would know the real story since not even Steven had ever told him the truth about that day.

"Well, yeah, I met him last night," Gabriel answered his mother's question. "But, I didn't get to talk to him. He's Steven's brother, Mom. If Steven introduces me to Matt, I can talk to him and get to know him."

"No. You have chores to do," Elizabeth heard herself say quietly and rather awkwardly.

"No, I don't. I've already done them this morning. Besides, I have time before..."

"Gabriel," she interjected strongly, "I told you, no!"

"Mom," he raised his voice, "I don't have any chores to do. I've already done them."

"Gabriel Smith!" Elizabeth shouted. She was surprised by her own tone, but she was desperate to keep him from going to town. "You get to your room! That's where you'll be today until your father gets home. He can deal with your disobedience!" She glared angrily at him as her heart suddenly began to race with a troubling anxiety.

"What disobedience, Mother?" Gabriel questioned innocently. He walked towards the steep narrow stairs that led up to his room confused and angry. "One of these days I'm going to pack my things and disappear!" he threatened.

Elizabeth tossed the dress she was mending to the floor and stood quickly. She erupted loudly, "What did you say, Gabriel? Tell me again what you just said!" she demanded.

"I said…" he paused to take a deep breath. He spoke in a normal tone, soft spoken and controlled, "Nothing."

Elizabeth's tone was harsh, "Are you thinking of running away Gabriel? Are you?" she demanded an answer.

"No," Gabriel answered, "I was…"

"And what would you do if you did?" she interrupted bitterly. "Drift around aimlessly like those boys in the jail? Meet the wrong people and follow them to the gallows, or do you think you'd become someone famous like Matt?" Gabriel's head lifted to meet her eyes. She could see she had hit the nail on the head.

"Gabriel," she sighed heavily. She placed her hands on her hips and took a deep breath to calm herself. She was about to tell him that he wasn't anything like Matt Bannister, but she couldn't. Gabriel was more like Matt than he'd ever know, Lord willing. Tears of frustration filled her eyes, she forced them back down. "Matt Bannister was raised by Charlie Ziegler, a gun fighter. Matt learned how to shoot and how to survive from him. You know nothing of that life style," she stated desperately.

"I could learn," Gabriel answered evenly. "I know how to shoot. I'm a good shot, Mom. I don't miss, you know that," Gabriel finished with pride.

It was true that Gabriel seldom missed when shooting targets and was even a better shot than Tom at distance shooting. There was no question that Gabriel had Matt's eye and accuracy with a rifle. "You shoot targets, Matt shoots men who are shooting back! Do you understand that, Gabriel? You would be killed because you don't know the first thing about it!" she spat out. "You should want to be a Godly husband and a loving father, like yours. Not a killer like Matt!" she spoke passionately and then froze. She had never referred to Matt as a killer in her life and for the first time she sounded just like her father.

"Dad's the sheriff of Willow Falls, Mom. Nothing ever happens here, we don't even need a sheriff," he griped too quickly.

"Don't you ever talk like that again!" Elizabeth snapped with her hard and angry eyes burning into him as she pointed a finger at him. "Your father is a respected man in this community and he sure was needed just last night, wasn't he? Quite possibly, one or two of those men rode in the Doyle Gang. So don't stand here in my house and tell me that they aren't dangerous or that my husband is useless as the sheriff! How dare you, Gabriel!" she yelled angrily. "Get to your room!"

"Fine! But I didn't say he was useless. I meant if he was in Dodge City or somewhere, he might have to use his gun like Matt and everyone else who's known outside of Willow Falls!"

"Gabriel!" Elizabeth gave a stern warning to not speak another word.

"I'm going!" Gabriel shouted back and ran upstairs.

Elizabeth wanted to burst into tears. Her world compressing with the arrival of Matt and the fear that it brought. Gabriel always went to town, there was nothing abnormal about that. The real issue was she was afraid that Matt being his father would come out in the open. To stop that from happening she'd keep Gabriel at home loaded with chores from dusk till dawn. It was wrong to punish Gabriel for being a boy, but in this case it was necessary to keep a larger, more consequential harm from happening. She pushed her thoughts aside and put her attention on her other children who pulled at her dress for her attention.

Upstairs, Gabriel sat on his bed and picked up his

favorite book about Matt Bannister from his bedside table. He wanted to get the marshal's autograph on it, inscribed to Gabriel himself. He wanted to ask the marshal about Pearl Creek, the Answar Saloon and Cinnamon Gulch in northern New Mexico. He wanted to hear the stories and be in awe of the man whom the stories were written about. He wanted to meet and talk to the legend himself, because as the line below the book's title proudly proclaimed: *"Every outlaw alive and breathing today has never had Matt Bannister on their trail."* Gabriel wanted to hear the stories from the man himself.

17

Tom Smith leaned back in his chair with his feet on the desk. His hands were clasped behind his head as he spoke to his prisoners. He enjoyed having prisoners in his seldom-used cells, it took away from the boredom of the job and even put a little excitement into it. Sitting in the sheriff's office all day waiting to be used wasn't a lot of fun, but it did pay well for a lot of sitting. He had been elected sheriff five years before and no one had seen fit to run against him in the last election.

Clyde Waltz had been the deputy for so long that he was a permanent fixture at the jail for as far back as Tom could remember. Clyde enjoyed the lazy days and getting paid for them. He had reached his sixty-sixth birthday, but was no more willing to give up his job, as he was willing to marry someone. Clyde was a different sort of man who didn't need or want much out of life. He simply filled the deputy position his whole law career and had worked under five different sheriffs doing so. Clyde never ran for sheriff because he didn't want the responsibility; he just wanted to sit on the front porch or behind his own desk and watch the time go by. He lived in a room in the sheriff's office and was there most of the time. Four or five times a year he'd leave town to go to his cabin up on Lake Jessup in the Blue Mountains. He'd stay a few days at a time, but every August he'd stay a full two weeks and then he'd come back down to work. He wasn't an authoritative lawman, but around Willow Falls he was respected just the same for being Clyde, the lifelong deputy.

Clyde had recently returned from the Anderson farm where he had collected the stolen horses and gotten testimony from the Andersons about the thieves. Clyde was presently down at the saloon having lunch where he spent a good portion of his time and salary on drinks and food.

Crime wasn't a large problem in Willow Falls, so a gang of horse thieves riding through town was actually big news. Tom looked at his prisoners proudly, he knew he had done his job and for the first time in the history of Willow Falls, he felt like the town's sheriff's office might get some real respect.

"Feel like talking, Mr. Birch?" Tom asked casually. Donovan Moskin had done all the talking and now Tom wanted to hear from the silent and hard man that watched and listened alertly, but offered nothing. John Birch laid on his bunk with his hands under his head, staring at the ceiling. "No?" asked Tom when John didn't answer. "Well, let me ask you, what part of Texas are you from?"

"Austin, thereabouts," John Birch finally answered after a silent pause. Donovan Moskin slept after eating his lunch.

"Austin, huh? How'd you get way up here?"

"Rode my horse mostly," John Birch replied casually without any emotion. He was tall, over six-foot and had broad shoulders, but his body was lean, muscular and hardened. He had straight brown hair that fell over his ears and had over a week's unshaven face. He obviously wore a mustache that turned down at the corner of his lips to end at his chin when he cleaned up. John's face was oval shaped with hardened gray eyes that looked more like steel than anything else. His demeanor had been calm, but Tom was weary of him. John was tough no doubt, but there was more to him than that; he was dangerous. All it took was one look at John to know that he could turn deadly at the drop of a hat.

Tom smiled, humored. "You don't say? Well, do you like our corner of the world?"

"No, I don't."

"Too cold?"

"Yep."

"That's because it's winter, John!" Tom explained sarcastically. "So how'd you meet up with Donovan?"

"I just did," John turned to look at Tom, annoyed.

Tom frowned thoughtfully. "I don't understand something, John. You guys have a pretty good amount of money on you, but you steal some horses." He paused, "Now you're all well-armed, traveling through our valley with, you know, enough money, so why steal the horses? It wasn't because you were broke and hungry."

"I don't know," John's voice sounded defensive.

"Were you looking to sell them?" Tom wondered.

"Don't know," John said uneasily.

"Huh! Well, I've done my job, it's all up to the judge now. However, I've been thinking about your friend's offer to the judge. Have you ever been to Coffee Canyon?"

"No."

"Does it exist?"

"Don't know."

"Ever been in jail before?" Tom pressed.

"Yep."

"What for if I may ask?"

"Different things," John answered simply without any interest in explaining.

"I wired the judge this morning, I hope to hear back from him soon enough about a hearing. He'll wire west for any information about you guys that you may not be totally honest about. So, if you're wanted, you're now found," Tom said with finality.

John Birch took a deep breath while a cold chill plummeted through his spine. He lay still, but his eyes widened at the prospect of his crimes being found out. The fact that he was a thousand miles from Texas meant nothing anymore, telegraph lines spread news faster than any horse could ride and even faster than a falcon could fly. They were facing prison time, perhaps years of prison time if the judge found out about the long string of robberies. They'd be hung if the law found out about the women they ravaged. That wasn't out of the question either since the nearest and the farthest ones were only a telegraph line away.

"Are you a wanted man, John?" Tom asked pointedly.

John lying calmly on his bed, shook his head. "Nope. Not to my knowledge."

"What about your friend, Donovan Moskin? He says he's famous. Is he?" Tom asked. "Because I've never heard of him."

"I don't know," John answered with a strained voice. "He might be."

"Well, you should know," Tom raised his voice, "you stoled horses with him! You ride with him. Come on, John; was he part of the Doyle Gang? Did he shoot what's his name?" Tom asked, turning towards his desk to read through his notes.

"Mark Chesney," John answered for Tom.

Tom double-checked his notes. "That's right, John! Mark Chesney. Was he someone important?"

"I guess," John said, "I don't know him."

Tom laughed sarcastically. "Well, I guess no one does! So tell me about the two boys. I don't understand why two drifters would buy horses and guns for two boys and take them on the road. Nor do I understand where the money comes from."

John didn't answer, nor would he. The sheriff could ask any question he wanted, but John was all too aware that he was saying too much. In the presence of the law any talk was too much talk, especially when he couldn't think as fast as Donovan. He wished Donovan would wake up and talk the sheriff's ear off. John himself wasn't an elegant speaker nor could he control the sinking feeling of panic in his chest when the pressure was on.

"Tough questions, John?" Tom asked intrigued. "Well, understand the judge isn't a fool. He'll ask the same kind of questions I did, and you'd better have some convincing answers. The more I think about it the more curious I get; I'll write that in my report too. In fact..." Tom turned his chair

toward his desk and grabbed his pen and ink bottle. "I'll do that right now." He wrote on the paper he'd been reading.

John wanted to say something, but he was too afraid of saying the wrong thing. It took all his strength to force himself to remain silent. He would tell Donovan later and together they would firm up a story and a plan. Donovan was a quick thinker; he'd brought John this far and he would get them through this. He always did.

18

Kyle Lenning was glad to be home. He had spent the last two nights in Branson at the Shady Ben's Hotel. It was a cheap hotel with simple plain rooms next door to Kyle's favorite gambling establishment, The Thirsty Toad Saloon, on Rose Street. It usually had a pretty good crowd of men who wanted to play a friendly game of poker without the wildness and rowdiness of most of the other saloons. Kyle usually played a fair game of poker, but this time he had played quite well and was coming home with eighty dollars more than he went to town with; even after buying needed supplies, Christmas presents, and two nights of drinking and gambling. He drove the wagon back home from Branson thirsting for water and feeling the same sickness he always felt after a couple of nights at The Thirsty Toad Saloon. It was good to be home, but he enjoyed going to Branson and getting away from his wife and kids for a few days to drink and gamble with his friends. A little fun away from the Big Z was needed occasionally and Kyle took every opportunity to go to town. Sometimes he'd go to the saloon in Willow Falls, but seldom was there a good card game going on. He liked the idea of having somewhere to go when he was bored at night and Willow Falls just wasn't Kyle's kind of town; he preferred the crowds and environment of Branson.

The Big Z was nothing, except a lot of work and little else. It was profitable sure enough, but it never failed to amaze Kyle how the profits went back into the cattle and the ranch. Charlie Zeigler was wealthy enough, but no one would know it by the looks of his home and the way he dressed. He never spent a dime on anything, except necessities. He paid Darius Jackson a handsome wage; as much as he paid Kyle and Annie. It was a sore complaint of Kyle's; no negro ranch-hand should make as much money as the heirs of the ranch. Kyle liked Darius and he couldn't complain about his work ethic, but his pay was too exorbitant. Negroes weren't supposed to make so much money. Apparently though, Kyle was the only one to think the way he did. Annie agreed with Darius' pay rate and even went so far as to say that when Darius passed away, Rory would inherit Darius' wages. Kyle strongly disagreed. It seemed to him that they made a living, but if they cut Darius' wages, they could make a lot more money. Kyle figured there was no reason to share his wages with colored folks who didn't earn half of what they made.

Kyle wanted to live in a big house decorated with the finest furniture and paintings to show the fruits of his labors and his success. He wanted to wear clean suits and sit in an office managing his business, while his wife dressed appropriately in a beautiful dress and perhaps a floral hat, as a lady should dress. He wanted his wife to act like a lady and raise their daughters appropriately. There were just certain expectations that he had for his future, including taking over his parent's hardware store in Branson.

However, Kyle had fallen in love with Annie Bannister almost as soon as he first seen her. She had come to a community dance with her brother, Albert and his family. Annie was the most beautiful young lady he had ever seen, and she literally took his breath and heart away. He swore then and there that he was going to marry her, and he would dedicate his life to making her smile, because her smile lit up his life. The first time he went to the Big Z Ranch to call upon her, he was surprised to learn that she wasn't just, for all practical purposes, a rancher's daughter, but a working hand on the ranch. She wore chaps over her pants, dirty boots on her feet, gloves and a man's wide-brimmed hat on her head, and she rode and roped efficiently as any man. Annie had made it known right up front that she would never move off of the Big Z Ranch for anyone. Her loyalty wasn't to Kyle, but to her aunt and uncle and to her friend, Rory. Despite being forewarned, Kyle asked Annie to marry him.

Annie wasn't exactly the kind of wife he'd dreamed of; she wasn't soft-spoken or mild-mannered. She didn't dress like a lady and she was embarrassingly enough, a better shot than he was. He wished she would take an interest in more feminine things, such as pictures for the walls or a new floral dress perhaps, but she had never changed. For Christmas, she didn't want a pearl necklace or a new quilt, Annie wanted a new saddle. He had bought her a saddle and had it in the barn under a tarp waiting for Christmas morning when he'd tie her horse outside of the house with the saddle on it. For his daughters he bought new dolls, because little girls are supposed to play with dolls, but more often than not his girls dressed like boys and learned to rope and ride. He was the only guy he knew, whose wife wore jeans, could break a horse and on occasion wore a gun belt too. Kyle had spent his youth wanting riches, but what he got was the life of a cowhand and all the dirty work that went with it. As frustrating as it could be, Kyle loved his wife enough to accept it.

Annie's world went no farther than the Big Z Ranch and her immediate family. Christmas was always a large family affair where the Fasana, Bannisters, and other relatives showed up at the Ziegler's for a few days. A strange strawberry roan mare settled in his barn didn't surprise him any nor did Steven's horse tethered to Charlie's hitching post. What did surprise him was the tall, well-built man with long dark hair and a neatly trimmed beard, sitting on Charlie and Mary's floor playing with Kyle's youngest daughter, Erika. Catherine, the next to oldest, jumped from the davenport onto the stranger's back as Kyle closed the front door.

The stranger looked at Kyle with a smile.

"Hi honey!" Annie said excitedly. She was sitting on the davenport in her jeans watching her daughters with a contented smile. "This is my brother, Matt. Matt, this is my husband, Kyle."

Matt stood up to shake Kyle's hand firmly. "Nice to meet you," Matt said with a smile. "You've got your hands full with these two." His two nieces sat on his feet holding on to his legs tightly, forcing him to drag them on his feet. Both girls were giggling.

Kyle stood wordlessly for a moment; his mind raced. For the eight years of his marriage to Annie he'd only heard references to Matt, but he certainly never expected to meet him. Kyle had told strangers in Branson whom he played poker with that Matt Bannister was his brother-in-law. It was a sort of bragging that always brought welcomed conversation and at least twice, had protected him from men who might have gotten violent without the threat of Matt Bannister being related to Kyle. He neglected to mention that he had never met his brother-in-law and if Matt had walked into the same saloon, he wouldn't have known who Kyle was.

"The marshal?" Kyle asked as he let go of the smiling man's hand.

"Uh huh," Matt replied. He directed his attention to Catherine, who was playfully biting his leg.

"Well, it's nice to meet you."

Annie smiled as she watched her daughters play. "Did you get my present?" she asked Kyle.

"Yeah, but you can't see it until Christmas."

"Wanna bet?" she challenged him.

Kyle scoffed, "Yeah!"

"What you get me, Daddy?" Erika jumped off Matt's foot to welcome her father home with a hug, followed by Catherine.

"Nothing. Isn't Santa Claus supposed to bring something?" Kyle asked.

"If that's the case," Charlie spoke, "all they'll get is a can of reindeer manure."

"No!" Catherine, the oldest said pointedly as she glared at Charlie severely. "We're not getting that!"

"No!" Erika copied.

Charlie laughed.

Matt, sat in Mary's cushioned chair beside Charlie, facing the davenport where Annie was sitting. Mary was in the kitchen making lunch. Annie had offered to help, but Mary had sent her in to talk to the men. Steven was out back to the privy momentarily.

"So Matt, did you come back for Christmas?" Kyle asked

softly, moving to sit by his wife. He sat putting his hand on her leg.

Matt nodded as he answered, "Yes."

"Where's your badge?" Kyle couldn't help but to ask curiously. Matt looked nothing like Kyle had pictured him, he looked younger than he pictured and had a friendly smile. He wasn't wearing a gun belt nor a badge and no matter how hard he tried, Kyle couldn't picture this man in front of him as the famous U.S. Marshal who was so feared. He expected a larger-than-life individual, who was mean as hell and so frightfully serious that no one would want to say a word to him. Kyle never expected to see someone of his reputation sitting on the floor playing with his nieces. He almost didn't believe it was Matt, however, he could see the resemblance to Steven and the rest of the Bannister's.

"In my saddle bag," Matt answered Kyle's question simply. "So you're the guy that married my sister? I've heard good things about you, so far."

"I hope so," Kyle answered. "I've heard a lot about you too."

Matt's smile faded. "Well, that might not all be true. Uncle Charlie told me you have a book that I might want to read. It was written by a Markus Swindle in Branson?"

"Yeah, I do. From what I understand you won't like it."

"I never do, but I'd like to read it just the same."

"Sure... I'll get it when I go home. He called..."

"Don't tell him!" Charlie interrupted sternly. "Let him read it."

"Okay!" Kyle said with a defensive laugh.

"It must be a bad book?" Matt replied curiously.

"You won't like it," Annie stated matter-of-factly.

"Huh!" Matt grunted and looked towards the back door as Steven came inside. He closed the door behind him.

"Aunt Mary, I think we should take Uncle Charlie's wood stove from his barn and put it in the privy. He doesn't use it for anything, except coffee anyway," Steven said to Mary loud enough to be heard by Charlie.

"You could do that?" Mary asked with interest in her voice.

"Why sure. So could Charlie," Steven offered.

"I don't think so!" Charlie's voice quickly answered from the living room.

"That's what you should have Uncle Charlie do, Aunt Mary," Steven suggested seriously as he stood in the kitchen.

"What a good idea," she considered quietly. "Would that really work?"

"A day's work and it could be done," Steven said with a simple shrug and walked into the living room with a smile towards Charlie. Charlie glared at him.

"Charlie," Mary's voice called from the kitchen as Annie and Kyle laughed, "Is that something you could do?"

"No!" is all he said.

"It gets really cold out there, so if that would work," she offered.

"No!" Charlie spoke again and then added, "I don't think that's feasible, sweetheart."

Annie shrugged and looked at Kyle. "It sounds like a great idea to me."

"Thanks, Steven," Kyle replied.

"No problem," Steven laughed. "I thought about doing that at my place when I was sitting out there one day, but if I did, I'd never leave the privy!"

"Oh, Steven!" Mary laughed and turned back to her preparing of lunch.

"What?" Steven answered, "I'm not kidding!"

"Right," Kyle answered sarcastically.

Matt spoke to Steven, "I haven't met your wife yet, but when I do, I'm telling her what you've said."

"So?" Steven stammered.

Annie laughed heartily. "So?" she imitated Stevens' voice. "You act so tough, but when Nora is here you say, 'what honey? okay honey, oh I love you too, honey.'" She looked at Matt and continued, "But as soon as she leaves the room, he'll say, 'I'm building a shed on my roof. I should nail the door shut when she's in the privy,'" Annie finished by mimicking his voice again, and then laughed.

Steven stood in place, turning red.

"Is that right?" Matt asked with a slight smile.

"No!"

"It is too!" Kyle exclaimed. "How many times have Charlie and I stood back and watched you run to do what Nora told you to do. And when she's gone, you tell a tall tale of how you sent her inside with the rest of the women or something. Huh, Charlie?"

Charlie nodded.

"I don't do that!" Steven denied their accusation. "I..."

"You're henpecked!" Charlie interrupted. "Exactly what I warned you not to be before you got married."

"I am not!" Steven argued.

"Baauuck, baauuck, baauuck," Annie imitated a chicken. She looked up at Steven with her wide brown eyes and tilted her head like a curious dog. "Baauuck, Baauuck."

"Shut up!" Steven told her with an embarrassed half smile.

"Baauuck! Uncle Steven's henpecked!" she told her daughters. "Baauuck!"

Mary's laughter could be heard from the kitchen.

19

The sheriff had gone home for the day, saying he would bring dinner back for the prisoners. It wasn't quite dark yet, but it would be in about an hour. Tom had done little all day, except sit at his desk and take notes on what his prisoners had said. Clyde Waltz sat at the sheriff's desk reading through the notes Tom had written. Tom was a very alert man with a keen memory and could analyze a story and tear it to shreds if it wasn't true. He seemed to be doing exactly that to these four horse thieves.

Clyde wasn't as passionate about the law as Tom was. He figured the horse thieves would go to trial and the judge could figure out the truth from the lies. His job was to make the arrests, report what he knew, and keep them in jail. Nothing more and nothing less, he got paid the same, no matter what. He figured that Tom analyzed out of boredom because it got mighty boring in Willow Falls sometimes. Now that there were four horse thieves in the jail it gave Tom something to work on and Tom was working too. He had five pages of notes, plus the original testimony, notes of statements, counter statements, almost everything that each one of them had stated.

Clyde finished reading the notes and sighed. He looked at the four horse thieves, John Birch and Donovan sat quietly on the bottom bunk talking quietly together in whispers. The two boys lay in their bunks quietly and worried.

"Are you thinking of an escape plan?" Clyde asked curiously, not liking the whispering between the two men.

Donovan smiled at him. "Now Clyde, you know as well as I do that there's no way out of here. Besides, it wouldn't do us any good to try. You and the sheriff are like those damn Apache Indians; you'd have us surrounded again before we even knew where we were. Then we'd be on trial for breaking out of jail! No thanks," he said casually, "I think we'll just stay right here and enjoy the warmth of the fire and the sheriff's wife's fine cooking."

"Sounds wise to me," Clyde commented without venturing farther. He had his own thoughts twirling around in his mind, thoughts that made him feel alone and lonely, as Christmas time always did.

Clyde had no family to speak of, so for him Christmas was rather lonely. He spent every Christmas in the sheriff's office while Tom spent the day with his family. Tom always invited him to come over for dinner, but Clyde never went. He had never been married, but if he had been, he wouldn't want someone like himself to drop in and interfere with their family meal. So Clyde would sit in the sheriff's office on Christmas Day, like he had done every year since he was hired as a deputy.

Like most folks, Clyde had fallen in love once in his lifetime, but he cheated himself out of a future with her, by not being honest with her about his feelings. He was still in love with her though, in love with her memory, anyway. That was all that was left; her memory and her children.

Ruth Fasana was the woman that Clyde had fallen in love with. It was true back then that every man, who wasn't a Fasana, wanted to marry a Fasana girl. Ruth was his closest friend, however she was engaged to his good friend Floyd Bannister. The day before their wedding Clyde and Ruth rode up to the Bannister's cabin on Jessup Lake for a picnic. It was there beside the lake on one August afternoon that she mentioned having doubts about marrying Floyd. She asked Clyde if he would marry her if she called the wedding off. Once in every man's life there is one moment he wished he could change, Clyde denied himself the chance to marry the only woman he would ever love. He didn't have anything to offer except his love, and maybe that would've been enough. She was never happy with all that the rich heir of the Bannister Cattle Ranch had to give her. He never loved and honored her the way she should've been. The way she would've been if he had the courage to be honest with her.

Life could be sad. His two old best friends had six beautiful children together, but Clyde was the only one who had watched those six precious children grow up and have children of their own. Clyde made it a point to buy the cabin beside Jessup Lake when Floyd sold out and moved to Portland. It had become a sacred place as that day beside the lake with Ruth was a little of both, the greatest and the saddest day of his life.

Clyde had seen Joel and Luther Fasana pass by in a covered wagon a little earlier heading towards the Big Z Ranch. Melancholy filled Clyde. If he had married her Ruth might even still be alive today, possibly. One thing Clyde knew for certain was Ruth would be so proud of her children and her grandchildren. He knew her well enough to know that.

Donovan Moskin's voice drew Clyde out of his thoughts, "Clyde? Hey, Clyde."

"Hmm, mm," Clyde answered sadly. He always felt blue when he thought about what might have been.

"Is something wrong, Clyde? You seem awfully quiet after reading that," Donovan asked, nodding to the papers on the sheriff's desk. He was curious as to what was written down. John had told him how the sheriff had been questioning him earlier while Donovan slept.

"No. Nothing's wrong," Clyde admitted. "Just thinking."

"About what if I may ask?" Donovan questioned.

Clyde smiled to himself and turned to look at Donovan. "Nothing..." he paused and then asked, "Are you a married man?"

"Me? No, no," Donovan scoffed. "Two or three dollars' worth is about all the woman I want around me. No, I ain't married." He paused, "But, if I was to meet a woman like the sheriff's, I might think about it."

Clyde ignored the statement and pulled his bowie knife out of its scabbard on his belt. It had a deer horn handle and a long blade. He pulled a sharpening stone out of a drawer and sharpened his knife. He did it often and for great lengths of time as it simply gave him something to do during the long lonely hours. He really didn't feel like talking.

"When you get that blade all honed up, maybe you could test it out on the sheriff's report there. What do you say?" Donovan asked with a smile.

"It's sharp enough, I shave with it."

"Yeah, but maybe you could slice it up, anyway. The paper that is."

KEN PRATT

"No. Tom might get mad about that."

"He might," Donovan agreed. "Tell me something, Clyde, reading those papers, what kind of case do you think that judge will have on us?"

"I don't know; I really couldn't tell you."

"Did the judge wire the sheriff back today?"

"Not that I know of. You can ask him when he comes back though," Clyde said uninterested.

"Yeah, I'll do that." Donovan paused and then added quickly, "The sheriff doesn't like us much, does he?"

"I can't read Tom's mind. He seems to like you fine though."

"Huh! I guess, I wouldn't know," Donovan said more to himself than to Clyde. "Can I see that report, Clyde? So I can make sure he has his facts right." He quickly added, as Clyde was about to answer, "I won't tear it up Clyde, I promise. I just want the judge to get the real story. I don't want the sheriff making things up about us just so he can make a name for himself." He stopped, and then added casually, "Some people do that, you know."

"You don't need to worry about that," Clyde replied, "Tom's the most honest man I know. I know a few, but Tom's the most honest. He only writes what you tell him."

"That's comforting, quite comforting," Donovan said quietly, sounding nearly sarcastic.

"Mr. Deputy," Young Evan Gray stated, "I need to use the outhouse."

"Sure," Clyde responded. He lay the sharpening stone down and replaced the knife into his scabbard. He grabbed his cell keys out of the top drawer of the desk and pulled on his gun belt. He went to the rear cell and told Rodney Gray to stay back as he opened the cell door to take Evan outside. He locked the door as he followed Evan out into the cold.

20

Joel Fasana was a big man; over six feet tall and built like a broad-shouldered bull with large hands that were thickly callused. He had short gray hair and a square shaped face that was clean shaven, aged and weathered. Joel was dressed in new black wool pants with suspenders over a new gray heavy flannel shirt. For nearly thirty years now Joel and his brother, Luther, owned the Fasana Granite Quarry that their father had founded. They made a wide assortment of granite goods including hitching posts, corner posts, benches, and blocks of all sizes, for new construction like the Monarch Hotel and a few other buildings in Branson. Of course, the main staple of the granite industry was memorial headstones, the shaping, engraving, smoothing and polishing of them for the local undertaker, Solomon Fasana their younger brother. The work was hard and laborious, but business was good.

Joel Fasana was a genuinely joyful man who loved children and had six of them of his own, four daughters, and two sons. All of his daughters were respectfully married and off raising their own families. His two sons were as different as night and day, Robert, the elder of the boys, was serious-minded and worked as a supervisor at the quarry. He was already a master in all phases of the trade and would take over running the company when Joel and Luther retired. William Fasana, the younger of the two boys, was a fancy-dressed, two-gun toting professional gambler. He could play cards better than most and if he was accused of cheating, he probably was. William had outdrawn and killed a man in Abilene three years before and that particular killing had added to his infamous reputation. He was also the only family member Matt had seen a few times in his long fifteen-year absence. William, like Matt, didn't stay in Branson, he was a drifter that followed the money to new towns and locations wherever it led him. Dragging granite out of the ground wasn't William's idea of fun or a living. Clean clothes, soft hands and a deck of cards at the best gambling halls in America was more to William's liking and the Monarch Hotel was a gambler's paradise.

Luther Fasana, like Joel, was big as an ox. He had the Fasana square shaped face, but wore a thick gray beard about three inches long. His hair was also cut short and mostly gray. Like his brother, Luther's face was aged and weathered by the sun and hours of hard work. His hands as well were big, powerful and heavily callused by his labors. Luther dressed in dark blue denim jeans with clear evidence of being worked in by the scuffs in the denim. A belt held them up, and he wore a red and black checkered flannel shirt. Luther had three grown children, his two sons, Luke and David were both in California at the moment testing their skills at running a store. His only daughter, Billie Jo, lived in Branson and was for all practical purposes married to Joe Thorne. Luther liked most folks just fine, but Joe was a lying drunkard who couldn't be faithful to a dog, let alone Billie Jo. Luther couldn't like a man that refused to marry the mother of his own children. Joe Thorne was a piece of human rubbish in Luther's opinion. However, Billie Jo was the one that chose to stay with Joe, despite her father's wishes.

It was good to see his two uncles again and to sit in the house listening to the family Matt hadn't seen in so long. It was pleasant to just sit, talk and laugh with them all.

Steven looked at the clock on the mantle and stood up slowly. "Well, I've been out here all day," Steven said. "Tomorrow I have to do a little work at the shop, since I didn't get anything done today. I probably need to go, I haven't seen my family all day and I need to milk the cow."

William Fasana spoke with a deep voice, "Oh, the chores of a farmer. That's why Matt and I headed East, we both agreed that a man's hand should never touch an animal's teat. Isn't that right, Matt?" William chuckled. He sat on a dining room table chair in the crowded living room, dressed in his expensive black suit and shined boots. William had thick long yellowish blond hair that was curly and always clean. His face was more oval than square, but had a tough and weathered face with a well-groomed mustache and goatee about two inches long on his chin. William had an arrogant nature about him that cared little of what others thought of him, or if anyone liked him at all. He dressed well, he shot well, and he played cards well and that was all that mattered to him.

"How would you know?" Steven responded to William quickly, "Your hands would start hurting not even half a pint into milking! It's a good thing you don't have to work for a living, because a day's work for you would end after the first chore was half done, milking! The cow would dry up." Steven emphasized.

"He'd starve to death, wouldn't he, Steven?" Joel Fasana asked in agreement over William's light laughter.

"Oh, quickly!" Steven scoffed with disgust.

"Well," Charlie spoke casually, "that's why I always said, even when you kids' were young, put the kids to work early in the morning, a chore at noon and after dinner, and they won't be afraid to work when they're older."

"Afraid to work?" William questioned, "I grew up working in the granite quarry. Believe me, it's not fear of work, it's despising work!"

"Oh, bull!" Luther argued. "Willy, you always looked for a reason to get out of a day's work. Even when you were little, you'd rather go look for spiders or snakes than to do your job."

"Well, what kid didn't?" William laughed. He despised being called "Willy" and didn't tolerated it from anyone, except from the elders in his family. He continued, "I just wasn't as afraid of you and Pa as everyone else was."

"Not of getting your butt whipped anyway," Joel added reflectively about his youngest son.

"I took my lashings, and I'd take them again the next day, but by golly, I wanted to do something else, so I did it!" William spoke proudly.

"I never knew a kid as determined to get his way as you," Charlie said fondly. "We were lucky that the Bannisters were all pretty good kids. They weren't perfect, and we had to give out some lashings too, but William, if you had lived here..." Charlie paused to nod at William knowingly.

William laughed. "I'd be milking cows and shoveling manure even now!"

"That's right," Charlie smiled.

"Well, I have to go," Steven said, still standing. "I'm sure my angry heifer's getting anxious for me."

Luther questioned Steven, "That cow likes to be milked, I take it?"

"Cow?" Steven faked surprise; glad somebody fell for his joke. "What cow? I was talking about my wife!"

William's voice was loud as he led the laughter.

"Wait up," Charlie called after Steven. "I need to stop by the mercantile, so I'll ride into town with you."

"I'll tag along," Luther said, as he got up off the floor. "I might want to get a few things myself. Willy? Matthew?" Luther invited.

"No, not me!" William exclaimed passionately while holding up his hands. "I've done enough riding on your wagon today."

"Matthew?"

"Yeah, I'll go," Matt said hesitantly, "but I'm riding my horse. Like William, I've done enough wagon riding today."

"I'll ride with you, Luther," Charlie said.

Charlie rode beside Luther on his covered wagon while Matt and Steven rode their horses beside it. It was late in the afternoon and the sun was fading fast as they made their way towards Willow Falls. The Mercantile would be closing before long, so Charlie asked Steven and Matt to ride quickly ahead to have William McDermott keep the store open until Luther and himself arrived.

It was then that Luther asked Matt, "Matthew, would it be alright with you, if Charlie rode your horse and you rode with me? I know you didn't want to, but I'd sure appreciate the time to visit," he explained.

Matt hesitated. "Sure," he said reluctantly and stepped out of the saddle. He held the reins for Charlie.

Charlie took the reins in his hands and swiftly swung up into the saddle. He asked, "What's her name?"

"Betty."

"Betty?" Charlie asked with a distasteful expression. "What kind of a name is that?"

"Female," Matt explained simply.

Charlie chuckled slightly as Matt stepped up on the wagon beside Luther. Charlie offered a few gentle introductory words to Betty before they galloped towards Willow Falls.

"How long are you staying, Matthew?" Luther asked as he started his mule team with a "Yah!"

"I don't know, Uncle Luther. After New Year's, I'll probably head back."

"Back to where?" Luther asked curiously. "I don't think I even know where you call home anymore. Every time I hear of you, you're someplace different."

Matt smiled slightly. "Cheyenne, Wyoming."

"Cheyenne, huh? What are you doing there that you can't do here?"

"Huh?" Matt was slightly confused by the question.

Luther looked at Matt. "I said, what's in Cheyenne, Wyoming, that keeps you there, that isn't right here?"

"Oh!" Matt said looking up the road towards Willow Falls in the far distance. The knowledge that Elizabeth could be somewhere within the town's city limits brought up a wave of anxiety that he couldn't quite control. He had planned to stay out of town and away from any possibility of seeing her, but it was getting dark and he knew most folks, at least most lady folks, would be in their homes making supper. He hadn't asked anyone about Elizabeth, how she was or how she looked, if she was happy or if she had become like her mother; quiet, humble and spineless in her own household. He didn't know which house was hers and he didn't ask for fear of finding himself watching it as he passed by hoping to see a glimpse of the girl that consumed him. He answered his uncle, "My job's in Cheyenne."

"Oh. So what's making you go back?"

"What do you mean?"

"I mean a job's a job. What else is in Cheyenne that you're going back to, a woman? A home?"

"No," Matt replied slowly, "none of that. I'm a deputy marshal in Cheyenne," Matt began to sound wary of the questions.

"Oh, I see," Luther sounded satisfied with Matt's answer. He continued sincerely, "So what's your joy in life, Matthew? What do you do to enjoy life?"

"I don't know, Uncle Luther. What do you do?" Matt suddenly sounded defensive.

Luther looked at Matt. "I'll tell you, Matthew and then you tell me. My joy in life is my kids and my grandkids. I take a lot of pride in teaching them how to fish and hunt. I enjoy teaching them how to shoot a bow straight or how to carve a piece of wood into something wonderful. It'll be my legacy when I'm dead and gone that they teach their children the things I taught them. It's the same things your grandfather taught your mother and me. The same things we taught you when you were little. Those are the things I enjoy. Times like these are great too, I love Christmas and all the family getting together. So now you tell me, what's your joy?"

"I don't know," Matt said solemnly. "All I do is work."

"I have a job," Luther ventured. "But I also know that work is only a part of living. We work to feed ourselves, but we live to enjoy ourselves. I love my life..." Luther said and then stopped as if to reconsider his words. He didn't want to cause any hard feelings, but someone had to be honest with the young man even if it hurt. He decided to continue. "Matthew, you don't laugh much, do you?"

"Some."

"But not often?"

"No, not too often," Matt admitted.

"You've been given some raw deals early on, but you shouldn't allow them to control your life now," Luther said with deep caring in his voice.

"I'm not," Matt replied defensively.

"You're not?" Luther questioned skeptically.

"No, I'm not. If this is about me leaving here, Uncle Luther, I was young and dumb. But now I'm a deputy marshal. It's nothing like your job; I'm not home every night by six. I was gone for four months straight one time. So if I'm not laughing, it's probably because I have a serious profession." He was growing more irritated with Luther's conversation.

"I bet. And no doubt you're good at what you do," Luther commented. "I think your mother would have been proud of every one of her kids. What do you think?"

"I suppose," Matt's voice was sharp and pointed like a waiting sword.

"I think so," Luther said confidently. Then he added, "But I wonder, do you think she'd be proud of the life you're living?"

"Yes, I do!" Matt sounded offended. "I'm doing what I want to do. Have I made something of myself? Absolutely! There are books written about me for crying out loud! Am I going back to Wyoming? Yes, I am. Now, I don't know what you're getting at Uncle Luther, but..." He paused to continue in a gentler, but still threatening tone, "I didn't come back here to be chastised by you. I made my choices and now I have to live with them. I'm not doing too badly and yeah; my mother would be proud of me." He stared at Luther irritably while Luther stopped the wagon.

Luther spoke calmly, "I'm not trying to chastise you. You're the one that rode away and disappeared for fifteen years. That's something you just don't do, not to your family." Matt rolled his head and was about to interrupt, but Luther continued sharply, "No, let me finish! If you go riding off next week back to Wyoming, the chances are I'll never have the chance to talk to you again..."

"Uncle Luth...

"Let me speak!" he ordered. "You're my sister's son and you will listen to me whether you like it or not! If not, then go back to Wyoming by all means, but you'll go back with my words burning in your ears! Let these words sink in; I don't think your mother's proud of you. I really don't. Sure, you're a famous marshal now. Big Deal!" Luther spat out distastefully. "You have no family, you have no children. You have no home or even laughter inside of you. You have no joy, Matthew! What you do have is a lonely soul and a lot of hurt to carry around. So you're always traveling from one place to another, tracking killers, you say... you know I'll bet you'd rather take a bullet in your heart than to risk loving some young lady, huh? The bullet would at least end your sorrow," Luther said coldly. He had watched Matt's expression become as hard as the granite blocks he drug out of the ground.

Luther took a deep breath and continued softly, "That's not the life your mother wanted for you. She wanted you to be able to laugh; she wanted you to be happy. Being a marshal means nothing. Those books you mentioned about you don't mean anything. A man's heart and soul are what matters and that's what your mother looked for most in you. Not a gun in your hand or a mean reputation. Now, I've said what I wanted to say, but if you think your job's what your family loves about you, you're wrong. That badge has kept you away far too long for us to respect it anymore. We never stopped loving you, Matthew. You just have to stay still long enough to take a chance in life, you might even find that life really doesn't have to be as lonely and hopeless as it might seem. And then perhaps that bullet in your heart wouldn't be so appealing anymore," Luther said pointedly. He knew Matthew was done listening, but it didn't matter. Luther had said all that he wanted to say.

21

The town was peaceful just as it had always been after dark. There were lanterns glowing through the windows of most of the houses, but the main street was dark and empty. The mercantile, sheriff's office, and the saloon were the only businesses with lit windows. Matt felt the pangs of reminiscence of long ago as he looked at the town's main street. Memories of his youth filled his thoughts, as he gazed momentarily at the schoolhouse, the saloon, the blacksmith shop and the other buildings that made up Willow Falls' main street. However, no other buildings in town held more memories than the white church with its tall steeple and the two-story white house next to it. It was the house where Elizabeth had lived and it was as if time had stood still, Willow Falls hadn't changed. Even the store was the same, it just had different owners.

A bell rang as Steven led the way into the store. He entered with all the confidence of a man without a single worry of running into anyone. Matt was the last to enter the mercantile, but did so with much apprehension of seeing certain people he didn't want to see. Reverend Ash, Tom, and Elizabeth were all nearer to him than they'd been in fifteen years. The Reverend was within a city block of him at the moment and Elizabeth could have been as well, he didn't know. He had never known what he would say to her if he saw her again or how he'd react if he saw the Reverend. Tom, he'd already exchanged words with, but the awkward possibility of seeing them again brought a touch of anxiety that he wasn't accustomed to. Just in case he ran into any of them, Matt fastened his badge onto his heavy buffalo skin coat. He didn't understand why exactly, but his badge was all he had to show for himself.

The mercantile was like many others, the shelves were stocked with foods and canned goods, spices and flour, linens, pots and pans – almost everything a frontier town would need. The owner, William McDermott, sounded excited to see Steven and Charlie. "Ah! Charlie, it's good to see you again!" William's eyes shifted past Charlie and Luther to Matt, who closed the entrance door behind him. Matt's eyes swept over the store, taking an inventory of his surroundings.

"You must be Matt! I've heard so much about you. What an honor it is to finally meet you." William held out his hand from behind the counter with a friendly smile. He was a medium height man with a slight build in his late fifties. He had short brown hair that was balding on top and a neatly trimmed mustache above his top lip. He wore spectacles and dressed in tan suit pants and vest over a white shirt.

Matt slipped off his glove to shake his hand. "Nice to meet you," he said as he gave a firm handshake.

"I'm Steven's father-in-law. He married my Nora, so we're kind of related, you are my granddaughter's uncle. Have you had a chance to meet your nieces and Nora yet?" William asked in an overly friendly manner.

"No, but, Steven's been talking about your daughter all day. I can't wait to see if she's all he claims her to be," he finished looking at Steven with a hint of a smile.

"Oh! I assure you," William offered confidently, "if God ever created a woman for a man, he created Nora for Steven and Steven for her. A happier couple I have never seen."

"That's the way it's supposed to be," Matt agreed.

Charlie leaned over the counter waiting to get William's attention. "Here's Mary's list," he said handing it to William. "I also have a few items of my own once you have Mary's things together. Do you still have that red ring I looked at once?"

"I believe I do. The red opal on silver?"

"I guess. It was red," Charlie said without William's enthusiasm.

Matt took the distraction to step away from the counter to look for anything that might make a nice present for Annie or Aunt Mary. Being so close to Christmas many of the clothing items and various pieces of cloth were sold out, but Matt looked around for something that Annie might like. It occurred to him that it was the first time he had looked for a present for anyone since he'd left so many years ago.

"So Matt, how long are you going to be here?" William asked as he filled Mary's order.

"Not too long. I just came home to see my family."

"It's too bad you're not staying longer. I'd be honored to get to know you. We don't get too many famous people around here."

"I suppose not," was all Matt said. He went back to looking for something, but he didn't know what.

"Nope," William continued, "your family's about the only famous people we've got around here. Charlie here, you, and Lee's going to be famous when he's governor, some day."

"Yeah," Matt agreed just to agree. He was looking at a purple robe that was rather heavy. He considered it an attractive robe that would keep Mary warm. It was expensive though and Matt kept it in mind as he stepped over to a display of dolls. Most of them were gone, but one or two were left.

"What else can I get you?" Matt heard William ask Charlie.

"A box of 44s."

"Going hunting?" William asked.

"Nope," Charlie replied without offering any explanation. Charlie never talked too much. He usually handed William the list from Mary and said less than ten words per visit.

"Oh, let me show you that ring," William said walking over to a glass counter, unlocking the lock and bringing out a ring in a nice white box with gold floral designs on it. "This is the nicest ring in the area and it's still just twenty-five dollars. It would look lovely on the missus finger."

"It would look better if it were ten dollars," Charlie stated.

William laughed. "Oh! That's not at all acceptable. The lowest I could go," he paused, "is twenty dollars, and that's giving you a great deal. Twenty-five dollars is cheap for what I could sell it in Branson for."

"How much are the chocolates?" Luther asked from down the long counter. He was looking at some chocolate candies in a glass case sitting on the counter.

"Fifty cents a dozen. Those are from the Branson Trust Candy Maker. Alicia's candies are like a fishing hook, one bite and you're caught. One piece is never enough," William explained.

"Give me three dozen if you got it, William," Luther said.

"Oh! Yes, sir, and Charlie, you think about that ring. I won't have it for long. I'll take it to Branson and sell it for fifty if it doesn't sell soon."

Charlie scoffed distastefully as Matt watched humorously. Steven nudged up close to Matt so he wouldn't be overheard. "Everything in here is overpriced; some things by a little, others by a lot. But he has the only store in town so he makes a profit, especially at Christmas time."

"I see," Matt agreed.

Charlie shook his head. "This ring's been here for over a year, no one's bought it. I'm not buying a ring no one else wants for twenty-five, or even twenty dollars. I won't do it! If you want to sell me that ring, then you'll do it for ten. I'll give you ten right now for it."

"Twenty's a fair price," William argued as he turned back to Luther with his chocolates all in one bag. "One dollar and fifty cents."

Luther paid him.

"Thank you," he said as he rang the till. "Charlie, do you think it's a beautiful ring?"

"Yeah, but it's just a ring. You can save it for next year. Maybe, it will depreciate down to ten by then."

"Now Charlie, a lady would love to receive a gift such as this from her husband. It makes them feel beautiful," William said with great sincerity.

"My wife is beautiful, and she doesn't need a ring to be it. Especially at twenty dollars," Charlie said matter-of-factly.

"Charlie, I heard you bought a bull for five hundred dollars. Now that's twenty times as much as this ring, but in your wife's eyes, this ring will be ten times more valuable than a bull."

Charlie rolled his head in exasperated laughter. He looked towards the window to his left and grew serious as his attention was suddenly elsewhere. He spoke with a serious tone as he watched outside the window, "I'm afraid, Mr. McDermott, that bull is far more valuable than this ring," Charlie slowly turned his head back to face William.

William started to argue, but paused as Charlie held up his hand to stop William. Charlie looked closely at the ring, but spoke to Matt through a concerned and tense voice, "Matt, ever so causally, look across the street behind that oak. No one else look," Charlie added quickly. "Do you see him?"

"Hmm," Matt hummed as he approached the purple robe which hung on a rack in the middle of the store. "He's got a pistol."

"Yip," Charlie said.

"Who does?" William asked, wanting to look.

"Don't look his way!" Charlie snapped at William. "Everyone just act normal. Steven, who is it?" he asked seriously.

"I can't tell for sure," Steven said from behind the wood stove that heated the mercantile. "But, it looks like Eli... Eli Barso."

"Eli!" William declared with surprise. "With a gun?" he asked unbelievably. He was about to turn around and look out the window.

"Don't look!" Charlie snapped roughly. He quickly shifted his eyes to look out the window. "That's him all right," he stated with contempt. "You got yourself an admirer Matt."

Matt nodded and then sighed. "Who is this Eli? Is he a good shot?"

Steven answered, "He's Johnny Barso's son. A friend of mine, I'll take care of this," he grunted and took two steps towards the door.

"Don't!" Matt spoke harshly stopping Steven in place. "How old is he?"

"Old enough to know better!" Steven said sternly. "I'll take him to his pa and he'll get his hide whipped off."

William McDermott answered Matt. He sounded nervous, "He's seventeen. He's a good boy. I don't know why he'd have a gun, but don't hurt him, he's a good kid."

"Well," Charlie spoke to William, "sometimes boys get foolish notions and this one might get young Eli killed." He then turned to Matt. "He's never killed before so he'll hesitate to shoot, but don't count on him freezing up."

"I never do," Matt replied sadly. "Uncle Luther, do you still hunt?"

"Yes!" Luther almost sounded offended. "Why?"

"Mister...?" Matt hesitated as he looked at William McDermott.

"McDermott. William McDermott."

"Mister. McDermott, can my uncle borrow one of your shotguns and two rounds?"

"Sure," William said uneasily. He turned around to show his stock of shotguns and other guns that he had hanging behind the counter between the windows.

"Don't turn around!" Charlie ordered under his breath sourly.

"Uncle Luther, will you crawl under the windows, collect a shotgun and two rounds. Then sneak out the back door, go down a ways, and come back up on the other side of the street. I'd like for you to move fast and as silently as you can over to the corner of that building." Matt nodded towards the corner of Steven's blacksmith shop. The young man hid behind a large oak tree in front it. "Keep him in your bead, but say nothing," Matt finished.

"You can't kill him!" William uttered aghast. "He's never hurt anyone!"

Matt sighed wearily. "Don't shoot him, Uncle Luther, just keep a bead on him. I'll come outside and talk to him. If he raises that pistol, I'll take care of him. Don't you shoot unless he fires first and I'm down. I don't want his blood on your hands."

Steven sounded afraid as he spoke, "We can avoid all of that, I'll go out there and whip his rear end for him. There doesn't need to be any shooting or bloodletting. I know him! He comes to my house and shop all the time. He wouldn't dare raise that gun on me! I'll take him to his father and you won't see him for a while and when you do, he'll still be black and blue. I can promise you that."

Matt looked at Steven sadly. "Steven, I'm sure you're right, but I can't do that. Go, Uncle Luther," he said to Luther and then turned back to Steven. "Remember when we were kids and Uncle Charlie told us not to shoot towards the cattle when we were squirrel hunting, but we did anyway? Remember we were whipped for it when we got caught? But the very next time we went shooting, the thrill of the hunt got us aiming towards the cattle again. Do remember that? We knew better, but our adrenalin was high and even after being whipped for the very same thing, the very next time we went out hunting I aimed towards the cattle, missed a squirrel, ricocheted and hit a steer. Do you remember that?"

"Yeah. What does that got to do with this?"

Charlie kept his face downward as though he was still

interested in the ring. He answered for Matt, "Matt's right, Steven. Young Eli over there is hungering to be famous," Charlie turned towards Steven, "killing your brother will give him that fame. Hung as well, but he's not thinking about that. All he sees is that squirrel; his one shot and chance to be more than a Willow Falls farm boy. A beating by his father won't cure him of that desire. It might just make him more dangerous." Charlie hesitated. "Eli has to have his opportunity. Stupid kid!" he added with disgust.

Matt waited for Luther to work his way around and over to Steven's shop. "What's the boy like?" he asked anyone who knew him. "Mean-spirited? Quiet?"

"He's a good kid!" Steven answered anxiously. "He's hardly ever in trouble and he does what his parents tell him."

"Well," Charlie offered from his place by the counter. "I doubt they told him to do this."

"They wouldn't!" William stated matter-of-factly. "Eli's a good Christian boy. He does like to hunt, but most boys do."

"Does he have friends that he does things with?" Matt asked.

"Oh yeah, a few of them," Steven answered. "They're all good, hard working, good-hearted boys. I've known Eli all his life. He's no killer!"

"We're about to find out, Steven," Matt said, as he carefully unbuttoned his long buffalo coat. Luther Fasana had hurried into place, Matt saw his bulk in the shadows with the shotgun aimed silently at the figure hiding behind the tree. From Luther's position, the boy was in clear view.

Matt walked to the door and paused to look at Mister McDermott. "You were mentioning fame a little earlier. If I'm killed on your doorstep, your establishment will become famous, do you know that? But if that boy across the street is killed, Steven's shop will become famous. So," he paused, "who do you want to become famous you or Steven?" Matt asked seriously as he un-thonged his revolver's hammer from the leather strap that held it in the holster.

"Neither!" William uttered in horror, "I don't... I..." he stumbled for words.

Matt smiled a small sad smile. "Unfair question?" he asked.

"Yes!" William answered.

"You were telling me how privileged you were to have me in town, someone famous, as you put it." He paused. "When the shooting's done and the blood's spilt and you smell the odor of death, then you tell me how privileged this kind of fame is. One of two things will happen; either he'll get lucky and gun me down on your doorstep and you'll benefit from my blood being spilt here, or more likely, that young boy is going to meet his maker tonight. But, I'm hoping he's as smart as you guys say and puts that weapon down. Start praying he is and stay here!" he said sharply. Taking a deep breath, he stepped towards the door.

"He's a good Christian boy! Certainly you don't have to do this! He's just a boy," William McDermott nearly begged Matt to stop.

Matt paused at the door and looked at William McDermott with an expression of deep sorrow. "So was I, Mister McDermott, so was I," Matt said and stepped outside into the cold darkness closing the door behind him.

He hesitated outside the door to allow his eyes to adjust to the night air and semi-darkness of the snow covered ground. Matt could see the young boy hiding behind the large oak tree slowly raising his pistol. The boy would have to step out from the cover of the tree to have a clear shot at him. Matt walked casually to his saddled mare, he kept his profile exposed to the boy to make a smaller target. He knew well that most people would miss taking a hurried shot with a revolver, especially if they were shooting at a man for the first time.

He turned his head to look at the boy. "Before you pull that trigger, I'd look to your left slowly," Matt spoke with complete control over his voice. He watched the boy's expressions change from fear to surprise and then panic. After seeing the shotgun's double barrel pointed at him from the corner of Stevens shop, the boy's face turned back to Matt in horror.

In one continuous motion, Matt had stepped his right foot towards the boy, twisting his body to offer only his right profile to shoot. In the same flash of movement, he drew his .45 caliber Colt revolver and had it aimed at the young man with blazing speed and ferocity. Matt's eyes burned with deadly venom while he had the boy clearly in his sights. "That's my uncle Luther. He's not much good with a pistol, but I've never seen him miss with a shotgun. Now!" Matt's voice was hard and dangerous. His eyes grew even more deadly. "You have until the count of three to drop your gun or start shooting. The choice is yours, one! Two!"

"Hey..." Eli cried hoarsely. His pistol dropped into the snow. "I dropped it!" he nearly yelled, filled with terror.

Matt stepped forward as he lowered his gun. "Come here!" he ordered. Eli stepped slowly as Luther Fasana walked up behind him.

"You almost got yourself killed, kid!" Luther said as he reached down for the boy's pistol.

Steven Bannister came running out of the store and jumped off of the steps. He ran by Matt and grabbed the boy by the coat collar. "What are you doing, Eli?" Steven snapped angrily. "Committing suicide or trying to kill my brother!" He pushed Eli back against the tree. He hit hard and fell terrified to the ground.

"Steven, I..." Eli began to speak, but Steven bent over and backhanded Eli's face viciously.

"Steven!" Charlie yelled, stopping him, "Don't," Charlie ordered and turned to William. "Go get the sheriff." William ran off and Charlie turned back to Steven. "This is Matt's fight, son."

Steven looked at Matt; he was standing back just a little and seemed to have perfect control over his emotions. He nodded to Steven wordlessly. Steven turned back to Eli. "You..." he spat out angrily and shook his head before turning away. "Do what you want with him!" Steven said to Matt as he walked back toward the store waving his arms in frustration.

"What's your name?" Matt asked calmly.

Eli sat in the snow at the base of the tree. He was visibly shaking in terror as he wiped blood off his split lip. "Eli... Eli Barso, sir."

Matt nodded, while gazing into the boy's eyes. "So what are you doing out here? Did you come to kill me?" Matt asked casually. His voice cracked concealing his true emotions.

"No, sir," Eli lied unconvincingly.

"Then *what*," Matt emphasized, "were you doing? Who'd you come to shoot - Steven? Charlie?" he asked with his eyes growing more enraged.

"No, sir," Eli answered. His voice cracked and was strained.

"Who then? It was me, huh!" Matt's voice rose to a loud authoritative demand for the truth. His adrenalin turned to anger.

"Yes, sir," Eli choked. He covered his face with his hands

and broke into tears.

Matt nodded slowly.

Steven, in a rage, once again approached Eli yelling, "What in the world were you thinking? You were going to shoot my brother, Eli? For what? Huh!" He stood beside Matt towering over the trapped boy. "Answer me!" Steven demanded loudly.

"I don't know," Eli cried weakly.

"You don't know? That's not an answer, Eli. Now answer me!" Steven demanded. His eyes were burning with rage. A small crowd of people began to assemble outside of the saloon and nearby houses to see what the noise was all about.

Matt could hear his name being whispered in the crowd as it grew. He refused to look at the crowd or even acknowledge their presence as they gathered. He knew the following day the entire Willow Falls community would hear about Eli and in a few days all of Jessup County and Branson would hear. Eventually the story would reach back to Wyoming, although, by then the story would've changed to another killing. Stories always grew the farther they went.

Eli looked up to glare at Steven with a pain-filled expression. He cried out, "I don't want to be like you, Steven! I want to become somebody like him!" Eli shouted pointing at Matt. Matt sighed and shook his head.

"So you're going to shoot him?" Steven asked astonished.

"At least I'd be famous!" Eli spat out. "And that's more than my dad or you'll ever be. And that's what he," Eli pointed at Matt, "did when he was my age."

"No, he didn't!" Steven yelled. "Matt didn't kill those men in cold-blood!"

Tom Smith shouted vehemently, "Well, it sure wasn't self-defense was it?" Tom came from the jail quickly, followed by William McDermott and Clyde Waltz. He had just come to town to bring supper for his four prisoners when William came running into his office. "Now tell me what's going on here." Tom was suddenly in a foul mood. Where Matt was, trouble followed, and that was exactly what he'd been afraid of.

Steven answered, "Eli was waiting to kill my brother. He was hiding behind that tree with his revolver." Steven's voice shook.

Tom eyed Matt harshly. "One day back and there's already trouble involving you! You need to stay on the Big Z until you leave," Tom said irritably.

"I intend to," Matt replied. "And no, Tom, it wasn't self-defense that day, was it?" Matt asked with his own venom to his voice.

"No," Tom replied coldly. "I'll take care of this boy, you all can leave now. You all, too," he said loudly to the crowd. He added specifically to Matt, "Get back to the ranch. I don't want to see you again, don't come near town." Tom's voice was threatening.

Matt's voice hardened, "Mind your place, Tom. You're stepping out of your jurisdiction."

"Stepping out of my jurisdiction?" Tom seemed to question, "It's my town! How dare you tell me I'm out of my jurisdiction in my own town?" Tom almost laughed. "Go home, Matt. Let's go, Eli," Tom said waving off Matt.

"This is Federal Marshal business, Tom," Matt spoke seriously. "Attempted murder of a Federal Marshal is a hanging offense and I take a dim look at it. Now, if you don't step away, I'll be forced to arrest you, Tom, for interfering."

"Arrest me? I'm the sheriff of this town. You can't arrest me. But if you don't leave Matt, I will arrest you for..."

Matt spoke irritably, "You're the Willow Falls Sheriff and

I'm a United States Deputy Marshal! I will treat you no differently than any other sheriff that gets in my way. I don't care about your personal feelings about me, I couldn't care less! But as long as I'm wearing this badge you will stay out of my way and you will do as I say. Otherwise, you will become a federal prisoner for interfering with the duties of a Deputy U.S. Marshal," he yelled.

Tom glared at Matt with what could only be described as hatred. "Fine, Matt! Go ahead and kill him, like you do everyone else. I will be contacting the federal office as a witness to your murderous abuse of power and I will not stop until they take your badge away! Then all you'll be is a simple murderer and I hope I'll have the pleasure to see you hang!"

Charlie Zeigler walked towards the two lawmen. "Watch your tongue, Tom!" he warned. "You're crossing lines I won't tolerate from anyone, not even you!"

Tom seemed to shrink back a little as he took a moment to calm down with a deep breath. Tom felt helpless, which in fact, he was at the moment. He shook his head in frustration and then looked at Eli, who was now standing. "I'm sorry, Eli. I can't do anything..." He looked at Matt with a great deal of disdain. "Right now, anyway!" Tom walked a few feet back over by where Clyde stood. Clyde looked nervous.

Matt looked at the boy, feeling the eyes of everyone upon him. "If you try this again I will shoot you. Make no mistake about that," he warned. "You almost met your maker tonight. Steven, take him to his parents, tell them he got lucky."

Matt walked quickly to his horse and stepped up into the saddle. He turned to Tom, who was glaring at him. "I'll stay on the ranch and we won't cross paths again. If I remember correctly though, it wasn't just me at Pearl Creek," Matt stated. He turned his horse towards the north end of town and rode through the small crowd that had gathered to watch. Matt kept his eyes on one figure as he rode towards him.

The Reverend Abraham Ash stood on his front porch watching from a distance. Although Matt recognized him immediately, he was surprised by how much the Reverend Ash had aged. The Reverend was once a figure of stern authority, but now in the evening's darkness, he looked pale and weak. The Reverend's eyes followed Matt like a hawk.

"Reverend," Matt said without any other acknowledgment. Their eyes locked as Matt rode by. The Reverend seemed to straighten an inch or so to put forth an aura of authority, but in his eyes there was only fear. Matt rode on, picking up to a gallop as he left the town.

Tom Smith stormed into the jail slamming the door behind him. He was red-faced and burned with indignation. He had never in his years of being the Willow Falls Sheriff been completely embarrassed and over-powered, as Matt had just left him. Every ounce of his blood boiled with a long dormant rage that cascaded through his veins like a torrential flash flood. His heart pounded, his hands shook and his breathing was heavy while he stood by his desk staring at the wall. For the first time, his prisoners were taken back and made aware of just how serious the sheriff could be.

Clyde Waltz stepped into the office with a strange, quiet demeanor. As soon as he closed the door, Tom spun around and yelled with a loud voice, "I told you! I told you he brought trouble! How did I know that something like this would happen? Everywhere he goes there's trouble, always has been. Thank God there were witnesses or Eli would be dead. Thieves have to steal and murderers have to kill! It's their nature. A bloody doggone murderer is all he is and yet he gets the glory!"

Clyde silently sat down at his own desk to listen.

Tom continued, "We decent folks are suddenly his victims when he shows up. However, no one else will think so; they all want to have a welcome home party for him! For crying out loud, maybe we should name the cemetery after him; he's filled it half way up!" Tom continued to vent to Clyde. "And yet, everyone thinks he's a hero! It's astounding to me; I wish these people could see him as he really is. Heck, half the people out there think he's more of a hero now than they did yesterday, I bet. And me... well, I can't match up to that. Lord, I wish they could see him as he really is!" Tom spit out and then paused to take a deep breath. He continued in a calmer voice, "You know, Clyde, there's a part of me that wishes Eli would have shot him. It would have saved us all a lot of trouble, but maybe, if we're lucky he'll keep his word and stay out of town, because I don't want to see him again. And I'll tell you this, if something like this happens again, I won't be so nice about it, I'll shoot him myself!" Tom said, finally sitting down and starting to relax. Exhaustion swept through him, but he didn't want to go home until he had gained control of himself. He knew he'd have to tell his wife and Gabriel, about what happened and it would irritate him all the more knowing Gabriel nearly worshiped Matt. It had always been a constant irritation to Tom how Gabriel idolized him, but he thought it would be a short lived fascination at most, he had been wrong. Perhaps now Gabriel would see that Matt was a cold-blooded killer. Even at the age of fifteen Matt had no remorse for killing. None!

22

It was a day like many others, a quiet, hot summer's day where the only excitement was being finished with the workday. Charlie Ziegler, Darius Jackson, the three oldest Bannister boys and hired hands had taken a herd of cattle up to Spokane, leaving Matt and Joseph Jackson to do the daily chores of the ranch. They didn't mind though, because with Charlie being away, it meant that they could quit work early and have more time to play with their friends.

Matt and Joseph came into town earlier than usual, they were sweat covered and dusty after a day's chores. They intended to ride out to Pearl Creek to the swimming hole commonly known as "The Lagoon". It was a large deep pool with a rope swing tied to an over-hanging branch of a large willow tree. Like most days, Tom rode behind Joseph and Elizabeth, naturally, rode behind Matt. The affection between the two was so well known throughout town that it bordered on being scandalous.

As they rode past the saloon on their way out of town, a stranger stepped out of the doorway. He was a man in his late thirties or early forties who was dressed poorly and wore a reversed butt two-gun set up on his gun belt. He wore a black hat and was unshaved with a long scar on his left cheek. He looked rough and held a tin cup of whiskey in his right hand. He called out stopping the four young riders. "Hey, you kids. I heard one of you was Charlie Ziegler's nephew. Which one of you is?"

"I am," Matt answered, halting his horse, "I'm Matt."

"I hear your uncle's not in town," the man said.

"No, he's up north. He should be back in a few days, though," Matt said ignoring Joseph's impatient nods to continue.

Four other men, all dressed in well-worn and dirty clothing like the first man, stepped out of the saloon, all four wore gun belts and looked as rough as the first. All five men seemed to eye the teenagers, especially Elizabeth, with great interest. "We're friends of his from the old days and we came to see him," the man explained without a smile. A couple of his friends smiled slightly as he said it.

"Come on, Matthew, let's get," Joseph suggested, eyeing the men nervously.

"Okay," Matt answered Joseph. He turned back to the men. "Give me your names, and I'll let him know you're in town."

The man shook his head. "Na, I'd like to surprise him. When's he due back?"

"In a few days, probably. Anyway, we need to go."

"It's about time," Joseph added uneasily.

"Wait up a sec. You didn't introduce your friends," the man called. He eyed Elizabeth particularly with interest.

Matt felt a stirring of uneasiness grow in his stomach. It was one that he couldn't quite ignore or hide. "This is Elizabeth, that's Tom and Joseph. Now we really must be going."

"Is that Charlie's nigger? I thought he was for the North,"

the man with the scar asked of Joseph. His friends laughed lightly.

"I'm no slave!" Joseph spoke defensively. "My family and me work and live on the Big Z."

"Look at that, fellas," the man said to his friends, "a nigger that thinks he's free. Where we're from you'd be shot for talking to us like that! You'd better watch yourself, boy, or I'll take a whip to you myself." the stranger warned with a cold glare at Joseph.

Joseph remained quiet, but was greatly troubled by the man's demeanor.

Matt cut in, "He's our friend and his name's Joseph. We're leaving now!" They rode off while the five men called out racial slurs to Joseph and sexual references toward Elizabeth.

"Joseph," Elizabeth said as they left town, "those men were drunk, don't listen to them," she finished with disgust in her voice.

"Those guys are idiots!" Tom tried to encourage Joseph.

"My Pa told me there were people like that in the world. I just haven't ever met them," Joseph said, obviously troubled by the men. "I don't believe they're Uncle Charlie's friends neither."

Matt looked at Joseph. "They won't be when we tell Uncle Charlie what they said. He would never be friends with people like that Joseph, you know that."

"Then why'd they say he was, Matthew?"

Tom offered his opinion, "They looked like gun fighters to me. And I didn't like the way they looked at Elizabeth, either."

"They gave me the chills," Elizabeth offered while she held onto Matt closely. He was her prince and protector, she always felt safe with Matt.

Matt felt Elizabeth's hands tighten around him. He smiled to himself as he said, "Uncle Charlie was a gun fighter, so it's possible they are gun fighters, Tom. They didn't give us their names though."

"Well, I got a bad feeling," Joseph offered, but not describing his feeling. "They aren't Charlie's friends. I can promise you that."

"It doesn't matter," Tom offered, "they're just passing through. Let's just forget about them and go swimming. It's too hot to worry about those idiots anyway, let's go have some fun!" he said from behind Joseph and kicked the horse. The horse jolting forward took Joseph by surprise. Tom yelled, "Let's race!" Joseph laughed and kicked his mare himself to get further ahead of Matt. Matt told Elizabeth to hold on while he urged his horse into a full run.

An half hour later, they were at the swimming hole enjoying the cool water in the afternoon sun. Tom and Joseph were taking turns swinging off of the rope swing out into the deeper side of the lagoon. The water had invigorated their spirits.

Matt had already swung off the rope a few times before he went over to the water's edge, where Elizabeth was wading barefoot in the shallow water. She held her light blue cotton dress out of the water to keep it dry while tossing playful glances at Matt. He smiled. "What's a lady like you doing in a place like this?" he asked playfully. He reached for her arms and drew close to her as the water dripped off of him.

"Oh, the Chief wants some water. So, I came on down to the stream to get him some," she responded with mock sincerity.

"Chief?" Matt questioned, "Why, are you an Indian princess, by chance?" he asked with some playful doubt.

Elizabeth tried not to smile. "Why, yes I am."

"Oh yeah, well, what's your name?" Matt asked as his hands slipped down into hers. The hem of her dress fell into the water as they drew nearer.

She laughed lightly and then stopped herself as she put on her best serious expression. "My name's..." she paused to think of a good name, "My name's Elizabeth Says."

Matt laughed. "Elizabeth Says! What kind of a name is that?"

Elizabeth eyed him affectionately as she drew even closer and kissed him slowly. "Elizabeth says she loves you, Matthew Bannister," she said softly and kissed him again as their arms went around each other in a long kiss.

Matt did not get the chance to say another word as the five men from the saloon interrupted their kiss abruptly. They rode their horses through the brush lines that circled the lagoon. They had obviously been watching the teenagers and spread out to cut off any exit that the kids might've tried to take.

Immediately, Elizabeth drew nearer Matt, and he encircled his arms around her protectively. "What do you want?" Matt asked nervously. He could feel a sense of great fear welling up within him and could hardly keep from breaking down into tears himself. Elizabeth trembled from the look in the men's eyes. Tom and Joseph both slowly walked through the water towards their friends with the same frightened expressions on their faces.

The man with a scar on his cheek, who had done the talking outside of the saloon, sat on his horse and looked at Elizabeth with a hungry grin, just like all four of his buddies did.

"What do you want?" Matt asked again, his voice cracked

with a growing anxiety. Tom and Joseph had joined them at the edge of the lagoon. The men on horseback were slowly corralling them into a small group, surrounded by the horsemen.

"We came for a pretty young girl," A big man with a gruff voice and a haggard, bearded face said through a large wad of chewing tobacco. He was a large heavy-set man of forty some. He walked his horse towards the four kids. "Come along pretty lady," he said and held his hand down to her to take.

Elizabeth began to tremble. "No," she cried weakly. She held onto Matt tighter.

"Honey," the man explained, "I'm afraid you ain't got a choice. Now come on!" he shouted and walked his horse closer and reached down to grab her arm.

Matt reacted quickly and grabbed his arm with both of his and spun his own body to the ground which yanked the large rider quickly out of the saddle. The man landed on the ground hard and knocked the wind out of him.

"Don't shoot him!" Matt heard a man yell quickly. It was the man with the scar ordering one of the men behind Matt. Matt turned to see one of the riders pointing his pistol at him. He froze with a petrifying fear that he never could've imagined if he wasn't staring at a loaded pistol that was pointed at him.

"What do you guys want?" Matt heard himself ask with a trembling voice and a quivering bottom lip. His emotions were getting the better of him.

"You son of a..." Matt heard a strained voice behind him. It was the big man that Matt had pulled off of his horse. Matt turned around just in time to have the barrel of the man's revolver ripped hard across his face. Matt stumbled backwards but kept his balance as Elizabeth screamed in terror. Matt straightened himself up as blood poured from an inch long cut on his left cheek. Matt glared at the big bearded man as he raised his pistol at Matt. The man hissed angrily, "I'm gonna kill ya, boy!"

"Don't you dare, Frank!" the man with a scar ordered. "We didn't come here for him. Put your gun away."

The man named Frank, hesitantly holstered his weapon and without a second thought stepped closer to Matt and threw a vicious right fist into Matt's face. Matt fell into the water as the force of the blow knocked him off of his feet. Elizabeth screamed and sobbed desperately as big Frank grabbed her and pulled her close to him. He drug her toward his horse.

Matt stood up at the sound of her cries. His nose was bleeding now and his eyes were watering heavily from a fractured nose. "Leave her be!" he shouted. "You're not my uncle's friends, are you?" He directed his question to the man with a scar who seemed to be the leader.

"No, we're not his friends. None of us have ever even met the man, in fact," the man explained with a cold glare at Matt. He continued over Elizabeth's screams and struggles to get away from Frank. "I'm Clay Dobson. This is my brother, Walt," he nodded to the man beside him. "That's Frank Walchester, Bill Nobel and that man behind you is Claude Magnus. We came to kill your uncle, son," Clay Dobson stated as easily as the Reverend said grace. "He gunned down my brother like the coward he is and Claude's brother too. We came to collect the debt he owes us."

Tom's mouth dropped open in recognition. "You're the Dobson Gang?" he stated more than asked. He and Joseph had been too scared to move, let alone say a word as they watched.

"You are?" Matt asked in disbelief.

"We are," Clay said simply.

"Let me go!" Elizabeth screamed as she fought against Frank.

"Let her go!" Matt yelled and took a step or two towards her.

Just then Elizabeth reached up and scratched Franks face with her finger nails. He cursed and threw a hard right into her abdomen, which knocked the wind out of her and quickly ended her struggling. Frank then gently lifted her face up with his left hand and threw a fast hard right fist into her face. Elizabeth dropped like a heavy rock.

Matt, in a fury of anger, ran and dove into Frank driving him backwards to the ground. Matt climbed on top of his chest and swung his right hand again and again into Frank's face. He didn't care about anything else, other than hurting the man. He couldn't hear anything except his heart pounding and Elizabeth desperately begging him to stop. He didn't notice anyone stepping closer to him until Claude Magnus slammed his pistol butt down across his head. Matt was stunned and easily pushed off by the embarrassed older man. Frank stood up and endured the laughter of his friends as he momentarily wiped the blood from his own face. Matt laid on the rock of the water's edge holding his head painfully. Blood ran heavily down across his face from the cut on his head. Frank cursed at Matt severely and began a series of hard and painful kicks to every part of Matt's body that wasn't protected.

"That's enough, Frank!" Clay shouted after a few moments. "Grab the girl and let's go."

"What?" Tom asked in horror. He froze when Clay looked at him.

Joseph went to help Matt up and spoke to Clay as he did so, "You should just leave!"

Elizabeth once again screamed when Frank grabbed her by the waist and began to carry her toward his horse.

Joseph helped Matt to stand and then went to help Elizabeth. He was stopped by the voice of Claude Magnus, who pointed his revolver at him, "What cha doing, boy?"

Joseph froze.

Matt again ran after Frank and grabbed the back of Frank's hair as he was setting Elizabeth across his saddle. Frank cried out as Matt forcefully pulled him away from Elizabeth relentlessly. Walt Dobson pulled out his carbine rifle and slammed the butt forcefully into Matt's shoulder blades. Matt stunned by the blow released Franks hair and was quickly hit to the ground and once again kicked mercilessly by Frank.

Clay Dobson spoke to Matt after Frank had finished beating him. "Boy, if you don't stay down and behave like your friends, I'm gonna shoot you myself. No more!" he warned with the coldest eyes Matt had ever seen.

Matt forced himself up onto his two feet and looked at Elizabeth. She was being held by Bill Noble and sobbing as she watched him being beaten. Matt was beaten, hurting and bleeding, but there was no defeat within him either.

It was as though someone else was speaking through him when he said, "You'll have to kill me if you want to take her! God as my witness, you will have to kill me! If you touch her, you'll be hunted down by every man in town." Matt paused momentarily to bend over and gasp for air painfully. Blood covered his face from his nose, mouth, his cheek, his head and a new cut above his left eye. He straightened himself and stared up at Clay as he continued, "If you kill me, my uncle will track you down. You won't leave this valley alive either way!" Matt's heart raced, but he showed no sign of cowardice; he was more than willing to sacrifice his life in the effort to keep Elizabeth safe. He knew the Lord Jesus Christ as his Savior and that security gave him the courage to die, if need be, to save the girl he loved.

Clay Dobson seemed to think it over a bit and then gave a small wave at Bill Noble. "Let her go, Bill. I think he's right about the girl, she'd only bring trouble. But a back-talking nigger is another thing, and look, they already have a rope hanging on a tree. String him up, boys."

"No!... Matthew!" Joseph yelled out, as he stepped backwards slowly with large petrified eyes.

"No, you'll have to kill me..." Matt began speaking urgently and stepped protectively toward Joseph. Big Frank Walchester punched Matt in the abdomen so hard that it sucked the wind out of him and dropped him to his hands and knees struggling to find his breath. Joseph, seeing Matt fall to the ground and Big Frank and Bill Noble stepping towards him, began to run towards the trail out of the swimming hole as fast as he could. Matt tried to stand, but Big Frank turned back and kicked him in the head and he fell backwards to the ground where he laid barely conscience.

Walt Dobson still holding his rifle, took aim at Joseph as he neared the trail and fired. Joseph fell to the ground and rolled in pain while reaching for the back of his thigh with a loud cry. "They shot me! Oh Lord Jesus, help me!" Joseph begged.

"What about the girl?" Frank asked Clay as he stood over Matt. "I didn't come all the way out here just to hang a nigger!"

"Joseph..." Matt said as he forced himself to sit up.

"Leave him alone, he's my friend," Matt said weakly. "Please, leave him alone."

Clay ignored Matt and looked sharply at Big Frank, "I said leave her alone! Now help Bill take him to the rope," Clay ordered Walt and Claude Magnus. "I want his friends to watch, especially that one!" he nodded at Matt.

"He's my friend," Matt begged, "He didn't do anything to you, please, just leave us alone!" Matt's voice cracked with emotion as he forced himself back up his feet. "Please, I'm asking you, don't..."

Claude Magnus had dismounted from his horse and suddenly kicked behind Matt's knee causing him to fall to his back on the river rock again. He arched in pain from landing on a larger rock. "Shut up!" Claude sneered.

"Please don't, sir. Please leave him alone!" Elizabeth begged as Big Frank and Bill Noble picked Joseph up by his arms and drug him towards the willow tree with the rope swing tied to it. He sobbed heavily as they did.

"Please," Tom pleaded, "We won't tell anyone anything. I promise." He wept.

"Help me, Matthew, help me!" Joseph screamed as they drug him by the arms past Matt. His face reflected pure terror and desperation as he sobbed between crying out for help.

"Don't!" Matt yelled fiercely, finding new strength to stand up and fight. "Hang me instead!" he pleaded and stepped quickly towards the two men who held Joseph. "I won't let you hurt my friends, so let him go and hang me!"

"Claude, can you hold him and shut him up!" Clay ordered as he climbed off his horse.

Matt was just about to reach for Bill Noble's arm when Claude once again kicked the back of Matt's knee from behind and dropped to his knees. Quickly Claude was behind him on his knees as well, with his right arm snuggly around Matt's neck and the other arm locking Matt's left arm behind his back. Matt was locked in a helpless position with only his right arm free to fight with, but despite his efforts, he was limited by Claude's superior strength and position.

Joseph tried to fight the two bigger and stronger men, but he was no match to their cruelty. Big Frank held him while Bill tied the rope swing around his neck. "Matthew!" Joseph yelled desperately, "Jesus help me!"

"Joseph!" Matt screamed loudly as they pushed Joseph forcefully off of the three-foot bank out over the water. Joseph tried desperately to loosen the knot as he helplessly clawed at the rope cutting into his neck while his feet cut through the top few inches of water like the pendulum of a clock. The incomprehensible cries of Elizabeth echoed through the trees, higher pitched than Tom and Matt's, but just as horrified. It seemed an eternity for Joseph to go limp and longer for his body to stop swinging through the water.

When Joseph's body hung lifeless and remained still with his toes in the water, Clay Dobson looked at Elizabeth. "You can tell them the Dobson Gang's waiting for Charlie Ziegler. Now get out of here and take your bloody boyfriend with you." He nodded to where Claude was still holding Matt from behind and forcing him to watch Joseph hang. He was sobbing bitterly.

"Let him go," Clay ordered.

Claude Magnus squeezed his arm around Matt's neck to choke him harder and spoke through his gritted teeth into his ear, "You ain't so tough! If it was me, I would've saved him, but you ain't nothing! Nothing at all!" he spat and released Matt by pushing his face down into the ground as he stood up over him. "Now get out of here!"

Sobbing the three friends rode up the trail through the brush and headed towards Willow Falls. They had not ridden even a hundred yards when they heard the Dobson Gang start shooting their guns and laughing. Matt pulled the reigns of his horse to a sudden halt and took a deep breath. "Tom wait. Lizzy, ride with Tom, I'm going back for Joseph."

"What?" Tom exclaimed. "You can't! They'll kill you too. Come on with us and get the sheriff."

"No!" Matt exclaimed, "I can't leave him there." He paused and waited for her to move from behind him, but she just held on to him tightly. "Go Elizabeth, please!"

"No, Matthew!"

"Go!" Matt yelled. Elizabeth slid down and Matt turned his horse and sprinted back to Pearl Creek without looking at her.

"Come on, Elizabeth. Let's get help!" Tom said with a hand extended to help her up behind him.

Matt rode straight back down the trail and the shooting stopped as he approached. The Dobson Gang turned their weapons on him, but held their fire as he came into view. Matt eyed each one of them as he rode slowly past them and into the shallow water. His face was covered with dried blood and his eyes were focused on the dead and bloody body of Joseph. They had used his body as target practice. Matt choked on his tears, and his body convulsed at the sight of Joseph's bullet riddled body. He rode up to Joseph's hanging body and dismounted.

The Dobson Gang watched him perplexed and speechless. They lowered their weapons and watched Matt try to do the impossible task of picking up Joseph's body and loosen the rope that was tightly knotted around his neck. He struggled to hold up the limp heavy body and reach the knot. Matt didn't say a word; he just kept trying to no avail.

Clay Dobson silently shook his head and mounted his horse and rode into the water where Matt lifted on Joseph's hips. Standing in his stirrups, Clay reached up with his knife and cut the rope. Joseph's body fell lifelessly into the water even with Matt holding onto it. Clay looked Matt in the eyes. "Take him home and dig two holes. Your uncle is next and anyone else who gets in our way."

Matt shook his head slowly as he stared up at Clay. "No, Joseph's blood is on your hands. You won't leave this valley alive, the Lord will see to that."

Clay smirked. "We'll see about that. You were right about the girl or either one of you two boys, it's amazing how fired up a town can get when one of their young ones are harmed. We came to kill your uncle, not a town."

"Why Joseph?" Matt asked with tears burning in his eyes.

Clay smiled. "No one's going to risk their life for a nigger, not even your uncle," Clay stated simply.

"His name's Joseph," Matt said. A tear fell, turning red as it mixed with the dried blood on his face.

"Not anymore," Clay said coldly. "Take him and go. And don't come back or I'll kill you."

"You should have killed me," Matt said with a nod as he glared at Clay. He then bent down to pick up his lifeless friend. Struggling, he picked Joseph up and laboriously, he heaved his body across the saddle of his horse. He climbed up behind Joseph uncomfortably and looked at every one of the men, who at the moment stared at him surprised by what they had witnessed.

Big Frank nodded admirably and said, "You've got grit,

boy, I'll give you that. You're not the smartest boy I've ever seen, but you are damn sure the grittiest."

Matt looked a Frank and then back at Clay. He spoke calmly, "You won't leave this valley alive."

Clay smirked deviously, "So you've said."

Big Frank chuckled and shook his head in disbelief as Matt rode away.

23

By the time a small posse was assembled by the Sheriff Lonnie Clark and deputy Clyde Waltz, Matt had led his horse by the reins for the near two miles back to Willow Falls. When the posse found him any ambition on the posse's part to track down the Dobson Gang was quickly ended by the sight of Joseph's lifeless, bullet riddled body lying over Matt's saddle. His blood ran freely down the saddle and dripped off the leather to the ground.

Matt was in shock when they found him and he fainted when the sheriff tried to question him. They hurriedly put him on a horse and took him back into town as fast as they could. Reverend Ash directed them to lay Matt on his bed, and sent for the closest to a doctor that Willow Falls had. The Reverend and his wife rode out to the Big Z Ranch to notify Mary Ziegler and Olivia Jackson of what had happened. It had been one of the hardest moments in the Reverend's career to tell Mrs. Jackson that her only son had been murdered for no reason. And for her own peace of mind, she wouldn't be allowed to see his ravaged body before his burial.

Matt awoke a few hours later in a darkened room surrounded by Aunt Mary, Missus Jackson and Missus Ash. When he asked if the sheriff had gotten the Dobson Gang, Mary mentioned that the men were currently meeting next door in the church to discuss it. Matt forced himself to stand up despite the women's pleas to lie still and the pain from his bruised ribs, fractured nose and the bruises and cuts on his face. He walked stiffly to the church and opened the door; his presence turned heads and widened eyes. A round of applause came as the town's citizens stood with smiles and some with tears. Some whistled while others hollered, "Praise the Lord!" as he entered the church.

"Matthew! Praise God you're all right," the Reverend said with a sad, but comforting smile. His voice always quieted the room. "We are all sorry about the loss of young Joseph. I know that's little comfort, Matthew, but you saved my daughter from those men and I can't thank you enough," the Reverend finished sincerely. The congregation applauded. Matt's pain-filled expression never changed as he looked around the room for Tom and Elizabeth. Neither one were in the church.

"You are a hero, Matthew!" the Reverend added while clapping his hands.

Matt couldn't care less about the applauding. He looked at the sheriff, who was clapping his hands with a large smile on his round face. "Sheriff, did you get the Dobson Gang?"

The Reverend answered, "We decided to call in the sheriff and the deputies from Branson. They should be here tomorrow afternoon, I'm guessing."

"Why?" asked Matt.

"Because we're not capable of arresting the Dobson Gang unassisted. They're too dangerous for us to arrest."

Matt raised his voice, "You don't need to arrest them!

Hang them, like they did to Joseph. You can't just wait for them to leave!"

"Matthew, I know you're upset," Reverend Ash spoke carefully, "but the law says they need to stand trial. That's the law."

"But..." Matt tried to interject.

The Reverend raised his voice, "I know they're guilty, we all saw Joseph's body. But we can't risk our lives foolishly either. Farmers picking up arms and taking aim against a gang of known gun fighters isn't wise. We need professionals."

"Reverend Ash," Matt spoke angrily, "If they had taken Elizabeth, would you be waiting for the Branson Sheriff or would you grab your rifle? What about you, Sheriff? You know if my uncle Charlie was here, he wouldn't be sitting in here talking. Those men would already be dead!"

The Reverend spoke frankly, "Your Uncle Charlie is the reason those men are here!"

"That's true," Sheriff Clark added meekly, "Matthew, your uncle's not here. So we have to do this our way."

"Which means you're doing nothing?" Matt questioned.

"Matt," Sheriff Clark said nervously, "nobody in this church has ever even aimed a gun at a person. The Reverend's right. Clyde and I have no choice, we have to go, but we won't endanger anyone else who's a citizen of this town. The Dobson Gang means business and they'll be expecting a posse. I ain't taking a posse after them!"

"Fine!" Matt said with contempt in his voice and walked out of the church. Outside he took a deep breath of fresh air and saw Tom sitting alone on the steps of the small schoolhouse across the street.

"Matthew!" Tom stated and began to weep as Matt

neared him. "I can't believe Joseph's dead!" he cried into his hands. "I guess we never should have gone swimming!"

Matt sat down slowly beside Tom and said, "They aren't going after them, Tom. So we have to."

"What?" Tom asked sounding horrified.

Matt looked Tom in the eyes. "Those men are going to leave and get away with murdering Joseph, unless we stop them. I need your help."

"No!" Tom exclaimed. "I'm never going back there!"

"Tom, I need your help."

"No, Matthew! We'll get killed, just like Joseph."

"No, we won't. Trust me."

"Matt..." Tom began to protest.

Matt interrupted him irritably, "Tom, they're going to kill my uncle Charlie and maybe my family. I need your help. Now, are you going to come with me or not, because, I'm going with or without you!" Matt said as he stood up slowly to leave.

"You can't even stand up without hurting, Matthew, so how are you going to go after them?"

Matt looked down at Tom with determination on his face. "I'm going. I may be killed without you watching my back, but I'm going to kill Clay Dobson before they get me. I can promise you that!"

Tom dropped his head and sighed heavily. "When?"

"Meet me at midnight at the fork in the road by the cemetery and bring your rifle. Tomorrow, we'll be heroes," Matt said without any emotion and walked a few steps before turning back to Tom. "You'll step quieter in moccasins; I'll bring you some. Meet me at midnight, Tom, and don't fall asleep on me," Matt said and walked towards the livery stable to get his horse.

Tom would never forget the look on Matt's beaten face.

His face was bruised, swollen and black and blue, but his eyes burned with a determined and fearless lust for vengeance that had taken Tom by surprise. Tom often wondered if it was guilt that forced him to agree to go with Matt that night, or the fear of saying "no" to him at that moment. The fact was he was more afraid of his friend at that moment on the school steps than he was of facing the five murderers again. At least at that moment he was.

24

Tom was pulled out of his memories by Clyde, who had asked him a question. "What?" he asked from his seat behind his desk.

"Are you going to answer them?" Clyde asked with a hint of a smile.

"Who?"

"Me!" Donovan Moskin exclaimed. "When you came storming in here a few minutes ago, you were talking about shooting someone. I'll make you a deal, let us out of here and I'll do it for you. We'll call it a promissory agreement and we won't say a word about it if you don't."

"I don't think so, Donovan," Tom said humorlessly.

Clyde Waltz added with a laugh to Donovan, "You wouldn't get very far if you did. Old Charlie and Darius would have you hung up before you got off the Big Z land, huh Tom?"

Tom stood up annoyed and started toward the door. "See you in the morning, Clyde."

"Come on, sheriff," Donovan chimed, "let me do you a favor. We'll take our chances on, what's it called, the Big Z?

Whatever that is. No one would ever know that you had anything to do with it. Just give me my horses and guns, tell me the name and I'll do the rest. No one will ever know."

"Oh, they'll know," the sheriff said sarcastically. He turned to face the jail cell and looked at Donovan. "His name's Matthew Bannister. Does that name mean anything to you?"

"Not a thing. Look, here's my deal; just tell me where he lives, let me go, and I'll go shoot him. When he's dead, I'll come back and we'll all say we were here at the jail. No questions, no doubt, and then tomorrow let us go. You're covered, I'm covered, the plan can't fail." Donovan looked hopeful as he proposed his latest offer.

Tom smirked tiredly. "Have you ever heard of Matt Bannister? He's a U. S. Deputy Marshal from Wyoming. Maybe you've heard of him?" Tom watched as Donovan's eyes grew big and his face seemed to grow faint. He didn't answer immediately and Tom continued sarcastically, "Still interested?"

"Matt's here?" Donovan asked quietly, "in this town?"

Tom nodded. "Yes, he is."

Clyde offered cheerfully, "Matthew grew up here! This is Willow Falls; where the entire Dobson Gang met its end. Surely you know that story?"

John Birch suddenly took an interest in the story. "The Dobson's were killed here? In this town? They died here?"

"Died and buried here," Clyde answered. "The whole gang including Claude Magnus."

"And the guy who killed them is here?" John asked to clarify.

"Matt Bannister! Yeah," Clyde said and then added just as excitedly, "he was just outside. One of our teenagers thought he might shoot him a marshal, and we almost lost a good teenage citizen."

"What's Matt doing here?" Donovan asked curiously. His voice had lost its determination.

"This is his home..." Clyde was cut off by Tom.

"You sound worried, Donovan. Do you still want to make a deal?" he asked sarcastically.

Donovan spoke in a low and sincere tone, "Matt's a hard man, I don't think I'll risk that. Does he know I'm in town?"

"Heck!" Tom spat out as he turned around stepping towards the door. "How would I know? He let you guys ride right by him. He knows I've made an arrest, but if he knows your names or not, I don't know. Why, is he looking for you?" All the talk of Matt angered him.

Donovan shook his head. "No, but I know him."

"You know Matt? How?" Tom asked. He was suddenly interested in what Donovan had to say.

"Cheyenne. He arrested me once or twice. He's a dangerous man, Sheriff. I suppose, I should be grateful that you found us instead of him," Donovan replied. His whole demeanor had changed significantly.

Tom looked at John Birch. "What about you? Do you know him, too?"

"No. I've heard of him though," John paused. "The Dobson's were from my part of Texas. I even met them a few times when I was young. I remember when I heard they fell, and it was a kid my age that did it. I couldn't believe it. It didn't seem possible. It still don't."

"If it's any consolation," Tom said, "they weren't armed."

"They were always armed," John stated.

"Not at five in the morning, they weren't," Tom said sharply. "Claude Magnus got two shots off and Walt Dobson got one. Bill Nobel, Frank Walchester, and Clay Dobson never fired a shot. They were gunned down like cows at the slaughter house."

"And this is what he told you?" John asked skeptically.

"No..." Tom said pausing.

Clyde answered for him, "He was there! He and Matt were both there."

"You were there?" John asked.

Tom nodded. "I was."

"Who'd you shoot?" John asked.

"No one. They were unarmed sleeping men."

"Tell me about it, Sheriff," Donovan said. "How'd Matt do it? Everyone knows Matt killed them, but no one's ever heard what really happened from a witness. Matt doesn't say much about it, he's not a real sociable guy, you know." Donovan paused before explaining, "He just tracks men down and that's what he does." He looked at Tom and asked, "How'd he kill the Dobson's?"

25

Tom had met Matt at the cemetery just after midnight. Matt was strangely quiet and led the way to Pearl Creek in the darkness. They spent three hours searching silently for the Dobson Gang. Finally, Matt caught the faint smell of wood smoke in the air three miles downstream from the lagoon. The Dobson's had camped down inside of a deep draw on a small brush covered sandbar in the middle of the creek.

Matt and Tom managed to get down into the draw as the Dobson Gang slept. When the first light came, Matt crawled closer to take position behind the roots of a large cedar tree that had fallen across the creek. It was about twenty yards from the little island that the Dobson Gang slept on. He aimed his uncle Charlie's sixteen shot model 1860 Henry rifle and wore his uncle's old .36 caliber Colt police revolver on his hip. Matt waited patiently until it was light enough to see clearly. Tom waited behind a rotting stump slightly upstream on the side of the steep bank. Tom's heart pounded in his chest as he held his father's Colt rifle with its revolving cylinder for repeating shots. He carefully watched the sleeping men and watched Matt, who reminded him of a starving tomcat stalking a field mouse. He was perched, loaded, and ready. Not long after the first rays of the sun lit the water inside of the ravine, Bill Noble woke up slapping at the mosquitoes that ate at them all. He stood to stretch and a bullet from Matt's rifle tore into his chest forcing him backward onto the sand at the water's edge. He was already dead with a bullet through his heart.

The four other men scrambled for cover with their guns in hand. Matt's second shot hit Walt Dobson in the upper left thigh just before he lunged forward to take refuge behind the brush and debris that had built up after the last spring's run-off. Walt's loud obscenities could be heard from the center of the small island as he looked at his wound. Matt's third shot was at Clay Dobson, who was running quickly toward the opposite bank across shallow water. The bullet missed. Matt quickly ejected the spent casing and reloaded another shell with the lever action. He aimed his fourth shot and fired, hitting Clay Dobson in the middle of his lower back. Clay fell down face first at the edge of the creek bank. He began yelling for his brother Walt to help him while he used his arms to drag himself out of the water. Walt yelled back becoming more desperate.

Claude Magnus stood up to get a better angle for a clear shot at Matt. Claude fired twice with his revolver, both shots were quick and close, but Claude Magnus met his own gun fighter's end. Matt's fifth shot hit him square in the chest. Claude spun around and fell dying next to where Walt laid hidden by the brush.

Tom Smith watched in horror as the gunshots echoed through the rivers deep draw and blood was being spilt before his eyes. With the screams of Clay Dobson echoing in his ear and the horror of watching real men meet death, Tom stood in shock and let his rifle drop to the ground. His mind told him to run, but his body remained much too terrified to move. Tom's most terrifying moment came when he saw Frank Walchester's rifle pointed directly at him. Tom stared into Frank's murderous eyes and waited for the bullet to pierce him. It seemed very surreal; eerily dreamlike while he waited to die. He was terrified moments before, but now he felt a peace pass through him, as there was nothing he could do to stop it from happening. He waited helplessly for the bullet's blow and to ascend to heaven like Joseph had. Suddenly, Frank's head imploded under the impact of a bullet from Matt's rifle. Frank crumbled to the ground lifeless. Tom looked over at Matt in horror, Matt was staring at him with an enraged expression on his face. It was an expression that Tom hoped to never see again.

For a moment, the shooting subsided as Matt searched the debris pile for Walt Dobson behind it. Then, Walt fired a single shot from his rifle toward Matt, it hit the fallen tree. Matt rested his rifle on the tree and aimed carefully as he patiently waited and listened like he used to do when they'd hunt ground squirrels. Walt began calling out for his brother to come help him, but then realized the magnitude of his brother's injury. Clay couldn't move his legs. In a rage, Walt screamed and stood up to take a shot. Matt ended Walt's life with an anticipated head shot as soon as he stood. After a moment, Matt laid the rifle against the tree roots and pulled out his revolver. He walked down the hill and crossed the shallow stream to the sandbar. He made sure all four of the other men were dead before he silently crossed to the other side of the creek where Clay Dobson still laid on his belly clawing at the bank. He was trying to pull his legs out of the water. Matt kicked Clay Dobson over onto his back to look at him. Clay was crying with terror in his eyes.

"I can't move my legs, get me to the doctor. I can't feel my legs!" Clay cried out. His cries echoed through the now silent ravine. Matt glared down at Clay without an ounce of mercy on his face. Clay didn't seem to recognize him as he continued to plead, "Go get the doctor! Walt!" he yelled out desperately, "Walt! Claude!" he yelled and then began to sob.

Matt spoke coldly, "They're not going to help you, they're dead."

Clay looked at Matt and focused for the first time on the boy standing over him. He asked, "Why are you doing this? What did I ever do to you?" His body began to tremble with terrified chills and his lips quiver.

"You don't remember hanging Joseph?" Matt spat out like it was venom.

"Who?" Clay asked incoherently. "Go get a doctor. I can't feel my legs!" he yelled out with tears streaming down his face. "Walt, where are you?"

"I told you, that you wouldn't leave this valley alive," Matt said and aimed his pistol at Clay Dobson's head and pulled the hammer back. The sound of the hammer locking into position seemed to echo throughout the ravine.

Clay looked at Matt with a perplexed expression that slowly grew in focus and his eyes widened in recognition. His face contorted into a desperate attempt to force out words that wouldn't come. Time had expired and his years of living were through. He would find out once and forever what was on the other side of life, whether he believed in it or not, he was about to face it. He was filled with a terror unlike any he had ever experienced before. It wasn't the terror of dying. No, it was the terror of what was waiting for him after he died, eternity.

Tom couldn't watch. He turned his head, covered his ears and somehow found himself curled into a fetal position on the ground, sobbing. The shot that killed Clay Dobson in cold-blood echoed loudly, followed by a haunting silence that felt like death itself. It was so silent that Tom had kept his ears covered so he couldn't hear it. Matt found Tom crying uncontrollably in a fetal position behind the stump while holding his ears tightly.

"Tom, go get the sheriff. Tell him the Dobson Gang is dead..." Tom heard Matt say. His voice was without pride, without joy, and without any hint of life at all.

Tom looked up at Matt and saw the splatters of Clay's blood spread across his face and shirt. Horrified, Tom scrambled on his hands and knees up the hill and then ran to his horse some distance away. He rode his horse hard all the way to town where he wept uncontrollably while he explained what he'd witnessed.

"And," Tom added softly, "that's it. They were all dead." He left out the parts about his actions and scrambling away from Matt to run into town. "Call him a hero if you want, but heroes don't kill unarmed men. Cowards do," he said as he stood up. "Good night boys, I'm going home."

After the sheriff left, Donovan asked Clyde, "So, why's the sheriff hate Matt so much? I mean, what's the real story? Killing a man like that wouldn't cause Tom to hate Matt, would it?"

"No, it's a longer story than that. I watched it all happen, you know, I've been the deputy for so long that I could tell you almost everything about anybody around here."

DONOVAN MOSKIN DID NOT SLEEP WELL. Any plans he had of deceiving the judge about Coffee Canyon would be lost if Matt Bannister heard of it. Its reputation as a secret place was still alive and well, but the fact was that it wasn't so secret any more. Donovan knew Matt couldn't be fooled by him. He had tried a few times, twice it had landed Donovan in jail and another time on the floor. Matt didn't seem to like him, so he did his best to stay out of Matt's way. He made it a point to keep Matt off his trail, and that was a large part of his leaving Wyoming for Texas and finally heading west. Unlike most other lawmen, Matt didn't stop looking for who he was determined to find. He was a hound dog of tenacity and a wolverine of ferocity, he was a man to be feared and Donovan did fear him.

If Matt heard that he was in the Willow Falls jail, he would come to the jail and start asking questions. Somehow he would find out what Donovan was doing and Matt would hang him for sure. Matt knew him as a liar and a thief and could see through him like a piece of clear glass. With Matt in town, the odds of being hung for their crimes increased greatly. The only comfort was the knowledge that Matt and the sheriff were old rivals. Donovan had witnessed the sheriff go into a rage over Matt, which meant they wouldn't be discussing the day's events with each other over coffee. There was the possibility that Matt would never know that he was in town. Clyde had stated the night before, "Heck, we'll probably not even see him again." All Donovan could do was hope Clyde was right.

26

The morning of Christmas Eve came early at the Smith house. Gabriel had to milk the cow and feed the other animals while Elizabeth gathered eggs in the chicken coop. Tom had slept little during the night and chose to sleep in for a bit longer than usual.

For Elizabeth, the news of Eli's attempt to shoot Matt was unbelievable. He was such a sweet boy, such a good friend to Gabriel and their family. It was inconceivable that Eli would dream up an idea to shoot Matt in cold blood! It was senseless, but then, young boys were often senseless. Sometimes they reacted much quicker than they could reason through their actions. By the grace of God though, no one got hurt, except Tom's pride.

Elizabeth was still amazed that Matt was back in town and at the mercantile the night before. Deep down she wanted to see him again. She was curious to know if Matthew had become the killer Tom made him out to be. He had once been her best friend and her first love. Was he really that different? She had to admit she didn't know Matt

Bannister, the lawman, she knew Matthew, the one who risked his life to save her from the Dobson Gang.

A part of her was scared of realizing that she wasn't really over him. What if those old feelings sprung to life again? What if she realized that she still hated her father for forcing her to marry Tom? Or maybe Tom was right and she'd despise Matt for what had become. More importantly, what if Tom found out that Gabriel was Matt's son and she'd been lying to him all these years? The risk for any or all of her worries weren't worth the consequences. So, she chose not to make herself available for going into town and accidently running into Matt. In a deeply selfish way she wished Eli had shot Matt, then there would be no more anxieties to fear.

Matt also weighed heavily on Tom's mind. He was troubled by Matt's presence and he mentioned Pearl Creek for the first time in years. Tom had spent the night tossing and turning, finally giving in to sleep only to be awakened by a nightmare which had kept him awake for a long time. When Elizabeth asked him what he had dreamed, he explained it was a nightmare about the Dobson Gang. It wasn't the Dobson Gang that scared him in his dream, it was the expression on Matt's blood covered face after killing Clay Dobson. But this time, Matt was standing over Tom aiming his revolver down at him, with a blood-thirsty rage in his eyes.

Gabriel was the only one excited to have Matt in town. He was anxious to meet him and would ride straight out to the Big Z to do so. The only thing keeping him from doing so was his fear of Charlie Ziegler. And at the moment she was glad of it.

Gabriel came inside with a bucket of fresh milk. "Hey,

Mom, can I go over to Eli's? I want to tell him what a fool he is. I think I know why he did that."

"Why?" Elizabeth asked, grateful for not having to give an answer right away.

"Because Matt killed the Dobson Gang and became famous. Eli told me once that whoever killed Matt would become famous too," Gabriel explained simply. "I guess he wants to be famous."

"Oh," Elizabeth said, "the difference is the Dobson Gang were outlaws and Matt's a marshal."

Gabriel laughed slightly. "Do you think Dad would have hung Eli for shooting Matt if he had?" he asked.

"Oh, Sweetie," Elizabeth paused uncomfortably, "I don't even want to think about it. But if he had shot him, then yes, your father would have to arrest him. The sentence would be up to Judge Jacoby, not your father."

"Boy, Eli's lucky! Can I go over there, Mother? I really need to tell him what a foolish thing he did."

"I don't know, Gabriel. Maybe you should ask your father."

"He's sleeping."

"Then you'll have to wait to ask him. Don't you think Eli might be in trouble with his father?"

"Yeah!" Gabriel exclaimed. "A lot of it."

"I think you had better ask your father, Gabriel. He'll know if Johnny will allow Eli to have any friends over or not. Okay?"

"I guess," Gabriel agreed. "I can't believe Eli actually tried that," he scoffed. "Like he could shoot Matt Bannister, that's ridiculous! Matt's too good of a gun fighter to be gunned down by Eli Barso," Gabriel said confidently.

Elizabeth spoke before thinking, "That's what people said about the Dobson Gang, Gabriel."

"Really? What'd they say?"

"Oh, I don't know. Never mind." Elizabeth had never talked about that day on Pearl Creek either. Much like Tom, she preferred to keep the memories carefully locked away.

"Well apparently," Gabriel explained, "the Dobson Gang picked on the wrong boy, because Matt Bannister sure took care of them. They were here to kill Charlie Ziegler you know. Matt ran into them first and they started harassing him and his girlfriend. He just pulled out this pistol and killed all five of them before they could get one shot off! Eli never would have had a chance!"

"Do you know who his girlfriend was?" Elizabeth asked with her back turned to him.

"No. Dad said she moved away right afterwards. Did you know her, Mom?"

"No. I don't even remember her name."

"Dad said she didn't live here for long."

Elizabeth closed her eyes and sank in the guilt of living with so many well intended lies. Gabriel's whole life was filled with lies. The Reverend had kept Elizabeth's and Tom's names out of the papers at the time to protect them from the stain of Matt Bannister. There was no written report in existence that affiliated them with the Dobson Gang. The Reverend made sure of that and urged the township to spare the two kids the burden of having to relive the horror of that day. That day had become a taboo subject to talk about in Willow Falls. Over the years, it was buried deep enough that it was nearly forgotten. But they would have to tell Gabriel the truth someday though, someday soon.

27

Coming back home was frightening enough, but Matt never expected to face an assassination attempt by a local boy. Uncle Luther's words rang like a church bell as he considered what might've happened if he'd been killed. His life up to this point truly had no value. He owned nothing; he loved no one nor did anyone love him. He wouldn't have left behind any children to carry on his name and the only child he apparently did have carried Tom's name. His life was empty. Fame, some would argue, would be his eternal legacy, but to Matt, his kind of fame was worthless. All it did was make him a target to foolish young men who wanted to be famous, so they too could become a target for some other young fool.

The words he exchanged with Tom and looking into Reverend Ash's eyes for the first time in years overwhelmed him. A flood of emotions tore and ripped inside of him until he could stand it no longer. He had come to the point where he had finally broken and on his knees up at the cemetery and poured his heart out to the Lord above. He had come home late far more at peace than when he left.

Now in the noon-day sun he felt good as he looked down the sights on his Single-Action Colt.45 revolver at the last of six cans that set on an old shot-up log. It was placed at the bottom of a hill beside the house. He fired and watched the can fly off the log. "Six for six, boys," he commented as he emptied his revolver onto the ground.

"Go set those up again, Ivan," Charlie Ziegler said to Ivan Lenning, Annie's seven-year-old boy.

"Watch this," William Fasana said when Ivan returned. He stepped forward and quickly drew both of his silver-plated .44s, firing both at once. A can flew off the log, then one more almost simultaneously, then after three or four shots another flew off. After eleven shots, he aimed his left hand and blew the last one off. William replaced his two revolvers into his twin holsters with a smile. "That's some deadly shooting, boys."

"Not bad," Matt agreed. "Four out of six cans with twelve shots, not bad at all," he said with a sarcastic smile.

"Oh, hush, they're new guns. Double-Action by the way did you notice that? Pretty nice, huh?"

"You missed eight shots!" Charlie exclaimed. He turned to Ivan. "Go set them up and let's see what you can do." Ivan ran to the log about thirty feet away to set the cans for his turn to shoot.

"That's impressive," Kyle Lenning said to William with a smile, and then asked more seriously, "Is that as fast as you can draw?"

"No," William answered, "I'm shooting at cans. In a real fight I tend to be faster. My life depends on it, huh Matt?"

"Usually," Matt uttered. He refilled the chambers of his Colt.

Kyle asked Matt. "Have you ever faced a faster gunman?"

Matt shook his head. "I don't test the speed of my hands against another man's."

"Oh bull!" William challenged. "You killed Johnny Meeks in the middle of the street. That was a draw," William stated.

"No, I had him in my sights and told him to drop his gun. He thought he was fast enough to draw and shoot before I could pull the trigger. He wasn't." Matt replaced his revolver into his holster.

"I heard you beat him in a quick draw?"

Matt shook his head. "No. I have never stood there waiting for someone to draw their weapon and fire at me. Nor have I ever heard of anyone doing that except in dime novels. You shouldn't believe everything you read, William. Johnny would still be alive if he wasn't so arrogant about his speed. Kind of like you."

Kyle laughed. "Was he fast?"

"Not fast enough obviously," Charlie said.

"No, not really," William answered, "but, he was stupid and that's why he's dead." William paused while Ivan took a turn shooting with Matt's revolver. "You know, Matt, you should get a set of guns like mine. If you rode into town wearing these, people would know you meant business," William spoke of his twin silver-plated Double-Action Colts with ivory handles reversed in his holsters.

"I can't afford them," Matt answered simply. "Besides, I don't wear a two-gun outfit."

"You look like a sodbuster with that old cherry wood-handled Colt. Start using one of these and you'll get attention. People respect these guns."

"People should respect any gun, whether they're pretty or not. The color doesn't make it any more or less deadly," Matt said with a little laugh. His eyes looked past William to a wagon coming up the road. It was Darius Jackson and his daughter, Rory.

Darius spoke loudly with his constant joy-filled smile, "I thought I heard some shooting going on and thought we'd come join the fun."

"About time," Charlie replied, "If we were under attack, we'd all be gunned down and burnt out by the time you got here to help."

Darius laughed. "I didn't see any smoke, but I thought I smelled dinner cooking. So we came rushing over."

"I don't know about dinner, but lunch should be ready soon enough. Until then, why don't you come over here and help me show these boys' how to shoot?"

Darius slowly and carefully stepped down from the wagon. "Charlie, don't you know them boys probably already know how? Those boys might even teach us a thing or two: if we weren't so hard-headed and knew better."

"I don't know about that," Charlie said with a smile. "Rory, come on over and take a shot."

"No thanks, Charlie," she said with an easy smile. "I'd better go help Mary with the food." She stepped carefully off the wagon in a blue dress with gray flowers as the pattern, covered by a long black flock coat. Her hair was up in a bun and she looked prettier than she normally did.

"What are you all dressed up for? It ain't Christmas yet," Charlie teased.

"Oh hush!" she quipped embarrassed by his remark and sent a quick glance at Matt before she walked quickly to Charlie's house.

"Now Charlie," Darius said, "you leave that girl alone. It's not often that she gets to wear that dress."

"Are you going to town?" William asked Darius as he watched Rory walking to the house. He had always been attracted to her like a fly to a horse, but she never heeded his attention. He didn't quite understand that, most women wanted more from William than he was willing to give. Rory acted like she wanted nothing to do with him.

"Na," Darius responded, "but if you're going, we could use a few things from McDermott's if you wouldn't mind."

William laughed. "I was hoping you'd pick up some whiskey for me, not send me!"

"Now you know better than that, Willy. I'll make a list if you're going."

"I guess, I'm going to town. Do you want to go, Matt?" William invited.

"Not a chance," he said firmly.

28

Tom slept in late and woke up in an irritable mood. He tried not to hurt Elizabeth's feelings, though he couldn't help sharing his crusty mood with her. After all, it was partly her fault. Their son looked just like Matt did at his age and it wouldn't take a biblical scholar or a Pinkerton detective to explain why. Seeing the anger burning in Matt's eyes last night, reminded him of that morning so many years ago. It was the same look that Gabriel glared at him with now, a fierce and angry expression that left little doubt of whose loins he had sprung from.

"You heard me," Tom said with complete authority over the boy. They were standing in the family room while Elizabeth and the other kids sat on the davenport watching father and son argue.

"Why not, Dad? What's the big deal? I'm not going to try to kill him, I just want to meet him! I know all about him, so why can't I go ask Steven if I can meet him?" Gabriel asked in a desperate plea of teenage reasoning.

"Because I said!" Tom hollered. "You don't know

anything about him, Gabriel! You read books, stupid, lying books that embellish the facts. Nothing happened like you read, I know. Now get to your room before I grab my belt!"

"Can I go to Eli's then? Can I go see him?"

"No! You can go to your room. Now get!" Tom yelled.

"Fine! But I'm not going to live here forever you know. I'll stay in my room for the rest of the day, but you can't keep me here forever!"

"Gabriel," Tom warned tiredly.

"I wasn't kidding when I told mom I'm going to run away. Just you wait and see!" Gabriel yelled out defiantly and then quickly ran upstairs before Tom could respond.

Tom turned to Elizabeth, frustrated and angry. "We need to have a talk, now! James," he spoke to their son who looked nothing like Gabriel, "watch your younger sisters. We'll be out in the barn."

"Wait here," Elizabeth said nervously to her youngest child, Alexis. She handed Alexis to six-year-old Rachael.

Tom waited for Elizabeth and then led the way out to the cold barn. Elizabeth was wise enough to grab her coat and her scarf and followed him silently out of the house. Tom held the barn door open for her to enter and closed the door to the barn behind him. He sighed heavily and then looked at Elizabeth as he leaned against the latched barn door.

"What is it?" Elizabeth asked nervously.

Tom seemed deeply disturbed. He sighed again looking for the strength to say the words. "Lizzie," he sounded broken. His breathing grew heavy and his voice cracked with tension, "I..." he stopped and put his hands in his pockets and looked up to say a quick prayer.

"What?" Elizabeth asked, greatly concerned and feeling the tension in the air. It scared her.

He looked at her with tears growing in his eyes. He spoke quickly, "I saw Matt last night. I saw his eyes. The very same eyes I just saw in Gabriel. I'm not Gabriel's father, am I?"

Elizabeth's heart fell like a rock and splashed right into the depths of her soul. Her breath was taken away and her heart beat rapidly as a numbing shock swept through her like an invisible wind. She was stunned and felt like running away, but there was nowhere for her to go. She couldn't hide it anymore, but she wasn't ready to admit the painful truth or face the consequences of it. "Tom... I can't believe you'd..."

"Lizzie!" he interrupted strongly. "Tell me the truth, I deserve that at least. Gabriel's not my son, is he?"

Elizabeth's eyes suddenly filled with thick warm tears and she bit her lip to hold her composure. She refused to look at Tom's face.

Tom gasped softly. "I'm not his father, am I?" His breathing deepened, as he watched Elizabeth fight her tears.

"Tom, please don't..." she uttered meekly.

"Oh Lord!" he exclaimed and walked across the barn to the horse stall and leaned his arms over the top rail. His heart pounded as he came to the realization that Gabriel wasn't his son. "He isn't mine, he's Matt's, isn't he?" He spun around to face Elizabeth harshly. "Isn't he!" Tom demanded loudly.

Elizabeth began to sob uncontrollably and nodded.

"Oh, Elizabeth," Tom whispered and turned back to the stall. He buried his face in his arms and wept silently.

"I swear it was a mistake, Tom. It happened only once and..." she explained quickly through her tears. "I'm sorry, I'm so sorry, Tom."

"Were we married?" he asked painfully lifting his face to look up at the low ceiling of the barn.

"Tom..." Elizabeth answered softly.

"Were we married?" he demanded loudly, suddenly turning around to look at her angrily.

"Yes," she said meekly, "but it wasn't like..."

"Adultery, Lizzie? You committed adultery and have been lying to me all these years? I knew it! I just didn't believe it, I never believed you'd commit adultery, never! Now I know better! And with Matt? Thanks a lot, Lizzie. You have deceived me and now after all this time I find out the truth." He paused to glare at Elizabeth with a trembling bottom lip. "Gabriel's not my son, Lizzie," he whispered painfully. Tears slid down his cheeks.

"Then whose son is he?" Elizabeth questioned with a piercing sorrow in her eyes. "He is not Matt's son. Tom, he's yours, Matt doesn't even know he exists. You're his father, Tom." She stepped towards Tom longing to comfort him.

He walked away from her to the other side of the barn. "No, I'm not and everyone knows it except for me. I'm sorry, Lizzie, but you have deceived me long enough," he spoke with disgust and shook his head. "How dare you? You should have married Matt since our marriage meant nothing to you!"

"Our marriage means everything to me! I love you more than I ever have," she cried.

"Oh really, what about Matt? You've always stuck up for him. Now I know why! You bore his son and then said he was mine! You adulteress pig! Maybe you should go tell Gabriel, he'll be excited, I'm sure. Then you can go to the Big Z and see Matt, maybe even give birth to another kid that I can raise! Why not, Lizzie? That's what happened with the first one!" he yelled. "But I'll tell you this, this time you can marry Matt or follow him back to wherever for all I care, because I don't want you around me anymore! You are a lying, adulteress whore!" he yelled with a finger pointed at her. He spoke firmly in a quieter tone, "I want you out of my life!"

Elizabeth's tears fell like a heavy rain down her distorted face. "Forgive me, Tom, please forgive me! I didn't mean to hurt you. I'm sorry," she lamented painfully. "Please forgive me, Tom. I love you!" she finished with her love for him genuinely being revealed through her yearning eyes and twisted, painful expression.

Tom shook his head slightly and looked at her with burning red eyes. "I can't. I just can't, Elizabeth. Now, if you'll excuse me, I'd rather not look at you, because you disgust me. You're a whore!" he said and left the barn leaving Elizabeth alone.

She dropped to her knees and bowed her head into the loose hay on the dusty floor sobbing. "Help me, please, help me to keep my family. Help me, Jesus. I am so foolish... I am so sorry. I don't want Tom to leave me..."

Rachael, Elizabeth's daughter, came into the barn. "Mother? Are you all right, Mother?" She ran quickly to Elizabeth. Elizabeth quickly stood up and wiped the tears from her eyes and the dust and hay from her dress.

"Yes, dear, I'm fine. You go on back inside and I'll be there in a minute."

"Why's Daddy mad," Rachael asked curiously.

"He just is, sweetheart."

"Why were you crying, Mother?" she asked with sensitive blue eyes.

"No reason. Now please go in," Elizabeth said with a

sniffle and wiped her red eyes. "Mommy's fine. I was just talking to Jesus."

"In the barn?" Rachael asked skeptically.

"Jesus listens no matter where we are honey, even in the barn."

29

Tom didn't say a word as he entered the Sheriff's Office. He took off his coat and hung it up on a wall hook. He reached for his gun belt and then realized he had forgotten it at home. He had never done that before, but then again, he'd never left his house as mad before.

"Morning," Clyde's voice irritated Tom immediately. Clyde was leaving the sheriff's comfortable chair to go sit in his own stiff chair behind his own desk.

"Go to lunch, Clyde," Tom ordered as he sat down.

Clyde paused momentarily. "Alright, Tom. Something wrong?" he asked slowly.

"Nope," Tom lied.

"What about us?" Donovan asked. "We didn't get breakfast, and you didn't bring us any lunch. We're a little hungry, Sheriff. Isn't that pretty wife of yours cooking today?"

"Clyde," Tom said, "order some extra plates for our prisoners. You don't need to hurry back."

"Yeah, he does!" Donovan exclaimed. "We're starving in here."

"Shut up!" Tom ordered Donovan. He turned to Clyde. "Well go, Clyde!"

After Clyde left, Tom leaned back in his chair and kicked his feet up on his desk. He put his hands behind his head and stewed in his innermost thoughts. Gabriel Abraham Smith was Matt's by-product of an adulterous affair with his wife. Tom had occasionally wondered over the years when he began to notice that Gabriel looked nothing like the other children and looked more like the Bannisters. Elizabeth's integrity was more solid than the anvil in the blacksmith's shop, so he had never doubted her.

Tom would have never believed that Elizabeth would be guilty of adultery; he never doubted Gabriel's legitimacy either, until last night. He had lain awake all night torn by his thoughts that wouldn't stop rotating in his mind. Matt's bitter scowl outside of the mercantile was identical to Gabriel's scowl when he was angry, and Tom recognized it immediately. He had tossed and turned while Elizabeth slept contentedly beside him. He watched her and listened to her peaceful breathing while battling the temptation to wake her up and demand to know if he was really Gabriel's father. After hours of anxious thinking, he had fallen asleep only to be woken by a nightmare. It was a terrible night, but the truth was far more unbearable to hear. Elizabeth's words devastated him with the force of a .50 caliber slug.

He couldn't stand to hear her say she was sorry. Should he have said he was sorry for marrying her? Should he have told her to get out of his house? Was she sorry? Most likely, but then again, she had nearly sixteen years to get used to her folly. He wasn't so fortunate or so ready to forgive. Tom had much to ponder; divorce was acceptable in the Bible in the case of adultery. Now that he knew Elizabeth was an adulteress and a liar, it became a likely option. How much forgiveness did she deserve for deceiving him for the entire nearly sixteen years of their marriage? As far as he was concerned she deserved none! Even though Gabriel was as innocent as Tom himself, he doubted that he could look at Gabriel in the same way. He doubted that he could ever call Gabriel "son" again. From now on, every time he'd look at Gabriel he'd see Matt. He'd be reminded for the rest of his life of his wife's infidelity and he would never forgive her for that.

"Tom," Donovan said from the jail cell, "you look a little angry today. What's up, bud?"

"I don't want to hear you today, Donovan," Tom spoke coarsely and looked over at him. "So keep quiet."

"Sure," Donovan said defensively, "but, I don't have much else to do being locked up in this cell like this. I mean, after all, you caught us before we got very far with them horses. No one got hurt, no damage was done. What do you say you let us out, Tom? I'd even give you the route to Coffee Canyon."

"I'm not in the mood, Donovan," Tom repeated.

"Mood for what?" Donovan asked innocently. "All you're doing is wasting our time and yours, you know that as well as I do. We'll get off on time served and a map to Coffee Canyon, which is probably more than we need to be set free. I mean you really haven't got a lot on us. What, attempted theft? Come on, Tom, have a heart, it's almost Christmas. Let us go. You haven't got anything on us, anyway."

"Horse theft is something," Tom replied simply. "In fact, it's something illegal here."

"You caught us! So how could it be theft?"

Tom shook his head. "Mr. Moskin, I'm looking forward to your day in front of the judge. I can't wait to see what line of bull you're going to use on Judge Jacoby."

"Bull?" Donovan questioned, taken back by the statement. "Sheriff, I am offended just a bit."

"I doubt that," Tom refuted.

"So when's our breakfast supposed to be here?" Donovan changed the subject.

"Soon."

"Yeah, well we're getting kind of hungry. We haven't eaten since last night you know. Where's some of that good home cooking your pretty wife makes? Has she taken ill?"

"Nope," Tom said simply.

"Well, where's the food, Tom?" Donovan asked sarcastically. He could see that the sheriff was angry, and he knew angry people often said too much when they were riled. Sometimes angry people could be easily manipulated into making rash decisions.

Tom looked at Donovan. "Clyde will bring you something soon enough."

"Mr. Sheriff," Rodney Gray called quietly, "I need to use the outhouse, sir."

"Fine," Tom said, planting his feet on the floor. He pulled the cell keys out of his drawer and walked to Rodney's cell. He unlocked it allowing Rodney to step out. "Do you have to go too?" he asked Evan.

"Yes, sir."

"Then come along."

As the sheriff led the two brothers past the other cell, Donovan offered, "You'd better take a rifle, Sheriff. A lawman without a gun is easy pickin's and you never know about prisoners, even young innocent ones."

30

Clyde Waltz ate his steak, potatoes, spinach, and biscuits hungrily. *The Saloon* was the only one in Willow Falls and lacked the flavor of Branson's many saloons, which competed to draw in the clientele. *The Saloon* was simply a gathering place with wooden tables and chairs, a bar and a few pictures. It served whiskey and beer, but the drinking population of Willow Falls was relatively small. Being the only restaurant in town, meals were the main source of it's income.

"More coffee, Clyde?" Constance Olhieser asked. She was a homely lady of some weight who owned the saloon with her husband, Barney. The Olhiesers were of German descent and were one of the few households that never joined the church. They were a loud-spoken couple that drank a large part of the liquor they stored and argued a lot. It wasn't all so unusual that Constance would have blackened eyes or bruises on her arms. After twenty years in the business, their only claim to fame, except for being the poorest saloon in Jessup County, was that it was the last saloon the Dobson Gang ever drank in.

"Yeah, a little more coffee would be good. I suppose missing my breakfast and being late for lunch deserves some more coffee and a quick shot of whiskey on the sheriff's bill today, Constance."

"Oh, the sheriff's buying today? Well good! We don't get enough of his business and we pay a part of his wages. It's about time he gives back to us. So what do you think, Clyde? Is the sheriff buying me a round?"

"Might as well. He told me to take my time," Clyde said with a laugh.

Constance poured two shot glasses of whiskey. "Does the sheriff mind you having some whiskey?"

"Oh, a drink or two is fine, but if I staggered into the office he might get a little upset. He's already upset about something, though, I haven't seen him so mad. He even forgot his gun today," Clyde chuckled.

"Well, he doesn't use it. Let me go check those steaks," she said and walked into the kitchen to check on the four other steak dinners that were being prepared for the prisoners.

Clyde sat alone at the bar finishing his meal and then checking for Constance quickly, he refilled his shot glass and then took a long swig from the bottle. "He may not use it, but it's good for a sheriff to have a gun," he spoke loudly toward the kitchen.

"Well if you ask me," Constance's voice boomed out of the kitchen, "this town's too small to have a sheriff and a deputy both sitting on their duff." She stepped out of the kitchen and up to the bar in front of Clyde and poured another drink for Clyde and herself as she talked. "Those fellas in the jail are the first ones in almost a year. Our town's not growing and we're paying quite a bit monthly for lawmen we don't need; yourself excluded of course. You should be the sheriff, Clyde," she said and then drank her shot of whisky.

"I've never wanted to be the sheriff," Clyde stated simply. "It brings too many problems, like you for instance. If I was the sheriff, you'd say the same things about me."

"Oh," she huffed with a playful slap to his arm. "I would not. I'd just keep you good and drunk. Then you'd be a good sheriff."

He laughed as the front door opened. William Fasana, the well-dressed, professional gambler of questionable couth, rambled in. His long blonde curly hair flowed over his shoulders underneath of his clean black hat with a silver band. He wore a black suit with a red vest over a white shirt. His golden pocket watch chain dangled across his chest into the vest pocket. William wore a long black coat, but as always, exposed his two silver-plated pistols with reversed ivory handles as he walked. He removed his black leather gloves as he approached the bar with a small smile.

Constance smiled. "Well, look at what the cat drug in. I haven't seen you in a while, William."

"Yeah," William said with his deep voice, "home for Christmas, and you know my family's not much for stocking whiskey. So I need a few bottles, Constance. Three for starters and a drink for now." He sat on a stool next to Clyde, slapping the old deputy on the back. "How are you, Clyde? Mind if I buy you a drink?"

"I don't mind at all, William. How's life treating you?"

"Like a dog in heat, Clyde. The last few months I've pretty much been living at Lee's Monarch Hotel. The place is a gold mine for guys like me. It's full of beautiful women and rich men who don't know how to play poker," William laughed. He put his shot glass down for a refill. "Constance, I'm used to the whiskey quality of the Monarch, but in times of desperation this rot gut will do. I'm praying Lee will bring a few bottles with him for Christmas."

"It's cheap," Constance said bitterly. "In this town we don't get enough business for better whiskey. Unlike Branson, most of these families around here think highly of church. Too highly in my opinion, no one drinks or gambles. The Reverend has a hold on every one of these people, except Clyde. He's our only regular, oh a few others, but very few."

"If you had better whiskey you might change that," William said bluntly.

Constance Olhieser left the bar suddenly heading toward the kitchen.

"So how's Matthew?" Clyde asked.

"Doing great! The boy can shoot about as fast as I can and about as sharp. Better tell that sheriff of yours to keep his nose out of Matt's affairs. Matt can shoot the end right off the sheriff's nose and next time he will!" William paused, "If I was Matt last night, I would've shot that young lad."

"Eli was just being foolish," Clyde answered.

"Foolish or not, I would have shot him!"

"Clyde, can you carry four plates?" Constance called from the kitchen.

"Yeah, just stack them up," Clyde hollered back.

"Hungry are you, Clyde?" William joked.

"No, we caught some fella's stealing horses. Hey, maybe you've heard of one of them named, Donovan Moskin? He says he ran with the Doyle Gang and killed someone named Mark Chesney?"

"Rusty Moskin! He's in jail, here?" William asked curiously.

"Yeah, he goes by that name too, I guess. You know of him?"

"Yeah," William said, "he stole some money and some blood from me. He's in jail, huh?"

"Yep, him and a fellow named John Birch," Clyde hesitated, "and two boys."

William nodded. "Well, Clyde, good talking to you. Tell Constance I'll be back for the bottles; I'm going to go say hello to an old friend of mine."

"The sheriff's in a bad mood, William," Clyde warned.

William smiled with a light chuckle. "When isn't he?"

31

"Sheriff, do you think Clyde will be back soon?" Rodney Gray asked respectfully.

"Yep," Tom answered without looking up. He leaned back in his chair with his feet on the desk staring at his boots with a mean scowl on his face. Whoever angered him had done a fine job. Donovan seemed to think it was either the marshal being back in town or his wife that had him so fired up, but the sheriff wasn't talking about it either way.

The front door opened and a well-dressed man with long blonde hair and two reversed silver guns stepped inside and closed the door behind him. The man's hardened face sent a chill down Rodney's spine. It must have everyone's as well, because even the sheriff dropped his feet on the floor and stood with unexpected surprise. Donovan at the same time dropped his cards and stood with an exasperated expression on his face. It was clear that both men knew the well-dressed stranger.

The sheriff didn't sound at all pleased to see him. "What are you doing here?"

William smirked a bit with his attention focusing on

Donovan. His smile grew. "I heard you had old Rusty Moskin in catch. I thought I'd come take a look for myself," he said happily enough. His voice was deep and confident.

The sheriff's eyes narrowed. "Now you've seen him. You can go now." He was in no mood to put up with William Fasana; another relative of Matt's that he couldn't stand.

"Mind if I visit with him?" William asked, motioning towards Donovan. Without waiting for an answer he scooped up Clyde's desk chair and walked to the cell bars setting the chair down with its back toward Donovan. He sat down with his arms folded across the back of the chair. "Hello Rusty," he sounded like an old friend who was happy to see him again.

"Hi," Donovan answered slowly. "William, what are you doing here?" he asked with an unsettled tone, as he slowly sat back down.

The sheriff walked up curiously behind William and asked, "Do you know him, William?"

William smiled slightly. "Sure I do! Everyone from Missouri down through Texas knows Rusty. In fact, Tom, he's even making himself known right here in your neck of the woods." He paused and then addressed Donovan, "Fate's an amazing thing, isn't it? I mean, the last time I saw you, you were rummaging through my pockets." He laughed lightly as he shook his head. "Of course, I was pretty drunk and bleeding from some coward busting my head open for forty-six dollars. It's been a while, hasn't it?"

"I was pretty drunk, William," Donovan explained apologetically. "That was a long time ago and I'm sorry. The sheriff has all our money and I'll have him give you the amount I took that night," he paused to swallow nervously. "I've felt bad ever since, William, really I have. You know how it is, I was down on my luck and had too much whiskey and…I don't know what I was thinking."

William answered in a calm and friendly tone, "What about, um I don't know… I crack this guy's head open and steal his money?"

"Ah…" Donovan exclaimed nervously, "William, I really didn't mean to do that. Believe me, we were friends. I don't know what to say… I was drunk. I'm sorry."

"You, ah… left town mighty quickly," William spoke slowly.

"Well, yeah! I woke up and realized what I did, or actually heard about what I did because I was too drunk," Donovan chuckled nervously as he continued, "to remember doing it. I knew when you recovered; I'd be in bad shape. So I left. But, I couldn't remember doing it! I still don't. I am sorry, William. Hey Tom," he addressed Tom, "will you pull out, what was it forty-six dollars you said? Can you give William forty-six dollars out of my money, I owe it to him." He turned back to William. "There, now we're even. So what are you doing in these parts? I can't imagine there's much gambling around here."

"He stole your money, William?" Tom asked, verifying what he'd heard.

William looked up at Tom. "Sure did, down in Arizona about two years ago. I got hit from behind with a board! Between my lights being knocked out and a bad case of double vision, this snake here robbed me of my money. I would have shot him, but I couldn't hardly see." William grimaced. "I was so drunk, Tom, that I passed out right there in the street bleeding all over myself. And worse, it happened on the one night in Arizona that it rains, so I got my suit so muddied up I had to throw it away! Anyway, for the next day or two I was so dizzy I couldn't stand up. Old

Rusty here is lucky he left town, but I knew we'd cross paths again. I just never expected it would be here!" William emphasized.

"He stole some horses, and we caught him and the others at the Anderson's home. They were eating dinner and planning on staying the night," Tom stated.

"Horse theft?" William questioned Donovan. "When'd you become a cowboy, Rusty?"

"I'm not," Donovan chuckled. "It was just a foolish choice. We didn't get far and hopefully we'll be set free after an honest trial."

William spoke seriously, "There's some folks around here that would've strung you up on the spot. No trial, no jury! If this goes to a local jury, you might be hung. You shouldn't take it so lightly."

"I'm not taking it lightly, but no harm was done. It's Christmas and we're taking care of those orphaned boys, there. I think a judge with any Christian charity will let us go." There was a hint of anxiety under his show of confidence. "And this seems like a Christian town."

"Oh it is! More than the saloon owners would want." William smiled. "But don't count on the judge's charity."

Tom returned with forty-six dollars, which he handed to William. "He's making a deal," Tom said simply.

William counted the money and put it in his vest pocket. "What kind of deal?"

"Oh nothing, really," Donovan chuckled, "I don't want to say until I'm facing the judge. Like you said, we can't take this lightly. Not to say I don't trust you, but I'd like to keep it quiet for now. You understand," he explained.

William smiled wider as he waited. "No, I don't. What are you up to?"

"I'm just protecting myself, I have the right to do that,"

Donovan said defensively. "What about you William? What are you doing around here?"

"I've been playing cards at the Monarch Hotel over in Branson for the last few months. In fact, about a week or two ago, I ran into a friend of ours, David Martin, old soft hands himself!" Donovan appeared to be shaken to his core as William eyed him knowingly. "He said you were coming this way, so I half expected you to show yourself around here. That's amazing, isn't it?"

Donovan recovered his composure and shook his head. "What? That you'd run into soft hands Martin? No, not really, gamblers run the same trails. Eventually they all meet."

William laughed. "Eventually," he agreed. "But a..." he shook his head with a wide smile. "He said you offered him a job to join up with your little gang or whatever. It sounds like you've found your calling. I suppose, I was your initial victim?"

Donovan shook his head, fronting a good show of ignorance. "I don't know what you're talking about."

"Okay!" William said tartly. He looked up at Tom as if he was going to say something, then looked back seriously at Donovan. "Rusty, I've been waiting for two years to run into you. Now I finally get to see you and you're in jail, right here in Willow Falls, ironically! I can't shoot you right now, unless the sheriff allows us to go outside, but Tom's no fun he won't. I know a little secret though, a secret Tom here, may not know and one that's going to leave you dangling like a plum-bob from a noose."

"We don't have any secrets; we're just passing through. I don't know what you're talking about!"

"Tom," William began, "Rusty here, has been robbing homes clear up from California. He does it at night."

"What?" yelled Donovan. "That's a lie! Sheriff, that's a lie!"

William stood quickly and in a flash pulled out his left side reversed revolver with his right-hand and had it pointed at Donovan. William's face was stone cold.

"Don't!" Donovan yelled as he stepped back out of the chair he was sitting on. He put up his hands to protect his face.

"William, put it down," Tom said nervously.

Donovan continued, "Don't do it, William! Matt Bannister's in town and if you shoot an unarmed man, Matt will track you down. You know he will!"

William laughed as he lowered his gun. "You don't say?"

"Yeah! Ask the sheriff, Matt's here, huh Tom?"

Tom glared at Donovan. "He knows that, they're cousins," he said simply.

"You're what?" Donovan asked in horror.

"We're cousins!" William laughed. "Heck, Matt and I were just target practicing this morning. You're right, though, Matt is a good tracker. I'll have him track your back trail for every home and store robbed. I think, Tom, you'll find a whole lot of unsolved robberies stretching from California to here. Rusty here, is a quick talker, but there's always a lie and a motive for every word he says. He's made it this far, but before you make a deal with him, you'd better check out everything he says. You'll find he's a wanted man."

Tom asked, "Have you ever heard of Coffee Canyon?"

"Sure."

"He's going to give us directions."

"For what?" William asked, puzzled.

"The outlaw hideout. Donovan says he knows the way to it," Tom explained.

"You mean he's going to tell you how to get to Coffee Canyon to be set free?"

"Yeah."

William laughed. "Tom, everyone knows where Coffee Canyon is. It's a bed stop along the Idaho and Utah border."

"What?"

William explained joyfully, "Coffee Canyon was a hideout and a famous one until 1877 when a group of lawmen found it. Coffee Canyon's now a hotel of sorts for travelers. I could tell you how to get there." He laughed. "I do believe Rusty's up to his old tricks again!"

"He's lying, Tom!" Donovan exclaimed loudly. "He just wants to see me..." he stopped suddenly as he was looking down the barrel of William's revolver again. Behind the sights, the hard blue penetrating eyes of William glared at him. "Am I lying?" he asked coldly.

"You won't shoot, that's murder," Donovan said slowly. "Sheriff, he's lying. Coffee Canyon's an isolated spot deep within the rock formations. It's not a hotel," he said nervously.

William put the gun away slowly. "Well Rusty, lie all you want. The fact is that if anyone knows the truth it is Matt and I will tell him about you and your newest career. I think he'll take a great interest in it. There's only one thing I can promise you... you and your gang won't leave here alive. You know Matt... tenacious! You boys now have the most dangerous U.S. Marshal in the United States checking out your back trail, and your story. You're going to hang."

"Search!" Donovan yelled, "You can't prove anything. We're innocent of all your accusations and you'll never be able to convict us!"

William smiled. "I won't, Matt will. Just do me a favor and remember me when the floor drops," William said, imitating the trap doors of the gallows with his hand. "Because I'll be watching!"

"There won't be a hanging! We'll ride out of this town alive and well. I don't know what you're trying to do William, but it isn't funny! I never saw soft hands Martin and I don't know what you're talking about! You're filling the sheriff's head with lies trying to convict me of things I've never done! You got your money back, so why are you trying to frame me? Us?" Donovan asked in a sincere almost pleading voice.

William laughed. "Yeah, keep it up. Say whatever you want, the fact is that there's a long trail of robberies and witnesses. Don't think that Matt won't travel to Portland to bring a victim here to identify you and don't think he won't have you held until then."

"William," Tom said irritably, "these are my prisoners! Matt has no business interfering in my business."

"That's fine, but they're wanted men. You might even get a reward for catching them, Tom. Check it out," he said walking toward the door. He turned back to Donovan. "See ya hanging," he said and imitated a trap door falling open with his hand.

"William!" Tom shouted. "Go!"

William laughed. "Okay, Sheriff. By the way, you're lucky Matt didn't shoot the end of your nose off last night for putting it where it didn't belong!"

"Get the hell out of here!" Tom yelled wildly. William laughed and stepped out the door, closing it behind him as Tom continued to yell in a rage.

Tom turned to Donovan and glared at him with his red bloodshot eyes. He walked quickly to the cell bars and spoke directly to Donovan, "If there's any truth to what he just said you will be hung! I will wire west to see if there's been any robberies and, if so, I will send for witnesses!"

"He's lying! Come on, Tom, you know we're not dangerous. He's just trying to get you to waste your time and maybe frame us for someone else's crimes. I don't know what he's talking about, he's crazy, absolutely crazy!" Donovan paused, "And soft-hands Martin is a thief. I mean, yeah we tried to take some horses, big deal. Soft-hands probably would rob people, that low down stinking rat. You gotta believe me, Tom. William is trying to frame us."

"What about Coffee Canyon, Donovan? Is it for real? Because, I could ride out to the Big Z and ask Matt. The truth's not hard to find."

Donovan hesitated. "Okay," he said, "Tom... I,"

Tom questioned angrily, "It's a hotel isn't it?"

Donovan nodded. "Now it is, kind of, but... "

Tom exploded into a loud rage, "You lied to me! Now you expect me to believe you about William? No, I'll take William's word for it and make some inquiries. But rest assured of one thing I'll find out. I promise you that!"

"Tom," Donovan said.

"Shut up Donovan! I don't want to hear another word, not another one! Got it?"

Clyde stepped inside with a smile on his face while carrying a wooden whiskey crate filled with four plates of food. Tom turned to Clyde. "It doesn't take an hour and a half to get some food!" Tom yelled irritably.

"You said to take my time, so I did." Clyde smiled slyly setting the box on his desk and taking out all four plates with forks, he walked towards the cells. The steaks were pre-cut into bite-size pieces for the prisoners.

Tom could tell by Clyde's smile that he was nearly drunk, but then he smelled the whiskey. "You're drunk!" he yelled. Clyde held the plates, waiting for Tom to open the cell doors so he could pass the plates to the two hungry boys.

"I had a drink," Clyde admitted, "I had to do something. The saloon's not a good spot for killing time," Clyde said with a smirk. "Is it Mr. Moskin?"

"I'd like to," Donovan replied, not sounding humored at all.

Tom was infuriated. "I told you before not to drink on the job. I don't want a drunken deputy and the town folks don't want to pay a deputy to sit around getting drunk!" Tom grabbed the whiskey box and threw it across the room as Clyde still held the plates of food. "I'm telling you, Clyde, if this ever happens again I'll fire you! I won't have it! If you want to get drunk, then you need to get your stuff and get out of here!"

"Are you firing me, Tom?" Clyde asked, sounding hurt.

"If you come in here drunk again, I will fire you!" Tom shouted. "Have no doubts about that!"

"Well, I'm sorry, Tom," Clyde said meekly. He knew he would be fired if Tom knew that all five meals and a bottle of whiskey were on his tab. Clyde figured it wasn't a good time to tell him about the whisky.

Donovan spoke, "Well, I've never seen anything like this before. Maybe you could slip us some food before the day is through."

"Shut up!" Tom yelled. "All of you just shut up and leave me alone. I don't want to hear anyone!" Tom sat down heavily and tossed the jail cell keys towards Clyde. They fell to the floor. Clyde had to set the plates on the floor as he opened the cell doors to feed his four prisoners. It was the first time Tom had ever spoken to him like that.

Tom now had to add more to his report. More lies to

figure out before Judge Jacoby heard a dozen different tales and threw out the case due to utter frustration. Donovan did all the talking and Tom couldn't tell the difference between a lie and the truth. He doubted Judge Jacoby could either when the time came, so Tom wrote it all down, every word he could remember. He rubbed his eyes tiredly. He was tired, very, very tired. He just wanted silence and some sleep, but then he'd have to go home and he didn't want to see Elizabeth. He didn't want to see Gabriel; he didn't want to see anyone. He just wanted to be left alone.

32
___

Gabriel lay upstairs on his bed reading his favorite adventure stories of Matt Bannister. He had read the same book dozens of times; it was a hardbound cover depicting a handsome, but capable looking marshal in a gunfight against two mortally wounded men who lay dying on the street. The real Matt Bannister was just down the road and Gabriel wanted to meet him. He wanted to ask questions and hear Matt tell his own version of the SeeSaw Saloon or what really happened on Pearl Creek. Now that he had his first real opportunity to meet Matt Bannister in person, his parents wouldn't let him go to town! He wanted to have his book inscribed by Matt, but he wouldn't be able do that if he couldn't go to town. Once Matt left, it would be too late and who knew if, or when, he'd ever come back to Willow Falls.

Gabriel didn't understand why he couldn't go to town or over to Eli's. His parents had no reason to refuse him from going, his chores were done and he had completed everything that he was told to do. Being sent to his room was a worse punishment than being whipped, being whipped hurt a bit, but it didn't hurt all day. Being stuck in his small room left him bored, and being bored was hard for a boy who'd rather be outside. After an hour of laying on his bed in silence, Gabriel decided it was time to try sweet-talking his mother into permission to go to town. His mother was empathetic usually and never stayed angry any longer than necessary. Oh, she could be fiery in her immediate response sometimes, but unlike his father, her temper didn't last long.

Downstairs, Elizabeth busily cut potatoes and other vegetables for a stew she was preparing. The younger kids played in the other room and she only glanced at Gabriel as he walked into the kitchen where she busied herself.

"What are you making Mother?" he asked with interest.

"Stew," she replied shortly.

"Do you need help?"

"Nope."

"Is there anything I can do?" he asked stepping around her. "Do you need anything from the mercantile? I'd like to go get some candy for the kids for Christmas." This was true enough, although he may have had another motive. He did have twenty cents, and he did intend to buy his brother and sisters some candy for Christmas.

Elizabeth answered shortly, "I don't need anything."

"Can I go anyway? Tomorrow is Christmas, you know."

"I'm aware of that," she said curtly. "Your father told you to stay in your room. So the answer is no, you can't go anywhere."

"But tomorrow's Christmas, I won't have any other time to buy them something."

"They don't need anything, Gabriel," Elizabeth said as she kept her attention on her slicing of a carrot.

"I'd like to buy it for them anyway, Mom. It's their

Christmas present. I've been planning on buying them some candy, but I haven't been able to go to town lately," he explained with frustration audible in his voice.

"I just told you no!" Elizabeth glared sternly at him. "Don't ask me again and get back upstairs!" She slammed her knife down flat and turned to Gabriel with a harsh expression on her face. Her eyes were moist with emotion and she appeared to tremble slightly, as she raised her voice to a high-pitched yell, higher pitched than he had ever heard from her before. "I am so sick and tired of you testing my patience against your father! He told you to stay in your room, so why are you down here questioning me? I am just so sick of you always wanting something! Can I go to town, Mom? Can I go to Steven's shop, Mom? Can I go to the Mercantile, Mom? Can I go to Eli's, Mom? Can I go, can I go? No, you cannot go, Gabriel! So quit asking damn it! Now you've made me curse! Just go to your room and get out of my sight!" She suddenly covered her face with her hands and wept bitterly.

Gabriel stood in awe of her actions. He had never seen his mother so upset and grew genuinely concerned. "Mother, are you all right?" he asked caringly, as he stepped forward to touch her shoulder.

"Go to your room and leave me alone!" she screamed loudly with a glare of contempt. "Now!"

"Fine!" Gabriel yelled in return and quickly ran upstairs visibly upset.

Elizabeth covered her face again with her hands and cried. Her world was falling apart.

Upstairs, Gabriel put on his coat and grabbed his book. He'd had enough, and he'd get out of her sight all right! He climbed out his window, closing it behind him and slid along the snow-covered slope of the roof and then jumped the eight feet down. He went to the barn in a hurry before his mother caught him and bridled their other horse. He led the bay mare out of the barn and jumped on bareback and rode off quickly towards town.

33

Steven Bannister had just finished repairing the plow he'd promised Mrs. Wilms he'd have done before Christmas. Now he had to load it on his wagon and deliver it to the Wilms' residence on his own way home. Steven was just putting his tools away when his front door opened and William Fasana stepped in. His black coat and hat had fresh snow flakes on them.

"I thought I heard some noise in here," William said with his boisterous voice. "You're working too hard, Steve. It's Christmas Eve, you're supposed to be getting drunk and losing money to me."

"You're just in time," Steven said, ignoring William's statement. "You can help me load this plow real quick."

William sighed. "I haven't touched a plow since I was a kid! I've made it my career never to touch one. You know, Steven, I don't understand how anyone can live their whole lives pushing a plow, barely making enough money to survive. All that hard work for so little. In one night I can win five hundred dollars or more, depending who I'm playing against, but these sodbusters hardly make a dollar.

Take you for example, you're slaving away here on Christmas Eve and I bet you're not making more than five dollars for that plow, are you?"

Steven smiled. "Seven dollars and a hound pup next spring."

William shook his head. "See? Albert has the right idea, let others sweat for wages while he's making a mint. He can afford to spend seven dollars a day for lunch if he wants to. He said he offered you a very fair wage for an easier position. Why'd you turn him down? You'd be making a heck of a lot more money than you do now."

"Oh, because I like it here," Steven answered honestly. "The people of Willow Falls need a blacksmith and I do a little work for our mill too, occasionally. I'm doing all right. I'm always busy."

"Of course you are," William said simply. "For a dollar here and a dollar there, Albert offered you a lot more money! I don't understand why you didn't take it."

"I don't want to leave Willow Falls, not for any price. This is my home."

"Well, if you ask me, you've missed a golden opportunity. I really can't believe you're content fixing plows and saw blades for free puppies and seven dollars," William offered sarcastically.

Steven laughed. "I also get free meat, vegetables and firewood. I guess I'm not too hard to please. I'm happy with my little shop." He shrugged, and then added more seriously, "The fact is, I'm supporting my family. We're not starving, obviously," he said as he touched his stout belly, "and I'm happy. I don't need the money."

"I don't get it," William said. "I guess sodbusters never had money, otherwise, they'd know they didn't have to work so hard. Maybe if you took Albert's offer, you'd realize there's easier ways to make a lot more money. And once you have more money, you'd realize how poverty stricken your ideas are."

"William," Steven answered sincerely, "my father was apparently quite rich for a time, and I can tell you I'm happier than he ever was. You can go make a fortune if you want to, so can Lee and Albert. Personally, I'm happy with a free hound pup, or a side of beef. The Bible tells me to help the poor, not to turn them away just because they can't pay. I'd fix this plow even if all I got was the free pup. That two hundred dollars a month wouldn't give me the same satisfaction that this does."

William frowned and shook his head while raising his hands in surrender. "So... Aunt Mary wants to know if you are bringing your family out to the Z tonight?" William asked changing the subject.

The door opened and Johnny Barso stepped inside of the shop.

"Hello, Johnny," Steven said awkwardly.

"Steven," Johnny answered quietly. "William," he said recognizing him, "it's been a very long time. How are you?"

"Good and you are?" William hesitated.

"Johnny Barso. I grew up with Steven," he explained while shaking hands with William.

"Oh. I never paid much attention to you little snots." William laughed.

Johnny smiled slightly and turned to Steven. "I came by to apologize for my son. I don't know what got into him, but he got a pretty good tanning. I really don't know what to say," he finished apologetically. He was obviously troubled by his son's actions the night before.

Steven nodded. "I figured you'd whip him. He was there

to kill Matt. I haven't seen Matt in a very long time, but I might've saved Eli's life last night."

"Wait a minute!" William interrupted. "You mean it was your son that tried to ambush Matt last night?"

Johnny nodded. "Yeah, I don't know what he was thinking."

William spoke frankly, "If he had done that to me, he'd be dead. I told Matt he should have shot the kid. Yeah, your boy's lucky to be alive! If it had happened anywhere else Matt would have shot him."

Johnny shrugged. "Unfortunately, if it had turned out differently, Matt would have been in the right. Eli...well, I don't understand the kid. Fortunately, Steven brought him home and I beat the devil out of him. At least I hope I did."

"How old is he?" William asked.

"Seventeen."

William smiled. "Your boy's stupid."

Johnny sighed with exasperation. "I know. I don't know what to say."

"Say you'll help me and William load this plow up," Steven offered, taking advantage of the help to lift the heavy plow.

"Sure."

"This is the last time I'm stopping by here," William said as he removed his hat and coat. He unbuckled his double gun set and laid it on a fairly clean space on Steven's workbench. "I just stopped by to see if you were bringing your family out to the Z. Aunt Mary would like to know if you're staying the night tonight or not. I didn't think I'd be stripping down to my bare minimums to lift a plow!"

"Stop complaining, William. You won't blister your hands by helping us lift this. And you can tell Aunt Mary we'll be there in an hour or two."

"Where's the wagon?" William asked as he rolled up his white shirtsleeves.

"Outside."

"Well, back it in here."

"Don't need to," Steven replied. "We'll just carry it out."

"No, let's back it in, then we won't have to carry it so far!"

"We're not carrying it very far. It's just outside."

"I didn't see it!" William argued.

"It's out back. I always load the wagon out back," Steven replied. He stepped over and opened the back doors to reveal an unhitched wagon sitting just outside. It could easily be pushed backwards to the plow.

"Grab a hold, boys. I added some extra weight so it'll dig deeper in the ground. Mr. Wilms uses oxen to plow with, William, in case you're curious, so they can handle the extra weight."

William scoffed. "I couldn't care less about that."

"Well, you might when you lift it. But let's get it loaded," Steven said as he reached down to grab a hold of the iron frame. They all lifted strenuously and stepped towards the wagon to set the front of the plow on the wagon bed.

"Need help?" Gabriel Smith asked as he stepped in through the front door.

"Yeah," Johnny answered, "jump in the wagon, and lift the front end as we push."

Gabriel did as he was instructed quickly. He eyed William several times wondering if he was Matt, but he didn't look the same as he did the other night.

"Now," Steven remarked happily as he slapped William on the back of his red vest, "Doesn't it feel good to sweat from honest labor?"

"No, Steve, it doesn't!"

Steven laughed. "Gabriel, you came at just the right

time. We should've used the pulley though," he stated to William with a smile.

"What pulley?" William asked surprised. Looking up, he saw a heavy steel pulley chained securely to a heavy beam centered above the shop. "Why didn't we use that?"

Steven smiled. "The rope broke when I unloaded this thing," he said putting his hand on the plow. "I haven't gotten a new rope yet."

"Is that your brother?" Gabriel asked skeptically as he looked at William.

"No, that's my cousin, William. William this is Gabriel Smith, the sheriff's boy." Steven introduced them.

William looked at Gabriel and then shook his hand. "Gabriel, I'm William Fasana, nice to meet you."

"It's nice to meet you, Mister Fasana."

"Call me William, my dad's Mister Fasana. You look familiar Gabriel. Have you ever spent much time in Wyoming?" William asked with a mischievous smirk.

Steven's eyes warned William to be careful of his words. It was believed that Gabriel was Matt's son within the family. But it would be wrong to publicly speculate that the boy was without evidence to prove it. Gabriel only looked like he could be Matt's son; it didn't mean he was.

"No..." Gabriel answered slowly as if it was the oddest question he'd ever been asked. He'd never been out of Jessup County.

"Oh," William mused, "I must have been thinking of someone else. Your father perhaps?"

Gabriel shook his head. "No. My father grew up here."

"Hmm!" William grunted.

Steven interrupted, "William, tell Aunt Mary that we'll be out there in an hour or two and thanks for your help. I do appreciate it," he said hinting for William to leave.

"Alright, Steve, I'll see you tonight. Johnny, it's good to see you again. Tell your boy he'd better stick to sharecropping." He turned to Gabriel. "It's good to meet you finally. I've heard a lot about you."

"Oh?" Gabriel questioned while he shook William's hand again.

William asked Gabriel as if a sudden thought had occurred to him, "Are you coming to the Z for Christmas?"

"No," answered Gabriel. He was a bit baffled by the question.

"You're not? You're part of the family aren't you?"

Gabriel shook his head with a puzzled expression.

"Huh! Well I'll be," he said turning toward the door. "I hope to see you at the Z someday, Gabriel. See you later, Steve." William pushed the front door open and stopped, as he looked up the street. "Well I'll be!"

"What?" Steven asked. He stepped forward to see.

"Your brothers," William stated with a smile.

Two black carriages were coming towards them. The first, pulled by two horses was driven by James, Lee's driver. He was bundled up warmly in thick clothes and a buffalo hide coat. Behind Lee's carriage another of the same type was being driven by a man that neither Steven nor William recognized.

"Is it Matt?" Gabriel asked, suddenly at Steven's side.

"No. This is Lee and Albert."

The carriage door opened and Lee stepped out into the falling snow wearing a dark suit under a long heavy black coat and derby hat. He smiled slightly. "William, good to see you. Steven," he said shaking Steve's hand with his gloved hand, "are you working today?"

"Just finished for the day. I thought you were staying home for Christmas this year?" He watched Albert step out of his carriage and walk towards them. He wore a tan suit that was perfectly fitted, but no hat to cover his bushy hair.

"We decided we'd better spend Christmas with Matt while he's here. Who knows when the next time will be?" Lee explained.

"Hey guys!" Albert greeted them. "Gabriel, my how you've grown! What are you doing here?" he asked curiously.

"Just talking to Steven," Gabriel answered. He couldn't believe Albert remembered him.

"You're Gabriel?" Lee asked, pulling his glove off to shake Gabriel's hand.

"Yes, sir, Gabriel Smith." He shook his hand. Lee was well known in the county, but Gabriel had never met him.

"It's nice to meet you, Mr. Bannister."

"No," Lee corrected, "I'm Lee. Call me, Lee, okay?"

"Okay."

William couldn't keep silent. "Looks familiar, doesn't he?"

"Yeah," Lee said and nodded at William.

Steven cut in to change the subject, "So are you all staying at the Z?"

"Yeah," Albert answered. His eleven-year-old son walked up to him.

Steven smiled. "Hello Josh," he said to his nephew, giving him a playful push.

"Better stop it, Uncle Steven or I'll box your ears off!" Josh Bannister said with a playful smile. He asked seriously, "Is Uncle Matt really here?"

"Sure is," Steve answered. "When you see him, give him a right hook to the jewels. I dare you," he challenged his husky nephew.

"No way! I'm not hitting him in the jewels."

William grinned. "I'll give you fifty cents."

"No way. I don't even know him!"

"Lee," Regina Bannister stepped out of the carriage into the snow. She wore a heavy dark coat similar to Lee's that covered her dress and leather boots with rabbit fur above the ankles. Her hair was up under a black felt hat decorated with a colorful array of feathers and black lace. She joined the men with a pleasant smile. "Hello," she said politely to Steven and William. "And you are?" she asked Gabriel though she already knew.

"My name's Gabriel, Gabriel Smith, ma'am," he answered respectfully. He was awestruck by her beauty; she was the most beautiful woman he'd ever seen.

"Gabriel, my name's Regina. Have you met Matt yet?" she asked pointedly.

He nodded. "Once. The other night I met him, but I was hoping to have him sign my book for me."

"And did he?" she asked.

"No, I didn't have it with me or I would've asked him. I was hoping Steven would have him sign it for me."

William spoke, "Well come out to the Big Z and ask him yourself. You don't need Steven to do it for you."

"I can't. I'm not even supposed to be in town. Besides, I don't want to..." he led off shaking his head. He didn't want to say he was afraid of Charlie Ziegler.

Regina replied, "Then let me. Do you have your book?"

"I'll get it," he said and walked quickly back into the blacksmith shop.

"Lee, the girls are cold and we need to get going. Aunt Mary will have a nice warm fire burning," Regina said softly hinting strongly to get on the way.

34

Reverend Ash took a sip of his warm tea. Usually he enjoyed a cup of coffee throughout his day, but he wasn't feeling as well as he usually did. His head was a little stuffy, and he had a slight chill, as he sat comfortably in his leather high-back cushioned chair. He had pushed it closer to the wood stove so the heat would quench his chill, as yet another cold front had moved down from the north bringing more snow. It seemed the older he got, the longer the winters became, and the cold brought more aches and pains to his aging body. Reverend Ash couldn't wait for spring to come and bring warmer weather. Every spring the whole valley came to life with wild flowers and blossoming trees. It wasn't heaven, but Reverend Ash couldn't imagine anywhere being more beautiful than Jessup County in the spring time. It was a beautiful valley during the winter too, but after a couple of weeks of the cold, he was ready for the sunshine and warmth of spring.

Reverend Ash was a busy man. If anyone thought that the clergy was a one-hour a week job, they truly had no idea what being a Reverend was about. He spent hours preparing for his Sunday service, and meeting the needs of his congregation was around the clock, seven days a week. He was also the superintendent of the schoolhouse and spent a great deal of time overseeing what was being taught to the Willow Falls children. As Abraham Lincoln had said, *"The philosophy taught in the classrooms of this generation, will be the philosophy of the next generation's government."* Reverend Ash agreed with the former President whole-heartedly. The kids of Willow Falls needed a good education founded strictly in the Word of God. Unlike the sin that had over-run Branson, leaving it infested with social lice, Willow Falls was a moral township that cared about their younger generations future morality.

Big businesses, such as the silver mine and the lumber industry opened up jobs in Branson, but now with gold being found, Branson was overflowing with strangers coming from everywhere to find prosperity. Entrepreneurs took every advantage to service the influx of strangers the easiest way they could. Money was all they cared about, even if it meant demoralizing the community in the name of success.

Lee Bannister was the worst of the entrepreneurs! He looked every part of decent well-to-do business man and had won a seat as a Jessup County Commissioner and also on the Branson City Planning Commission. Despite his likable public appearance, he was a venomous viper out to destroy anyone for his own gain. His political positions and professional connections had solidified his monopoly on the county real estate market through his Branson Home and Land Broker's Office. The newly operating Monarch Hotel was supposed to be a symbol of Branson's economic success, luxury and higher society, but all the Reverend saw was vanity. Lee had stock in every one of the big companies that supported Branson and had enough financial power to squeeze out whomever he wished. Lee was one of the seven men in an elite little group that worshipped money above anything else, and led Branson and Jessup County in a godless direction that benefited only them.

Branson was once a wonderful town, but now it was a haven for all sorts of criminal elements and morally deprived men and women, who cared nothing of the Lord. It had taken such a short amount of time for Branson to plunder into the depths of depravity like a modern day Gomorrah. Lee Bannister wasn't the only man to blame for it of course, but he definitely played a leading role in its demise.

Fear sometimes strikes unexpectedly. Reverend Ash had stood up to refill his teacup when a passing glance out the window revealed a potential nightmare before him. It was no wonder that panic struck the Reverend's heart when he saw his grandson, Gabriel, standing outside of Steven's blacksmith shop talking to Lee Bannister.

The Reverend quickly walked to his front door and stepped out onto his covered porch. "Gabriel!" he shouted gruffly, "get over here!"

Gabriel's face expressed worry. His attention was pulled away from his grandfather by Lee, who shook his hand followed by Albert and William. Lee's wife, Regina, hugged him unexpectedly. It was all the Reverend could handle. "Come here, Gabriel!" he yelled angrily.

William waved. "Hello Reverend," he finished with a distasteful laugh. Lee waved sarcastically.

Gabriel walked casually toward his grandfather with a smug grin. He didn't realize how angry his grandfather was until he was closer. His grandfather glared at him until he was at the bottom step of the front porch. "Hi Granddad," he said carefully.

"What are you doing talking to those people?" the Reverend asked accusingly. "What has your father told you about them? What have I told you about the Bannisters, Gabriel? Get inside!" he ordered as he realized all of the Bannisters were listening to him.

"How dare you disobey your parents and me?" he stated as he closed the door behind Gabriel. "Those men are not to be on friendly terms with you. They are an abomination to God! Cursed men who can only corrupt your soul with worldly desires and trap you into hell! Those pagans don't care about God or righteousness; all they care about is their money. That's their god and they don't care how they get it. Those people are all trouble! You stay away from them, Gabriel! But don't take my word for it; let's go see your father."

"Granddad, Steven's the one I was talking to," Gabriel argued carefully.

"Really? I saw you talking to Lee! I saw his wife hug you! Now, what did they say to you, Gabriel? What were they talking about?"

"Nothing. I just met them that's all."

Reverend Ash turned to look out his window and watched the two black carriages move past his house. William Fasana rode inside one of them with his horse tied to the first carriage. He watched, despising the men and the sin that they represented. "Why did she hug you?" he asked, in control of his voice.

35

Tom sat at his desk staring at Gabriel quietly, while the Reverend told him his concerns about Gabriel becoming friendly with Lee Bannister and emphasized Lee's wife giving Gabriel a hug after handing her a book that he wanted Matt to sign.

Tom heard the Reverend's words, but he concentrated on Gabriel. For the first time Tom could see how obvious it truly was that Gabriel looked like Matt. The boy had Matt's height, broad shoulders, brown eyes on a handsome face and dark hair. The truth had always been plain to see for anyone who looked, but Tom had been blinded by the love he had for a lying and adulteress woman. It was no wonder Lee and the rest of the family would be so interested in him that Lee's wife would even hug the boy. He had been betrayed and life as he knew it was over. Gabriel was not his son.

He slowly stood from his desk and walked over to Gabriel as the Reverend finished speaking. "I told you to stay in your room!" Tom spat out viciously and then he threw a hard right open-handed strike across Gabriel's face.

Gabriel fell quickly to the wood plank floor and rubbed his cheek in disbelief; his father had never hit him before. Tom's wrath got the better of him and he quickly stepped over to Gabriel and yanked him up by the coat collar and slammed the boy's back against the wall. He yelled into Gabriel's face, "Don't you know how to listen? I gave you an order!" Without waiting for Gabriel to answer Tom stepped backwards pulling Gabriel with him and spinning around forcefully he threw Gabriel over his desk viciously. Tom followed after him with a reddened face full of rage and his eyes bulged in fury.

Clyde jumped up. "Tom, stop it!"

Tom pulled Gabriel up off the floor by his coat collar and again slammed him against the wall forcefully. "Do you want to be a Bannister, Gabriel? Well, do you?" he yelled. Tom clinched his right fist and gritted his teeth and then threw a hard right fist into Gabriel's left eye. It happened so fast that he cocked his hand back to strike Gabriel again, but stopped as if an invisible hand had grabbed his arm. He wanted to beat him like he would Matt, if Matt had walked in. Tom's breathing was heavy and his heart pounded with a rage he had never felt before. He was about to hit Gabriel again when Gabriel's broken plea stopped Tom's fist from striking.

"Stop, Dad! I didn't do anything wrong," Gabriel cried out. Tears ran down his face and his eye was already beginning to swell.

Tom tossed Gabriel to the floor by his coat lapel without any care. "Get out of my sight. Go!" he yelled forcefully and kicked the boy in the rear to get him moving. Gabriel ran across the floor and out the door quickly, beginning to sob as he ran.

Tom glared at the Reverend, who looked disturbed by his son-in-law's reaction. "What?" he yelled at the Reverend.

The Reverend Abraham Ash spoke frankly, "I didn't bring my grandson here to be beaten like a criminal."

"Then why did you?" Tom snapped. He was breathing hard like an angry and dangerous bull.

"To be corrected by his father, not beaten. You threw the boy around like a rag doll! I expected more from you," he said frankly and left without saying another word.

Tom stood in the middle of the room with everyone's eyes silently on him. He stepped to his desk and picked up the papers that had fallen to the floor when Gabriel had rolled over it. He sat heavily in his chair.

"Wow!" Donovan said from within his cell, "that was your boy?"

"Don't you say it!" Tom ordered as he spun around to face Donovan. He looked meaner than Donovan had expected.

"Say what?" Donovan asked, not waiting for an answer. "Sheriff, all I was going to say is that it looks like you could use a drink. Send Clyde over for a bottle and let's have a drink, play some cards and talk about the one thing we have in common."

"Shut up!" Tom ordered firmly, not falling into Donovan's verbal enticement. "I don't want to hear you or you!" he pointed at Clyde.

Clyde spoke anyway, "Little rough with young Gabe, weren't you?"

Tom stood up quickly and yelled, "Is it any business of yours, Clyde? Is it? I am his father, not you and I'll damn well do as I wish! The kid wants to be a Bannister, so I'll treat him like a Bannister. Gabriel..." Tom said loudly and then stopped suddenly. The reality of not being Gabriel's father sank into his heart to the deepest part of his soul. It weighed more than Tom could bear and he sank heavily back down onto his chair. The realization that Matt Bannister was Gabriel's father very literally took the words right out of Tom's mouth. He sat quietly fighting the emotions that yearned for him to give in to his tears.

Donovan offered, "I couldn't help over hearing what your father-in-law was saying about Matt and his family. I don't think Matt or his cousin William are all that great myself. Tom, you've treated us quite fair, and I appreciate it. So how about you let us help you out a bit. If you let us out of here, we'll take care of your problem and they'll never bother you or your family again."

Tom sat with his face buried in his hands.

Clyde answered for Tom, "Donovan, can't you see that Tom doesn't want to listen to you?" He spoke gently to Tom, "Are you all right, Tom? You haven't been yourself all day."

Donovan seeing an opportunity spoke quickly, "Of course, he's not all right, Clyde. It doesn't take a certified doctor to know that! But, it only takes one well-placed bullet to end all this trouble. Drop the charges, Tom, and Matt will be history."

Tom laughed in spite of himself. "Mister Moskin, are you a cold-blooded killer along with a horse thief, robber, and whatever else William was saying?"

"Of course not!" Donovan said sharply. "I don't know what William was talking about, he's a lying trouble-maker as you probably know. If there were any robberies like he said, no one could prove it was us, because we're innocent. And I don't think much will come out of the horse theft charges either. Like I said, you've been fair to us, and I like you. Let me help you and we'll call it even."

"I'm not letting you out. But I am going to wire west for

any unsolved robberies taking place at night. I don't like William much myself, but his story sounds convincing."

"It's not!" Donovan said innocently. "Don't waste your time, Tom. You'll be better off letting us out right now and we'll take care of Matt for you before he...I don't know... steals your wife away or something."

Tom glared at Donovan for a moment with a dark scowl upon his face. He sighed and smirked just a touch. "I'm a Christian, Mr. Moskin. I don't care how much I dislike someone; it is not within my God-given power or right to have them assassinated or injured in any way. Nor is it acceptable for me to even listen to such talk. However, your offer will go on record. And if you did commit any robberies, I will find out about it." Tom's face meant business.

John Birch spoke from his top bunk, "Tomorrow's Christmas."

"So it is," Tom said, uncaring. "Well," he turned to Clyde, "I'm going home and going to bed. I'll have Elizabeth bring Christmas *Eve's*," he emphasized to John Birch, "dinner to you guys. Good night."

"About what time," Donovan asked with a shrug, "can we expect this great dinner?"

"Six probably. I'm going to bed; I couldn't sleep last night. Tonight I will," he yawned and turned to Clyde. "See you later, Clyde."

36

Adultery, lies, illegitimate son, deception, lies, adultery, was all Tom could focus on. He rode home slowly not caring about the cold or the coming darkness of late afternoon. He didn't care that his pockets were empty of candy for his children or that it was Christmas Eve. He longed for sleep and had every intention of going to bed when he got home despite any complaints from his wife.

"Wife"- that was a funny word he thought. In definition it meant a woman who pledged her life to her husband. Marriage, isn't to be taken lightly, it's the joining of two lives into one that's expected to last a lifetime. Tom took his vows seriously when he promised to love, honor and be faithful to his bride. He had married sacrificially and gave his life over to supporting her financially and every other way he knew how. He had lived his life as a good man, a good husband, and a good father, to provide a good home for her and be the kind of man that she could be proud of. Their life together was never in want, nor in great excess, but he had always been content and most of all, he had loved Elizabeth.

During their wedding vows, she had promised to be faithful to him. Tom had always believed that she had loved him, but it had become clear that Elizabeth had committed adultery within days of their wedding. Tom knew that because she was a virgin on their wedding night and Matt had left town a week after they married.

How proud he had been to become a father too! What father isn't proud the moment he holds his newborn son in his arms for the first time? Unimaginably, for nearly sixteen years she had been lying to him day in and day out. She knew Gabriel was not his son, but Matt's. The conniving, lying, adulteress harlot had turned him into the town fool and he would not spare her his wrath for the sake of the children! It was better for his daughters and his son to be separated from such a woman than to grow up exposed to her self-corrupting ways!

He had no intention of allowing her to stay in his house, he wanted her and Gabriel both out as soon as possible. She could explain the reason why to their kids. It was her decision after all and the pain it would cause would be her doing. A divorce was imminent! He didn't care where she went or how she earned a living; he just wanted her out! However, she would not take his children; he was perfectly able to raise them alone. He was more than willing to endure the tears when their mother walked out the door.

What a scandal it would be though. Willow Falls, like most communities, had its share of gossips and those who loved to see others hit hard times. Tom and Elizabeth getting a divorce would be the biggest news in Willow Falls since the day the Dobson Gang was killed. How ironic that the two incidents should have the same man as the common denominator. The news of a divorce would be small news compared to the public acknowledgment that Gabriel was

Matt's son. That would be the big news that spread across the county like a wildfire. Elizabeth was an adulteress! She only did it once that she'd admitted to, but she had lied for so long, that he couldn't trust a word she said anymore. She certainly wasn't devoted to him when they married, and now that Matt was back in town, she could go fulfill her devotion to him, like she should've back then. Tom didn't care anymore.

He put his horse in the barn and fed the animals for the night. He noticed Gabriel's horse was gone, but its saddle was in place and by the looks of their cow's udder it hadn't been milked since that morning. Normally, Tom would be fuming that it hadn't been done by now, but he was too tired to care. Elizabeth could get her son to milk it or do it herself. He was going to sleep.

As Tom entered the warm cozy home, his two youngest daughters ran to him wanting his attention and hugged his legs tightly at the door. They spoke rapidly trying to gain his attention over the other with the excitement that only Christmas Eve brings to children. In the excitement, their voices rose into a non-stop verbal competition just to talk to him. Tom had no patience for them. "Hey!" he yelled, "go sit down, both of you! My gosh, I can't even step into my own house without you two getting into a fight. Now go!" he shouted to his youngest blue-eyed daughter, Alexis. She ran to her mother, who was in the kitchen preparing the table for Tom's favorite dinner. Alexis hugged her mother's leg crying.

Elizabeth bent down to comfort her little one. She looked up at Tom as he removed his hat, coat, and boots at the door. He looked tired and absolutely worn down. "She was just saying hello, Tom," she said meekly.

He glared at Elizabeth, but didn't reply.

"Dinner is ready. I made..."

"Doesn't matter," Tom responded dully. "I'm going to bed. Gabriel or you need to milk the cow and the prisoners at the jail need to be fed." He glared at her with hard reddened eyes. "Personally, I don't care if they eat or not. But the cow needs milked and those two boys would appreciate something to eat."

"I'll take them some food," Elizabeth said quietly. "Have you seen Gabriel, Tom? He ran off hours ago and I haven't seen him since."

"Try the Big Z, Elizabeth! William Fasana invited him out there for Christmas. Lee Bannister and his wife invited him to stay at their place too, probably. Lee's wife was hugging on him. She took his book out to the Big Z so Matt could inscribe it for him. I'd check there, Elizabeth. There's a family reunion going on," he said sarcastically.

Elizabeth's jaw sagged as her heart fell to the floor. Every one of Tom's words struck her with more fear of losing her family. "What are you talking about? He doesn't know any of those people," she stated, bewildered.

"Maybe not," Tom shrugged tiredly, "but they know him." He wanted to say more, he wanted to say everything that came to mind, but he didn't. It was Christmas Eve and he would allow one last Christmas morning before he unloaded his wrath onto her.

Elizabeth was perplexed. Certainly her admission to Tom could not have reached the Big Z already. She was tempted to ask him if he had told anyone, but chose not to. He looked angry enough already.

"I'm going to bed. Don't bother me," he said simply.

"Tom," she stated quickly, "we need to talk." He looked at her irritably as she continued, "Can't you wait until tonight? It's Christmas Eve," she added desperately.

Tom took a deep breath, and answered in a controlled voice, "I won't have anything to say to you until after Christmas. The kids need to enjoy it, but after Christmas, believe me, we'll talk. As for right now, I'm going to bed. Don't wake me up for any reason." He stepped into his room wordlessly as he heard Elizabeth say, "I love you, Tom." He would never say those words to her again. She didn't deserve a roof over her head, let alone his love or kindness. He closed the door.

Elizabeth paused. Tom's silent response didn't go unnoticed. She had never seen him more hurt than he was earlier in the barn, nor had she ever seen him so devastated, so completely broken as he was now. She wished with all of her being that Gabriel was Tom's son. She could wish, but it didn't change a thing.

She had always wanted to tell Tom the truth. It had nagged at her for years, but she could never find the courage do so. In a very personal way, despite Tom's agony, she was relieved to have the truth out in the open. The consequences of the truth being known could be a different story. Tom, by all rights, could order a divorce and she would understand it if he did. He had every right to be angry and every reason to despise her. Even if he had no grace in his heart and became embittered and hateful towards her, she would never stop loving him. She had made a mistake many years ago, but she loved Tom like she had never loved Matt. True, Matt was her first love, but Tom was her real love. Despite the circumstances at the time, she was thankful that she had married Tom.

What Tom said about Lee and Regina taking an interest in Gabriel left no doubt that the whole Bannister family knew he was related to them. Her fears were becoming a nightmare and she wondered what Matt would say, feel or do now that he knew he had a son. Would he be excited or completely indifferent? As the stories presented him, he'd become pretty indifferent about everything, including life. It scared her to think Matt would want to get to know Gabriel now.

What about Gabriel? How would he react if he found out that his hero was his father? Elizabeth truly didn't want to think about it. It would be hard enough for Tom to forgive her as it was. It would be impossible for him to forgive her if Gabriel took a paternal interest in Matt.

Later, Elizabeth set her kids to cleaning up the dishes and slipped into her room to change out of her dress and into a pair of riding pants, the warmest ones she had. She put on one of Tom's heavy cotton shirts and her riding boots, tied a scarf around her face, and put on a heavy coat. Town wasn't too far away, but it was cold outside. She thought she would look for Gabriel while she was in town as well. He had never run away or been gone for so long before. He had Matt's blood in him, so to think he wouldn't run away for good someday was foolish. He was too much like Matt in some ways, but in some others he was just like Tom.

"I'll be home shortly," she told her children and walked outside. To her surprise, Gabriel was standing in the barn. In the lamps light, she could see he'd been crying and his face was marked up. "What happened to you?" she asked while looking at his darkened and swollen eye.

Gabriel began to sob. "Dad, beat me, Mom. I was talking to Steven and..." He paused as Elizabeth put her arms around him.

"Lee," Elizabeth finished.

He nodded his head crying bitterly. "Dad beat me. I didn't do anything," he paused. "Ask Granddad."

Elizabeth grabbed the boy's face with both hands and

looked into it. She spoke strongly, "Listen to me. Your father's going through a very hard time." She stopped as the air was sucked out of her. Tears welled in her eyes momentarily, but she fought them back down. She wished she could tell him why and explain a life-long lie. She was no longer able look into his pain-filled eyes as her shame filled her completely. Her voice struggled to keep from cracking. "I'm so sorry, Gabriel," is all she could say and held him tight as her tears fell.

"Is he in a better mood?" Gabriel asked.

"He's asleep. It was a mistake, Gabriel. Now go in and eat, be quiet though. I'm going to town and I'll be back."

"Do you want me to go for you?"

"No, I need the time alone. Please saddle my horse and would you milk the cow, please." Elizabeth picked up the basket of food for the prisoners and Clyde.

On the snow covered road to town, Elizabeth's tears fell freely. It was inconceivable that Tom had beaten their son. It wasn't right, but nothing was feeling right. She stopped her horse to stare up into a dark sky of thick falling snow flakes. "Father, please help me. My family's falling apart and I can't keep it together. It's all my fault. But Lord, please help me keep my family together somehow, please." She wept.

37

"Not much activity in this town, is there? In other places I've been, the saloons are full and rowdy on Christmas Eve. This town is silent! I haven't seen a head pass by the windows for hours. Come on, Clyde, let me have a swig of that," Donovan Moskin said as Clyde Waltz took a drink from the bottle of whiskey he had bought.

Clyde smiled widely. "Tom might expect me to get drunk on Christmas Eve, but he might be a sight madder if you got drunk too."

"Yeah, well then, you shouldn't be having a bottle in front of me," Donovan replied. "Come on, Clyde, it's Christmas Eve. What harm can a drink do?"

Clyde laughed. "None! That's why I'm having one."

"What time is it, Clyde?" Donovan asked shaking his head with frustration.

Clyde looked at his pocket watch. "Five-thirty, time for a drink." He laughed and took another sip.

John Birch spoke seriously, "It's a little early to be hitting the bottle, isn't it? What if you pass out and we have to use the outhouse? We'll be stuck in here," he complained.

"That won't bother me none," Clyde replied with a smile.

John continued, "And what if the walls catch fire and you're too drunk to move. We'll all die!"

Clyde shrugged. "You'd better hope that doesn't happen then."

Donovan asked nonchalantly, "Where's your cabin, Clyde? You said it was up in the mountains somewhere? Didn't you say Tom and his wife used to go up there for church or something?"

"Yeah, years ago they did. It's up on Lake Jessup, about twelve miles southeast of here up in the Blues. I spend every summer there," he said thoughtfully. "It's the prettiest place in the world."

"Let's go up there right now!" Donovan suggested.

Clyde chuckled. "I might, but you boys can't, I'm afraid."

"How do you get there?" Donovan asked.

"Just this side of where we arrested you there's a trail that goes up to it. It used to belong to Floyd Bannister when he owned the ranch. Old Fredrick, Floyd's father, built a wagon road wide enough for his carriage to go up to it, that was a long time ago though. I bought it from Floyd when he sold everything and moved on." He took a drink with a somber expression on his face.

"So how many folks are in town tonight, anyway? I can't believe how quiet it is, Clyde," Donovan asked.

"Not many are out and about," Clyde answered. "Most folks are with their families for dinner. This isn't what you'd call a wild saloon town."

"Isn't anything open right now?"

Clyde shook his head with a smile. "The Sheriff's Office."

Donovan laughed. "What time is it, Clyde?"

"Five forty-five," Clyde answered. "Why? Are you

expecting Santa Claus?" Clyde laughed heartily at his own joke.

"Maybe," Donovan answered. "Clyde, I have to use the privy and we'd better make it quick!"

"Well," Clyde said before taking a long drink, "let's go." He set the bottle down and stood a little wobbly. He got the keys and came to the door, unlocked it and pulled it open. Donovan stepped out of the cell quickly and pushed Clyde up against the wall forcefully, knocking the wind out of him. The whiskey had dulled Clyde's precautionary skills and before he realized what was happening, he felt Donovan unsheathe his own Bowie knife and thrust it into his abdomen. Clyde watched as Donovan pulled the blade out and thrust it back into Clyde's abdomen again driving the knife's point into the wooden wall behind him. He looked up with horror into Donovan's face; his eyes were cold and fierce. Clyde knew then that Donovan intended to kill him. Clyde's eyes fell down to his knife as it was thrust in and out again. Its wide razor-sharp blade was slicing through him like he was paper, blood poured out over the blade and onto the floor. He heard familiar voices frantically yelling in the background. It was the two boys begging Donovan to stop, but the knife went in again. He noticed the horror on the two young brother's faces and the slight smirk on John's. He didn't hurt. He felt numb and growing weaker as he slid down the wall, leaving a wide bloody smear from the knife's exit wounds. Clyde lost the strength to ask why and surrendered to the darkness that came.

"What are you doing?" were the last words he heard. Rodney Gray had yelled them.

Donovan turned around to John. "We haven't got much time. Go to the stable and get our horses, all four of them, the boys are coming with us. Stay out of sight until I call you. The sheriff's wife is coming, don't let her see you. Now go!"

John went straight to the gun cabinet and put on his gun belt. He looked out the window and then stepped out the door and drifted across the snowy street.

Time was short, but he didn't know how short. The sheriff's wife could come at any time and Donovan wasn't prepared for her arrival yet. The key to his successful jailbreak depended upon her arrival and his foresight.

Donovan took the jail key out of the door and opened the other cell door for the two Gray brothers. "Come on," he ordered. "Grab all the blankets and take them over there," he pointed to the front of the jail.

"You killed him!" Evan Gray uttered, unmoving with fear.

"Yes, I did!" Donovan stated impatiently. "Look, you can either wait here and hang or go with us. Remember, I told you, if you'd help me I'd put you on a train for New York? They're going to hang you; they were going to hang all of us. I didn't have a choice! But you do, go back to New York or hang!" Donovan grew increasingly impatient.

"I don't want to hang," Rodney answered. He was frightened.

"Then do what I tell you! Get all the blankets over there." He pointed towards the windows at the front of the jail, "Then watch for the sheriff's wife and tell me when you see her. Hurry up!" he yelled.

Evan Gray grabbed blankets and carried them to the front of the jail while Rodney stood by a window looking out from behind an orange curtain. Donovan loosened Clyde's belt, took the bloody sheath for the knife, and put it on his own belt. He pulled the Bowie knife from Clyde's body, wiped the blood on Clyde's shirt, and sheathed it. "I'm sorry, Clyde. I did like you," he said and left the body.

As the boys watched the windows, Donovan opened the sheriff's desk and took out the things that belonged to them. He went to the gun cabinet put on his gun belt and grabbed their rifles and made sure they were loaded. He went back to Clyde and took his pocket watch; it was five after six. He checked Clyde's wallet and took his two dollars, and then he paused. There was no time to haste. He grabbed the sheriff's report and tossed it into the wood stove before taking a long pull from Clyde's bottle. It was perfect for the moment, so he had another long drink. Frantically he thought through his plan. If the sheriff showed up instead of Elizabeth it would ruin everything. He could only wait and hope that it was Elizabeth that brought their dinner.

He looked over at Clyde's lifeless body. His head and shoulders were against the wall while his body was sprawled across the floor in a pool of blood. He had liked Clyde, but he was forced to take Clyde's life to save his own. There was no other way out of Willow Falls since William Fasana had called his bluff. If the sheriff inquired about robberies, Donovan and his friends would be hung. At least now, with Clyde's death, they had a chance to get away and Donovan still had a hand to play. He had bluffed his way through card games, prostitutes, widow's money, and even a few judges along the way. They, like Clyde, came to trust him just enough to let their guard down. It was the friendship Donovan had made with Clyde that gave him all the advantage he needed. He had once again beaten the odds, and now he was one deal of the cards away from playing his hand. Killing Clyde was part of a calculated plan that was founded on this one desperate gamble.

"Somebody's coming into town. One horse," Rodney announced anxiously.

Donovan took another long drink that nearly finished the bottle. It was time. It was all or nothing.

38

Elizabeth rode slowly towards town with a heavy heart laden with an unyielding fear of losing everything she knew and loved. Time had caught up with her and it felt like a tsunami mercilessly washing over her. What rubble was left behind from a once beautiful home was yet to be seen. She had grown up as a Minister's daughter and knew that the Bible forewarned that adultery would have consequences, but she had chosen not to heed them. True, at the time, she was seventeen and believed that she was in the right, but oddly enough, the simple words of scripture prevailed again. It was amazing what almost sixteen years could do to change a person's heart and way of thinking.

Elizabeth rode up to the jail and hitched her mare before carrying the basket of food to the front door. She took a moment to compose herself, wipe her nose, and put on a cheery smile before she opened the door and stepped inside.

From behind her, a hand covered her mouth tightly, and she was pulled into a heavyset body. Her eyes scanned the jail; the cells were empty. The two young boys she had liked so much were against the far wall staring at her with fear in their eyes. Clyde lay dead in a pool of his own blood, partly propped against the wall. From her right side, the large shiny blade of Clyde's Bowie knife came close to her throat. Her breathing quickened. She dropped the basket to the floor and froze with fear.

Donovan spoke into her ear, "Don't move and don't yell or you'll end up like Clyde." He spoke to the boys, "Get me the shackles in the sheriff's top drawer."

Rodney searched the desk quickly, his hands were shaking. He brought a pair of metal shackles.

"Put them around her wrists tightly," Donovan ordered. As Rodney did so, Elizabeth began to sob into Donovan's hand.

"Evan," Donovan called, "go tell John to bring the horses!" Evan walked quickly out the door.

"Listen to me, Elizabeth," Donovan spoke quietly, but firmly. "I know you are scared, but I want you to listen. I don't want to hurt you; it's your decision, okay?"

She nodded fearfully. Tears ran down her face.

"Rodney, grab me a paper from over there." Donovan nodded towards the wood stove, where a small stack of newsprint was. He spoke into Elizabeth's ear, "I'm going to remove my hand from your mouth. If you scream, it will be your last breath." He pulled his hand away slowly.

Elizabeth whispered frantically, "Please don't! Please! Oh Lord Jesus, help me. Please let me go, I have children who need me, please!" she begged. She tried to turn to face Donovan, but he quickly crinkled up the paper and forcefully shoved it into her mouth. Her cries turned to muffled screams. "Shh," he ordered forcefully, "we need to go." At his words she brought her shackled hands up to her mouth to pull out the paper and scream in desperation. Donovan caught her wrists just in time. "Do that again and I'll shackle your hands behind your back and shove that paper down your throat! Do you understand me?" he snarled.

Elizabeth nodded. She was jerked outside by Donovan and helped roughly upon her horse. John held her horse's reins nervously.

"Rodney, grab John's rifle and put it in his scabbard and get Evan a rifle too. Hurry!" he ordered. Rodney quickly did as he was told and delivered the weapons while Donovan spoke to John, "Leave town. Stay near the road, but stay away from any houses. Get back to the main road we were on and head towards Branson. Rodney and I will be right along. Hurry, but whatever you do, don't let her go. And you," he paused looking at Elizabeth, "wait..." He pulled out Clyde's pocket watch and broke off its chain. He tied her shackled wrists tightly to the saddle horn. He jerked her hands attempting to break them free, they held. "Now go," he said to John. John kicked his horse and led her away, they were followed by Evan. Donovan looked around at the silent town, so far, so good.

"Get the other rifles and blankets," he said to Rodney, as he went inside to leave a note for the sheriff. Once back outside, he wrapped a blanket around himself, and rode off into the night. The tracks in the snow were clear for anyone to follow, but it was still snowing. Donovan hoped the note he left would buy enough time, at the very least, for the snow to cover their tracks. He was counting on it, in part, for their jailbreak to go smoothly. They had broken out of jail, but now they had to get away and that part of his gamble was up to the sheriff. Tom had tracked them down in the cold, snow, and darkness before, the question was would he do it again, now that his wife was a hostage. Donovan didn't think so, but he wasn't going to count on it. He would not be taken by surprise again.

39

Reverend Ash consoled his wife with a loving warm hug before he started his buggy down the street. It was after dinner time and really too late to be going to Tom and Elizabeth's unexpected, but the Reverend had seen a violent side of Tom he'd not seen before. There was a wildness in Tom's eyes that he didn't recognize.

The Reverend had learned over the years to mind his own affairs and leave the kids to settle their own troubles, but he was worried. Tom didn't act like himself today, he acted more like a man controlled by rage. A man enraged enough to beat his own son like Tom did, might be enraged enough to lay his hands on others, namely Elizabeth. If he were a betting man, he'd wager against it, but it was the "what if" that nagged at him. It was just that one percent chance that Tom had taken that rage home with him that bothered the Reverend. To settle that concern he asked his neighbor to go to the stable and bring his horse and buggy to him.

Under the pretense of excited grandparents who couldn't wait until Christmas they loaded the buggy with wrapped presents and headed towards their daughter's home.

"It's so cold, Abraham," Darla commented, even though she was bundled thickly in blankets.

Abraham stopped the buggy a block from their home and looked at the snow around the jail. Multiple fresh footprints and horse tracks led to and from the livery stable and jail before leaving town. It was unusual for that much activity between the jail and stable at that time of night. Especially on Christmas Eve when everyone would normally be at home, and that was what made him stop.

"I'll be right back, dear; I just want to say Merry Christmas to Clyde." The Reverend slowly and carefully climbed out of the buggy and stepped carefully to the jail's door. "Hello, Clyde," he said as he entered. He froze in horror at the sight of Clyde's body and the empty jail cells. "Good Lord!" he exclaimed and ran quickly out the door. He slipped and nearly fell as he ran off the wooden porch. His face was white as his hair.

"What's wrong?" Darla quickly asked, immediately concerned.

He quickly climbed onto the buggy seat and urged his horse into a quick pace. "Clyde's been murdered!" he gasped. "He's..." he couldn't continue.

"Murdered?" his wife asked in surprise, "By whom?"

"Those men! They're gone, I have to get Tom!" he answered and rushed out of town urging the horse into a full gallop.

"Slow down!" Darla yelled. She feared the old buggy at such speeds. Even on dry ground she hated speed, but in the snow she feared it even more.

The Reverend ignored her, he focused straight ahead in a hurry to get to Tom's. Clyde's murderer had gotten away, but with fresh tracks still visible in the snow, he knew Tom could catch them easily enough. Before long, the Reverend pulled into the yard of the Smith home. He jumped down and ran to the door, opened it and went quickly inside. "Where's your pa?" he asked his grandchildren, who were playing quietly in the main room. He had startled them. "Where's your pa? Tom," he yelled out for Tom.

"He's sleeping," Gabriel answered. "What's wrong?"

The Reverend walked past Gabriel to Tom's room and stuck his head inside. "Tom, Tom wake up!"

Tom stirred.

"Tom!" the Reverend yelled. "Get up, Clyde's been killed!"

"What?" Gabriel asked in shock. "By who?"

The Reverend ignored him and walked into Tom's room. "Tom, did you hear me? Clyde's dead. Tom!"

"What?" Tom yelled back angrily. He opened his eyes and glared at the Reverend. "Leave me alone," he said uncomprehendingly.

"Clyde's dead, Tom!"

"What?" Tom asked, starting to pull himself out of his deep sleep. "What are you doing here? I told you to stay in the water," he said, still influenced by sleep.

"Tom, wake up! Clyde's been killed by your prisoners and they're gone!"

"Huh?" Tom grunted trying to comprehend what he heard. He sat up on the edge of his bed and shook his head. "What?" he asked.

The Reverend sighed, frustrated. "Clyde's dead! He's been killed by your prisoners!"

"They're in jail."

"Not anymore! They are gone and Clyde's dead. Now get up and let's go!"

"Clyde's dead?" Tom asked in disbelief.

"Yes!"

"Dad..." Gabriel spoke anxiously, "Mom never came home."

"What?" Tom asked Gabriel.

"Mom's not here," Gabriel's voice shook nervously.

Abraham seemed to understand. "Where's Elizabeth?" he asked. A wave of terror settled within him.

Tom stood up as if a rattlesnake had just bit him. "Oh, my Lord!" he proclaimed fearfully. "Gabriel," he called as he quickly dressed, "go saddle my horse. Get my guns ready and hurry!"

"Where's Elizabeth?" the Reverend asked again. The strength of his voice was gone.

Tom stopped dressing and looked at him. "I sent her to feed those men. She hasn't come home."

"Oh, Lord Jesus!" the Reverend cried. His wife Darla gasped and began to weep as she overheard from the doorway.

Tom dressed quickly. "Abraham, go round up every man that you can find and take them to the church for a meeting. I'm going to the jail." Tom sat on the bed to put on his socks then walked quickly to the front door to put on his coat, boots, hat and gun belt. "Tell them I need a posse as fast as possible," he said and ran outside to meet Gabriel, who was almost finished saddling the horse.

Tom had run his horse into town as fast as he could. He could see through the closed curtains that the lanterns were still lit in the jail as he slowly hitched his horse. Cautiously, he stepped inside not knowing what to expect, but knew what he'd find. Clyde's body lay where it had fallen, his entire abdomen was pierced apart leaving a large pool of blood with Clyde's wallet laying in the middle of it. Obviously it had been emptied and tossed aside. It took a while for Tom to pull his eyes away from Clyde's bloody remains, but it was clear that one of the men, either Donovan or John, had grabbed Clyde's Bowie knife and used it on him a number of times. Clyde's knife was missing, whoever had the knife, Tom thought, was the one who killed him.

The jail cells were open, and the blankets were gone from each bed. His desk drawers were all open, and the rifles were gone from the gun cabinet as well as the gun belts and ammunition for each weapon. Tom's arrest report was missing also, which he found curious. It was then he noticed the piece of paper that was left on his desk. He walked over to read it and the strength left his legs as he read. He sat down heavily and covered his face with his hands, nearly breaking down into tears. He would have, except that the door opened and Gabriel stepped cautiously inside. He gasped in horror at the sight of Clyde.

"They killed him," Tom said softly. "He's dead."

Gabriel spoke carefully, "Are we going after them?"

Tom sighed. "A posse's being formed right now. They're going to meet us at the church. Why don't you go over there and wait for them? I'll be along in a bit."

"Where's Mom?" Gabriel asked with great concern.

Tom looked at Gabriel. "Go on over there, Gabe."

Tom watched Gabriel close the door behind him obediently. He then noticed the basket of food that was setting on the floor by the door. It was still full of food and the physical proof that Elizabeth had been there. It was his fault; he never should've asked her to do his job. He put his face back into his hands. His breathing grew heavy as he read the note again.

40

Half an hour later, the church was well lit with oil lamps and twelve men sitting in the pews talking anxiously about the news of the jailbreak and the murder of Clyde. They all had guns and were willing and ready to hunt the murderers down. Some of the men tried to go over to the jail to see Clyde for themselves, but Tom had locked the door. The Reverend and Gabriel had described what they had seen.

Finally, Tom entered the church, ignoring the few questions that were asked. He walked straight up to the podium and waited until it was quiet.

"Clyde's dead. He was stabbed numerous times with his own Bowie knife. We all know how sharp it was, so you can imagine what it did to him," he stopped, sounding troubled.

"What are we waiting for? Let's go get them!" Johnny Barso expressed.

"They're well-armed," Tom continued. "Between the four of them they have five six-shooters and five rifles, two shotguns and ammunition for all of them. They took everything from the jail's gun cabinet."

"We've got guns too!" someone shouted.

"We can't let them get away with this!"

"Amen."

Tom lowered his head and then looked up. "They also have Elizabeth." All the talk stopped.

"They have Mom?" Gabriel shouted reactively.

"Dear Lord, no!" the Reverend said with distress.

"They left a note," Tom continued loudly to quiet those who spoke. He took it out of his pocket.

"I'll read it:

Sheriff,

We have your pretty wife. You have my word that she'll be released unharmed if you do as we say. Don't follow us and don't let Matt come after us, otherwise she'll end up like Clyde. Don't wire ahead or behind. Don't be a fool. Go home Tom and wait for Elizabeth to come home unharmed. That is your only choice for the safety of your wife, or you can come ahead and find her dead."

He paused after reading it. The silence in the church was deafening. "I..." Tom began slowly, "I don't know what to do."

"We need to go get Mom! *That's* what we need to do!" Gabriel stated plainly with fire burning in his eyes.

'*Déjà vu*,' the Reverend thought. Suddenly he was back in the same church nearly twenty years before when it was a young Matt who demanded quick retribution while the congregation sat in fear of the Dobson Gang.

"Gabriel," Tom stated firmly, "listen to me. They killed Clyde and they mean it. We can't just ride after them, son. They'll kill her."

"Then go get Matt Bannister, he'll go get her!" Gabriel insisted.

"Hell no!" Tom snapped bitterly. "I'll not have him going after those guys and get Elizabeth killed. It's his damn fault they took her to begin with! William Fasana..." he explained to the men in the pews, "came into the jail today and told Donovan that Matt was in town. Apparently they all know each other. William told Donovan he was going to tell Matt he was in the jail and they would hang for something Donovan and his gang were doing or had done...I don't know. All I know it obviously scared Donovan enough to kill Clyde and kidnap Elizabeth."

Johnny Barso spoke angerly, "What are we going to do, Tom? You're the sheriff."

"I don't know," Tom admitted.

"I say we go after them," Cliff Jorgensen offered. "I think they'll let her go and run like cowards when they see us coming!"

"I agree!" Walt Delaney concurred. "Let's go after them!"

Tom sighed. "She's my wife. If anything happened to her," he stopped and bit his lip tightly.

Cliff Jorgenson shouted emotionally, "We have to do something! Clyde's dead! We can't let his murderers go free."

"I agree with Cliff, Tom," Johnny Barso said. "They weren't hard to catch last time."

"I don't know. If you guys saw Clyde's body, you wouldn't be so anxious to go," Tom argued.

"Are you the sheriff or not?" Cliff Jorgensen asked appalled by Tom's hesitation. "If they had taken my wife, I'd already be on their trail to get her back or die trying! But there's no way in hell I'd be sitting in here like a damn coward!"

Tom slammed his fist on the podium and yelled angrily, "Do you think I don't want to? Do you think I want to stay here? It's not your wife they took, Cliff, she's mine! Those men aren't kidding around. Do you think I could live with myself if they killed her because of me?" He glared at Cliff as he continued, "I don't know what to do, okay? Those murderers have my wife! They may not hurt her if we just wait...I don't know. And I'll be honest, all I care about right now is Elizabeth."

"What about Clyde?" Barney Olhieser asked of his long-time friend.

"Clyde's dead."

Cliff Jorgensen stood up and yelled, "Yeah, and his murderers are getting away!"

"They have my wife, Cliff! Do you not understand that? You can go home and your wife's there. Mine's not!" Tom yelled.

"Enough!" the Reverend roared loudly. "I saw Clyde's body and my daughter's out there in the hands of the men capable of doing that to another human being. I will not sit here and hope for a safe return! How long would you wait, Tom?" the Reverend asked heatedly. "Nor will I let you men pretend to be experienced trackers and risk my daughter's life!"

"Then what do you want to do, Abe?" Tom asked irritably. "You're certainly not a tracker either."

"Let's ask Matthew," the Reverend suggested.

"No!" snapped Tom. "I won't..."

"Matthew knows those men, you said so yourself! He could tell us what we should do and he'll know if this man keeps his word or not. You can always find another wife, Tom. But, I can never replace my daughter! I won't allow you to risk her life. We're asking Matthew!" Reverend Ash said with finality.

Tom sighed. "Okay fine, we'll ask him, but do know he's

no better than those men who took her. But we'll be risking her life on the word of another killer!"

The Reverend explained simply, "He may be a godless pagan, but he hunts men like these down for a living."

"Yeah," Johnny Barso agreed, "let's go out to the Big Z. He's out there tonight."

41

————————

Mary Ziegler sat quietly in her bedroom reading the nativity story from the book of Luke to the children. She had read that story every Christmas Eve as long as anyone could remember and now the next generation of kids sat around her while she read the story and answered their questions. Matt stood in the doorway watching his nephews and nieces while listening intently. When she had finished answering their questions she sent them out of her room to have one more piece of peach-cobbler before bedtime. It was then that Mary saw Matt leaning against the wall in the darkened hallway listening. She smiled, "How long have you been standing there?"

"Long enough to hear the story," he answered quietly. "You used to read that in the family room though."

She patted her bed. "Come sit with me. When you were little the house wasn't so full. It's just nicer and quieter to read it in here now. The older you get the faster time seems to go. Before you know it, you will be my age and those children will be your age and have kids of their own. It's the way of life. Maybe someday you'll have some of your own children in here for me to read to."

"Maybe, but I don't think I'd make a very good father."

"When the day comes, you'll feel differently. I always knew you boys would make good husbands and wonderful fathers. You all have your mother's heart."

"I went by her grave last night," Matt offered quietly. "Do you ever wonder what would have happened if the Dobson Gang never came here? I keep thinking about that. Joseph would be alive and I'd be..." he trailed off unwilling to finish his sentence.

"Married to Elizabeth?" Mary asked knowingly.

"Yeah," Matt admitted sadly. "Life would be good. Sometimes I think God has a vendetta against me for some reason. I was the happiest I've ever been when the Dobson Gang came here. I wasn't convicted for murder by the courts, but I was sentenced for it by everyone I knew. I am still guilty of murder in this town. I'll never be able to walk out from under the shadow of the Dobson Gang here. They were unarmed and just waking up, I'd arrest someone for that myself, probably. But you know, I'd do it again. I do not regret killing those men even though it ruined my life."

Mary was troubled. "So are you trying to say you're going back to Wyoming?"

Matt nodded. "Yeah, I am. I'm not welcome here. I can't even go to the store without some kid wanting to shoot me and the sheriff making a scene about killing the Dobson Gang."

"Hmm," Mary spoke sadly. "Sometimes, I do think of what life would be like if things didn't happen the way that they did. I guess it's different for me though. If your mother hadn't of passed away, for instance, then we wouldn't have had you kids.

I loved my sister very much, but I am so thankful to the Lord for his foresight. Charlie and I were never able to have children and I could never understand why not? I used to pray every day and for a time I was so angry with God, I thought it was so unfair that everyone else could have children, but not me. Then, one day, our big empty house was filled with you kids and then I understood. God knew that one day our big home was going to be full and there wouldn't be room for one or two of my own. I've thanked Him ever since."

She spoke in a stronger and more authoritative tone, "And now about the Dobson Gang. Those momentarily unarmed men were coming here to kill Charlie. Charlie told me they would have killed me and everyone else who lived in this house and burned it all down. They were hate filled cold-blooded murderers and you saved our lives. They killed Joseph, but they could have killed many more people and they would have. Matthew, I don't regret that you did that either. We'd all be dead if you didn't."

Matt nodded his head. "I know, but it doesn't help. I can never forget that day, Aunt Mary. I remember everything: the sound of the river, the first shot and every scream, especially Joseph's and Elizabeth's. I remember it all like it was yesterday."

Mary tapped Matt's knee lovingly. "It was a horrible thing that happened."

Matt smiled sadly. "That's my whole point. Why would God let such a thing happen and make me suffer for it the rest of my life? Why am I the one who had to go through something like that? What purpose did it serve other than profiting writers who write lies about me? It ruined my life."

"It spared our lives," Mary said simply. "Maybe that's why God allowed it. Just to save the lives of this family." She paused before continuing, "One time I took a look inside of

Charlie's pocket watch and I thought 'what an ingenious thing!' There were all these little gears and these wind-up thingy's and they all worked together somehow to keep the time. It was very complicated, but the pocket watch kept perfect time." She paused to look at Matt. "If a man can make something so complicated, yet so useful and beautiful out of metal, then can't the Lord above create lives that are complicated, yet useful and beautiful all at the same time? Maybe it all depends on how we are looking at it."

"Maybe," Matt answered. "The question is will he in my life? I have been praying for years for the Lord to give me something worth living for, but I have accomplished nothing and I have nothing. Not even a real friend."

"Matthew," Mary began with a sad smile, "from what I understand you don't give anyone the chance to become your friend."

The dog began to bark and Mary commented, "It must be Billy Jo. Well, better late than never. What would you like to accomplish in life, Matt? Really?"

"I don't know, Aunt Mary. I really don't know, but I know this, the Lord hasn't kept me alive all of these years for nothing. He must have a plan because I really don't."

Mary frowned. "Then let's pray that Jesus will reveal his plan for your life. You will never find contentment until you are walking with the Lord on the path he wants you to walk down."

42

As the posse crested the hill overlooking the Big Z Ranch, the two big homes came into view. Although it had been a long time since Tom had been there, he looked with some familiarity down at the Ziegler home and the large hay barn. Annie's house and a few other structures were new. Tom took a deep breath and started down the steep road that leveled out at the first of the three barns.

A dog barked consistently as they rode up to the Ziegler home. They were surprised to see Charlie Ziegler open the door and step outside onto the front porch with a revolver in his hand. He was followed by Lee, Albert and Adam Bannister who were all unarmed. William Fasana, however, came out buckling his double gun belt around his waist and then held his right hand near his left revolver when finished. Luther Fasana carried Charlie's shotgun that hung above the door, as he joined his relatives.

Charlie held his pistol down at his side as he spoke, "Hello, Tom, can I help you?" It sounded more like a warning than a greeting. It was highly unusual for the sheriff to bring a bunch of his friends out to the ranch after dark. It put Charlie on edge.

"We came to get Matt," Tom said. Gabriel rode up beside him, his blackened eye was visible.

Charlie looked at Gabriel then back at Tom. It didn't seem right, and he got a bad feeling in his stomach, which was something he always trusted. "Matt? What for?" There was an icy edge to his voice.

"Clyde's dead and..."

"Matt didn't kill him!" William exclaimed. His blue eyes grew mean and his right hand fingers seemed to dance nearer to the ivory handle of his revolver. It sent a shiver down the spines of the posse.

"Clyde's dead?" Charlie asked, ignoring William.

Tom nodded and was about to speak when the Reverend blurted out, "Those men took my daughter, Charlie. We need Matt and you to go get her back. Give him the note!" Abraham ordered Tom from his buggy. "I want my daughter back," he added softly as Charlie took the letter.

William asked Tom with surprise, "Rusty Moskin did that?"

"Yeah," Tom said.

Matt walked slowly onto the porch with his Colt .45 in his hand. His eyes roamed over the members of the posse. He stepped between Charlie and William and looked at Cliff Jorgensen, who had his hand resting on the butt of his revolver. "Cover your gun," he spoke firmly to Cliff and waited until he removed his hand and covered the holster with his coat. "What's going on?" Matt asked no one in particular.

William answered, "Rusty Moskin broke out of jail, killed Clyde and kidnapped Tom's wife."

Matt looked at Tom with a surprised expression on his face. "Donovan Moskin?"

"Yeah," Tom nodded, "he left a note."

Charlie handed it to Matt. He read it while Charlie asked, "Do you know what direction they're going?"

"Southeast towards Branson," Tom answered. "They took all the guns and bullets from the jail. They also took blankets, and...Elizabeth."

"Who are they?" Matt asked as he handed the letter to William.

"Donovan Moskin!" Tom spat out the name, irritated by the foolish question.

"Who are the others?" Matt asked, simplifying his question. "William told me you arrested him. I'm assuming he's your horse thief from the other night?"

"Yeah," Tom said. "The others are John Birch, he's from Texas apparently, and two teenage boys they picked up in The Dalles. The boys seem pretty harmless, orphans," Tom explained.

"How old?" Matt asked.

"Seventeen and fifteen. Their names are Rodney and Evan Gray," Tom answered. "Elizabeth took an immediate liking to those boys."

"Those boys will have guns," Matt said simply.

"I know," Tom replied. "I have my posse though. We'll out number them almost four to one if you guys ride with us."

Matt shook his head. "I don't ride with posse's. Never have and never will."

Tom rolled his eyes in frustration. "Matt, I don't have time to argue with you! I intend to get Elizabeth back, I don't believe they'll let her go and we need your experience. Now, will you help us or not?" Tom asked irritably.

"Of course, I will. But do it my way and you'll have a much better chance of getting her back alive. You're right, they won't let Elizabeth go, but they won't kill her until they're safely out of this area." He paused. "If you take this posse and go after them, you're going to get half of these men killed, and probably Lizzie too!" Matt expressed a sense of urgency.

"If we surround them they'll have no choice, but to surrender," Tom argued.

"No, they'll have no choice but to fight. They'll be better prepared, better covered, warmer and have hostages. They won't give up and you won't win!"

Charlie voiced his opinion, "Posse's also make a lot more noise and targets, Tom. You need to send those men home."

The Reverend spoke to Matt for the first time. "Matthew, will those men kill Elizabeth if they see the posse?" His voice was weak.

Matt thought for a moment and then looked at the Reverend. "Donovan is a snake," he said slowly, "he's running for his life and it is hard not to leave a trail in the snow. Right now he's as dangerous as a rattlesnake trapped in a corner. He's fighting for his life and he'll do whatever he has to do to survive, make no mistake about that. That includes killing Elizabeth," he finished seriously.

"So he will?" the Reverend asked to clarify it for himself.

"He's not going to let her go," Matt answered simply.

"Then we need to go!" Tom stated anxiously. "Are you coming with us?"

"Tom, you wanted my experience, right? Then listen to my advice and send your posse home. They'll only get themselves killed and Lizzie too."

"Then what do you suggest?" Tom spat towards Matt.

"Send the posse home and we'll track them down tomorrow at first light."

Tom shouted desperately, "I'm not letting my wife stay with those men tonight! We need to go, now!" He angrily turned his horse around to leave.

Matt spoke loudly, "Tom! I understand what you're feeling…"

"No, you don't!" Tom yelled as he wheeled his horse back towards Matt. "Elizabeth's out there somewhere held at gunpoint by murderers! Maybe you can go back inside and enjoy yourself, but I can't! My wife's in danger and I can't go home and sleep like nothing's happened. I came out here because I need your help, but understand I don't want it! You can go to bed and dream about Christmas morning hot cakes if you want to, but we're going to save Elizabeth. Let's go, boys!" He again turned his horse to leave.

Matt raised his voice to be heard, "They're going back to the same house you arrested them in. They'll be watching for you all night tonight." Matt lowered his tone, "They're expecting you to follow them just like you did last time. Elizabeth won't be harmed tonight, Tom. They're too worried about you to take the time to molest her."

Tom turned his horse. "How do you know, Matt? How do you know where they're going? If you know so much about them then you should've recognized them when they rode right past you!" Tom yelled.

Matt ignored his statement. "Moskin knows I'm in town and he knows William's in town, but he doesn't know where. Nor does he know where your house is. He's going to the only place he knows for sure he won't find any of us. He'll stay up all night waiting for you, because that's where they went wrong last time. In the morning, they'll all be tired, too tired to think clearly." He added, "Give him some room to relax. You only get one chance to get her back alive, Tom. Just one!" he emphasized strongly by holding up one finger to make his point. "Tomorrow morning, we'll ride out and pick up their trail. I promise you only one thing, we will have a better chance of bringing her home alive tomorrow, then if you go racing out there tonight with inexperienced men."

Tom shook his head. "I don't want to leave her out there," he said fearfully.

"Thomas," Mary Ziegler said compassionately from the doorway, "why don't you send those men home to their families. You, the Reverend and Gabriel come inside and have some coffee and peach cobbler."

"No," Tom replied softly, "we can't, Mary."

"Oh, hog wash!" Charlie Ziegler scoffed. "You men go home. Tom, Matt, and I are going after Elizabeth in the morning. None of you are going and don't go after her tonight or I swear I'll shoot you myself! You'll get her killed is what you'll do," he snarled at the men making up the posse. He then spoke to Tom, "Come on inside. It's cold and I don't want to stand out here. I need to know all about those men if you expect me to ride into the line of fire."

Barney Olhieser exclaimed heatedly, "What about us? We can't just do nothing! Clyde's my friend, and I ain't gonna sit back and do nothing!"

Matt glared at Barney dangerously, "The hell you won't! You heard Charlie and now you'd better hear me, go home and stay there! If any of you try going after them tonight, I will personally hold you accountable for Elizabeth's life! Now go home."

"You're the sheriff, what do you say, Tom?"

Tom sighed. "Go home guys. Thanks for your willingness, but I think Matt and Charlie are right. We're going to do it their way."

Tom hesitantly climbed off his horse as his posse begrudgingly turned their horses to leave. "I need a shot or two more than coffee tonight," Tom mumbled as they left.

"Well, you've come to the right place!" William laughed.

"Gabriel," Tom said, as Gabriel stepped out of his saddle, "go back home and let your Grandmother have my bed."

"But Pa..." Gabriel's disappointment showed on his face.

"I'll not have that," Mary said firmly. She crossed the porch and took Gabriel by the arm. "This poor boy's been through enough tonight! I have some cobbler that will keep you coming back for more, Gabriel. Come on inside," she said and led him through the door into the assembled crowd within the Ziegler home.

Matt spoke to Tom as they entered the warm house, "Tell me about the others, the two boys and the one called John Birch. I already know Donovan."

43

John Birch stood beside one of the family room windows with his Winchester rifle in hand. He peeked out the window at the silent white landscape for any trace of movement. His attention was focused on the right. "See anything?" he asked without looking back.

"Obviously not," Donovan answered from the kitchen. He was watching the door the sheriff had snuck in through the last time he'd hid at the Anderson home.

"Well, I don't like it. It's too quiet! Are you boys sleeping or just not answering when you're called?" John Birch hollered loud enough to be heard upstairs.

"No. Nothing," one of them replied.

"I'm awake," replied the other from upstairs. He sounded sleepy.

John answered, "If you see something, don't yell out too loud, but let us know. Rusty, do you think your letter worked?" John asked sounding hopeful.

"I don't know," Donovan answered truthfully. "We put Tom between a rock and a hard place. If he was anyone else, I'd say he wasn't coming, but he's is a very determined man, so a part of me thinks he is. He's tricky though, so watch carefully."

The oil lamps and the candles had been extinguished leaving the house dark. If they did come, Donovan wasn't about to compromise his position by leaving the lights on. Tom had outwitted them once and Donovan wasn't going to make the same mistake twice. There was no doubt that they could be easily tracked in the snow straight back to the Anderson home.

It was snowing outside though and Donovan hoped it kept snowing. His escape would be much easier if the snow covered all signs of their tracks. He hoped that the sheriff stayed in town long enough for that to happen. Donovan would now be wanted for the murder of Clyde and the kidnapping of Elizabeth; both were hanging offenses. Every sheriff, deputy, marshal, and bounty hunter in the West would be looking for him now. His days west of Missouri were over, he couldn't go any place where he'd be recognized again. His life wasn't quite over though, he could hop on a train under an assumed name and take up a new life in Massachusetts or Florida, the farthest points from the West that he could think of. However, the fastest route to safety was to run straight up into Canada while he still had time to flee. His options were few, but he still had some.

He may have dug his own grave by killing Clyde, but it was an easy decision to make despite Clyde being a likable old coot. It was a shame to have to kill someone he liked, but if it saved his neck from a rope, it wasn't so shameful after all. At least now he had a chance at surviving. Sitting in jail waiting for the sheriff to backtrack his trail wasn't an option he could risk because it would end with him being hung. Hanging was a humiliating and shameful way to die. Donovan had decided to take a chance at living or go down fighting rather than being hung. He spoke from the darkness of the kitchen, "Tom's possibly on his way, maybe even watching us right now."

"Not unless he's a ghost," John replied sharply. "Nothing is moving out there."

"He may be waiting. He's a smart man with unusual techniques. Hell he might just come sneaking up here at three in the morning. We'll be ready for him though."

"I intend to greet him with my Winchester right in his big chest," he answered confidently. He looked at Elizabeth, who was tied tightly to a kitchen chair. She had hardly said a word since they had left Willow Falls. There was a red mark across her cheek where John had slapped her earlier in the evening. It was the only way to stop her from screaming when she watched Donovan murder the old Anderson couple when they opened their door. He stabbed both of them multiple times. It was quick and completely unexpected, just like he had done to Clyde. She hadn't spoken a word since then.

John spoke to her coldly, "You'll be a widow by morning most likely. So I might as well drag you down to Mexico and make you my wife or sell you to the highest bidding Mexican. Pretty blond haired, blue eyed, white skinned beauties are a rarity down there. I'd make a pretty penny off of you."

Donovan answered from the kitchen, "Better count Mexico out. We need to go north, up to Canada, I think."

"Canada?" John questioned. "I'm not going to Canada; I'm heading straight back to Texas. I'm done with the snow and ice. I'm going back home."

"Well, the first thing we have to do is get out of here. Maybe what we should do is try to find Clyde's cabin tonight." Donovan walked into the family room where Elizabeth was. "Have you been to Clyde's cabin?" She didn't answer. "Hey!" he raised his voice, "Clyde said you've been to his cabin, is that right?"

Elizabeth looked at Donovan with a blank stare. "He's not coming," she answered without any emotion.

"Who... your husband? He's coming," Donovan stated. "You just don't want us to think he's coming. That way tricky Tom can save your pretty face and put ropes around our necks." He smiled wickedly at Elizabeth. "That, my dear, will never happen."

Elizabeth frowned sadly and water filled her eyes. "He's not coming for me. He has no reason to; he's going to divorce me anyway," she uttered quietly.

Donovan appeared puzzled. "What are you talking about? Why was he so upset today?"

Elizabeth cast her eyes downward, sniffled, and then looked back up at Donovan. "I told him the truth..." was all she could say.

"What's the truth?" he asked, bemused by her statement. John listened with interest.

A tear fell down her cheek. "Gabriel's not his son. He's Matthew's."

"What?" Donovan gasped highly amused.

"Gabriel, my oldest, is not Tom's. He's Matthew's son," Elizabeth said with a painful expression contorting her face at the admission.

Donovan laughed. "Well, that might piss off the sheriff, huh John?"

John laughed. "I'd say so."

"So who's Matthew? One of your local farm boys, Tom's brother perhaps?" Donovan asked with a smile.

Elizabeth caught the gleam in Donovan's eye and smiled slightly herself. She couldn't wait to watch his expression. "You know him as Matt. Matt Bannister."

Donovan's smile faded for a moment and then returned. "You don't say...Well that explains why your husband has a passionate dislike for the marshal."

"Tom won't come for me, but Matt will," she said simply. "If you hurt me, Matt will track you down no matter where you go." She stated the words, but she didn't believe they were true.

Donovan tightened his lips. He knew Matt personally to be a tireless bloodhound who was not bothered by time, distance or weather. He was the last man Donovan wanted on his trail. Donovan hid any sign of his anxiety and said, "Well, Missus, let's just hope your husband takes my note to heart. If not, he, Matt or whoever, will get a bullet in their chest. I gave them fair warning."

John spoke confidently from the window, "They're not coming. We've got his wife and they aren't going to risk it. We're safe as long as we have her."

"Keep your eyes open, John. You might think no one's coming, start dozing off and look up at the window just in time to see Matt Bannister pointing his side arm at you."

"Oh Yeah? Well, I'm looking forward to killing him. I'd like to go home and say I killed the man that murdered the Dobson Gang. Justice would be served."

Elizabeth said, "You guys won't get away with this. The only way out of the valley is east or west and both ways will have people looking for you."

Donovan responded sarcastically, "I thought you said your husband wasn't gonna be looking for you?"

"He won't be the only one looking," she said quickly. "You murdered Clyde."

"I did, and I took you as my wild card too. Tomorrow you're going to help us find Clyde's cabin. When things settle down, we'll cut out north across the valley towards

Washington and into Canada. Then my sweet Elizabeth, you'll be free to leave us if you want to."

"You're not going to cut across the valley into Washington. You'll never make it across the Wallowa Mountains in the middle of winter. Like I said, there's only two ways out of the valley and that's either east or west. What makes you think they won't check Clyde's cabin anyway? Everyone knows about it."

Donovan laughed. "In this weather? No half-witted white man would climb to the top of a mountain in this freezing cold."

"Then why are you wanting to?" she asked spitefully.

"Because they'll never expect it," Donovan explained simply.

44

While Tom and the Reverend talked to the men in the family room, the women had taken an interest in Gabriel. Mary sat him down at the kitchen table to eat a large plate of dinner and then some cobbler. While he ate, she sat at the table and talked with him with great interest. Gabriel was a bit overwhelmed by the graciousness of Mary. He didn't know the lady, but she was warm, kind and oddly affectionate. The attention that he was receiving wasn't so much uncomfortable as it was unexpected. He put his plate and spoon next to the washbasin in the kitchen after thanking Mary for the delicious food.

Gabriel had watched Matt carry the book he handed Regina into the kitchen and lay it down on the counter to get some more cobbler himself. He had left it on the counter and Gabriel picked it up and flipped through the pages to discover that Matt had not inscribed it.

Regina was quickly at his side. She was wearing a dark-green dress with black lace around the shoulders and upper chest. Her hair had been pulled back in a bun and her large dark brown eyes made him nervous under her gaze. She was such a beautiful woman that Gabriel couldn't keep eye contact with her.

"Did he sign it?" she asked softly. She did not want to be overheard by the men in the other room.

"No, not yet," he responded.

"Leave it here until he does. So what do you know about Matt?" Her eyes watched Gabriel carefully.

"A lot," he admitted. "I've read almost everything about him."

"Then you know more about him than I do. I just met him myself and the only gunfight I know about is when he shot the Dobson Gang. Lee had to tell me about that though. I suppose you might loan me the book to read?" she asked. "I don't know anything about my brother-in-law."

He handed the book to her. "What did happen with the Dobson Gang? I've read three or four different stories about that and they are all different."

"You don't know?" she asked in disbelief.

"No, I don't know which story is true."

"Did you ask your parents?"

"They don't know. They said he saved his girlfriend, one other story says he did too, but none of the other stories mention a girl at all. The Dobson Gang apparently came here to kill Mr. Ziegler and ran into Matt on Pearl Creek. One story said they killed a runaway slave which doesn't make sense to me. Another one said it was vengeance for killing his horse, so I really don't know." He smiled as he shrugged his shoulders.

"You really don't know, do you?" Regina asked astonished.

"No," Gabriel laughed slightly.

Regina recognized the same sad smile she'd seen on Matt's face. "Well, you're right, Joseph wasn't a runaway slave. That's his father, Darius, right in there talking to yours and his sister is helping Annie put the kids to bed." Regina noticed the questioning look on Gabriel's face and explained, "Joseph was the boy killed by the Dobson Gang. He was Matt's friend."

Gabriel seemed astounded. "He was Miss Jackson's brother? I never knew that!"

"There seems to be a lot of things you don't know Gabriel. But I'm not the one who should tell you about all of that. Didn't Steven ever tell you about it, or anyone?"

"No. Steven always changes the subject. All he ever said was Matt did what he had to do. I don't know exactly what that means. No one talks about it." He paused to change the subject. "My dad and granddad don't like him or Mister Ziegler much. We wouldn't even be here, except those men took my mother. It sounds like they're going to help get my mom back, huh?" Anxiety showed on his young handsome face as he asked for reassurance.

Regina gave him an unexpected hug. "Yes, they'll help and they'll bring her home."

Annie Lenning came into the house with Rory and entered the kitchen. "How are you holding up, Gabriel? This has been an awful night, but I'm glad you're here."

"I'm okay," Gabriel answered, sounding stronger than he really was. "I just hope Mister Ziegler and Matt can bring my mother home before those men hurt her. The letter they left said they'd kill her if my father came after them."

Annie smirked. "Well now, they don't have just the sheriff coming for them, they have Charlie Ziegler and Matt Bannister on their trail. And possibly a few other guys like William Fasana and all of my brothers and uncles. Either way, they won't get far. If they only knew the war party that's coming they'd lay their guns down and come back on their own, right now." She emphasized by raising her eyebrows and saying, "So relax. I know your mom's a very Godly woman, and the Lord takes care of His own."

"That's true," Rory added softly. "I've been praying for her safe return and I won't stop until she's safe at home."

"Thank you, Miss Jackson. I didn't know..." he stopped short. He realized how insensitive it would be to mention her brother.

"What?" she asked with a waiting smile.

"Ah, nothing..." he sounded hesitant.

Regina answered for him. "He didn't know Joseph was killed by the Dobson Gang. He's never heard the true story of what happened, he's only read about it in books and all the stories contradict each other. He was curious to know what really happened."

Rory's smile faded. "Yes," she nodded, "Joseph was my older brother. The Dobson Gang shot him twenty-seven times after they hung him," she finished softly.

"Twenty-seven times?" Gabriel asked appalled. "After they hung him? For what?"

Annie answered quickly, "For being black, which is quite a crime to some people. You don't know what happened?"

"No," Gabriel said defensively. He explained the many versions to Annie and Rory.

Annie chuckled, "Well, I think Matt's going to have a few words about Swindoll's version. Matt and Joseph were best friends with your father," she finished sincerely.

"My dad?" Gabriel asked puzzled. "He knew Joseph?"

Rory frowned with disgust. "Of course."

Annie spoke, "They were all best friends; didn't you know that?"

"No! My dad said he didn't know Matt too well, and he never mentioned Joseph."

Annie glanced at Tom indignantly from the kitchen and looked back to Gabriel. "So they never told you anything? What did your parents say about Matt and what happened at Pearl Creek?"

Gabriel shrugged uneasily. "Nothing really, they don't know too much about it."

"Hmm, it's interesting how no one in this town knows anything about that day, isn't it? Maybe like they're trying to hide something." Annie stated sarcastically. She looked at him intently and then whispered, "I'll let you in on a little secret, ask your parents, they were both there."

Gabriel's eyes grew wide. "They were?"

Annie nodded. "Ask them."

"I have! They said they really didn't know."

Annie shook her head. "Gabriel, tell them that I'll tell you what really happened if they don't. Then we'll compare notes, okay?"

"My parents were there?" he asked again. "Why would they say they didn't know what happened?"

"They probably don't want to talk about it, but ask them for the truth."

"Will Matt talk about it?" he asked.

Annie shook her head. "Probably not."

45

Gabriel shook the men's hands on the porch. It was after eleven and the Reverend, Tom, and Gabriel were leaving. Gabriel didn't get a chance to talk to the men as the women had kept him cornered in the kitchen for most of the evening. He had met everyone in the house briefly and now shook their hands as he was leaving, except for the women who hugged him affectionately. Especially Mary who held him tightly for a long moment. He couldn't figure out the reason why, other than she was very friendly. Matt was the only one Gabriel really wanted to get to know, but as yet, he had very little conversation with him.

"Gabriel," Charlie Ziegler said, as he shook Gabriel's hand, "you should say hello once in a while."

"I will," Gabriel said. He looked over at Matt, who was talking with Tom. He wanted to talk to Matt quickly before he had to leave.

"Good," Charlie stated and then continued just as Gabriel tried to step towards Matt, "If you need a job this summer, I'll have one for you. If it's all right with your pa that is. I'll need a good hand, so if you want to work, the invitations open. And don't worry about your ma, we'll bring her home."

"Thank you," Gabriel said sincerely. He was a little taken back and surprised by Charlie's job offer, it seemed out of place, maybe even inappropriate as they'd come to ask for their help to get his mother back, not a summer job. He had always thought Charlie was mean and according to his grandfather, Charlie was dangerous, but after tonight he would know better.

He stepped closer to Matt and got his attention by extending his hand to shake. "Mister Bannister, thank you for going after my mother, I know you will bring her back." Though Gabriel tried to squeeze Matt's hand tightly, his own hand seemed to crumble in Matt's strong grasp. "I've read everything about you. It's an honor to meet you in person and I'm glad you're going after my mother. I know that you'll save her."

Matt looked into the boy's eyes and saw his own reflection combined with Elizabeth's. There was no mistake about it;

Matt was looking at his own son. A son he never knew he had.

"Don't believe everything you read, especially about me," he responded as he let go of the young man's hand. "I'm no different than anyone else. It's a pleasure to meet you, too."

"I..." Gabriel spoke nervously, "I left a book inside, will you sign it for me?" he asked awkwardly.

Matt slightly gave a sad smile. "You had better get on your saddle," he said with a nod towards Gabriel's horse. "Let me bring your mother home, then we'll talk about the book."

"Let's go, Gabe," Tom spoke in a fatherly tone.

"It's an honor to meet you, Mr. Bannister. Have a good night," Gabriel said again before stepping into his stirrup to pull himself up into the saddle.

Tom asked, "Matt, what time should we meet, sun up?"

"We'll meet you at the jail at seven," Charlie answered for Matt.

"Seven it is," Tom agreed.

Reverend Ash looked tired and worn down as he sat on his buggy's seat. His eyes grew moist as he spoke softly, "Gentlemen, please, bring my baby girl home. Please," he begged with dignity.

"We'll do our best to bring her home," Charlie stated with finality.

Matt addressed Tom with a sobering tone, "Tom, there will be shooting tomorrow. Just so you know there will be killing." It was a statement with no question of doubt.

Tom nodded understandingly. "By law, I'm obliged to bring them in alive, if I can. But I do know how to shoot if that's what you're getting at, Matt," Tom answered offended.

"I know that," Matt said quickly. "All I'm saying is be prepared. You may have to kill a man tomorrow."

Tom glared at Matt. "They killed my friend and kidnapped my wife. Believe me, Matt, I have never been more prepared to kill than I am right now!"

Matt nodded. "I understand, Tom."

"I am going to try to bring them back alive. I want them convicted by a trial."

"If we can," Matt agreed. "But expect gun play, because they're not giving up without a fight."

"Then we'll fight. I won't come home without Elizabeth though." Tom's eyes were determined.

"Me either," Matt agreed.

"Déjà vu, huh?" Tom asked as he turned his horse. "See you in the morning."

Matt took a deep breath as he thought about Tom's parting words. He watched him ride away with Gabriel beside him.

"Are you all right, Matthew?" Mary asked, putting her arms around him.

"Yeah."

"You'd better come inside before you get too sick to do anything tomorrow," she advised.

William Fasana stepped out of the doorway. "I know you want to save the damsel in distress, but since the sun's not coming up for another seven or eight hours, I say we play a game of poker. It'll take the edge off for a while." He already had a game started, but he wanted Matt to join in.

Matt shook his head. "I don't gamble, William. You know that."

"You can always start."

Matt smiled sadly. "No thanks. I have other things on my mind."

46

Surprisingly, Elizabeth had dozed off tied uncomfortably to the padded rocking chair, but a sharp smack across her face stunned her back to life. Donovan Moskin began untying her. "Wake-up, darlin'. I need you to get in there and cook us up some grub. We're leaving soon, so hurry up!"

"Cook what?" she asked startled.

"I don't care, but make it fast!" He led her into the kitchen where the cookstove was already burning. "John, go get those boys and tell them to get the horses saddled."

"I'd rather watch her," he sounded tired.

"Not tonight. Once we get up in the mountains we'll be safe enough, but I want to get there while the snow is still falling," Donovan explained. John disappeared up the stairs.

"We'll need to take food with us," Donovan told Elizabeth. "You're in charge of that."

"What makes you think I'll feed you?" she asked fiercely. "You took me against my will."

"That's right, doll, and we'll probably do a lot more against your will too. But if you ever want to see your beautiful little girl again, then you'd better do what you're told.

Look, I don't care about anything except getting up to Canada. You can either be helpful and be let loose to go home or not! Not, means I kill you right now. What do you want it to be?" Donovan was obviously tired and under a heavy burden.

"I want to go home to my family!" she yelled emotionally.

"Then cook us up something to eat and pack up some food. That'll be a good start!"

While Elizabeth started to cook breakfast, the two Gray brothers saddled up all the horses and got a pack horse ready to be loaded with food, guns, blankets and kindling for a fire. Donovan and John scurried around the house taking things they found: money, guns, powder, and clothes - anything that seemed useful. Elizabeth was left alone in the kitchen and was tempted to run out into the semi-darkness of the snowy night. She doubted that she would get far and she couldn't hide due to the snow. Maybe she'd run into help, though it was doubtful, it was three in the morning after all. It had become evident that Tom wasn't coming, but it didn't surprise her. He had made it clear that he intended to divorce her. Perhaps being kidnapped was a blessing to him. He would be spared the embarrassment of a divorce and wouldn't have to put the children through one either. Tom would use the note Donovan had left as an excuse not come after her. He wasn't a coward, but if he made up his mind to divorce her, then he wasn't coming. She had tried to frighten her kidnappers by using Matt's name, but the cruel reality was that he probably hated her more than Tom did; he certainly had every reason to. Even if Matt wanted to come after her, it was likely that Tom and him would get into a fist fight if not something more serious.

In the meantime, Donovan would lead her up to Clyde's

cabin, where no one would think to look and she'd be at his mercy for the duration of their stay. Elizabeth knew one thing and that was she'd have a much better chance of successfully escaping now than if she was isolated up on the mountain. Any attempt to escape would be dangerous, but in the valley there were homes and people who could help her. There was no one to help her if she was taken to Clyde's cabin. If she wanted to go home then now was the time.

Evan Gray brought two of the horses to the back door of the house and went back to the barn to help his brother. The opportunity was a wide open window to break free. She didn't grab a coat, being cold would be the price she'd pay for her freedom. She quietly opened the back door and climbed up on a fresh mare. She took the reins in her hands and kicked the horse hard, forcing it into a quick run back towards Willow Falls. She heard John Birch yell from upstairs and knew he'd be coming after her. She raced as fast as the horse could go towards the main road and then quickly turned towards home five miles away. She had broken free momentarily, but now she had to stay ahead of them.

John Birch hopped on the other horse which happened to be his own and sped away kicking his mare and whipping her with his split reigns to catch up to Elizabeth. Donovan Moskin ran outside, looking for a horse and then ran to the barn.

Elizabeth leaned forward as she kicked the speeding horse. She had made her escape, but she had a long way to go to get home with John not far behind her. She could see the road she was riding on clearly and the bushes and trees draped with brilliant snow passed by her quickly. The night was silent, but despite the serenity of nature, Elizabeth's heart pounded with fear. She looked back and saw John cutting the distance between them fast. She expected to hear him shout or shoot a warning shot or something, but he steadily chased after her. He was getting closer and she could see the wrath in his face when she looked back. He meant to harm her.

She kicked the mare harder. "Help me, Jesus," she prayed fearfully, "help me to get home." She looked back again and seen John reaching down where his rifle would be sheathed on his saddle. In a state of panic, she kicked harder and cried out to the Lord silently. If there was anywhere nearby for her to go, she would go there, but the closest home to the Anderson's was two miles away. She had only that far to go!

Out of nowhere, a rope fell over her head and shoulders, it tightened forcefully, like a vice around her bosom. She was ripped off of the speeding horse and floated nearly dreamlike until the shattering collision of her back hitting the frozen ground. An explosion of pain immediately knocked the wind out of her and sent a jolting pain through her chest and neck. She lay there unable to speak while trying to take a breath of air.

John sat in his saddle with a dangerous smirk on his face and the rope wrapped around his saddle horn. He began slowly walking his horse backwards, increasing the tightness of the rope around her chest making it impossible for her to breath and drug her through the snow.

"Wanna run?" John asked harshly, "then let's run!" John turned his horse and kicked it, causing his horse to gallop. Suddenly Elizabeth was bouncing uncontrollably and painfully through the snow. It was Donovan Moskin's angry voice that brought John to a stop.

"What are you doing?" Donovan yelled. "What are you trying to do, kill her? We need her, you idiot!"

"She wanted to run away. I was just showing her how we can run her back!" John said full of venom. "She won't try it again!"

Elizabeth was struggling to catch her breath and weeping bitterly from the pain by the time Donovan loosened the rope and looked at her face. Her face had a few abrasions and small cuts, but she didn't look too badly beat up. She was too weak to move at the moment, but she didn't appear to have any broken bones. He only hoped she didn't have any internal injuries.

"Let me see your hands," Donovan demanded. He started to tie them together.

"Please," Elizabeth wept, "let me go. Please, I have children. They need me. Oh God, please help me!" She dropped her head into the snow and wailed loudly. It was hopeless; she couldn't get away.

"We need you to take us to Clyde's cabin. If you try anything like this again, I'll rip your boots off your feet and you'll walk in the snow. Believe me, Missus, I'm done being nice!" Donovan threatened unsympathetically.

Elizabeth lifted her head to look at him. She yelled loudly, "I don't know where Clyde's cabin is!" A sharp slap struck her face.

"Shut up!" Donovan ordered. "I know you do, and you will lead us to it! Now get up."

Elizabeth glared dangerously at him. "I hope I get to see you hang," she spat out bitterly.

"The only way they'll catch me is over your dead body. I'm afraid you're my ticket to freedom," Donovan said. He pulled her to her feet roughly. "Now let's go! Like it or not, doll, for the next week or so, we're stuck together like husband and wife."

John glared at Donovan severely. "Don't be trying to keep her all to yourself."

"I'm keeping her for us!" Donovan replied sharply. "She's our only hope, especially if Matt Bannister gets scent of us."

"Yeah, you keep talking about him," John said, while Donovan lifted Elizabeth up onto her horse. "I hope he does come. I'd like to go home and tell the folks that the man that killed the Dobson Gang was finally avenged. It would be my honor to kill that man."

"Well," Donovan said while climbing onto his horse, "you go for it. Myself, I'm going to keep the Missus here between him and me." He led her horse by the reins.

"Dangerous man, is he?" John asked. He already knew Matt's reputation, but had never seen him.

Donovan took a deep breath. "He's deadly."

"Well," John answered, "so am I."

47

"I hope she got away," Evan Gray commented. He waited in the doorway of the barn with his older brother for the men to return. It was cold outside, but they were too anxious to wait comfortably in the kitchen where the stove burned.

Rodney nodded in agreement. "She knows her way home and as long as her horse holds out, she should."

"What will they do if they catch her, kill her like the others?" Evan asked. He was obviously afraid.

Rodney shook his head. "No, she knows where the deputy's cabin is and Mister Moskin's counting on her to lead us to it."

"We should have stayed in The Dalles, Rodney. We might have slept in a stable and went hungry a lot, but we hadn't killed anybody either." Evan was deeply disturbed by the night's events and wanted to have no part of it. He had witnessed three cold-blooded murders, and it terrified him.

"We didn't kill anyone, Evan, Mister Moskin did. We didn't kidnap Missus Smith either. If we just do what they want for a few days, Mister Moskin promised to buy us a ticket back to New York on the train. That sounds a lot better than being stuck here cold and hungry with no place to go. So let's just try to get back to New York," he suggested.

"I don't want them to kill Missus Smith," Evan stated with a frightened voice.

"Me either," Rodney agreed. "Just remember, Evan, if help comes don't shoot at them. We'd be hung for sure then."

"I don't want to stay here!" Evan exclaimed. "Let's go. Let's just go anywhere, but here. Mister Moskin's a killer, Rodney, not just a thief! He could kill us too, you know. You heard what he said about Coffee Canyon, it was all lies. Pa always said you can't trust a liar, so what are we doing with him?" Evan asked, bewildered. "He's a killer."

Rodney shrugged uneasily. "Trying to get back to New York," he said softly. He knew Evan was right, but what else could he do? He and Evan could part company with Donovan and John, but with no money or anywhere to go, it wouldn't be long until they were freezing to death or arrested. Another option was to turn themselves in and hope for mercy. But even if they were cleared of any charges and set free, they'd still be three-thousand miles from home with no money or any place to go. The only other option Rodney had was for him and Evan to remain with Moskin and Birch. They seemed to have a good enough plan to escape from the valley and then Donovan promised to put the two boys on the train back to New York. Then Rodney could forget all about Oregon and the nightmare it had been for him and his family.

"Evan," he said softly, "let's just get back to New York and forget all about this, okay?"

"What if they catch us, Rodney?"

"Then we'll tell the truth. We haven't done anything wrong, Evan. We haven't!"

"Then let's leave, let's just go! I don't want to be killed because of them! Let's go talk to the sheriff and tell him where they are going or something, anything! I don't want to stay with those guys anymore."

"What would we do, Evan? Where would we go? We don't have a home anymore. We don't have anything, except for what Mister Moskin and Mister Birch got us! Mister Moskin's a smart man and he'll get out of this and when he does, we're going home. I don't like them either, but sometimes we have to do what doesn't seem right to us. The train's the only chance we have to get back home and I want to go back to New York." Rodney paused, and then added softly, "I wish Pa had never brought us here."

"I'm not going with them," Evan volunteered.

"What do you mean, you're not going?"

"I'm not going!" He was about to say more when he heard the sound of horses in the distance. His heart quickened while he waited to see if they had caught Elizabeth or not. "They caught her," he sounded disappointed as he watched Donovan leading Elizabeth's horse behind his.

Rodney sighed.

"Hello, boys," Donovan sounded tired. "Let's get the food loaded and more blankets and stuff. We need to get moving, I want to be up in the mountains by sunup."

"Mister Moskin," Rodney spoke carefully, "Evan, and me decided we don't want to go. So you can leave us here and we'll find our own way back to New York."

Donovan looked at him appalled. "Are you crazy? There'll be a lynch mob coming in the morning and they'll string you up without a care! Your only chance is sticking with me," he maintained with finality. "So help us get the supplies loaded, we need to move quickly!"

Rodney continued, "We haven't done anything..."

"What?" Donovan sounded surprised. "Breaking out of jail, horse theft, not counting kidnapping and murder. You boys are guilty of doing some things and they'll string you up without asking a question! I promise you, you boys won't even get a trial."

"We didn't do any of that!" Rodney argued weakly.

"No?" Donovan questioned. "You're not in the jail, are you? That's the only thing they'll consider. If you want to stay here, fine, but you'll be decorating an oak limb by noon. If you don't believe me, wait here and see. Make a run for it and find out, but we're going! Good luck kids," Donovan said and dismounted. "John, let's get our things. Evan hold my horse for a minute, and don't let her go!" he warned pointing at Elizabeth, before the two men went back to the house.

Rodney and Evan looked at the scraped up face of Elizabeth compassionately. She was staring down at her hands which were tied uncomfortably to the saddle horn. It was evident that she had been roughed up and severely troubled.

"Missus Smith," Evan said touching her leg softly, "are you all right?"

She closed her eyes as a tear fell down her cheek.

"Missus Smith, will they hang my brother and me if we stay here?" Rodney asked. He also touched her pant leg gently to get her attention. "Will they?" he asked again.

She shook her head slowly at first and then quicker as she realized if the two boys stayed behind, she'd be left alone with the two men. She looked at them with desperation in her eyes. "Don't leave me alone with them, please!" she pleaded and started to cry, "Please don't leave me alone with them!"

"Shh, we'll go," Rodney whispered. He feared they

would be overheard by either John or Donovan as they came out of the house. "But you have to promise me you won't let your husband hang us."

She nodded quickly and tried to regain her composure. "I won't let him, I promise you. Just don't leave me with them, please," she begged.

Evan felt a surge of anger boil within him. "Did they hurt you?"

"Not yet," she cried with a grimace. "But I'm scared they will."

48

Tom Smith couldn't sleep. More than anything he wanted to grab his guns and ride after the men that took his wife. He wanted to leave right now while their tracks might still be evident in the snow, but Matt's words kept him sitting at home agonizingly watching the clock in the family room.

He had every reason to hate Matt, but he also knew Matt wouldn't risk Elizabeth's life unnecessarily. He had no doubt that Matt would sacrifice his own life to save Elizabeth's and probably even Tom's if it came to it. All the hostility he had for Matt was put aside to confront the situation at hand. A situation which was caused by having his wife do his job.

The moment she admitted Gabriel was Matt's son, it was like his whole life was ripped away from him. He thought it couldn't get any worse, but now he understood just how quickly it could. Despite his earlier words, Elizabeth was the love of his life and now that she'd been kidnapped nothing else mattered, except getting her back. Somehow life and death situations quickly place priorities where they belong. Forgiving Elizabeth would be a lot easier than he ever imagined it could be, especially knowing that he may never have the opportunity to tell her that he forgave her. She was the other half of who he had become and he would never be the same if anything happened to her. She was his best friend, and he loved her as a man should love his wife: truly, deeply, and for life. All Tom wanted was Elizabeth back home; they'd get through everything else.

Prayer became his first priority, and he hadn't prayed so sincerely in years. How he longed for the ears of God and wished he'd been in the Word daily as eagerly as he was now. He longed for the confidence that his prayers would be answered and the reassurance that the Lord was listening. In times of trouble people always pray with a greater depth and seek the face of God far more earnestly than they usually do. Tom's first priority was to put his trust in the Lord God Almighty.

His second priority was his children. He was responsible to feed, comfort, love and reassure them that everything would be okay. They needed their father as much as he needed them and holding his children brought a comfort that he found fulfilling in the absence of his wife. Nothing was more core-centered in his life right now than his relationship with the Lord and with his family. They were the two things that made his life worth living.

In the dim light of his kerosene lamp, Tom quietly closed his Bible. He pulled on his boots and collected the belongings he thought he'd need for the day ahead. Though sunup was still an hour away, Tom was growing restless. He gathered a little food, warm clothing, a bedroll, and of course his weapons and ammunition. He put on his coat and hat and paused at the front door to make sure he hadn't wakened anyone. He wouldn't be leaving right away, but waiting was more than he could bear, at least he could prepare himself while he had time. He carried his bundle of necessities to the barn quietly and stepped inside. He laid his belongings down and lit a lantern that hung near the door. His horse snorted at his untimely entrance.

"Shh, girl," he said softly. He closed the barn door and then went and rubbed his mare's neck gently. He stared at the spot where Elizabeth stood when she told him Matt was Gabriel's father. Sadness filled his heart, and he wished he could take every word he had said to her back. He wished he would've cried on her shoulder rather than condemning her with words that he thought he meant. Now less than twelve hours later all he cared about was getting her back alive.

Outside, the snow was falling heavily and the tracks from the night before would be covered by fresh snow. It would've been nearly impossible for Tom to track them without fresh tracks, as he'd spent very little time tracking anyone. As sheriff of Willow Falls he'd spent his career mostly as a symbol of the law. Actual necessity of law enforcement was rarely needed in Willow Falls. Occasionally, he'd been needed for some minor offense, but he'd never had a murder or a kidnapping take place before. Tom had never even drawn his weapon in the years that he'd been the sheriff, except for when he recently arrested the "Moskin Gang" as the townsfolk were calling Donovan and his gang. Tom was overwhelmed by what was happening in his once peaceful and quiet town. For the first time in his career he felt utterly incompetent to do his labors. He had no idea how to handle the search, and even less knowledge on how to rescue his wife. He had seen what Donovan could do to a person, and he feared for Elizabeth's life. He had no doubt Donovan would kill Elizabeth too.

Matt was right; this was beyond Tom's ability. The tracking and rescuing would have to be left up to Matt and Charlie. They had far superior experience with tracking than Tom did. Matt had said some key sentences that made sense; waiting until morning was one. Even though it was the hardest night of Tom's life, he thought it was the wisest choice to make. Matt also said there'd be shooting. Not maybe or possibly so, but definitely there would be shooting, again it was out of Tom's range of experience. The last time Matt said there'd be shooting, Tom froze in terror. Now as he thought of it, a deep-seated anxiety swept through him, what if he froze up like he did when he was a kid? Tom shook the doubt from his mind, this time his family was the one in danger, he would do what he had to do to protect his family. He wouldn't freeze when push came to shove, his family came first!

The barn door opened and his mother-in-law stepped into the barn wrapped in a heavy wool blanket. Darla Ash was a tall and thin woman of sixty years of age. She had a kind face and a quiet countenance that always seemed peaceful, even now when her only daughter was in the hands of wicked men. Her dark hair was tied in a tight bun and she wore round spectacles with silver rims. She closed the door behind her and then leaned against it. She looked tired. "You're not going after her right now are you?" she asked quietly.

Tom shook his head. "No, not yet. What are you doing up, can't sleep?"

"I was sleeping. You woke me up when you came outside. So what are you doing out here?" she asked.

He spoke quietly. "We had a fight today, a serious one."

"What was it about, if I may ask?"

Tom swallowed. He didn't want to say, but he couldn't keep it in any longer. He couldn't stand to bear the burden, but he also didn't want to shame Elizabeth, not to her mother, not to anyone. "You can't tell anyone, because it will shatter our family and her reputation, Darla."

Darla frowned. "I won't tell. She's my daughter, Tom."

He struggled to speak. "Gabriel's..." he heaved with a compressed sob, "not my son." Tears immediately grew thick in his eyes. "He's Matt's," he uttered weakly before his shoulders began to tremble and he began to sob.

Darla came forward to hold him. Despite his efforts to control himself, he wrapped his arms around Darla and sobbed.

"I called her a lot of bad things! I told her I wanted a divorce. God forgive me if anything happens to her. I love her so much..." he cried.

"I know," Darla answered gently. "She should have told you years ago."

"You knew?" Tom asked, surprised. He let her go and stepped back to look at her. "She told you!"

"She never said so, and I never asked, but Abraham and I could tell. He looks like Matthew."

Tom turned around to lean on the stall railing as he digested Darla's words. "You knew?" he asked again.

"I suspected." She explained, "Elizabeth was Abraham's only child and he did what he thought was best. Elizabeth would've run away and married Matthew, if Abraham hadn't of persuaded you to ask for her hand in marriage. She was in love with him, Thomas," she stated pointedly. "I know Gabriel is Matthew's son, but I also know you are his father. You are his only father and my daughter's husband. Forgive her, Thomas, because she loves you with a far greater and more mature love than she ever had for him."

Tom spoke slowly, "All I want is Lizzie home safely. If we can just bring her back alive and unharmed, I'll never yell at her again. I never have until today." He stopped to ponder his thoughts sadly. "I have forgiven her, Darla. I forgave her the moment they took her."

His shook his head slowly as he continued, "The Dobson Gang wanted to take her too and Matt wouldn't let them touch her. He was willing to die for her honor, Joseph's too. I was too scared and frozen. Matt saved Elizabeth that day, and he tried to save Joseph." He fought the choking sensation that built in his throat. "I never understood it until now. I didn't want to be his friend after that day. I was probably the first person to call him a murderer, but he's not. I understand now what he felt." A tear slipped from Tom's eyes. "Those men deserved what they got. I watched all of them die and I saw the rage on Matt's face that day and quite frankly, he scared me more than the Dobson's did. Now I feel the way that he did." He took a deep breath and exhaled. "Matt said there would be shooting today, and I hope so, because I want to kill Donovan Moskin as much as Matt wanted to kill Clay Dobson."

Darla spoke softly, "Matthew didn't have the legal right to go after them."

"Matt had more of a right to go after them than any sheriff in the nation did." He looked at her determinedly. "I'm leaving my badge at home. I'm not going up there to arrest them."

49

Elizabeth screamed as Donovan Moskin threw her down into a snowdrift and wrestled her coat off her. Expecting him to rip off her husband's heavy flannel shirt, she covered her breasts tightly with her arms. Instead, Donovan grabbed snow with both hands and forcibly rubbed it through her hair and across her face, neck and down the back of her shirt.

"Now," he demanded while standing over her, "your only chance of getting warm again is finding the cabin. Take your time if you want!" he shouted. They had been riding for an hour and a half and it was far too cold to be wandering aimlessly on the side of a mountain. She darnwell knew where the cabin was, Clyde had told him as much. He was motivating Elizabeth to find it a bit quicker than she was.

Elizabeth stood up and tried to wipe the snow out of her shirt and off of her messed up long yellow-blonde hair. She yelled, "I'm not taking my time! I don't know where it is from here. Everything is covered with snow!"

"You had better look harder, because you're not getting

your coat back until we're in the cabin. Now you better start searching!"

"I haven't been there since I was a kid!" she protested. "It belonged to Floyd Bannister; it's on his property some-where, but I don't know where we are!" she cried in frus-tration.

"Clyde said you knew," Donovan stated. "You're wasting time, woman. I untied your hands, but if you try to escape, I'll shoot the horse out from under you and you can walk or be drug behind, either one, but I'm running out of patience." Donovan warned severely.

Elizabeth stared at Donovan with contempt. "I'll do my best! But they'll find you eventually and I doubt you'll be so tough then!"

Donovan threw a hard right open-handed slap that echoed loudly through the trees. Elizabeth fell forcefully into the snow. She held her stinging cheek that reddened immediately. Despite its sharp sting she refused to cry and looked up at him defiantly. "Get on your horse!" he demanded.

"Fine!" she shouted. Elizabeth stood and climbed up on her horse angrily. "Ha!" she yelled, kicking the horse to an abrupt start. John and the two Gray brothers immediately followed her. Both boys huddled under blankets trying to keep warm in the freezing temperature that grew colder the higher they climbed. Donovan climbed back on his horse, covered himself with a blanket and followed the other riders.

Elizabeth couldn't navigate the terrain as the landmarks she would recognize were either covered by the clouds or by the thick snow. She was disoriented and simply lost. She had been cold long before losing her coat, but now the bitter cold had a doorway under her skin and she shivered uncontrollably. It had been twenty years, at least, since she'd been to the lake and the cabin Frederick Bannister had built. She remembered a narrow road that twisted its way up the mountainside that eventually led to a beautiful lake, just below a large looming rock formation that could be seen throughout the valley, known as Pillar Rock. If she could see it she'd know exactly where the cabin was, but all she could see was snow, falling snow and low gray clouds releasing snow.

The road up to the cabin was on the old Bannister Ranch which was west of the Anderson's by a couple of miles. However, she couldn't tell how far west they had come or if they were close to, on or past the Bannister Ranch land. The road she hoped to find was wide enough to take a wagon all the way to the top, at least it was twenty years ago. In the snow, she doubted she'd recognize it even if they were on it. In truth, there was little chance of finding it if she couldn't see Pillar Rock. She rode west and immediately her horse stumbled over some unseen object under the blanket of snow, which had become a common hazard slowing their progress. The falling snow continued to wet Elizabeth's hair and body and she knew that they would have to find the cabin soon or she'd freeze to death. It hadn't been five minutes, and she was already shivering and felt her teeth chattering. She stopped and looked back at Donovan. "Give me my coat," she pleaded slowly through her chattering teeth.

Donovan moved up in front of the boys next to John. "No," he answered coldly. "Find the cabin."

Tears of frustration filled her eyes. "I can't! I can't see the top and I don't know where we are!" she cried. "I'm freezing. Please give me my coat or a blanket. Please!" she begged.

Donovan shook his head. "Find the cabin!" he demanded forcefully.

Evan Gray had seen enough. "Here," he offered, pulling the dark wool blanket off of his head and started towards her. "You can have mine."

"Don't give that to her!" Donovan ordered roughly. "She knows exactly where the cabin is. She's just taking us around in circles. She'll find it when she's cold enough!"

"She'll freeze to death long before we will. Look at her! She's frozen to the bone. Here." He handed the blanket to her. She immediately bundled it around her with grateful tears. "Thank you," she said with a shivering voice.

"Maybe, you're right," Donovan agreed, and then tossed her the blanket she had been using before he took it. "You'll get your coat back when you find it. If I was you, I'd be finding it soon, or you'll be losing fingers and toes to frost bite. The games over, dear, now you'd better find it!"

"I'm trying," she stated weakly.

"Maybe she doesn't know where it is," Evan pointed out to Donovan. He was tired, freezing, and in a foul mood.

"Oh, she knows, and you'd better watch yourself, kid! I won't put up with you and your mouth, got it?" Donovan questioned with a threatening tone.

"Yeah, I got it," Evan replied with disgust.

Elizabeth rode through trees and more trees, through clearings and into trees. She changed to a southwest direction with the thought that she would eventually reach the top and recognize something, particularly Pillar Rock. Donovan's plan was working as she was desperately trying her best to find the cabin. Shivering and chattering teeth were just a symptom, it was her fingers and toes that burned with the cold numbing pain that concerned her the most. She had been praying constantly and every few minutes she reworded her prayers. She prayed to be rescued, to be kept safe, to even escape perhaps, at the moment though, she prayed for warmth and to find the cabin. She was miserable and she couldn't imagine getting any colder than she was.

She led the riders out of a tree line into a wide steep clearing. Just before entering the tree line on the other side of the clearing, she glanced up the mountain and stopped suddenly. Up the steep incline were a series of rocky crags that jutted out of the ground. They were close together and anywhere from a few feet to twenty feet tall in the middle of the clearing. It was a familiar sight from her childhood. She remembered always expecting Indians to be hiding behind them when her parents made the trip up to the Bannister's cabin to spend a weekend on the lake. It wasn't Pillar Rock, but it was a landmark that she had been looking for to point her towards the cabin. She was on the very trail to the cabin! She turned her horse up the mountain and spoke with a new energy to her voice. "The cabin's up there," she exclaimed suddenly excited, "This is the trail!"

"See?" Donovan questioned Evan and Rodney with a smile. "We'd still be circling somewhere back there if we hadn't wet her down. It won't be long now, boys!" he remarked cheerfully.

Relief was on the faces of all of them as they rode up what seemed to be quite a long distance until they climbed over a bluff and then dropped gently down a hill ending at a lake partly frozen over. Beside the lake was a medium sized cabin that appeared to be in good shape with a small barn behind it and an outhouse. They hurried to the cabin.

"Get the kindling, Rodney, I need a fire," Donovan said as they entered the cabin. He was freezing.

Elizabeth sat in a rocking chair with both blankets wrapped tightly around her trying to get warm. She thanked the Lord that she had looked up just at the right moment to see the jagged rocks on the trail. Once a fire was going in the small kitchen stove, and a larger fire burning in the fireplace to heat the cabin up quicker, Donovan looked at Elizabeth. "Go make some breakfast and make it quick," he ordered. He lay down on Clyde's single bed not far from the fireplace and covered up under Clyde's dry blankets. "No," he added as a second thought, "we'll eat later."

John Birch walked in with more firewood to add to the already growing pile of dry wood waiting to be burned. "The horses are put away, but there's nothing to feed them. What are you doing?" he asked Donovan irritably.

"Getting some sleep."

"What about me, I'm just as tired as you are," John challenged.

"There's another bed in the back room, go sleep there, but tie her up first," he paused. "Let me sleep for a couple of hours, then you can sleep for a while. I don't want the boys watching her."

"Why not?" Rodney asked timidly.

Donovan looked at him severely. "I just don't! Now one of you boys go get some sleep."

"What are the chances of them tracking us up here?" John asked. He was just as exhausted as everyone else.

"With the snow falling like it is, not too likely. They'll be looking for us down in the valley, not up here."

"Well," John stated, "I don't think we should be sleeping if a posse rides up."

Donovan looked annoyed. "Relax, we're safe here." He closed his eyes. "You all be quiet; I need some sleep. And remember to tie her up."

50

Tom Smith was waiting somewhat impatiently at the jail. He was standing outside with Reverend Ash waiting for the arrival of Matt and Charlie. It was light out and the snow had covered the tracks of the outlaws, sure enough. At the moment, Tom wasn't panicking about it, but he was fighting the fear of never finding Elizabeth. He thought Matt had a reasonable theory that they'd find Donovan at the Anderson farm. Where else would they be? Tom was nervous and had a thousand butterflies floating in his stomach. His wife was out there and he knew in a few short hours he might have to shoot a man or be killed trying to save her. His anxieties were fueled by the memories of the Dobson Gang. He could not forget how terrified he had been on that morning. He had spent his life trying to block out the memories of that day, but now he was about to relive it to a certain extent. Once again Matt would be beside him.

"Morning," Tom said as Charlie and Matt rode up to the jail.

"Morning," Matt replied as Tom climbed up into his saddle.

Reverend Ash stepped up close to Matt's horse. "Matthew, do you remember this?" He held up the river rock vaguely shaped like a heart that Elizabeth had given him many years before.

Matt looked at it and shook his head.

The Reverend spoke softly, "Elizabeth gave it to me the day you three...four, Joseph was there. The day we had a church picnic along the river and you four disappeared. Do you remember that day?"

Matt thought back and nodded slowly. "Yeah, you beat her. She told me about it," he said coldly.

The Reverend's face contorted slightly as guilt ran through him. "Yes, I did," he admitted weakly. He looked up at Matt with desperation in his eyes. "She came into my office late that night and handed me this rock as a gift. It is in the shape of a heart so she got it for me." He paused, with tears swelling in his eyes and pressed his quivering lips together tightly. "Bring her home, Matthew, please. Whatever it takes, please just bring her home."

"I'll do my best, but it's the Lord's to give. You're a Reverend, you know that," Matt stated mercilessly and kicked his horse. "Let's go, gentlemen."

Charlie rode in silence between Tom and Matt. There was a combination of tiredness and discomfort on both of their faces. Charlie could read the stark contrast of Tom's frightened stoical expression, to the pointed concentration of Matt's. They all had separate thoughts to ponder and prayers to say. There were no promises that any of them would make the return trip to Willow Falls alive, except for the promises they'd made to their loved ones. But as they all knew, those promises weren't theirs to give.

Charlie looked to his right at Tom. "You still owe me two

days of hay cutting, you know," he said to break the uncomfortable silence.

"What?" Tom was pulled out of his thoughts. He was experiencing the very real fear that they might find Elizabeth dead, or not at all. His confidence in his professional partners was a great comfort, but did nothing to calm his fears.

Charlie explained, "I once paid you for a week's worth of work and you only worked three days. Remember? You and Matt said you wanted to be paid early. I wrote it all down, you can look at my billings if you don't believe me."

"Charlie," Tom began, "if we get Elizabeth back, I'll cut as much hay as you want. I'll even bring lunch."

Charlie chuckled. "I'll sharpen the scythes. You don't need to bring lunch though," he said comfortingly, "I just want what you owe me."

Tom smiled slightly. "If I recall correctly, we made twenty-five cents a day. I'll pay you back fifty cents."

Charlie scoffed. "If I was a banker, it would be cheaper for you to work for two weeks." He explained with a smile, "The interest over the years you know."

It had been years since he had seen Charlie's old playful smile. It was a comforting gesture. "I'm glad you're not a banker," Tom replied finally. He then added, out of curiosity, "Have either you guys ever been in a situation like this? I mean a woman being stolen like Elizabeth was?"

Charlie shook his head. "Nope. Have you Matt?"

"Once, but I wasn't fresh on the trail. I was a week or two behind," he finished.

"Did the men let her go? Were you able to save her?" Tom asked.

Matt shook his head slowly. "There was a couple of buffalo hunters who took a young woman who was out for a buggy ride with her husband. They killed her husband and took her. I started to trail them about a week after the incident," he hesitated for a moment. "I found the men, but they had buried her out on the prairie the same day they took her." He looked at Tom. "The men were hung, but like I said, I wasn't fresh on their trail."

Tom seemed disturbed. "What do you think are our chances of getting Elizabeth back alive?" he asked frankly.

"I don't know, Tom. But I do know that she's still alive, at least through today."

"Do you think they'll try for Branson? That seems like the only logical place to escape."

"Most likely," Matt agreed. "They had to hide out somewhere and I doubt they rode through the night."

"And you think the Anderson place is it?"

Matt nodded. "I do. Donovan's a big talker, but he's not too brave, really. He only victimizes people weaker than himself. And like I said, he already knows who lives there."

"They won't let her go, will they?" Tom asked already knowing the answer.

"No." Matt continued softly, "She's too valuable to them right now to kill her though. As long as they have her they know they're...fairly safe. But I can't promise you that we'll find her alive either, Tom."

"I understand that," Tom said tiredly. "If she's still with them, how are we going to get her back without putting her in harm's way? I'll be honest; all I care about is getting her back alive."

"We know, Tom," Charlie answered for Matt. "We'll figure all that out when we find them. That's the reason a posse like you had last night is a bad idea in situations like this one. Someone is bound to take a shot or draw attention to themselves before a plan is made. A bad plan always ends up with bad results, you can count on it. So when we get close to the Anderson's, we'll slow down and watch a bit before doing anything. It's possible they've left the house by now, but we'll talk to the Anderson's and be on their trail."

Tom asked anxiously, "What if they never went to the Anderson's, then what?"

"Then," said Matt as if the idea had never occurred to him, "we'll have to ride a bit harder to find their trail and hope we weren't too far off."

"What do you usually do in a situation like this?"

"I've never been in a situation like this," Matt replied simply.

"So we hope they're at the Anderson's homestead?" Tom asked, unimpressed.

Matt looked at Tom. "I'm counting on it."

51

Gabriel Smith sat nervously on his horse, waiting for the three riders as they drew near. He'd left soon after his father; but instead of following Tom into town, he had ridden two miles east towards Branson. Gabriel was dressed warmly and carried his small caliber-hunting rifle across his lap. He waited on top of a hill where the road gave a good view of the area below it. He had every intention of going with his father to get his mother back, in fact he was determined to go and would not be refused! He reminded himself of that when he saw his father glaring at him.

"Gabriel, what are you doing here?" Tom asked and then yelled, "What's that for?" He pointed at the rifle.

Gabriel's voice cracked, "I'm going with you."

Tom was growing angry. "The hell you are! Now get your butt back to the house right now before I drag you off that horse and whip you like a child!"

Gabriel looked at Charlie, who stared at Gabriel sternly.

"Go!" Tom ordered.

"No," Gabriel said defiantly.

"What?" Tom questioned and climbed off his horse to walk over to Gabriel.

Gabriel spoke quickly, "I won't go home. My mother's out there somewhere and I won't go home!" He flinched as Tom pulled him down off of his horse. Gabriel yelled as Tom raised his hand to strike him, "Hit me again if you want to! I don't care anymore, but you won't stop me from following you! No matter how bad you beat me. You'll have to kill me to keep me from coming with you!"

Tom's arm fell to his side. Gabriel's facial expression, tone and choice of words brought flashbacks of Matt from so many years before. The fear, rage, and determination on Gabriel's face was the same as Matt's when he refused to let Frank Walchester lift Elizabeth up onto his horse. Tom stood still momentarily, looking at his son, perplexed.

"Please Dad, let me come," Gabriel begged.

Charlie's voice penetrated Tom's ears, "Ah...let him ride along. The boy's got to grow up sometime."

Tom turned to look at Charlie. "I don't want him to see the things I've seen."

Gabriel spoke accusingly, "Are you talking about Pearl Creek, Dad?"

"What?" Tom asked surprised.

"Pearl Creek! Annie told me that you and Mom were both there! Miss Jackson's brother was killed, his name was Joseph, right? You were there, Dad, you knew him, and so was Mom! You both lied to me! You said you didn't know Matt very well, but you were best friends! You said his girl-friend had moved away after the Dobson's were killed, but Mom was Matt's girlfriend, wasn't she?" He looked up at Matt and asked accusingly, "Wasn't she?"

"Gabriel..." the secret he had tried so hard to keep was now out, "I..." Tom started to say.

"I'm going with you Dad, and you won't stop me!" Gabriel said determinedly. He looked at Matt. "My mother was your girlfriend, wasn't she?" he asked pointedly.

Matt's eyes grew hard and his voice wasn't any kinder. "If you're coming with us, let's get an understanding right now. You follow behind us and keep your mouth shut! If we say stay, you stay! If I have to tell you to be quiet even once, I will send you home and you will go!" Matt's eyes burned into Gabriel's. "This is not a pleasure hunt, boy! We have one chance," he held up a gloved finger, "just one to get your mother back alive. If you screw that up, it will be your fault. So, if you're coming, do what you're told and only what you're told! Do you understand me?" Matt snarled.

Gabriel stared at Matt frightened by the authority in his voice and the hardness that blazed in his eyes. "Yes, sir," he responded meekly.

"Then get on your horse! Tom, let's go," Matt ordered angrily. He looked over at Charlie, who smiled and then laughed quietly. He kicked his horse to move forward.

52

The sunlight broke through the clouds and woke Elizabeth up as it reflected through the glass. By the placement of the sun, she guessed it to be around ten in the morning. She had slept for a while despite being tied uncomfortably to a wooden chair. She could tell by their breathing and the snoring that her captors still slept soundly. She was bruised, scraped up and her shoulders and neck ached with sharp pains when she moved. Despite her discomfort and dire circumstances, she appreciated the natural beauty of the cabin's view of Lake Jessup and the mighty granite face of Pillar Rock, which rose high above the blue waters of the lake surrounded by a white blanket of snow. The cabin was built with small square paneled windows that ran the length of the wall in the small kitchen and dining room to give the view.

It was a comfortable log cabin with a stone fireplace and chimney in the open main living area, which consisted of a single bed, and a rocking chair. There a private bedroom with a double bed, and a kitchen area with a small woodstove for cooking and counters to prepare the meals on. The dining table was small with three chairs and close to the back door that led to the out buildings, and luckily, more than a cord of dry wood stacked up on the back porch under a steep lean-to roof. The cabin was smaller than she remembered, but the view was far more spectacular than she ever imagined. It was a shame that the only person to ever use the cabin was Clyde.

She feared Donovan was right, the cabin was too far out of the way to be remembered by anyone, including Tom. Every lawman in the county would be looking for them in the valley or low lying hills, but none would venture up into the Blue Mountains to the base of Pillar Rock to check a little forgotten cabin. Donovan was right, he and the others could sit comfortably in Clyde's cabin, until the beehive of searchers called it quits in the valley below. In a week or so, they could leave the safety of their hideaway and ride towards Seattle, Canada or wherever they would go to out run the law. Elizabeth hated to admit it, but she was starting to believe that Donovan might slip away and remain free.

She thought of her children at home and realized suddenly that it was Christmas morning. Her children were probably terrified without her being home and she wondered how Tom was dealing with them about her absence. Most agonizingly, she wondered if Tom was treating Gabriel decently or was he rejecting him now as well. Elizabeth had come to terms with her own fate if Tom divorced her. She'd take Gabriel and go to her parent's home to live. She would have to explain the truth to him and the church's congregation too, as her public divorce would not only be an embarrassment to her and her parents, but a shame that wouldn't easily be washed away.

Of course, that was only if her captors let her go. She knew exactly how easy it was for Donovan to murder someone, even someone as elderly and helpless as Arthur and Gladys Anderson. He had brutally stabbed them to death in their own home for absolutely no reason at all. There was no credibility for Elizabeth to believe that he would spare her when it was time for them to leave. She would fight for her life, but she was ready to face the Lord if that was the fate ahead of her. She had put her future, her family and her life into God's hands. The only thing she asked was that He watched over her children, each and every one of them.

She took in the glorious view and welcomed the Creator of it all to take her home if that was what He desired. The words of Esther came to mind, which brought a sense of peace oddly enough, "*If I die, then I die.*"

Christians, for the most part, look forward to going to Heaven to be with Jesus. It is what the purpose and meaning of life is all about. Life isn't about owning the most land or building up a fortune of the nicest things money can buy. Life is about getting to know the Creator of our souls, the One who loved us enough to suffer and die for us. What was it the psalmist wrote? "*Life is like a night's dream, then we wake up for eternity.*" Life is a limited time we have to live in the here and now on earth with family and friends, but as everyone knows there is an end. Death is without a doubt terrifying, because unlike an icy cold riverbank, there is no way to step back out of it, if you don't like it. Death is final.

But yet, the Book of Psalms compares it to waking up and our life on earth to a single night's dream. Our lives are quick, like a wisp of wind cutting across a wheat field, and then we face death. It's the fateful journey that we all will face at our appointed time. Our life, whether it is short or long, will then only be a memory, like a dream. According to the Bible, there is an eternal life and those who choose Jesus will enter into Heaven, those who don't, choose instead eternal darkness apart from God.

Elizabeth had lived a good night's dream. She'd seen wonderful times that she had loved and she'd seen miserable times when happiness was hard to find. Overall, God blessed her night's dream with a loving husband and four beautiful children. The Lord had been good to her, and He still was. She was thankful for good friends and the very sunshine that lit this Christmas morning, and for finding the cabin when she did. She sat quietly, staring at the snow covered Pillar Rock and half frozen lake. It was truly a beautiful view and she knew the Lord had hand-crafted this beautiful scene like an artist does a painting. 'Oh yes,' she thought, 'You are amazing God!' Despite her situation, she felt a joy in knowing that God wasn't a mysterious and far off notion, but rather that she knew the creator personally in the man of Jesus, the Christ. If her time on earth was through, then she would take comfort in knowing that she was going home to the Lord.

53

"What do you think?" Charlie asked Matt. They were on horseback a good distance away and behind some brush watching the Anderson homestead. The small, weathered and unpainted two-story home seemed to be very still with no movement or any other sign of life. There was no trace of smoke coming from the chimney which was suspicious on a cold Christmas morning.

Matt watched it carefully. "It's a little late in the morning not to have a fire going, isn't it?"

"My thoughts exactly," Charlie said and then turned to Tom. "What are your thoughts, Tom?"

"There'd be a fire if they were home."

Matt nodded without taking his eyes off of the house. "I agree. Just in case though, you two go around the back like you did last night, and I'll draw their attention to the front if they're there. Donovan knows I ride alone, so he won't expect you coming in the back door."

MATT'S EYES scanned everything as he rode slowly and

cautiously closer to the Anderson's home. The front side of the narrow two story home had four windows that were the only places that Donovan and his gang could shoot from. Matt intentionally rode to the left side of the front door to place his horse between him and the windows if need be.

His eyes searched the windows for shadows, movement, or anything that resembled danger. He carried his Winchester across his lap for a quick response, his feet were light in the stirrups and his adrenalin was high. With any sign of movement in the house he'd be out of the saddle and firing at the sidewalls of the windows. He knew every gun Donovan had would be drawn to the front of the house, leaving the back door unprotected for Charlie and Tom to enter the house behind them. He didn't have much faith in Tom, but he knew Charlie would shoot to kill in controlled fashion and speed.

It was a rare individual who was able to stay clear-headed and in control of their emotions when fear turned to terror in a gunfight. Matt had always had that ability; he never panicked or let his nerves be bent by fear. A level head during the fast pace of a gunfight made all the difference between life and death. Fear made most men's hands shake which caused firing prematurely and a missed target left a lot of time, whether a second or two, for the target to shoot back. It was panicking during a gunfight that most often opened the door to one's own grave. Matt wasn't always the first to fire, but so far he'd always been the last one standing. He had a plan and was ready to react. He hoped that Donovan and his gang would be startled to see him and in their panic; he hoped their aim would be off. Even if they killed his mare, he could fall to the ground and use her for cover long enough for Charlie to even the odds.

As he got closer to the front porch and the solid wood

door, he doubted that the outlaws were inside. The pressure would have caused Donovan to fire. He was the kind of man that was run by his emotions.

Matt momentarily kept his mare between the bottom windows and himself as he dismounted and placed his rifle in its scabbard and then pulled out his revolver as he stepped up on the porch. Cautiously, he unlatched the door and softly pushed it open. As the door opened, Matt immediately saw a large puddle of dried blood on the floor. A blood trail of two bodies being dragged through the front room, around the staircase left no doubt in Matt's mind as to what had happened and who was responsible.

He stepped lightly through the living room of the silent house, his eyes searching for clues, but nothing stood out more than the blood trail. It circled back behind the staircase to a recessed closet built under the stairs. He opened the door knowing what he'd find. The aged bodies of the Andersons were covered in blood and thrown together without care. Their eyes were open and lifeless.

The back door opened and Charlie was quickly at his side, gazing at his long-time friends.

"Good Lord!" gasped Tom in horror.

"Tom," Matt spoke softly, "check upstairs."

Tom nodded and turned the corner; his heavy footsteps could be heard climbing up the stairs.

Charlie knelt down and closed the eyes of his friends. "They went up on the mountain. Five or six horses cut a trail south, looks like they're heading up the mountain." He stood up and nodded toward the bodies. "They've been dead for a while."

"They were murdered at the door. I don't think Donovan and his gang gave them a chance."

Charlie's voice was strained, "Well, their time's coming

quick, but right now we need to close the door and get moving before we find Elizabeth in this condition. I expect to find them first!" He knew the savagery of certain kinds of people and what a group of men of that character could do to an attractive woman in their control. He knew in the end she would meet the same fate as the others if they didn't stop them.

Tom's footsteps echoed down the stairs. "There's nothing upstairs," he said nearly out of breath. "We saw their tracks heading up the mountain."

Matt looked at Charlie. "Chances are they'll turn east towards Branson."

"There's only one way to find out," Charlie stated shortly. He addressed Tom with the same sharpness to his voice, "Tom, just so you know before we leave here, those men aren't coming back alive. Even if they surrender, I'm gonna hang them where they stand!" he paused to glare at Tom. "So if your badge gets in the way, you'd better turn for home now!"

Tom replied seriously, "I already left it at home. They have my wife, Charlie, whether they hang out here, or in town makes no difference to me."

Charlie nodded approvingly.

"How fresh are the tracks?" Matt asked.

"I'd say five or six hours old. They must have left pretty early, before sunup."

Matt frowned. "They must've thought we wouldn't find their tracks if it snowed enough."

Tom's face reflected some hope. "We can cut them off in Branson."

"No," Charlie said softly, "it's better to follow their trail. Then there's no question of where they are."

Tom grew frustrated. "What about Elizabeth? You

already said they were hours ahead of us. If we follow their trail, we could be stumbling around in the brush for hours while they're already in Branson. Time's important, Charlie, it's my wife is in their hands. We don't have time to casually waltz behind hoping we'll find them in Branson. I say we just go and stop pussyfooting around. We know where they're going, so let's go!"

Charlie replied gruffly, "You cannot tell me for a fact that they're going to Branson! You can assume or reason all you like, but you don't know! We follow their trail!" Charlie walked through the kitchen out the back door and whistled loudly and waved for Gabriel to come.

Tom was irritated. "Matt, you said yourself that they're not going to just any house. The only logical place is Branson."

Matt frowned and put his hand on Tom's thick shoulder. "Let's go. We have to follow the tracks because not only does it lead us to them, but it will also tell us how careful they're being, how scared they are and how confident they are of escaping."

"What about Elizabeth?"

"Lord willing, we won't find her cut up like these folks. That's the other reason though, we'll find whatever they leave behind."

54

Elizabeth had fallen back to sleep and the bright sunlight glaring off the snow onto her face woke her up along with the near unbearable pain she felt. Being yanked off of the horse had severely jarred her body and her upper back and neck were stiff and aching. Being tied tightly to the wooden chair for hours caused her tailbone to hurt as well. Aside from the aching and soreness, she was also quite thirsty. She hadn't had any water since her capture, and her mouth was dry to the point where it was hard to swallow.

She could hear the snoring and breathing of the others who slept soundly. She prayed that they would sleep all day although she was nearly thirsty enough to wake them up herself. If she could have untied herself, she could've ridden back down the mountain without her kidnappers even realizing it until she was safely at home. But John had tied the knots so solidly that she could barely move as it was.

She guessed that it had been about eighteen hours since she had been abducted and by now the whole community knew Clyde was dead and that she was taken. Donovan had left a note and Elizabeth knew the letter would be pretty convincing to anyone who had seen Clyde's body. She wondered if anyone would risk looking for her.

She knew Tom wasn't coming, not by his own will power, anyway. He was the sheriff and the town council did have the authority to send him after her, even if he didn't want to. Her father would certainly have the influence to insist that Tom went to look for her, but it wasn't his decision alone. There were two other council members, and at least one would have to agree with the Reverend before Tom was forced to look for her. Under most circumstances, Tom would not hesitate to come after her, but under the current circumstances it was questionable at best. Even if Tom did come, he'd never find their tracks and search for them in Branson like Donovan said he would. He and everyone else would search everywhere in the valley, but they wouldn't search Clyde's cabin. They would find the bodies of Mr. and Mrs. Anderson, but there would be no clues as to where they took Elizabeth. Donovan was right, he could sleep easily.

Elizabeth was trapped; she was totally at the mercy of her captors. The only hope she had was in Jesus. No matter how it ended, whether she was saved, escaped, let go, or killed, she would put her hope in the Lord.

"Oh Lord," she whispered, "help me through this. I want to raise my children, I want to see Alexis grow up and marry," she whispered as a tear fell down her cheek. She stared out the window at Pillar Rock. "I'm sorry for the lies I've told, and the pain I've caused. I don't want to lose my family, Jesus. I want to be home with my husband and my children. Your word promises that I can trust you. So help me please... I need you," she whispered desperately. She kept her eyes upward to the blue sky and the snow-covered granite of Pillar Rock. A Bible verse flashed through her memory: *Be still and know that I am God.*

"I don't have much of a choice," she said aloud. A chill ran through her spine as she realized she had spoken too loud and Donovan Moskin was suddenly awake.

He sat up quickly on the bed that was in the main room. Evan and Rodney Gray were asleep on the floor. Donovan jumped out of bed alertly, went to the windows and peeked outside. He opened Clyde's pocket watch and grew angry with a curse. He kicked Rodney in the ribs and yelled with his deep voice, "Wake up, you no good bag of crap!"

Rodney leaped up from his comfortable fetal position on the floor with a fear-filled expression on his face. Evan jumped up quickly as well. John Birch ran out of the bedroom with his revolver in his hand as Donovan's voice continued to shatter the silence. "I told you to keep watch!" he yelled at Rodney. "We're lucky the sheriff didn't march up here and wake us up with his shotgun! If you ever fall asleep when you are told to keep watch again, I'll cut you open like a rabbit! Do you understand me?" he yelled.

"Yes, sir," Rodney gasped, "but I..." he tried to explain.

"We're all tired! We could have been hanging on a noose because of you!" Donovan sneered.

"I'm sorry, but," Rodney said discouraged, "you told John to keep watch, not me."

"I know what I said, damn it!" Donovan yelled. "You messed up! There could be a posse outside right now just watching. We don't know because you were sleeping!" He glared angrily at Rodney. "You put us at risk! When I tell you to do something, you need to do it. It won't happen again! If I catch you sleeping on your watch again, you won't wake up, I will promise you that! Now, get some wood in the cook stove, let's see if you can do that right," he yelled. He looked at Evan. "You help! You boys need to start helping out. John and I are doing all the work around here."

John glared tiredly at Rodney with his cold eyes; his voice was calm, but threatening, "Don't ever put the blame on me for your mistake again, boy! I won't tolerate it. Now go get that wood."

"I woke up and caught the boy sleeping," Donovan explained irritably to John. "I..." he paused to yawn.

"The sun's shining. Do you think our tracks are covered?" John asked, while the two brothers quietly went out to gather some wood from the woodpile.

Donovan looked out a window. "Yeah, if they're looking, they're looking down in the valley. They didn't come for her last night, so old Tom might be waiting at home for his pretty little wife to return," he said with a slight smirk.

"What about your marshal friend?"

"If he's searching, he's down in the valley too. If he knew where we were, he'd be here by now..." He shot a hard glance at Rodney, as he carried an armload of wood back to the wood stove. "And with no one keeping *look-out*, we'd all be dead! That U. S. Marshal, Rodney, is the last man you want to see because by the time you see him, you're dying! He's killed more men than any other marshal or lawman, period. Dead or alive!" he said glaring at Rodney. He then stepped up behind Elizabeth and put his hands on her shoulders. "Isn't that right sweetheart? The sheriff's little wife here knows Matt pretty well, since she had a child with him and all. Do you think he's coming sweetheart? I'm sure he's looking."

"Matt has no reason to come after me, he doesn't even know Gabriel is his," Elizabeth replied solemnly. She kept her gaze upward on Pillar Rock. Her cries inwardly went to the Lord as the feel of Donovan's hands resting upon her shoulders frightened her.

Donovan chuckled. "Tom knows we'd kill you if anyone comes, at least, that's what he thinks. We know something else though, don't we?" he asked affectionately. He stepped around in front of her and knelt down to look into her eyes.

"What?" she asked weakly. Her eyes watered from the fear that crept into her as she stared into his eyes. Under different circumstances she might've considered Donovan's face as friendly, perhaps even harmless. It was a very deceptive face.

He slowly smiled at her and stood back up. He spoke cheerfully as he walked back behind her, "How about some breakfast, I'm starving. How about you making up some bacon and eggs, that would be a good start to your day." He untied the rope that held her in place.

Elizabeth breathed heavily as he untied her. She feared the worst, but she was too frightened to argue about making them breakfast; she was hungry too. However, she prayed Donovan wouldn't want more from her than bacon and eggs.

55

They had been trailing the faint tracks of a half dozen horses for a few miles. It was apparent that Donovan left the Anderson home while it was still snowing with the hope that the snow would cover their tracks, but a faint trail was left to follow. Their trail showed little interest in either coming down into the valley or doubling back towards Branson. They didn't seem to have a good sense of direction or any clear idea of where they were going. The tracks zigzagged up the slope then back down again without any explanation as to why. Matt followed slowly as no one knew what the next hill, creek or tree line would hold. Sometimes people caught in the snow found a decent place to hole up under a fallen tree perhaps, or a cave, even a snow cave dug out by hand, was sufficient for a potential ambush.

Tom pulled the reins of his horse to a sudden stop. "I know where they went! Look!" He pointed at the rough granite face of Pillar Rock. It stood like a giant tombstone in the near distance. "They're going to Clyde's cabin," he announced simply.

"Clyde's cabin?" Matt asked unknowingly.

"Clyde bought your father's cabin on Lake Jessup. He must have told them about it. He talks about it all the time." Clyde's death would have moved him deeply, if he hadn't been so worried about Elizabeth. It dawned on him that he'd never get to sit and listen to Clyde tell the same stories all day long for the sixty-eighth time again. He shook his head slightly to shake it off and then continued, "It's the only place up here," he explained.

"Clyde bought the lake cabin?" Matt asked as he looked at the mountain peak.

"A long time ago, but that's where they're going I'll bet you. They're looking for the cabin!"

Matt hadn't forgotten about the cabin, in fact, he'd been thinking about it since seeing Pillar Rock earlier that morning. However, he had never considered his family's old lake cabin as being Donovan's destination. The thought had never even occurred to him.

"You know I'll bet you're right, Tom," Charlie said. "I'll bet they're sitting up there in the cabin watching their back trail with an ambush."

Matt looked over at Charlie. "You think they're at the cabin?"

"Matt, so far these guys seem smarter than your average criminal running for their lives. They seem to have everything planned out from killing Clyde to the kidnapping, the note, killing Arthur and Gladys at the front door and leaving long before we got there. These guys aren't just running for their lives, they're thinking about escaping the area. Hiding out at Clyde's cabin, well now, that's smart. If we hadn't found their tracks in the woods or it had snowed a few inches deeper we'd be in Branson and all over this valley, but we'd never consider Clyde's cabin as a possibility."

Gabriel sounded hopeful, "Like Dad said, Clyde's always talking about it. I'd be sure he told them about it."

Matt hesitated and then looked at Pillar Rock. "It was cloudy this morning. With the clouds as low as they were, they wouldn't be able to see Pillar Rock."

"Nope," Charlie agreed. "That would explain all the erratic shifts in direction."

Matt nodded. "Tom, do you think Elizabeth remembers how to get there?"

"Not from here. Well, she knows it's in front of Pillar Rock, but she hasn't been up there since we were kids."

Charlie quipped, "Well, Pillar Rock's in clear sight now, they won't have any trouble finding it."

"Matt," Tom began, "I'd like to get there as fast as possible. Couldn't we follow a ways more and then cut up from their trail to get to the cabin, it would be faster."

Matt shook his head thoughtfully. "We'd be coming in from the east and Charlie may be right about an ambush. Donovan knows you, William and I will be looking for him. So he might be watching the east in case we're tracking him. The trail from the old ranch comes in from the west side of the cabin if I remember correctly. If we come in from the west it'll give us a better chance of getting close without being seen."

Tom said, "That's going to take more time than just riding up there now."

Matt nodded. "Yeah, but a little extra time's worth avoiding a possible ambush. Rest assured, Tom, before the day is through the battle will be fought and we'll get Elizabeth back."

56

The Reverend Abraham Ash wasn't the kind of man who could sit idly in his study and worry, nor was he the kind who could sit in his comfortable chair and relax knowing the Lord was in control. He knew that, of course, but he was the kind of Reverend who was found on his knees in front of the altar praying. With his wife, Darla, beside him, they prayed earnestly for the safe return of their daughter. They prayed for the men who went after her including, they assumed, Gabriel, who disappeared shortly after Tom had left. There was much to pray for and many of their friends joined with them in the pews to pray for Elizabeth.

The Reverend wasn't the pillar of spiritual strength he'd been every Sunday for over thirty years. He was on his knees with his head bowed and holding hands with his treasured wife while the congregation took turns praying over them. For the first time he was the one who was hurting and in need.

Lettie Snow and her husband, Carl, like everyone else in the church, had left their homes on Christmas to come comfort and pray for their friends. Lettie prayed with surprising strength in her voice despite of her aging body, "Lord, you know the fear and heartbreak that has overcome our town. We lost Clyde, and we hope he's with You. But we know Elizabeth is your daughter and we ask you to bring her back safely to us and fill her parents with your peace. Jesus, we come to you on our knees to intervene on Elizabeth's behalf. You brought Matthew home, Lord, and I can't help wondering if his leaving our town was to prepare him for this day. We put our trust and confidence in Jesus. In your name we pray, Amen."

Reverend Ash began to sob on his knees with his head buried into his hands on the floor. Darla Ash held him comfortingly with her arm over his back. She spoke softly, "Let's go fix some lunch. We've been praying all morning, and that's all we can do for Elizabeth. Our grandchildren are in the house and probably getting hungry. I say we send our friends home and salvage what we can of this Christmas," she suggested with a subtle strength. She leaned her face close to her husband's ear. "Come inside and eat, Abraham. You need to keep your strength up."

He lifted his head revealing a tear-streaked face as his red eyes found hers and grasped her hands softly. "I will fast until she's home," he said weakly. "Darla, I'm the one that ran Matthew out of this town," he stated with conviction.

"That was a long time ago," she answered softly.

Lettie Snow spoke to the others in the church, "Come, let's leave them alone with the Lord. Darla, we'll feed your grandchildren."

"Thank you, Lettie," she said, as their friends left the church and closed the door.

Reverend Ash spoke as the door closed, "This morning Matthew looked at me with such indignation, but there was more, there was so much more." He looked at Darla with desperation in his eyes. "Was I wrong, Darla, to forbid him from seeing Elizabeth? Was I wrong to remove him from our church?" he asked, feeling a heavy burden.

Darla sighed. "I told you then that you were wrong," she spoke as sensitively as she could. He looked at her with a perplexed expression. She continued, "You are such a hard-headed man that sees what you want to see and hears only what you want to hear. Matthew went through hell to save our daughter's life. Abraham, Matthew needed you more right then, than anyone has ever needed you. And you weren't there for him."

He closed his eyes tightly. "God forgive me."

"Abraham," Darla spoke while placing her hand on his cheek to have his attention. "Now, you need him more than you have ever needed anyone, don't you?"

"We need him!" he snapped sharply and slowly rose to his feet slowly. He spoke pointedly, "Darla, he stood above Clay Dobson and murdered an unarmed man in cold blood! He killed five men without giving them the chance to surrender. That's murder! What was I supposed to do? I looked into his eyes and he had no regret, absolutely no remorse! I didn't want him around my daughter."

"Don't justify yourself, Abraham," Darla said softly.

He shouted loudly, "I was justified!"

"Then why are you asking me if you were wrong?"

He sighed and then sat down on a pew tiredly. "Because my soul is in torment. I have never felt as though I was wrong." He looked at his wife with a painful expression. "Darla, I insinuated for him to kill those men who have Elizabeth this morning. I have never felt the way I do. Lord forgive me, but if those men were here, I'd shoot them myself. I would to save my daughter."

Darla smiled slightly. "Matthew loved her very much,

Abraham. He will risk his life to save her now, just like he did years ago."

Abraham sighed deeply. "I've been praying for years that Matthew would never come back here."

"Praise God that he did, Abraham. Praise God!" she said pointedly.

57

John Birch finished his meal as he watched Elizabeth busy herself scrubbing the pan she had cooked the eggs and bacon in. She stood with her back to him with the sleeves of her heavy flannel shirt rolled up. She was well shaped and had beautiful blonde curly hair that hung, loosely tied, down to the middle of her back. John Birch eyed her with a passion he'd not felt for anyone in a long time. It was a rare that such a pretty woman showed her structure in brown riding pants.

"You know your husband would be a fool, to not try to get you back. You're a fine looking woman for having four kids too," he stated from the table. Elizabeth's shoulders tensed at his words. He continued, "Most women seem to plump up with every kid, but quite frankly, I like a little extra on a woman. Not too much, though, you're about right for my taste. I understand the Dobson Gang took a liking to you, too. They were from Texas, you know, the same area I'm from. I guess they raise boys like us to like girls like you down there. The Dobson's were my heroes, you know, and you were the last pretty thing to see them alive." She slowly continued to wash the pan intentionally ignoring his words. He continued, "The story that the deputy gave us was that Marshal Bannister saved you from them. I'm surprised Walt and Clay didn't kill him. I just don't see one boy killing those men, nor do I see them letting you go because of some bleeding boy. I knew those men; they wouldn't let you go that easily. They had good taste in girls just like I do."

Donovan laughed a low-pitched guttural laugh as he leaned back in his chair at the table watching Elizabeth. The two boys watched the men nervously.

John scooted his chair back and kicked his boots up on the table and clasped his hands behind his head. "It seems to me, that you had your chance to be with some great historical men. Big Donovan and me, we're not famous like they were, but there's no other invitation except us right here." He paused to watch her reaction. Her shoulders were tense, but she never replied.

Donovan spoke sarcastically to John, "You mean it's just us up here by our lonesome for a week or two?"

"Well, that's right," he replied. "But at least we got ourselves a pretty woman to cook, clean, and keep us warm at night. Isn't that right, sweetheart?" he asked pointedly. Elizabeth seemed to cringe, but still didn't reply. "I guess she's not talking to us right now," he spoke to Donovan with a chuckle. "I like it better that way myself, don't you?"

Donovan smiled. "It's a fine quality sure enough, but even if she screams, no one's going to hear her up here. Besides, she said it herself, her husband's not coming for her, and neither is Matt, not if he's smart, anyway. It's just us, like one big happy family."

"Oh, the marshal," John replied, "it's too bad I didn't get the chance to see him, I would've done Texas proud to kill that man. If the chance ever comes, I will." He added sarcastically, "One thing's for sure, the deputy won't be coming to your rescue. I don't think you're going to get out of this one, sweetheart."

Elizabeth laughed lightly taking them by surprise. She moved the frying pan to her right hand and grasped it firmly and then explained, "You killed Clyde. Tom won't come for me, that's true. But he can't stop Matt from coming. He may not come for me, but he will come for Clyde's murderers and if Matt doesn't, Charlie will. Clyde was his oldest friend."

"Do you think anyone will travel up here, sweetheart? It's much more likely that they'll search the next town. I hear it's pretty good- sized, almost a city," John spoke casually.

"Who's Charlie, Clyde's drinking buddy I assume?" Donovan asked without concern.

Elizabeth's voice was stronger as she answered, "Charlie Ziegler. The man the Dobson Gang came here to kill." She turned and faced the two men with the pan still in her hand. "He's the bounty hunter that killed the brothers of the Dobson's and Claude Magnus." She continued, "He's also Matt's uncle."

"He's dead," John replied simply. "Lemon Skin O'Malley shot him on the Pike River."

"No, he's been ranching right here. Charlie's alive and well and if you think this place is so well hidden, let me tell you a secret. Matt used to live here and Charlie's been here a thousand times. I wouldn't get too comfortable if I was you. And if you touch me someone will track you down, even if I have to hire them myself!"

Donovan and John both laughed. It was John who spoke first, "Your tune's changed. Where's this hope coming from, anyway? This morning you were hopeless and now all of a sudden you're talking about being rescued by a dead man and maybe even a marshal."

"I don't care what you've heard, Charlie's alive. Like I've said, they'll come for Clyde, if not for me, but they will come. And I will be rescued, I know my Lord will rescue me somehow."

John raised his eyebrow questioningly. "From my experience, sweetheart, the only thing the lord rescues is Bible print shops from starving. I don't think he can save you from us, but if so, where is he?" He lifted his hands questioningly.

"Jesus protected me from the Dobson Gang and he will protect me from you, too."

John laughed for the first time. "Well, if there is a god, he would've been on the Dobson's side, sweetheart."

Elizabeth raised her voice angered. "They were murderers! They were wicked horrible men who got what they deserved. They didn't deserve the gallows, they died like rats in a water barrel and they deserved it! I wish you would've run into Matt because you'd be lying in the cemetery next to your long forgotten heroes, dead! And I would spit on your grave like I do theirs," she spoke squarely to John.

"You'd like that, wouldn't you?" John asked dangerously.

Elizabeth stood tall and spoke frankly, "I would! And I will when Matt finds you."

John raised his eyebrows. "I look forward to the opportunity to kill that son of a..."

"So do I!" she shouted loudly, cutting him off. "You might get away for a while, but you can't outrun the law."

John laughed. "The law? Honey, we've been out-running the law clear from South Texas. Nobody, including the law, knew who we were all the way up here. The only trouble we've had with the law was here with your husband, and I don't think we'll hear anymore from him. Don't forget, sweetheart, even if they do come for you, they'll leave when they see that knife to your throat. They should have no doubt that we'll use it."

"Then use it!" she challenged. "You kidnapped the wrong woman if you think you can frighten me. I am a born again Christian! You cannot kill me, not unless my Lord allows it."

A perplexed expression appeared on John's face.

Donovan laughed. "There you have it, John. She's the only person I've ever met that only god can kill!" He laughed.

John smirked slightly. "Well, Christians aren't supposed to commit adultery are they? Last night you said you had, so you must not be all that great of a Christian."

Elizabeth felt a rush of shame. "I made a mistake."

John stood up. "Oh, that's right, your god forgives the wrongs of you high and mighty Christians, doesn't he?" He stepped towards her with his eyes full of hatred and what she would recognize as evil.

"Don't you come near me! You've already done enough wrong, leave now and you might get away with your lives." she stated fearfully. She held the black cast iron frying pan in her right hand ready to swing it as a weapon.

Donovan's eyes glazed over with fierce wickedness. He also stood up, unable to control his perverse hunger.

John laughed lightly. "Well before we go running off into the cold again, I think we'll have a little fun. Come here, sweetheart." He stepped closer reaching out for her.

Elizabeth swung the frying pan as hard as she could at John's head, but missed. When the momentum of her swing came to its full extent, she tried to pull it back towards his head, but John lunged forward and entrapped her with his arms. She couldn't get out of his clutches and

Donovan was quickly there to strip the frying pan out of her hand.

Elizabeth screamed and brought a hard knee up into John's groin. He momentarily released her and doubled over in pain. She stepped quickly back to the counter and picked up the knife she used to cut the bacon with. She pointed it at Donovan. "Come near me and I'll stab you!" she hissed like a frightened badger in a corner.

Donovan glared at her harshly and faked a forward lunge. She jabbed the knife outward awkwardly. As she drew it back, Donovan lunged at her to grab for the short knife. She jabbed it forward desperately and stabbed the palm of his hand. He cursed and backed away looking at his bleeding hand. "She cut me!" he shouted more surprised than concerned.

John stepped forward quickly and despite Elizabeth's best attempt to stab him, he was too fast for her. He grabbed her wrist and twisted her arm until the knife fell to the floor. He released her arm and threw a hard right fist into her face, which propelled her across the counter then down to the floor. He kicked her in the stomach and then grabbed a handful of her hair and pulled her up to her feet. He wrapped his hands around her and pulled her close to him. She struggled and tried again to knee his groin, but he was expecting it and turned slightly to her side.

"You committed adultery before so it won't hurt you to do it again. Your god will forgive you, now come on!" He began to drag her towards the bedroom he'd slept in.

She dropped down to the floor unwilling to be escorted in there on her own two feet. "Let me go!" she screamed as she struggled to get away from him.

Evan Gray couldn't stand it. He stood by the table concerned and pleaded, "Come on, let her go. You promised you wouldn't hurt her, Mister Birch. Don't!" he yelled. "Donovan, please," he begged.

"Get lost you little pup!" John sneered viciously while he fought Elizabeth for control.

"Let me go!" She fought to free herself.

"Grab her legs!" John ordered Donovan. She screamed helplessly as her body was pulled easily up off of the floor. They carried her towards the cabin's bedroom.

"Help me! Lord, please help me!" she cried out. She glanced desperately at Evan and Rodney Gray. Both of the boys watched in horror as she was quickly carried across the room.

"Guys, don't," Evan pleaded. "She didn't do anything wrong. Let her go!" He grabbed Donovan's arm to stop them.

Donovan shot a fierce glance at Evan. "Get away from me! When we're done, you can have a turn!" He followed John into the bedroom and with his foot kicked the door shut. It slammed hard in Evan's face.

Evan turned to his older brother with a quivering voice, "We have to do something!"

Rodney was scared. "Evan..." He motioned with his empty hands that he didn't know what to do. "Evan, just stay out of it."

Evan grimaced with disgust at his brother. "We can't just sit here and do nothing or we're as guilty as they are. I can't stay out of it. She needs our help and we can't just let them hurt her. It isn't right. So sit there if you want, but I'm helping her."

INSIDE THE ROOM, Elizabeth struggled and fought with everything she could, arms, fingernails, teeth, and legs, while the two men struggled to hold her down on the bed.

Donovan had gotten her boots off, but was having trouble grasping the buttons of her riding pants with her fighting them as she was.

John held her arms roughly and sneered at Donovan impatiently, "Hurry up!"

"I'm trying," Donovan gasped.

She screamed, "Let me go, you bastards!" She fought to break free from John's grasp and twisted her body from side to side and kicked her legs to keep Donovan from unbuttoning her pants.

Suddenly, Donovan cursed in frustration and layed heavily upon her and tried to kiss her. She turned her face away from him, but she couldn't struggle against his weight that crushed down on her. He began to force his hands under her flannel shirt as John cheered him on.

Both men paused to glance at the door as it opened quickly. Evan Gray stepped into the room with Donovan's revolver in his hands and pointed towards the men. "Get off of her!" he said with an attempt to sound authoritative. The revolver shook, despite using both hands to hold it. His eyes revealed the amount of fear in them.

Donovan slowly climbed off Elizabeth and onto his feet. "Evan, put that away," he said softly, nervously. Being on the receiving end of the barrel of his own gun was frightening.

"Not until you let her go. Let her go, Mister Birch," Evan ordered with a cracking voice.

John smiled dangerously. "Go sit down before I take that gun away from you and whip your ass!" His hostility was evident in his voice.

Donovan spoke nervously, "Let her go, John."

"He ain't going to shoot," John scoffed. "I can see it in his scared little eyes. Besides, the idiot doesn't have the hammer cocked. Now backhand the boy and get him out of here!"

"Let her go, Mister Birch," Evan tried to say with more authority and pulled the hammer back until it clicked. "I won't let you do this."

"Let her go, John. Now!" Donovan shouted and physically slapped John's hands off of Elizabeth's wrists. She scrambled at the first feel of freedom and tried to leap off of the bed, but Donovan grabbed a hand-full of her hair to hold her in place. She grimaced in pain with her knees on the hard floor beside the bed. "Okay, Evan, now what?" he asked. "And you better take your finger off that trigger because it doesn't take much to pull it. You don't want to shoot me on accident, not after all I've done for you and your brother."

"Let her go, I said." Evan pointed the gun at Donovan as John slowly stepped closer. His breathing was growing heavy.

Donovan spoke softly, "If I let her go and she takes the gun, then we'll all hang. I'll make you a deal though. We won't touch her, but give me the gun." Donovan held out a hand towards him.

Evan shook his head with large frightened tears growing in his eyes.

Rodney stepped in behind Evan, he looked as scared as Evan did. He was also holding a revolver down at his side. "Mister Moskin, you won't hurt Evan will you?" he asked.

"Of course not," Donovan said sounding sincere. "We got carried away and you're right, we shouldn't have treated her like that. I shouldn't be treating her like this..." He looked at the fistful of blond hair in his hand while she kneeled painfully on the floor. "But, I won't let her go until we have the guns, both of them." He nodded at the one Rodney held.

Rodney spoke anxiously, "How do I know you won't hurt Evan?"

"Oh, for peats sake!" John snapped and stepped forward quickly.

Evan swung the gun towards John and spoke desperately, "Stay back, Mister Birch! I don't want to shoot you."

"Evan!" Donovan scolded. "We're like family, you, me, John and Rodney, nobody's going to shoot anyone. Now please lower the gun. Evan, please," he sounded genuinely caring.

"Don't do it, Evan!" Elizabeth shouted and then cried out in pain as Donovan squeezed his handful of hair and shook her head.

Evan turned the gun back on Donovan. "Let her go!" he yelled, "You said you wouldn't hurt her."

John took advantage of Evan's attention being shifted and quickly stepped forward. Evan tried to bring the gun back towards him, but John was too fast. In one swift motion John kicked Evan's wrists forcing his hands around the gun up towards the ceiling, inadvertently firing the weapon on impact. The bullet went over Donovan's head and into the wall near the ceiling. Shocked by the speed of John's kick and the thunderous percussion, Evan dropped the gun in horror and stumbled backwards and fell against the opened door. John picked up the .44 caliber revolver, cocked the hammer and pointed it at Evan with rage boiling in his eyes. Evan sat terrified.

"Don't shoot him!" Donovan yelled and quickly pulled John's arm down. He had let go of Elizabeth's hair momentarily, and she scrambled on her hands and knees quickly towards the gun Rodney held by the door. Donovan kicked Elizabeth in the stomach and she collapsed to the floor beginning to cry as she curled into a ball.

"Give me that gun!" he ordered Rodney. The revolver was handed over to him immediately.

"Why not shoot him? He tried to shoot me!" John replied angrily.

"Because," Donovan shouted, "that shot just gave our position away!" He cursed and then kicked Evan in the face. Evan immediately covered his face with his hands and curled up on his side while Donovan continued to kick him in a rage. "We would've had our fun and let her go, but no! Now, they'll know where we are and it's your fault!" He finished with another hard kick to Evan's ribs.

"So what?" John asked. "If a posse comes up here, we can out last them. We're warm at least," he offered.

Donovan paced back and forth in thought. "Okay..." he announced, "Rodney, go saddle two horses, quickly."

"Just two?" Rodney asked anxiously.

"Yes, two! You and John are going for a ride." He turned to John. "Remember that rock formation down the trail a mile or so? Set Rodney within those rocks for an ambush, then get back up here."

"Ambush?" Rodney asked awkwardly.

Donovan turned to Rodney and spoke quite seriously, "Yes, an ambush. And if I don't hear you shooting and someone rides up here, my first shot will be at point blank range at Evan! Do you understand what I'm telling you?" he paused for effect. "If you see anyone riding up here, you shoot them or your brother's dead!" Donovan clarified any confusion. He turned back to John. "Give him the Winchester and set up some kind of code that you'll both remember. Hurry up, I'll feel better once he's in place."

"But," Rodney stated fearfully, "I've never shot anyone before."

"Hey," Donovan said cynically, "your brother wanted to

be a hero. So if you want to see him alive again, you'll shoot anyone that rides up that trail. That's the only option you have!" he finished coldly.

"Evan," Rodney spoke while helping his little brother up, "I'll see you later, okay?" He smiled reassuringly to his little brother. "I love you, Evan."

"I love you, too," was all that Evan could say as a tear slipped from his eyes.

Rodney stepped close and whispered in Evans ear, "Stay by Missus Smith. I'll do what I have to, but you stay with Missus Smith. You were right. I'll be back and then we can go home. I promise."

Evan smiled with bloody teeth. "I'll see you soon, Rodney."

58

Matt sat on his horse and stared down below at what used to be the Bannister Ranch. The back of the two-story block style house looked all too familiar, very much as it had when he had lived there as a child. He looked at the large oak tree that his older brothers used to climb on and his mother used to sit under to watch him swing on a rope his father had tied to a thick branch. Matt's chest tightened as he reminisced.

Tom waited quietly for Matt while Charlie and Gabriel rode ahead. After a few minutes, Tom asked, "Has it changed much?"

Matt shook his head sadly without removing his eyes from the property. "Who owns it now?"

"David and Sue Lyman."

Matt nodded. "It's interesting how different a father and son can be. My grandfather built that house and made the Bannister Ranch into the largest and most successful one in the valley. He had a hand in making this State too and built a small empire. He was a man of solid character to say the least. My father lost it. Every acre of it," he said softly. "Well, forgive me, Tom for reminiscing. Let's catch up with Charlie and Gabriel. The last thing you want is Charlie encouraging your son to put on a gun belt."

"A gun belt doesn't worry me too much, just as long as he doesn't teach him to rely on it. Gabriel's a little too interested in gunfighters, especially you," he said with disgust despite himself.

Matt smirked slightly as he rode forward. "Maybe now that he realizes that I'm no different than anyone else, he'll lose interest."

"You've become more famous than Charlie ever was. There's books about you and Gabriel has every one," Tom stated with an edge to his voice again. It didn't go unnoticed by Matt.

Matt shook his head. "I've never sought to be famous. I just did my job." He looked at Tom seriously. "I understand there's an author right down there in Branson who wrote a book about me that called Joseph my nigger?"

Tom shrugged. "I don't know, I never read it." He pulled his reins to a stop and spoke frankly, "The fact is, I've never read anything about you. I've never wanted to. The truth is if I didn't need your help to get Elizabeth back, you wouldn't be here. So let's stop acting like old friends and you're coming over to my house for dinner, because you won't ever be invited!" He continued with a growing venom, "And don't bring up Joseph. I've tried to forget about that day and I've never wanted Gabriel or anyone else to know that Elizabeth and I were there. But your sister ruined that. I swear!" he exclaimed. "My whole life is falling down around me and it's all because of you!"

"Me?" Matt asked inquiringly. "All I did was come home,

Tom. We are old friends by the way or are you trying to bury that too?"

"Friends, Matt?" Tom asked intentionally keeping his volume low. "Yesterday, Elizabeth told me Gabriel wasn't my son. He's yours!" He grimaced painfully. "Now, you tell me what kind of a friend you are!"

A shameful expression crossed over Matt's face as he looked away from Tom buried in guilt.

"Yeah, Matt, it was news to me too. I have no desire to be your friend. On the contrary, after we get Elizabeth back, I don't ever want to see you again!"

Matt nodded, silently pressing his lips together in shame. He had no words to say.

Tom continued, "You had no business being with Elizabeth, you knew she was married! I raised Gabriel for fifteen years thinking he was my son." Tom's heart was broken. His eyes moistened and his voice cracked, "You stay away from him!" He kicked his horse lightly walking past Matt.

"I'm sorry, Tom," Matt said softly. He looked back at Matt with disgust and kept riding. Matt spoke quickly, "I was a kid, Tom."

Tom turned his horse to face him. "I wish I could blame everything I did on being a kid! That's exactly what she said by the way. I guess adulteress minds do think alike! There's nothing you can say that could justify your actions. Absolutely nothing!"

Matt spoke softly, "I won't justify it."

"You can't justify it!" Tom stated harshly, struggling to keep his voice down. "I raised Gabriel thinking he was my son and now I'm told he's not!" he hissed. "You committed adultery with my wife! At least your father destroyed his own family, not someone else's!"

"I didn't mean for things to happen the way they did. I

loved Elizabeth just as much as you did, if not more. Yeah, I wanted her to marry me, I begged her to leave with me..."

"She was married to me!"

"She was miserably married to you! I'm sorry it all turned out like this, but I had no idea about Gabriel. I am sorry, Tom. You don't know how sorry I am, but don't forget you're the one who got to marry her, not me!"

"You just got her pregnant and left town. I was the one deceived," Tom seethed with anger. "While you were out becoming famous killing people, I was raising your kid! Now you're back and I'm paying the price for knowing you, yet again!" Tom shook his head. "Well, one thing's for sure, you're no better father than your own."

"I didn't know I was a father, Tom! And I'm getting tired of the insinuations of being a murderer too by the way," Matt interjected angrily.

"Maybe I should write my side of the Pearl Creek story. Maybe then you wouldn't be such a hero, would you?"

"They were coming after my family!"

"Well, I know what that feels like," Tom snapped. "You prowled around my wife enough! If we save her you better not start prowling around her again either or I'll... Well, I promise you I won't stand for it."

"I'm not prowling around your wife," Matt said calmly. "But if you ever threaten me again I will pull you off that horse and beat you senseless. That, I *can* promise you!"

"I want you out of my town! You've..." A distant gunshot echoed down the mountain. Tom's fury suddenly melted into fear.

Matt's face also transferred back to concern as he looked up the mountain where the sound originated from. He kicked his horse hard to gallop past Tom.

Tom followed right behind him. "Think they shot her?"

he asked anxiously. All of the bitterness against Matt was suddenly gone.

Matt didn't look back. "I don't know," he answered. "I don't know."

59

Matt followed the tracks left in the snow by Charlie and Gabriel and even though he rode quickly, it still took him nearly ten minutes to catch up to them.

Charlie shook his head irritated. "It's about time you boys showed up!" He was disappointed by the length of time it took them to get there.

Matt asked quickly, "It came from the cabin?"

Charlie nodded. "It was dinner, an accident or an execution," he explained simply. His words weren't unheard by either Gabriel or Tom.

"Elizabeth?" Tom asked with dread in his voice.

Matt addressed Tom quickly, "We don't know. A single shot could be anything like Charlie was saying." He turned back to speak to Charlie, "Once we get up there, we better come up with a plan because we're not going to be able to wait them out and I doubt that they're going to invite us in from the cold. With clear skies it's going to be downright cold tonight."

Charlie nodded. "We'll have an hour or two of sunlight

at best, so whatever the plan we come up with had better work. We can only surprise them once."

"We could wait until after dark. They'll feel more comfortable if we do," Matt offered.

"I don't feel like waiting around till midnight," Charlie said sharply.

Tom joined in anxiously, "We need to get up there! Every minute she's with them is a minute closer to her being murdered. It may not be too late to save her if we go now," he spoke anxiously.

"Tom..." Matt said calmly.

Tom interrupted firmly, "I want my wife back, Matt! If you want to wait for the perfect moment then you wait, but I'm going to get my wife. I cannot wait any longer, I won't wait any longer!"

Matt responded quickly, "Don't let your emotions control you! If you go barreling up there like some kind of raging fool, then you're going to get yourself and Elizabeth killed!"

Tom grimaced. "Now that she's my wife you don't want to save her?"

Matt smiled devilishly as he said, "You know, when this is all over, I'm going to pull you off of your horse and knock some common sense into you, Tom."

Tom raised his eyebrows daringly. "I'll look forward to it. You have no idea how much so," he said with a straight face.

Charlie scolded, "You two knock it off! We don't have time for your petty crap!"

Matt chuckled lightly. "We'll settle our score later. Right now let's ride on up. And Tom, we're not forcing anything up there until I say so. Do you understand me?"

"Fine," Tom agreed. "Don't you mess this one up, Matt,

Elizabeth's life is on the line. If she's still alive," he added quietly.

"She's alive." Gabriel refused to believe otherwise.

Tom looked at Gabriel and nodded in agreement.

"Let's get going," Matt said.

60

John Birch had set Rodney in a position within the large granite rocks protruding from the ground. It would give him a good view of the clearing and still be well hidden. Rodney didn't care so much about the view or being hidden, what he did care about was trying to stay warm. The afternoon sun was burning bright in a cloudless blue sky, but it was bitterly cold outside. His fingers and toes were numb, despite wearing his winter jacket and thin wool gloves. He wished he had thought of bringing a blanket or two. He took a moment to peer around the large rock at the tree line he was supposed to watch and waited for someone, who he hoped would not come.

"If someone comes," John had told him when he walked him behind the rock, "you wait until they're close enough to put the bead on their chest and pull the trigger. Donovan says the marshal rides alone, so your best bet is making that first shot a killing one. If you miss, you may not get another shot, so aim well. Stay behind this rock and keep shooting if that happens. If you get him and everything is fine, you fire your gun three times to let us know everything's okay. Three quick shots in procession that'll be our code. Don't forget it's three shots!" he emphasized by holding up three fingers. "If there's shooting and we don't hear three shots, then your brother's dead and you had better be too! Do you understand me?"

"Yes, three shots," Rodney replied. "But what if I'm shot?" he asked anxiously.

John shrugged uncaringly. "Then we won't hear the three-shot code and you won't live long enough to care what happens to your brother. Three shots," John stressed emphasizing by raising three fingers again. He left Rodney to stand alone while he rode back up to the warm cabin leading Rodney's horse behind him.

Rodney would have to wait until it was dark. He didn't have any other choice because his brother's life was dependent upon him doing so. He considered his options, but other than staying in place and doing what he was told, there was nothing else he could do.

He was scared and knew they had made a huge mistake by leaving The Dalles to join up with Donovan and John. All he wanted to do now was leave with Evan and get away from the mess they were in. The sheriff's wife, was a nice lady, but she wasn't Rodney's concern, Evan was. He hoped she would get away too, but he wasn't willing to risk his life or Evan's to save her. Evan, of course, had, but he was always a little more courageous and outspoken than Rodney was. Evan sometimes acted first and then thought about what he'd done later, where Rodney always tried to think things over first. He worried about Evan's safety now that he was alone with Donovan and John. Evan did not have Rodney's cool head to bail him out of trouble if he got into more. It weighed heavily on his mind as he stayed in place watching a frozen clearing amidst the silent trees.

If anyone came up the mountain they would be coming to condemn them all, including Evan and himself. There was a great gamble in letting them pass by or even running to them for help. They could shoot him on sight and that would lead to Evan being killed when he didn't fire the three shots. Even if they listened to him and promised to save Evan, they wouldn't care if Donovan killed him. The Sheriff's wife would be their only concern. On the contrary, if he aimed well and just shot the man down, he and Evan could get away and go home. If anyone came or not, Rodney swore he'd never pick up a gun again. The West had already taken his family and was threatening to take his last surviving sibling and his own life as well. He would not risk his brother's life by allowing anyone to pass by him.

He could not wait for this day to come to an end. He had watched the sun as it slowly crossed the sky and in another hour at most probably, he could go back to the warmth of the cabin. In a few days when it was safe to do so, they could part company with the men and go back home where they belonged. He wished his father had stayed in New York and never heard of the Willamette Valley. Apparently the valley wasn't full yet because it was still drawing people from all over the country. That so-called paradise hadn't been seen by anyone in his family and it wouldn't be either, Rodney was taking Evan back where they came from.

Suddenly, like a slap across the face, he realized that it was Christmas! He had forgotten all about it until now and regretted not telling his brother, *"Merry Christmas"* at the very least. Growing up in a Christian home, he remembered the joy of just being with his parents and three younger siblings on their last Christmas together. It was two years ago and it was a day filled with love, joy and laughter. Now the silence of the forest was the only sound that filled Christmas Day.

As the hour wore on he felt frozen in places that he never knew existed. His teeth chattered and his fingers and toes were numb despite his efforts to keep the blood flowing through them. He was miserable to say the least, but he'd stay out there all night to save his little brother's life if he had to. He couldn't afford to complain about the conditions, he had no choice, but to do as he was told.

He stood up to shake some warmth into his body and as he did, movement from the left side of his peripheral vision drew his attention to four horsemen riding out of a small opening in the trees. He dropped quickly to the ground behind the rock and grabbed his rifle and held it close to his chest. His heart raced with a terror he had never known and his breathing quickened as he peeked down the hill to his left. He would not have seen them if he hadn't of stood up when he did, because he was told to watch the tree line to the east that they had entered the clearing from. The four horsemen rode in from the west side of the clearing which was practically behind him as he watched the east side of the timber line. Rodney recognized the sheriff Tom Smith immediately and his son, Gabriel, who rode beside him. Riding in front of them were two men whom he had never seen before. Both men were wearing long buffalo skin coats and rode slowly as they carefully watched the terrain. Rodney had no choice, he had to save Evan's life. He stood up and aimed the rifle remembering the words of John Birch, "Aim well."

61

"How much farther is it?" Gabriel asked Tom. "It's freezing out here."

Tom shrugged. "Well, the higher we go the colder it gets. Where we're going is up on top, it's not far, maybe another mile. I haven't been up here since I was a kid. Our church used to come up here for a picnic every summer."

"It seems very far for a picnic."

Tom smiled for the first time. "It is. We used to come up here on a Saturday and camp out by the lake and have worship service Sunday morning. It was really a lot of fun back then. We went every year, my parents loved it."

"They went?" Gabriel asked questionably.

"Yeah, they were younger then. Heck, your mother and I were just kids."

"How come we still don't? I didn't know there was a lake up here until Clyde told me."

"Lots of reasons," Tom said simply.

"Oh," Gabriel sounded disappointed.

A shot rang out unexpectedly and Tom fell quickly from his horse. The sound of the bullet hitting its target echoed in Gabriel's ears. He watched in disbelief as his father landed in the snow. Matt and Charlie were both automatically off of their horses with their rifles in their hands. Matt fervently waved Gabriel down off of his horse, but it was happening too fast for Gabriel's mind to comprehend. He looked down at his father and yelled, "Dad!"

Gabriel felt himself being pulled carelessly off of his horse and thrown into the snow by Matt. His eyes were hard and frightening as he yelled angrily, "Get down and stay down!" He looked quickly at Tom.

Tom stared wild-eyed at the blood coming through the fingers of his gloved right hand over his left shoulder. "I've been shot!" he announced weakly, "I've been shot!"

"Stay by him," Matt ordered. Another shot sounded, and the bullet whizzed closely past them, followed by another.

Charlie ran through the snow across the open clearing towards the cover of a large rock more centered to where the shooter was. The depth of the snow and the terrain slowed him down considerably. Knowing that, Matt raised his rifle and fired at the vertical rock formation the two shots had come from. He saw movement behind it and fired again. Quickly he ejected the spent cartridge, and he fired his Winchester again. He knew his shots were ricocheting off the rocks, but his purpose was to keep the shooter occupied until Charlie got behind some cover.

The unknown shooter fired from behind the rock, it was well over Matt's head. Matt returned fire hitting the rock's edge close to where the shot had come from. He ejected the spent cartridge and fired again. It had given Charlie enough time to take refuge behind the rock he was running for. Matt then ran quickly uphill and dove behind a dead stump just as the figure behind the rock fired at him. It was closer, but the bullet whizzed by. With Charlie safely behind some cover and behind a stump himself, Matt took a moment to aim carefully; he didn't have a clear shot, but he could hit close to the shooter. He pulled the trigger and his bullet hit the edge of the rock and ricocheted a few inches from his target's face, the man took a few steps backwards in response. Charlie fired his Spencer rifle and Matt saw the man behind the rock fall quickly to the ground.

Matt jumped up and ran forward with is rifle pointed towards where the man fell behind the vertical rock formation. He reached the edge of the rock and aimed his rifle at the prostrate body of a boy who was no longer a threat. He lay on his back holding is lower right abdomen as blood spilled out onto the snow. The boy's face was youthful and clearly in shock. He appeared to be somewhat coherent though.

"Help me, I'm hit," he begged with the urgency of a dying man.

Matt lowered his rifle and stepped forward quickly. "Is she alive?" he asked, and then demanded forcefully, "Is she alive?"

He nodded, looking at Matt with desperation. "They're going to kill Evan. Please save him. Don't let them kill Evan, please..." he begged weakly. Tears were filling his terrified eyes.

Matt shook his head slightly. "Who's Evan?"

"My brother. I... I'm sorry. I... ha had to shoot or, or they're going to kill..." he swallowed, "my brother... I, I'm sorry."

"They're going to kill your brother if you didn't shoot us?" Matt asked as Charlie arrived. Charlie was out of breath and looked surprised, then troubled to see the young boy lying in a pool of steaming blood sinking into the snow. He was dying fast.

Rodney nodded once to answer Matt.

Charlie interrupted urgently, "Son, do you have a code in case there was shooting?" He grabbed the boy's rifle.

Matt added strenuously, "Come on do you?" Rodney nodded and held up three fingers weakly.

Charlie immediately fired three quick consecutive shots out over the clearing and then tossed the gun aside. He looked at the dying boy. "Stupid damn kid."

Matt spoke softly over Rodney's troubled breathing, "They're apparently going to kill his brother if he didn't shoot."

Charlie frowned.

Matt touched the boy's arm, pressed his lips together forcefully. He spoke softly, "Listen, we'll save your brother. I promise you if we can."

Rodney looked at him with heavy eyes that were growing dim. "Te... tell him I'm sorry, and... I... I love him," he whispered.

"I will," Matt replied softly. He put his gloved hand on the boy's forehead. "Do you know the Lord, son? because you're about to meet him."

Rodney smiled slightly and nodded once. "I know," he whispered and breathed his last. Matt closed his now empty eyes.

Gabriel ran up the hill behind Matt and stopped when he saw Matt kneeling beside the body of Rodney. "My dad's hit bad! He's bleeding a lot. Good Lord, I know him!" Gabriel declared suddenly as he stared at Rodney's lifeless body.

"He's gone," was all Matt said. He stood and picked up his rifle.

"Tend to Tom. I'll take care of the boy," Charlie said sadly.

Matt quickly walked towards where Tom laid, but constantly looked up hill with the expectation of the others riding down. He had seen Tom's shoulder momentarily, but at the time he was far more concerned about the person shooting at them.

"My dad's been hit. He's hurting!" Gabriel explained with emotion taking over in his voice while he followed Matt. Tom was lying in the snow with a fearful grimace on his face. Matt stepped quickly and silently to Tom's side and pulled Tom's hand off of the wound. Matt's expression was cold and focused. "I won't lie to you, Tom, you're losing a lot of blood. We need to stop the bleeding." He stood and walked over to his horse.

"How bad is it? Am I...?" Tom paused taking deep breaths.

Matt ignored him and dug through his saddlebag and pulled out a small ball of twine, he tossed it to Gabriel, who dropped it into the snow. Matt untied his tarpaulin bedroll from the back of his saddle and rolled it open to reach his dry woolen blanket. He took his knife and quickly cut a piece out of his blanket, then replaced his knife in its sheath on his belt. He quickly went back to Tom and knelt beside him with a glance up the mountain side. "Gabriel, keep watch up that mountain! Tom, if we can stop the bleeding, you'll live, but we still need to get you to a doctor, the sooner the better. Let's get that coat off and see what it looks like." Tom sat up with a painful grimace while Matt unbuttoned his heavy brown coat. Carefully, he pulled Tom's left coat sleeve over his shoulder.

Tom cried out as the sleeve came off his arm. Blood soaked his two shirts and seemed to be all over his left side. It streamed down his left arm and all over his right hand which he had been holding over the wound. A tear in his shirt revealed where the bullet had entered into his shoulder, but there was no exit wound.

"The bullets still in there," Matt said as he quickly placed snow onto the piece of blanket. "The cold will help stop the bleeding, hopefully, but you need to get down the mountain as fast as possible, Tom. How are feeling, dizzy, tired?"

"A little dizzy, but I'm not going down the mountain, not until I find out what's happened with Elizabeth. She could be dead for all I know. I won't leave until I have those men in my custody," he spoke defiantly, but he sounded much weaker than Gabriel expected.

Matt draped the piece of blanket around Tom's shoulder vertically and tied it tightly. "She's alive."

Tom turned his head. "How do you know?" he questioned painfully though gritted teeth.

"I asked that boy up there. He also said they were going to kill his brother if he didn't shoot us when we came."

"Who shot me?" He grimaced while Matt pulled his coat sleeve back over his arm. "Which boy?"

Matt called to Gabriel and tossed his knife into the snow in front of him. "Cut me about three feet of that twine." Gabriel took it and hastened to do so.

Matt answered, "I don't know his name, but he said to tell Evan he loved him."

Tom sighed. "Then that's Rodney Gray up there. Is he dead? And won't those men come down here now?"

Matt shrugged. "He is and they could. So let's get you on your horse. Charlie's going to have to run you back to town."

"No, I'm not going!" he protested.

Matt spoke softly, "You have a family, Tom." Gabriel handed him a piece of the twine. Matt took it and tied a rough sling around Tom's neck as he spoke, "That wound needs attention before an infection sets in, and I think your family wants you coming back alive."

"I came up here to get my wife."

"I know you did. But bleeding to death isn't going to save her, now is it? I won't let you risk your life; you have to go."

Charlie Ziegler carried his rifle as he walked quickly through the snow to join them. "How's the shoulder?" His eyes were sharp and alert, but had a new shade of sadness in them.

"He's losing a lot of blood," Matt said. "He needs a doctor, so you're going to have to lead him to town. Gabriel and I will have to finish this."

"Gabriel's not staying here!" Tom protested fiercely. "No way! I don't want my son getting shot. I won't allow it!" For the first time Gabriel didn't argue.

Charlie sighed. "I don't like that idea either! Those men could be setting up another ambush as we speak. If you go get yourself killed, our whole little posse would have failed. They'll cut her throat and high tail it out of here and that's two deaths I don't intend on seeing! I haven't got time to take him down to town. Gabriel can do that just as easily as I can."

"That's right," Tom agreed. "I want you both to go after Elizabeth. You're the only ones who can save her."

"And what if he loses consciousness?" Matt retorted sharply to Charlie. "Gabriel's not going to know what to do, nor does he know the trail down. Tom hasn't got time to question whether he can make it or not, he needs a doctor, and he needs one now! The bullet's still in his shoulder and you know the signs to look for, Gabriel doesn't. I know we all want to get these men, but Tom needs a doctor!" he finished sternly.

Charlie shook his head in frustration. "Get on your horse, Tom." He turned to Matt. "I'm coming back!"

Matt nodded and helped Gabriel to lift Tom onto his saddle. "I want to keep Gabriel with me," he said to Tom.

"No. I told you I don't want him hurt and those men aren't going to care how old he is. If they see Gabriel they're going to kill him just as easily as everyone else they've killed."

Charlie rode his mount over to Tom and grabbed his reins. He looked at Matt with worry in his eyes. "You be careful and watch out for an ambush. That code may not have been right; that boy was in shock. He probably didn't even understand what I asked."

Matt nodded. "I'm not going up the trail, I'm going to circle around to the back side of the cabin. They won't know what hit them." He turned back to Tom and explained, "Tom, I will not risk the boy's life. The only reason I want him here is in case I'm killed. But I promise you, I will get one of them and that leaves only one for Gabriel to shoot with my rifle. Then he can take Elizabeth home. If I go alone and don't succeed, you will never see her again." He paused momentarily, "I'm thinking of your family."

Tom frowned emotionally. "What, that he can kill someone at fifteen and grow up to be like you?"

Matt looked down at the ground momentarily and then looked squarely at Tom. "I pray not. He should grow up having a mother, don't you think?"

Tom's face softened, and he nodded as the emotions slowly filled his eyes. "Gabriel," he said getting is son's attention, "stay with Matt and do what he says." Then he looked back down at Matt, "Take care of my son. I'll never forgive you if anything happens to him." His bottom lip quivered.

Matt agreed with a nod. "Get going you two," he said to

Charlie. Words on both sides were few and hard to say. Charlie kicked his horse and Tom looked back at Gabriel until they were out of sight.

"Well, Gabriel," Matt said, "before anything else, we'd better get off the trail before they do come riding down here."

"Is my dad going to be all right?" Gabriel asked trembling.

"He should be fine. Charlie will take good care of him," Matt said as confidently as he could. Although he knew all too well that gunshot wounds were sometimes deceiving. It was the infection that often ended a man's life and not the wound itself.

62

Donovan Moskin had said little since John took Rodney down the mountain. He mostly paced back and forth or stood nervously peeking out the opened door waiting for John to return. The discharging of the gun Evan held compromised the security of the cabin's location if anyone down the mountain heard it. If they could get through the next twenty-four hours without being found, he'd know they were safe, however the sooner Rodney was in place the better he'd feel. He closed the door and looked over at Elizabeth and Evan. They were sitting in two chairs facing the fireplace with their backs to Donovan. It was the way he told them to sit, so he could keep an eye on them without their eyes burning into him in return.

Evan was frightened and it showed in his skittish blue eyes. Donovan had forcefully put him on the chair in front of the fireplace and he hadn't moved or spoken a word since. He had never seen Donovan react so angrily and it scared him because he knew he was in trouble when John returned. John had never been overly friendly with the boys, but seemed to tolerate Rodney more than him. He didn't know why exactly, but John didn't like Evan much and he was wary of John coming back to the cabin.

Elizabeth tried to comfort him with a warm smile and put a reassuring hand on his knee, but it seemed to do little good. He looked quickly at her and then looked away anxiously. She understood the reason he was frightened, but she was forever grateful to him for his courage to protect her the way that he had. His courage had earned her loyalty, and she was committed to not allow anyone to hurt him or his brother if she could help it, including her husband or Matt. She reached over and tapped Evan's leg. "Hey, Merry Christmas," she spoke quietly with a sad, but sincere smile. "We've both had better ones I'm sure."

He nodded anxiously with a frightened expression.

She continued softly, "When we get back to town, how about I cook you and Rodney the biggest Christmas dinner you've ever seen?" He nodded with a nervous tight-lipped smile. She grabbed hold of his cold hand. "It'll be okay," she reassured him.

He whispered through his emotional strain, "They're going to kill me."

Her eyes narrowed. "No, they're not, Evan. I won't let them. You and Rodney are coming to live with me when this is all over."

"You mean that?" he said a little too loudly. He was amazed by her words.

She nodded with a warm motherly smile. It immediately disappeared when Donovan's big hand landed on her shoulder from behind. She immediately shrugged his hand away.

"What are you two whispering about?" Donovan demanded.

"Nothing," Evan said meekly.

"What did you say?" Donovan demanded roughly.

Elizabeth looked back at Donovan with a stern expression. "I said help's probably on the way!"

"Don't get your hopes up. If anyone comes up this mountain they're going to get shot, shot at anyway. And that's all the warning we need. Besides, they all know the consequences for following after us, so if they're shot at... well, I doubt they'll be so determined to keep coming. Not if they care about you, anyway."

"What about Matt?" Elizabeth asked questioningly.

"Matt's a human being," he said as he walked back over to the door to peer outside. "A bullet will stop him just as quickly as it does anyone. Besides, we have you, you seem to forget about that fact fairly often." He smiled as he held the door open and looked outside. "John's back. By the way, he'd love to see Matt come up here."

John Birch came in the back door shortly thereafter. He was cold and stood next to the fireplace in front of Elizabeth and Evan to warm himself. Evan stared at the floor holding perfectly still, trying to appear invisible, Elizabeth thought.

John took notice of him just the same. "Yeah, you just sit there and shake, you little yellow bastard," he said with great indignation in his voice and hatred in his eyes. "You're not such a brave little boy now that I'm armed, are you? I should slap the snot out of you!" He quickly slapped the side of Evan's head with his right hand.

Evan put his hand to his cheek and fought the tears that filled his eyes. He refused to look up, but it was obvious that he wanted to sob.

John asked with disgust. "Are you crying? What are you a little girl? Maybe we should ride back down to that old woman's house and grab you a dress! I think I'll start calling you Sarah, does that sound all right with you, Sarah? Well?" he demanded an answer.

Evan shook his head as a tear dropped from his eyes onto his hand. He quickly wiped his eyes without lifting his head. "No," he said meekly.

John bend over to speak close to Evan's ear, "I have never seen a weaker boy than you, Sarah. You make me sick!"

Evan's body convulsed, and he broke into unexpected sobbing with his face buried in his hands. Elizabeth reached over to comfort him and wrapped her arms around him.

She glared at John with disgust. "Why don't you leave him alone? He's just a boy, for crying out loud!"

"I don't know about that," John said questionably. "He cries like a little girl if you ask me."

"You're a pathetic excuse for a man, do you know that? It must be common for men from Texas to get a feeling of strength from terrorizing young boys. I'd like to see how scary you really are when you meet Matt someday. We'll see how scary you are then!"

John's eyes were empty, except for a hollow rage that left no doubt that he was no stranger to hurting others. "Woman, I don't try to scare anyone... I just do. And for good reason, because it wouldn't bother me none to shoot you, that kid, or his brother! But as far as that marshal goes, it's a good thing we haven't met yet. He wouldn't be as famous as he is if we had. I look forward to killing him if he has the guts to come up here."

"That letter might work on Tom, but Matt's not naïve about men like you." Elizabeth looked back towards Donovan. "What about you, Mister Moskin? You apparently know him; do you really think you two will be the ones to finally kill Matt Bannister? Do you really think you can out smart him on the same mountain he grew up on?" she asked with disgust.

Donovan hesitated before answering. "The difference is, we expect him. We already have an ambush waiting, and if he comes up here, he'll meet the author of that Bible he carries around."

"Bible?" John questioned unknowingly, "He's a Christian or is that some kind of joke? He can't be all that dangerous if he's a Christian!" he smirked.

Donovan answered with a shrug, "It's not a joke."

John smiled humorously. "I've never met a Christian who was a threat to me; hell, all of the Christians I've met were pretty well threatened *by* me. You didn't tell me he was a Christian. Hell, if he comes up here we'll just set a plate of food outside and when he gets down on his knees to give thanks, we'll shoot him," he finished with a sarcastic smile.

"Yeah, you do that," Donovan said without humor.

"Oh come on, Donovan! If he brings a posse up here, we'll start singing a hymn or two and when they stand up to join in, we'll open fire!" he laughed for the first time.

Donovan shook his head with a smile. "Yeah, that's funny, but don't take him lightly. He really is the last person we want to have on our trail."

"He's very dead if he comes near me," John promised. "I don't know what you're worried about. Christians are soft like little Sarah here, weak little crybabies," he mocked Evan before looking back up to Donovan. "Christians are a bunch of fools in my opinion! Hell, they're so weak minded that a book dictates their life, a badly written book at that. I've heard preachers talk their nonsense and then ask for an offering, like I'm going to buy into their sales pitch. I would rather spend my money on a bottle of whiskey and a good time. At least I'd get something for my money, even if it is just a headache the next morning," he laughed.

John looked at Elizabeth and continued, "My god doesn't expect me to cower down to anyone. I'm my own god, sweetheart! A real man makes his own decisions and backs his own words up with action." He emphasized by revealing a tightened fist. "You folks read those stories in the Bible and devote your lives to an ancient book and get walked on and spit on for what? To make some invisible sun-shiny god happy?" He paused to look distastefully at Elizabeth. "It takes a weak man to be a Christian. And I am not a weak man! Like I said, I make my own way."

Elizabeth looked at John evenly. "Matt was a Christian when he killed the Dobson Gang. In fact, he wanted to be a Reverend, unluckily for you, he didn't become one."

"I'm getting sick of hearing about the marshal! Where is he?" John yelled lifting his empty hands. "He's not here, and he's not coming! And even if he does, he's not riding back down!"

Elizabeth answered calmly, "I believe in God and I do believe what the Bible says, every word of it. You can mock it if you want to, but the Bible says you won't get away with mocking God. I don't know if the Lord will lead Matt up here or not, but I do know Jesus will save me."

John's eyes hardened as he took off his gun belt and tossed it onto the bed close to Donovan. "You think Jesus is going to save you? Let me show you how well you can depend on your invisible god!" he snarled and quickly grabbed Elizabeth by her hair and viciously yanked her out of her chair.

She screamed and tried to pry his hand loose, but to no avail. Evan stood up quickly to help her, but he was stopped cold by John's eyes, they were savage and unrelenting. John's voice was cold, "Sit down! Donovan tie him up."

He pulled Elizabeth's face close to his by her hair and snarled, "I'm sick and tired of listening to you!" He yanked her across the room and flung her onto the bed forcefully. He then jumped on top of her and sat on her chest to hold her arms down. "Hurry up!" John yelled at Donovan as he stared down at Elizabeth's struggling face.

"Get off of me!" she screamed and struggled to break free.

Evan screamed, "Get off of her, you son of a bitch!" He was putting up a fight until Donovan hit him with a hard right-handed fist. Evan fell to the ground holding the side of his head, and Donovan easily picked him up by his hair and forced him into the chair. Evan sobbed while Donovan tied him up with the same rope Elizabeth was tied with earlier. Big Donovan Moskin was soon standing by the bed with a childlike excitement on his face. "Here," he said, "I'll hold her arms."

Elizabeth screamed loudly and tried to fight desperately, but Donovan's strong arms held her pinned tightly to the hard mattress, leaving John's hands free. He put both of his hands on her cheeks and forced her to look at him while he leaned down and glared at her with a sneer on his lips. "Where's your invisible god now, huh?" he snarled. "Where is this Jesus? Call to him!"

Elizabeth spit into his face.

He threw a viciously hard opened right hand downward across her face, which immediately reddened her cheek. He followed through with a hard fist into her face, causing her nose to bleed. Elizabeth was stunned momentarily by John's blow. "Where's your god, woman?" John breathed heavily. "Huh?"

Evan began to yell for them to stop. His cries were desperate, pitiful and helpless.

Elizabeth recovered from the blow and felt the warmth of her blood run down her cheek towards her ear. She may have been overpowered and helpless, but she refused to lay there and endure what they had in mind. It was better to fight and die trying to survive than to lay still and surrender before dying. They were not going to let her go either way. She was a Christian and had nothing to fear of death, so she would fight them to her last breath. She struggled with all the rage she could find and yelled out, "Jesus help me!"

John paused and smiled bitterly. "My name's John, not Jesus. I don't think Jesus can help you anyway, darling." He laughed with sadistic delight. He used his hands to hold her face and leaned forward to kiss her... Then a rifle shot echoed up the mountain.

Both men quickly let her go as they jumped up off of the bed. They were suddenly much more concerned about the gunshot than her. More shots followed one after another then a single shot rang out sounding different from the others and then silence.

"That wasn't my Winchester," John said worriedly.

Elizabeth quickly went over to Evan and began to untie him. She wiped the blood from her upper lip and continued with the rope while the two men opened the door to look outside.

"By my count there are at least two people that fired back. We might have some company." John buckled his gun belt around his waist.

Evan's voice grew with anxiety. "Were they shooting at Rodney?" he asked and then repeated more urgently, "Were they shooting at Rodney?"

"Yes!" Donovan yelled towards Evan and stared back out

the opened door. "Why the hell they didn't put windows anywhere else except for the back of the cabin I don't understand!" he complained. It was obvious that he was concerned.

John said, "That wasn't my gun, someone's coming."

Donovan nodded.

"The marshal?" John asked.

Donovan nodded. "Maybe," he answered softly, "But he usually rides alone."

John took a deep breath. "Well, if he's got the guts to come up here now, we'll be ready for him."

Evan asked his toughest question yet, "What about Rodney? Where's Rodney?" No one answered him.

Elizabeth was stunned. She didn't expect to hear gunshots echoing up the mountain, but it was one of the most beautiful sounds she'd ever heard. Her spirit was rejuvenated with each bullet fired, but now her spirit fell with the realization that Rodney could be dead. She sighed heavily and was about to comfort Evan when three quick shots echoed up from below.

John Birch smiled and spoke with great relief evident in his voice, "It's all right, Rodney's okay! Whoever came up here is either dead or on the run." He laughed before explaining, "That's the signal that everything's okay!"

Suddenly Elizabeth's hope of being rescued fell. Whoever came up after her was either dead or leaving her behind. Through her own tears of hopelessness, she watched Evan's face spark to life with relief and excitement. His brother was all right.

"Whew!" Donovan laughed, "I'm glad Rodney's down there. We might have been caught with our pants down!" He laughed, joined by John.

John turned to Evan with a pleased smile. "Sarah, your

brother has just won your life back." He sat heavily on the edge of the bed and grabbed his head with both hands and sighed heavily. "I think I'll wait a half hour or so, then ride down and find out what happened. I don't want to ride straight into a gun fight just in case Rodney's got the taste for killing now." John spoke sarcastically to Elizabeth, "Maybe Rodney is the one that'll end the marshal's life, right here on the mountain he grew up on. If so, I'll bring the dead marshal's badge up here for you."

Elizabeth sat in the chair beside Evan and began to sob into her hands. Evan, now untied, put a hand on her shoulder to comfort her like a concerned son would his mother.

"Where's your faith now?" John asked in a belittling manner. "Where's this lord of yours, anyway? The only thing that can save you now is how cooperative you are willing to be a little later tonight," he said with the same predator eyes he had earlier.

63

Matt and Gabriel followed Charlie and Tom down the mountain for about two hundred yards before turning back up the mountain through the cover of the trees. Matt was alert and watchful as he pondered every possible option the outlaws could have. He hadn't spoken to Gabriel nor did he have time to feel awkward about being alone with his son. His thoughts were on what Donovan might try to do when he realized his back was against the wall. The most dangerous people and animals alike were trapped ones that had no other alternative than to fight for their life. Donovan knew even if he surrendered, he would be hung for murder. Matt had given him a large enough lead to gain some confidence in his escape and let his guard down a bit, but he hadn't. He set up an ambush with the expectation of being trailed. Matt smiled slightly when he realized Donovan was expecting him.

"Marshal Bannister, is my dad going to be all right?"

Matt had almost forgotten about Gabriel riding behind him. "Should be."

"Is my mother really, okay?"

"According to that boy, she's still alive," he replied as he ducked under a branch.

"I hope so," Gabriel stated. He couldn't tell if his chattering teeth were caused by his nerves or from the cold, but it was obvious when he spoke. "I didn't know until last night that my parents were the ones with you. I didn't know it was Miss Jackson's brother that they killed either."

Matt stopped his horse and turned towards Gabriel. His eyes didn't look mean nor angry, just quite sincere. He nodded with a sad expression. "His name was Joseph, and he was my best friend. We were all best friends. Then one day everything changed." He took a deep breath and continued, "I was your age, Gabriel. And I was a thousand times more terrified than you are right now. If you can imagine that. They murdered my friend, and by the grace of God, they let your parents go. I went back for Joseph, and then I went back for blood. No one talks about it because no one wants to. Me either, but I'm not that lucky. I'm the one that shot those men."

"Is that why you left Willow Falls?" Gabriel asked curiously.

Matt looked at the familiar facial features of his own son. How could Matt tell Gabriel that the moment of his own conception was the reason he had left Willow Falls? Tears filled his eyes unexpectedly as the old heartache of leaving Willow Falls and Elizabeth behind was exhumed. The unexpected tears grew so thick that Gabriel became blurred. Matt smiled painfully and then shook his head. He struggled to sound strong; "No," he said softly and turned his horse quickly. "No more questions, Gabriel. We have to go."

"Is it true that you were courting my mother?" Gabriel asked quickly. "Mister Ziegler said my grandfather wouldn't allow her to see you anymore after you killed the Dobson Gang."

"Gabriel," he turned his horse to look at Gabriel impatiently, "we don't have time to talk. We need to get up to that cabin before dark or before one of them rides down and finds that boy. So no more talking! We need to hurry," he said frankly.

"I'm sorry, Marshal Bannister. I just can't believe that no one's ever told me these things. Just the other night I asked my mother who the girl was that was there that day. How was I supposed to know it was her? I can't believe it was my own mother and father." He paused and asked quietly, "Did you love her?"

Matt frowned noticeably. "I did," he said simply. "Listen, when we get your mother back home, I'll answer any questions you have. I'll even sign that book if you want me to, but right now, I haven't got time. I need you to shut up and ride!" he finished sharply.

64

Elizabeth sat in a chair beside Evan staring at the far wall lost in her own thoughts. Unknown to the others, she was devastated. For a moment, hope had shown its face, but it had disappeared as quickly as it had risen. Whoever came to rescue her had apparently failed and left her in the hands of two men who would terrorize her and then send her to face the Lord, eventually. She had believed that God would deliver her from the hands of these godless men, but God hadn't deliver her. She had held on to the Bible's promises like a flame on a dark night, but those three consecutive gunshots were like a God-given slap across her face. Her fate was simply in the hands of her captors and they could do as they wished since there was no one coming stop them. In a moment of despair, she considered doing exactly what they wanted, but it was only a brief thought. She would fight them to the death no matter what. It was better to die fighting than to surrender to the torture of their abuse, only to be killed anyway. She would never live to go back down the mountain and see the faces of those she loved the most, her children and her husband.

Maybe it was an act of mercy the Lord was choosing not to rescue her. The good Reverend would be able to keep his reputation and Tom would be able to keep his honor without divorcing her. The town of Willow Falls may never know, but what a shame that his last memory of her would be blackened by her confession of adultery. What a painful sting it was knowing her legacy would be remembered for that. She had lost everything that was important to her in a single day and nothing was more painful than realizing that she'd never see her four children again. It was too much to bear, and she buried her face into her hands and began sobbing heavily from deep within.

"Ohhh..." Donovan mocked her with a smile, "What's the matter, sweets, are you afraid?" he asked without any compassion to his voice. "Crying isn't going to do you any good. We're not moved by your tears. Tom might be, but he's not here. I mean that literally, he could be face down in the snow!" He laughed.

"They know where we are," John said soberly. "And I'm not confident that boy didn't miss every shot he took now that I think about it. So I wouldn't count on anyone being dead quite yet."

"It's freezing outside. No one's coming up here after dark. Hell, by the time they get here tomorrow, if they come at all, we'll be halfway to Canada."

John shook his head. "After we catch a boat back to California, you mean. I'm never coming back to this part of the country again."

Donovan chuckled. "That's pretty brave talk from a guy who hates water."

"I don't like being cold either. If you're thinking Canada, I'm going my own way," he stated determinedly.

Donovan smiled. "Our welcome's up here in the West

for sure. We'll have to travel east and settle in New York or Florida. Some place where the chances of running into somebody we know on the street isn't too likely."

John nodded towards Evan. "Cry baby Sarah there and Rodney will be in New York."

Donovan tightened his lips thoughtfully. He spoke without any conviction in his tone, "They won't say anything to anyone."

"I don't believe that," John said with a threatening tone to his voice. "They'll only slow us down. We need to dispose of them up here and disappear. You know as well as I do that this one's going to turn us in as soon as he can. I'm not going to risk that happening."

Evan stared at the floor as a wave of petrifying fear rolled through him. He looked up at Donovan with desperation in his eyes.

Donovan looked at Evan and spoke softly, "We'd better keep him around, he's a good pawn to hold over his brother. And that young fella down the hill earned his dinner tonight. He'll be useful later, too."

"We haven't got any dinner tonight! This worthless pawn, as you called him, forgot to pack up the food I put on the counter! He was too concerned about the misses there! Speaking of which, I ain't taking no for an answer tonight, sweetheart. So you might as well start thinking about enjoying it. And you," he snarled at Evan, "might wanna stay curled up in the corner like a whipped pup, or I'll put you out of your misery tonight! We should've left both of you snot-nosed toe-heads in the gutter where we found you."

John then looked at Elizabeth with disgust as she cried softly into her hands. "What are you crying about? You said your husband was going to divorce you anyway. So look at the bright side, if the boy actually killed him, you'll be free."

She slowly turned her head to look up at him hopelessly. "Why don't you just kill me and run? If you left now, you'd get away,"

"Oh, when the times right we will. But I have plans that you may not appreciate as much as I do. If you're nice about it you might just live to go home and raise your kids."

Donovan smiled wickedly. "You're gonna have to earn the right to go home. You might be the only woman in the world who had Matt Bannister's baby and Donovan Moskin's. That would be something, huh?" he chuckled.

"Yeah, she could join a freak show with all those babies by different daddy's," John said coldly.

Donovan smiled. "The traveling whore show," he offered with a laugh.

John smirked. "For a pious Christian woman, you sure get around. Hell, play nice and I might even toss you a dollar or two to get your new life started. If your husbands dead, you'll be whoring before the New Years to feed all of those bastard kids you have." He addressed Donovan, "We should take her with us and rent her out along the way."

Elizabeth glared at John vehemently. "You'll have to kill me first."

John laughed. "You wouldn't be the first woman I killed. So don't think I won't. You're a pretty woman, but that's all the use I have for you. That and cooking up some food if we *had* some!" he emphasized to Evan.

"I wouldn't cook for you anyway," Elizabeth stated dryly.

"You'll do what you're told!" John snapped quickly with hardened eyes as he glared at her.

Elizabeth held eye contact as she spoke slowly, but with every word her disdain was evident, "I cooked what we had this morning. If you're hungry there's a few eggs and a jar of peaches, go make it yourself. I'm not afraid of you. You're nothing more than a waste of human flesh. You disgust me and I never hated anyone more than I hate you and your disgusting friend!"

For a moment, John said nothing leaving a tense silence in the cabin. Donovan snickered lightly and said, "You know my brother and his wife hated each other when they met too. It happens sometimes, people hate each other at first and then they fall in love. The sheriff's got a broad chest and it would be hard for Rodney to miss. If he hit his mark, she's more than likely a single woman now. You might want to think about that John, she could be the love of your life. You know what they say, the lord works in mysterious ways," he laughed.

John smirked. "Could be. What do you think, sweetheart? Do you think if I rode down the mountain and found that you're a widow we could make a go of it? Well, if I find him down there, I'll bring his badge back, and we'll just consider that it's your gods will for us to team up. We'll have to skip the wedding and just have the honeymoon in the back room for now. Of course, we'll have to leave your bastard children behind because I don't like kids. Yeah, under the right circumstances, I think I could come to like you."

Elizabeth stared at the floor while a helpless void opened up in her soul. She felt like she was falling further down into a bottomless pit of pure blackness. "Would you please just leave me alone," she said quietly and wiped the tears from her eyes.

"Well actually now that I'm getting excited to know what's down there and our future, yes! I'll leave you alone. But I'll be back in about half an hour probably to get started on our lives together. I mean even if he's not dead, he's still going to divorce you. So either way, I think it's meant to be.

Trust me, love, you'll be thanking your god before you know it," he said with a sarcastic smile. He looked at Donovan. "I'm going down to get him."

"Hold up a minute," Donovan said. "I gotta go use the privy while there's some light out. It'll be nice to use one without the deputy standing by the door. Wait here until I come back, I won't be long." He grabbed some old newspaper by the wood stove and walked out the back door.

As the back door closed, John looked at Elizabeth and said, "Won't it be kind of ironic if I bring Rodney back and he killed your husband? How you gonna feel about those two bastards then?" John mused.

Evan looked up quickly and said, "He wouldn't do that intentionally. He only would because you guys made him!"

"Shut up!" John yelled and suddenly back handed Evan across the face with an unexpected right hand. The force of it knocked him out of his chair onto the floor. He remained on his hands and knees with his face down in his hands. He cried silently.

John continued to yell at him, "I didn't ask you, did I? I told you just a few minutes ago to curl up in the corner and stay there! Don't speak, don't move, don't even look at me, you little piece of..."

"Leave him alone!" Elizabeth screamed loudly as she stood up and glared at John. "Just leave him alone! You are the piece of crap, not him! He is more of a man right now at fifteen then you will ever be! Are you such a coward that you have to manhandle women and children to feel like a man? You make me sick!"

John tilted his head slightly and glared at her. "Sit down," he ordered slowly, but dangerously.

"No," she replied.

"Woman, I am telling you to sit down! I won't say it again."

Elizabeth looked unwaveringly into his fierce eyes. "Go to hell!"

John slapped her with a hard right hand, that sounded as painful as it was. The fierce blow knocked her to the floor leaving her momentarily stunned with a stinging cheek and the taste of blood in her mouth. She looked up at John with fiery eyes layered by tears. "You're a coward! You can hit a woman and smack a boy around, but I bet you didn't say much when Tom was around did you?" she asked as she slowly stood back up. "I bet you were scared to death when you were arrested. Tom told me you didn't say much, but you haven't shut up since we've been here. It must be easy to be the tough man when it's just you and that tub of lard, Donovan. It's easy to be a big man when it's just two soft-hearted boys and a woman to intimidate! Well, I'm not scared of you anymore. I grew up around tough guys, and I mean real tough guys, like Charlie Ziegler, Darius Jackson, Matt Bannister and his brothers, Cliff Jorgensen, and of course my husband. And perhaps the toughest of them all on me, was my father. So don't think you can slap me around and threaten to kill me because I see through you! Oh yeah, you're tough, but underneath of all of that fury and hatred for life, you're nothing more than a scared coward!" she spat out furiously. She added quickly, "Maybe you're the one who should be called, Sarah."

John immediately threw a hard right fist towards her face. Expecting him to do precisely that, Elizabeth brought her left arm up to protect herself. The blow was hard and powerful, and although it connected with her forearm she was knocked to the ground by its force. Though not as stunned as she was a moment before, her forearm ached severely.

John stood over her and yelled, "I'm not afraid of anyone or anything! I have never backed down from a fight from any man, woman or child! You're damn right, I haven't! Do you want to call me Sarah? Go ahead and say it, you self-righteous whore!" he yelled loudly and kicked her in the stomach. She curled up in a ball to protect herself as he kicked her again. The square toe of his boot hit her with great force as she squeezed her body into the tightest ball she could trying to protect her ribs and face with her arms.

Evan stood up and ran forward without thinking about it and pushed John away from her with all the strength he could. "Stop it! You're going to kill her..." He stopped with his mouth still opened and stared at John's revolver which was suddenly pointed at him. John had pulled it and had it aimed at Evan in the few seconds it took for him to regain his balance after being pushed.

"I've had it with you! That was the last straw and now you're gone!" he said coldly with every intent of shooting him.

"Don't, please!" Elizabeth said from the floor. "John, he's just a kid. Please don't. I will do anything, but don't shoot him."

"Anything?" he emphasized while sneering at Evan.

"Yes, anything. But only if you don't hurt him or his brother."

Evan shook his head. "No, Misses Smith, don't do that."

"Shut up!" John ordered him. He spoke to Elizabeth, "Donovan was right, the boy is a pawn of value. My day just couldn't get any better than that." He smiled slightly and holstered his revolver. He spoke to Evan, "Go back to your corner, pup."

Elizabeth slowly stood back up to her feet. Her arms ached from the kicks they received and it showed on her tired and still reddened face from the earlier slap she had received. "You let those boys go and I'll do whatever you want."

John smiled. "Now you're making...." he stopped as he heard a noise outside of the cabin. He listened...

"You let Evan ride out of here right..."

"Shh!" he demanded and drew his revolver slowly. He walked slowly towards the front door. "I heard someone walking outside and I don't think it's Donovan."

65

Gabriel was cold even though he lay on Matt's tarpaulin and was covered by his blanket. They had left their horses some distance back in the forest and carefully crept to a position well hidden behind the tree line, on a slight hill that over-looked the cabin. The side of the cabin that they watched had no windows to see inside, it was just a log wall with a large river rock fireplace at its center. They waited and listened for any sound coming from inside. Donovan's natu-rally loud voice carried, but was seldom heard over the raised voice of another man.

"What's the plan?" Gabriel asked softly, in a shivering voice. He was getting colder by the minute and didn't think he could stand it for much longer. He had dressed in his warmest clothes, but they were proving to be very insuffi-cient against the cold. The longer they waited, the grayer the shade of day became and the colder he felt.

Matt seemed perfectly content to lie in the snow with his gloved hands and warmth of his buffalo hide coat with his head covered by the thick hood. "There's no plan, just opportunities," Matt whispered. "We wait."

"Wait for what?" Gabriel asked, his voice trembled.

Matt frowned slightly. "For the Lord to give us an opportunity."

"Like what?"

"I don't know. We'll wait and see."

"It's freezing out here. I'm freezing to death!" Gabriel whined with a shivering body.

Matt looked at Gabriel irritably. "Not yet you're not, but it was just as cold earlier when you had the chance to leave!"

"Yeah, but I wasn't this cold!"

Matt sighed with frustration and rolled to his back and pulled his thick buffalo hide gloves off to unbutton his coat. "Wear this for a while," he sounded quite irritated about it, as he sat up to pull the coat down over his shoulders.

The sound of the cabin's back door opening caused Matt to lie down onto his back quickly with his coat caught half way down at his elbows. Both of his arms were pinned beneath him. He tried to free them and peek over the snow at the same time, but his body weight on the long coat made it nearly impossible to move. He dared not breathe a whisper and laid motionless as he watched Donovan Moskin walk loudly across the twenty yards between the cabin and the privy. Matt's heart pounded fearfully. If Donovan looked up the hill to his right, Matt would be in clear view and helpless with his arms pinned underneath him. He had never been more vulnerable in his career, and all because of a cold and whining boy. Matt's life hinged on Donovan's peripheral vision and Gabriel remaining absolutely silent and still. If the boy moved or whispered to any degree Matt knew his life could be ended, and if not his, Elizabeth's very well could be. They would lose the element of surprise if a single motion or sound was noticed by Donovan. The very contrast of his dark coat against the snow had a probability of being noticed. Knowing the risks and helpless to do anything about it, Matt could only watch Donovan walk closer to the outhouse and pray that he would not look towards him. If he did, Donovan would be able to pull his revolver and shoot two or three times before Matt could get his coat off and return fire. Matt exhaled a relieved heavy stream of steamed breath as Donovan reached the outhouse door and stepped inside without so much as glancing up towards him.

Matt rolled to his knees and stood up quickly to pull his arms free and tossed the coat carelessly down to Gabriel. He kept his eyes on the privy while he knelt down on one knee close to Gabriel to whisper, "Do you know how to use a rifle?" he asked while handing his rifle to Gabriel.

Gabriel nodded. He could tell Matt was upset by the close call with the coat.

Matt stared pointedly into Gabriel's eyes. "I'm going down there. If I fail, it will be up to you to save your mother, do you understand that?" he asked, and then continued without waiting for a response. "Don't shoot at anyone or let them know you're here until they go to get their horses. Shoot the one who's nearest to your mother first. Don't miss!" His eyes burned into Gabriel the importance of not missing. "If you have to, shoot her horse or shoot her, but don't you dare let them take her! Aim and shoot, don't think about it or hesitate, just put the bead on their chest and pull the trigger. And don't shoot at anyone until you have a shot. Got it?"

Gabriel nodded. He felt more frightened than cold.

Matt took a deep breath and exhaled. "My gloves are there, wear them to warm your hands up. Remember, stay calm, it doesn't do any good to panic, ever! Like God says, *be strong and courageous.*"

427

Matt then drew his revolver and stepped cautiously down the hill through knee deep snow towards the side of the cabin. His eyes watched alertly, turning his head from the outhouse in the back of the cabin to the cabin's front corner. As he neared the fireplace, his pace slowed considerably to approach the wall as quietly as possible. His time was short, and he'd have to act fast due to the knowledge that his tracks would be seen by Donovan as soon as he stepped out of the privy. Matt listened to the pleading voice of Elizabeth to spare someone and the bitter and mean voice of another man, who had to be John Birch. Matt's Colt was in his right hand, while his left-hand fingers twitched nervously. He decided to go around to the front of the cabin and go in through the door to avoid a cross fire if he got between John and Donovan. He stepped towards the corner cringing with every slow step as it crunched loudly under his feet despite his efforts to keep his feet light. His heart pounded as it suddenly went quiet inside of the cabin and his footsteps sounded all the louder. He looked behind him towards the back corner to make sure Donovan hadn't yet noticed him and stepped forward slowly. The only sound Matt could hear was his own pounding heart and the snow crunching under his feet as he stepped closer to the corner of the cabin. He took a deep breath when he heard boot steps inside moving slowly, lightly towards the front door. Matt's thumb pulled the hammer of his Colt back until it clicked far too loudly in the deadening silence of the mountain. Whatever the caliber of man that was inside, knew Matt was there, and with one more step Matt would be at the front corner where they would meet. Matt said a silent prayer, took a deep breath and stepped to the corner and turned towards the door.

The front door exploded open and John Birch ran

outside with his revolver pointed towards the corner of the cabin. He fired quickly in a fanning motion at the sight of Matt, he got one shot off, narrowly missing him, but Matt was already leveling his revolver at John. Matt fired almost simultaneously in quick return. The explosion in the center of John's chest was rapidly followed by another. Matt had placed two shots into John's chest and watched John's face contort into terror as he fell backwards into the snow. He was already dead.

Matt quickly slipped around the corner of the front door with his revolver immediately pointed at a young blonde haired boy who stood near the foot of the bed in the middle of the room. The boy wasn't armed and stared with wide petrified blue eyes at the barrel of Matt's Colt.45 and then up at the hard and dangerous eyes that glared at him behind the revolver. Matt's eyes softened a touch when he saw Elizabeth standing against the wall beside the fireplace. A surge of anger burned within him as he noticed the abrasions and bruises on her face. His eyes went back to Evan burning hotter than they did before.

"Matthew don't!" Elizabeth blurted out quickly. "He's my friend!" She looked at him with utter disbelief that he was really there.

"Get out of the way!" he ordered Evan, as his eyes focused towards the windows at the back of the cabin. Elizabeth stepped forward and pulled Evan by the back of his coat collar towards the wall where she was.

Donovan Moskin was running quickly towards the back door. They could see him through the kitchen windows. Donovan could have seen Matt plainly standing in the cabin had he looked, but he was too terror struck to be observant. He ran to the back door with his revolver in his hand.

Matt stepped to the middle of the room and raised his

gun expectantly. The back door flew open and Donovan burst through it in a frantic rush. His worry turned to horror when he saw Matt standing side-ways before him with the barrel of his Colt already aimed at him. Donovan in a sudden panic tried to raise his revolver as fast as he could.

Donovan felt the compression in his chest and fell to his back almost in a dream state. He saw the ceiling boards and tried to get back up, but he couldn't catch a breath of air nor could he find the strength to sit up. It was then that he realized that he'd been shot and the knowledge of what terror really was, began to fill him. He could see the gun smoke fan out across the ceiling and Matt Bannister walking slowly to his side, his famous Colt hanging loose in his hand. Matt knelt down to one knee beside him.

Donovan looked at him in shock. "Matt..." Donovan said with disbelief in his voice. He sounded weak and out of breath.

Matt spoke softly, "You don't have long. It's too late for your friend, but it's not too late for you, yet. You are about to stand before the Almighty, Donovan. You can be sent to hell for your sins or you can be like the thief on the cross and ask Jesus to forgive you. Do that and today you'll be in paradise. Do you hear me?"

Donovan nodded slightly with his terrified eyes staring into Matt's.

"Salvation is a gift from God, and all you have to do is believe that Jesus is the Lord and died for your sins, just so you can be with him. But you have to ask him to forgive you and to save you. He won't do it if you don't ask. Will you ask Jesus to forgive you and become your Savior?"

A large wet tear fell from Donovan's eye down to his ear. "Yes," he forced out through his bloody lips. His lungs were quickly filling with blood. "Matt..." he whispered.

Matt put his hand on Donovan's forehead, lowered his own head, and prayed, "Thank you, Father, for hearing Donovan's heart. I pray he'll face you with a clean robe of forgiveness like you did for the thief on the cross. In Jesus name, Amen," he finished and looked at Donovan's fading face. "The Lord's willing to forgive you, Donovan. No matter what you've done."

Donovan tried to speak, but could barely whisper, "I... sorry," he said with a touch of a small sad smile as another tear dropped. He gasped and coughed as speckles of blood flew out of his mouth. "Sss...." He motioned with his eyes toward Elizabeth.

Matt nodded. "I know."

Donovan seemed to smile slightly and breathed his last.

Matt paused for a moment and then reached over and closed Donovan's eyes. He stood up and holstered his gun. He turned to Elizabeth, who stood in the center of the cabin holding the blonde teenage boy at her side, they both appeared to be in shock.

"Are you all right?" Matt asked awkwardly.

She tried to smile, but her lips began to quiver as her emotions overtook her. Overcome by relief and weakness, she sat heavily on the same chair to which she had been tied earlier and began to cry into her hands. Evan Gray stood uneasily beside her exchanging awkward looks between her and Matt. Matt stepped forward and knelt down in front of Elizabeth. He cast a casual glance at Evan before putting a hand on her knee. Her face was buried in her opened palms.

"Lizzy," he asked softly, "are you all right?"

She pulled her tear-streaked face up from her hands and nodded quickly. Then, with a crooked smile, she fell forward to hug Matt tightly. She buried her face into his shoulder sobbing.

"Shh," he whispered, "you're safe now."

After a moment, she slowly gained some composure and released him while wiping the tears from her battered and bruised face. With a nervous laugh, she said, "I never wanted you to see me like this."

Matt replied softly, "Under the circumstances, I think it's acceptable. You're safe now and you'll be back home tomorrow."

"I didn't think anyone was coming for me," she uttered and began to cry again.

He smiled compassionately. "I would have come running from Cheyenne if I hadn't already been here. Tom would be here too, except Charlie had to take him back to town." The perplexed look on Elizabeth's face brought her an explanation. "We were ambushed down the mountain and Tom got hit in the shoulder. He needs a doctor, but he should be okay."

"Is he all right?" she asked worriedly.

"Should be. I've seen worse."

"But he'll live?" she asked quickly.

"I'm sure he will. He was bleeding a bit, but Charlie's knowledgeable about things like that." Matt paused, "So Gabriel and I came on up here."

Elizabeth's eyes widened. "Gabriel's here?"

Matt nodded with a slight smile. "He's up on the hill."

Elizabeth's face lit up, but Evan interrupted before she had the chance to reply. His voice trembled with fear, "Sir, it was my brother that shot Sheriff Smith." He added quickly, "But he didn't mean to. Mister Moskin and Mister Birch forced him to. They told him they'd kill me if he let anyone by. I'm sure he really didn't mean to hurt the sheriff. When he comes back you can talk to him. Missus Smith can tell you my brother's not like these men. He wouldn't hurt anyone intentionally. So please don't arrest him or me. We didn't have anything to do with any of this. Ask Missus Smith," Evan pleaded with sincere and desperate blue eyes.

Matt frowned and stood slowly. He looked at Evan with true compassion. "Your name is Evan?" he asked softly.

"Yeah. How'd you know?"

"Your brother told me," Matt stated quietly.

"You arrested Rodney?" Evan asked, bewildered.

Matt shook his head slowly. "Your brother's dead, son. He wanted me to tell you that he loved you," he said as gently as he could.

Evan backed over to the bed and sat down heavily. "He can't be dead, Mister Birch said he was fine. He fired those shots. He was fine!"

Matt shook his head. "We returned fire, and he was shot. He died while I was speaking to him." Evan's eyes filled with thick and painful tears. Elizabeth quickly went to Evan's side and held him while Matt finished speaking. "He made me promise to save you; he loved you very much, Evan. I'm sorry."

Evan's face grew strangely contorted. "Was it you?"

Matt shook his head. "No. We didn't have a choice, son. I'm afraid those men put your brother in an unfair position." He paused and looked at Evan. "I wish it could have been different. I wish he would've talked to us instead of shooting at us."

Evan whimpered, "What about those shots? Mister Birch said it was a code," he choked out the words as his tears began to fall.

"There sometimes is, son. Three shots are the most common."

"So it was you!" Evan accused, angrily.

Matt nodded sadly. "I'll go get Gabriel," he said while

Evan began a deep guttural wail that turned into heavy mourning on Elizabeth's shoulder.

Outside in the cold, Matt closed the door behind him. Donovan Moskin and John Birch were both dead and Elizabeth was alive and safe. Matt took a deep breath and leaned against the wall tiredly, he closed his eyes and thanked the Lord. However, the sound of Evan's excruciating cries echoing through the forest, tore at Matt's heart.

66

Gabriel had watched John run out of the front door and fire his gun at Matt. Within seconds he had watched John's lifeless body fall into the snow. Gabriel couldn't take his eyes off of John's body until he heard Donovan burst out of the outhouse carrying his revolver in his hand. One shot later Donovan was dead, and it was over. His mother was safe, and it was all over.

Although, he'd read stories about Matt's gunfights and those of others, he was surprised by how quickly it ended. It was over very fast and then the cries of Evan began to echo through the silent mountain. Gabriel was thankful to have his mother back alive and despite his relief and joyous reunion with her, he could not help but to feel empathy for Evan.

It wasn't long until Matt called him to help put the two outlaws over their saddles for the night. The odor of the fresh deaths was unpleasant to Gabriel, and he choked on the acidic smell that left a distinct taste in his mouth as well. Matt explained that the bodies needed to be tied over the saddles while they were still warm. It was a job Gabriel despised, but Matt didn't seem bothered by it at all. While they walked their horses down to get Rodney's body Matt said, "You're awfully quiet. You wouldn't stop talking earlier, and now you won't talk."

"I've never seen anyone die before," Gabriel said quietly.

"It's not as glamorous as your story books make it out to be is it?"

Gabriel shook his head slowly. "No, sir."

"Maybe now you'll understand why I didn't sign your book. It's not something I'm proud of."

"It doesn't seem to bother you," Gabriel observed flatly.

"Not outwardly, I suppose. But this isn't my first time either, like it is yours."

Gabriel asked pointedly, "So was it a pleasure to kill those men?"

"What?" Matt asked with a questionable expression on his face.

"Mister Ziegler said it would be a pleasure to kill those men," Gabriel explained.

Matt smiled slightly for the first time. "I think he meant that it would be rightly justified, not necessarily fun." He chuckled and continued, "Most folks, don't enjoy killing anyone, but they have to on occasion, especially lawmen."

"Does it bother you?" Gabriel asked looking at Matt.

"The young man lying down here in the snow bothers me. The two men back up there... no."

"But you killed the two men. And twenty-five others?" Gabriel seemed to asked.

Matt nodded. "Yeah."

"That's a lot of people."

"It is."

"Were all the men you've shot killers?" Gabriel asked.

"Most, but not all," he sounded regretful, but he didn't elaborate any further. They rode the rest of the way down to the rock formation and found Rodney's body where it had lain. Even though it was dark, Rodney's body was quite visible against the snow under the bright moon. Matt walked around the body and knelt down almost affectionately as he looked at Rodney's face. "Gabriel, I want you to take a good look at this boy," he said, looking up at Gabriel. "Do you know why he's dead?"

"He got shot," Gabriel answered from a few feet back. His voice shook from the cold.

"Ultimately," Matt agreed. "No, it's because he didn't have solid character. You have to stand up for what you believe in, otherwise, you'll follow whoever takes the lead. If I'm ever able to teach you anything, then you'd better listen to me now. The world's full of people who will lie, cheat and steal. They'll seem like great people and even a caring friend perhaps, but they'll deceive you, use you, and like this young man, kill you for their own gain. The Bible refers to them as wolves in sheep's clothing. Be very aware of them, because you will run into them, I promise you. Donovan Moskin was one of them, and this boy and his brother paid the price for following him. So do not make friends too quickly or trust anyone blindly, let them earn your trust. Most importantly of all, stand up for what you believe in. Don't allow anyone to compromise your integrity, because that's all you have, and there's nothing else about being a man that matters."

Matt paused and then added, "The simple truth is it's too easy to follow an immoral man into a lifestyle of immorality. So you had better keep your feet planted firmly on God's word and your convictions strong. Be a man of integrity, Gabriel. Stand strong for what's right or this world's going to tear you up. Integrity...Gabriel, is what separates the sheep from the wolves."

67

It didn't take very long after eating a few canned peaches and half of a shared egg for Gabriel to fall asleep beside his mother, while she consoled Evan on the bed. It had been a long twenty-four-hour period for all of them with very little, if any, sleep, but now both of the boys slept soundly.

Matt refused to eat, saving what was left of the jar of home-canned peaches for the boys to have in the morning. Matt made a pot of coffee to fill the emptiness of his stomach. He was tired, perhaps more so than he'd been in a long time. He could go into the back room to lie down and sleep, but he hoped to talk with Elizabeth while he could. Tomorrow morning, they would ride down the mountain and their lives would go back to normal. He'd probably never have the opportunity to talk to her again. He sat at the kitchen table sipping a cup of the hot coffee watching Elizabeth sleeping with her arm over Evan.

Matt took another sip of coffee and looked around the cabin reflecting on the few memories of his childhood that it held. The cabin was in good shape. Clyde had taken decent care of it over the years. He wondered if one of his brothers would be interested in buying it from Clyde's estate to keep it in the family, since their grandfather had built it, after all. He was fairly confident that one of his older brothers would since they'd have more memories of it than he did.

His attention went back to the bed as Elizabeth sat up tiredly. She forced herself out of bed and walked exhaustedly to the kitchen table and sat on a chair. She smiled slightly and then rubbed her face with her hands, struggling to keep her eyes open.

"Want some coffee?" Matt asked. She nodded and Matt got up to get her a tin cup of hot coffee. He set it down in front of her and said, "It's pretty warm."

She took a sip and looked at Matt sincerely. "Thank you."

"You're welcome. I'm sure Lee's big hotel makes it better, but it's good enough for times like these."

"No," Elizabeth murmured shaking her head, "I mean thank you for coming up here. They would have killed me and Evan," she yawned.

"You're welcome."

Elizabeth took another sip of coffee. "Is Tom going to live?" Her red eyes showed great concern as they went to Matt's.

"He should. I can't say how good his arm will be, but he'll live, I'm sure."

Elizabeth sighed. "I wasn't expecting you and Tom to come together. In fact, I wasn't really expecting anyone to come. I just kept praying."

"You didn't think I'd come after you?" Matt asked with a soft smile. "Like I said, I would have come from Cheyenne in record time if I had been there."

"You had no reason to," she spoke weakly.

"I couldn't think of a reason not to. Someone had to come get you and Tom would have gotten himself and half of the town's men killed." He added quickly, "I'm not saying he's incompetent, he just hasn't been in enough situations like this to know better. He had the whole town coming after you."

She rolled her eyes. "Tom was probably trying to make sure I was killed; he must have seen the note that they left. I would have thought he'd be happy I was gone. I'm surprised that he came with you though, he's hated you for a very long time," she stated and took a sip of her coffee.

Matt shook his head. "No, he was pretty insistent on coming. He made his feelings clear between him and I, but we had the same goal; we wanted to get you back home alive. Tomorrow you'll be welcomed home like... a... I don't know, a queen, I suppose."

She sighed with a downcast smile while her eyes filled with unexpected moisture. She cast a quick glance over toward the two sleeping boys and then spoke quietly, "No, Matthew, I'll be welcomed home by my children..." She paused to bite her lower lip and fight her tears from falling. She wiped her eyes to regain her composure. "I don't know if Tom will still want to be married to me when he finds out I'm adopting one of my kidnappers," she said with a troubled laugh.

"You're keeping Evan?"

"I have to, he risked his life for me. He's seen enough hard times to last awhile, and I'd like to see him smile as carefree as my own children. I don't know how Tom will react to that, but he can either be a part of it or... divorce me," she said with a shrug.

Matt smiled and spoke as he yawned, "He's not going to divorce you."

"Well, we'll see," she answered questionably. It was obvious that she was intentionally leaving something out of the conversation. There was an uncomfortable silence between them that hovered like a thick fog of not knowing where to begin a long overdue explanation. Elizabeth spoke first, "Can I ask you something?"

Matt nodded.

"Why would you lead Donovan to the Lord before he died? Do you really think he deserves to be in paradise, as you put it?" Her words took an angry turn, "Men like him and John are meant to go to hell! He got what he deserved, but he doesn't deserve to be saved, he was a reprehensible murderer, Matthew. He was a cruel and evil man! And I resent you for telling him about the Lord and I know Jesus won't accept a man like that!" Her eyes burned into Matt.

Matt asked softly, "Did they...?"

"No!" she answered firmly with steel in her eyes, "but they tried. Evan saved me the first time they tried, and those gun shots drew their attention from me the second time they had me held down." Her voice deepened as she looked angrily at him, "But they had the look of demons in their eyes and I know how evil they were! I cannot believe you'd tell that murdering pig about the Lord, Matthew! That just doesn't make sense to me how you might think he could reap the rewards of a life he never sowed." Her voice cracked as she continued, "All you cared about was his eternal fate, and he doesn't deserve it!"

Matt spoke softly, "Let me tell you something, Lizzy. A long time ago I stood over Clay Dobson, with only one thing on my mind, retribution. I saw the fear in his eyes; he was terrified because he knew I was going to kill him. I can't explain to you the look of desperation that was on his face, but I aimed at his head, right between the eyes, and I fired."

He took a deep breath and his voice softened, "I watched his head explode, but that's not what haunts me. I'm the last person Clay Dobson saw before he died, I'm the one that killed him... and he went before the Lord and judgment not knowing the truth of salvation. His soul was lost." He paused pointedly. "The thing that haunts me is the look that was in his eyes when I pulled the trigger. The same desperation that was on Clay's face was on Donovan's and others that I've shot over the years. The real terror isn't of me, it's of what's coming for them next. I sent Clay into eternity without telling him about Jesus; that is what haunts me. So now, I tell people like Donovan about the Lord. Sure, he was a bad man, he was a murderer and other things too, but you know, Jesus still loves him. And if Jesus loves him then I have an obligation to tell him so before he stands in front of Jesus. The Bible says that God wishes no man to perish, not one person... I take that to mean He wants to save everyone, including Donovan."

"Matthew," Elizabeth explained emphatically, "he took me from my family! He killed Clyde and murdered the Andersons for just being home! He threatened my life and got a young innocent boy killed because it benefited him. He's ruined Evan's life and maybe even my husband's." She paused and then asked pointedly, "So how can you sit there and tell me his lousy soul is worth saving?"

"Because someday I'm going to stand before the Lord and He's going to ask me why I didn't."

Elizabeth closed her eyes and sighed tiredly. "Oh, Matthew," she said gently, "you haven't changed have you?"

"I've changed a lot. I think we all do as we grow up."

"Are you going to leave again?" she asked suddenly with a hint of anxiety revealing itself in her eyes.

Matt laughed at the suddenness of her question. "Yes,

after New Year's I am," he said with a smile. He elaborated, "I thought it was time to see the family since I haven't seen anyone for so long. It's good to see them all, but yes, after New Year's I'm going back to Cheyenne."

"Are you glad to see me?" she asked softly.

His smile faded as he spoke, "I'm very glad to see you. I didn't know if I was going to get here in time or not."

"No," she said slowly, "I mean did you want to see me after all these years?"

He was silent. He looked at the two boys sleeping and listened to their slow heavy breathing. He couldn't avoid the question, yet there was a heaviness that filled his chest. "No," he admitted quietly, "I didn't want to see you."

She frowned sadly as her eyes shifted down to the table. "Do you ever think about me?"

He nodded slowly. "Sure, but I try not to."

"Because you hate me?" she whispered.

"No, I've never hated you, Lizzie. I loved you way too much too ever hate you."

"What about now?"

"You're married," he stated simply and stood up to get more coffee. He took Elizabeth's cup as well and continued to speak, "What I feel doesn't matter anymore, does it?" he asked as he poured the coffee.

She waited until Matt carried the two cups of coffee back to the table and sat down across from her. "Thank you," she said taking a hold of the coffee cup. "I don't know how to say this, so let me just start at the beginning..."

"Lizzy, you don't..."

"No, let me talk, Matthew. Just so you know, I married Tom to please my father. I didn't love him. And you don't know how many nights I laid awake wishing I had left with you for months after you were gone. I dreamed you would come back and ask me to go with you one more time, but you never did. Matthew, you took a part of me with you when you left.... but you left a piece of you with me." She looked at him with the greatest sincerity. "Gabriel is your son," she whispered softly.

Matt smiled sadly and lowered his head emotionally.

Elizabeth continued, "Tom just found out. I never told him until yesterday. He's going to divorce me," she said as a tear fell softly from her eyes. "I'm going to lose my family."

Matt reached over and took her hand in his. The feel of the warmth of her soft skin sent a rush of nostalgia of long ago within him. His heart felt like it skipped a beat as he gazed into Elizabeth's eyes for the first time in fifteen years. "Tom told me," was all he said.

"He did?" she was surprised.

He nodded. "Tom loves you, Lizzie. He doesn't want a divorce. The only thing he cared about was getting you back alive. He might've considered divorcing you, but he came close to losing you today and that puts everything in perspective. He was angry when you told him obviously, but anger's a surface emotion. You think you hate, but the truth is when you get to the meat of the matter, love is the only emotion that matters. If love is an emotion at all and I don't think it is, I think love is a living part of who we are. But anger itself, is just an emotion that comes and goes like a smile or a frown."

Elizabeth looked at Matt incredulously. "He told you?"

"He did. Tom has every reason to hate me and he let me know that." Matt smiled slightly. "But he loves you. You're his wife and Gabriel's his son."

"No, he's yours," she insisted to clarify any doubts.

Matt nodded. "Everyone in my family already knows

445

that. Aunt Mary wants him to become a regular part of the family, but..."

"How do they know?" Elizabeth questioned abruptly.

"Because he looks like me," he answered with a sad smile. He looked at her hand in his. "Listen to me, Lizzy. I don't regret that day, but I left Willow Falls and my family because of it. I loved you too much to stay in the same town with you and Tom living together. I left so I could survive without the pain, but it didn't work." Matt squeezed her hand softly and looked at her scraped up and bruised face. She was still as beautiful as she had been the day he left. "I've pictured your face every day for fifteen years and have never forgotten that day, because it was the greatest day of my life. I've measured every girl that I've ever met to you and not one has ever measured up close. I am honored to have a son with you, but I'm not his father, Tom is. Tom has raised him and loved him his whole life, so don't tell Gabriel about me being his father."

"You don't want him to know?" She seemed both surprised and relieved at the same time.

"For what purpose? Seriously what good would it do him? Your kidnapping has shaken up his world enough, let's not shatter it."

"I don't know if it would shatter it. You don't know how much he idolizes you."

Matt shook his head. "He won't anymore. Gabriel has seen enough death today to last a lifetime and there's a big difference between reading about a gun fight and seeing one. He won't be so interested in me or them anymore."

Elizabeth closed her eyes. "Matthew, I'm so sorry that I couldn't have told you about him a long time ago. I know it must be hard to come home and learn that you have a fifteen-year-old son, but I would've told you then if you were here. I knew he was your son the moment I first held him and looked into his eyes, but I couldn't mention it to anyone. Tom would have divorced me if I had told the truth and my father would have disowned me. I didn't love Tom, but I was too scared to leave him because I didn't have anywhere else to go." She looked up at him with sorrow filled eyes. "Will you forgive me, for the hurt I caused you? If you can."

An appearance of anguish crossed his face. "You couldn't have told me even if you wanted to. I ran far enough away to make sure of that. There's no forgiveness needed, my friend, but I wish I would have known."

"Why?"

He took a slow deep breath before answering. "Because maybe then you would have come with me," he said as his eyes glossed over with a slight moisture. "I wanted to marry you, Lizzy. I have never loved anyone as much as I loved you. And you know, I never asked the Lord for fame or fortune, a pretty house or a thousand cows, I asked him for you. That's all I ever wanted was to just spend the rest of my life being married to you. Whether we were rich or poor, accepted by your father or rejected, it didn't matter to me. I just wanted to live every day of my life in love with you, that's all!" He paused momentarily, "But your father robbed me of that when you and Tom got married. And oddly enough, I don't remember you being in love with him."

Elizabeth let go of his hand and wiped a tear from her eyes. "I wasn't," she said softly.

"Then why did you marry him? We were supposed to raise a family together, Lizzy, you and me! I know your father rigged up a wedding plan, but you didn't have to agree to it. For a long time, I blamed your father, but you had a choice in it too. You didn't have to marry him. If you loved me, then why'd you marry Tom?"

"I've already told you why," she said softly and then continued with a stronger tone, "My father made me marry him! I loved you, Matthew, you know that, but what was I supposed to do? I was forced to marry him! I hated my father and Tom for what they did to me, but when I really needed you, you were gone!" She shook her head slowly with a hurt expression in her eyes. "If you would've stayed here and been my friend, I would have come to you after Gabriel was born. If I would have known where you were, I would have come to your door. You're the one I was in love with, Matthew."

"I was your friend," Matt said sadly.

"You were my best friend, but you abandoned me when I needed you the most. We would've been married a long time ago if you had stayed here and waited for me. I loved you, and I couldn't have stayed married to someone else if you were here. You know the hurt may have been hard for you, but the guilt was excruciating for me."

"And now?" he asked painfully.

She closed her eyes tiredly and then she looked at him sincerely. "I love Tom; I love him very much. He's a wonderful man and I wouldn't want my life any different than it was. I don't know what's going to happen now that he knows about Gabriel..." she stated with a nervous shrug, "But we'll see."

"Do you really love him?" Matt asked softly.

"Yes, I do," she said looking into his eyes. "Matthew, understand that I waited for you and I hoped and prayed every day that you'd come back to take me away. But one day I realized that you weren't coming back for me, so I gave up waiting for you. Gradually, I fell in love with my husband. Honestly, I can't say I wish things were different, except I do wish that Gabriel was Tom's son." She spoke to

Matt in a sensitive manner, "We made a mistake, Matthew, which I do regret."

Matt took a deep breath and looked down at the floor while her words cut their way into his soul. He sighed lightly. "You were everything to me, Lizzy. Absolutely everything."

"And you were everything to me until I found someone else... my husband."

"Usually, people are supposed to marry the person they love. You must be one of the few who are happier marrying someone they didn't love," he said with a touch of bitterness to his voice.

"Usually, that's true," she said with a slight smile, "but Matthew, I'm thankful it worked out the way it did. I think we prayed for the same thing, but God in His wisdom had other plans that we didn't understand. Now I just hope you'll find someone to fall in love with and marry."

Matt frowned. "I don't think that's in God's plans for me; not everyone's created to be married, and I think I'm one. Besides, I guess, I keep thinking about what we had, and I know I'll never have that with anyone else, not like what you and I had. I've had a few suitors over the years who wanted me to court them, but it just isn't the same." He looked at her and smiled slightly. "They're not you."

"Matt Bannister, life is too short to waste it on the past. Do you realize that we were their age back then?" she said waving at the sleeping boys. "We were a little older, but not much. I won't say we were just kids, because the love was as real as it could get, but it didn't end up the way either one of us wanted it to. What we had was wonderful, but that was a long time ago. Matthew, honestly, don't waste another day comparing what we had to what you *could* have if you just allowed yourself to take a chance. I don't believe you're not the marrying kind or this conversation wouldn't even be happening. So please, put the past behind you, and let's just start over again as friends, okay?"

Matt smiled slightly. "I still love you, Lizzy."

"And I still love you, but not like I used to. You don't have anything to run from, not anymore. And there's nothing to compare another lady to anymore either, So don't."

Matt's eyes alertly went to the front of the cabin when they heard a muffled sound coming from outside.

"What's that?" Elizabeth asked urgently.

"I believe that would be Uncle Charlie coming back up here. Well, Elizabeth," he said taking her hand in his again, "if we never get to talk like this again, I guess I should say thank you..." he stopped, not really knowing what to thank her for or what else to say. He looked at her softly. "I still love you though."

Elizabeth nodded. "I know. I've always known, but you have to move on, Matthew. I sure would like to keep you around for a friend though," she spoke sincerely.

He let go of her hand and stood up with his coffee cup in his other hand. He paused in front of her and said, "I am your friend, and will be until the moment eternity comes to an end."

"Eternity never ends," she responded fondly.

Matt looked into her eyes and offered a small seemingly sad smile. "Precisely," he said and walked to the front door and opened it to look out into the night. "You boys are too late. We just drank the last of the coffee," he called out as the three horses approached the cabin.

His cousin, William Fasana replied, "We didn't ride all the way up here just to freeze our butts off! There better be some coffee brewing or somebody left to shoot!" William tried to sound irritable, but his relief was obvious in his voice.

"Well, there might be a little coffee left, but it's getting cold," Matt replied with a smile.

"It will be plenty warm compared to me," William answered as he rode his horse up to the door along with Charlie and Adam. They had a relieved smile on their faces.

"Go put your horses in the barn and come on inside. I'll make some more coffee. I'm getting cold standing out here."

William scoffed with mock disbelief, "Hear that, Uncle Charlie he's getting cold! We ride all the way up here in the freezing cold to make sure he's alive and all the appreciation we get is what's left of the cold coffee."

68

It was mighty late and the Reverend Ash's home was quiet, except for the tall grandfather clock with its consistent ticking and the crackling of the wood stove. Tom slept off and on under the watchful eye of Walt Delaney, who was the closest to a real doctor that Willow Falls had. Walt had some medical training in his younger years, but he found a more fitting career managing the *Willow Falls Bank and Postal Office*. In a crisis, Walt had more knowledge than anyone else and kept a bag of medicine and doctoring instruments close by for when he was needed. His knowledge was needed more often than he would've liked as suturing wounds and broken limbs happened occasionally. Gun-shot wounds were few and far between though, in fact he had never dealt with one. He had successfully pulled the bullet out of Tom's shoulder and cleaned the wound as best that he could. However, with his limited knowledge, he could not say to what extent Tom would recover the use of his arm. All he knew for sure was Tom could still move his arm and fingers, but the shoulder might not rotate like it once did. He had sent an urgent wire for the Branson doctor to come tomorrow to look at Tom's wound. As it was, Tom slept under the influence of some morphine. He had spent some time cleaning the wound to the best of his ability, but the fact was that he wasn't a doctor and there was much that he didn't know. Walt sat by Tom's side fighting the urge to go home and sleep himself, but if he slept at all, it would be in the chair beside Tom.

Reverend Ash, Darla and their friend, Lettie Snow did what God-fearing people do in desperate times - they prayed. They were on their knees and crying out for the Lord's mercy to deliver their daughter safely back to them. In the Reverend's hand the heart shaped rock that Elizabeth had given him was clenched tightly. He would continue to pray until his daughter was home safely or news came of her going home to be with the Lord. But while there was yet hope, they would pray.

A loud knocking on the front door late at night frightened the three of them. The Reverend got to his feet slowly. He was joined by his exhausted wife and Lettie Snow when he opened the door. He was surprised to see the long-bearded face of Adam Bannister dressed warmly in a cow's hide coat. He was a big man and appeared to be quite cold, but he smiled none the less.

"Adam," Reverend Ash said awkwardly, "my goodness boy, come inside. You're freezing." He opened the door to make way.

"No, thank you, Reverend Ash, Missus Ash," he nodded to Darla. "I just thought you'd like to know that Elizabeth is fine and she'll be coming home tomorrow!"

"What? Really?" The Reverend's face lit up as he quickly took hold of his wife to hug her. She began to cry joyfully.

"Yeah," Adam announced, "Matthew rescued her! Her

face is a little bruised up, but they didn't harm her and she's just fine."

"Praise the Lord," Reverend Ash said softly, and then repeated it as his emotions swelled, "Praise the Lord!" He looked at his wife's tear-streaked face with a large joyful smile and hugged her with a child-like excitement he hadn't shown in years. "Thank you, Jesus, thank you."

Adam added, "They'll be here in the morning. I thought you'd like to know."

"Oh yes! Thank you, Adam. Please come inside," Darla said with deep appreciation.

"No, I have to let my family know. Aunt Mary's beside herself by now, I'm sure. Well, have a good night."

"Adam," Lettie Snow spoke, "what time do you think they'll be riding into town?"

He shrugged. "Nine, ten probably, could be later. But Elizabeth's coming home tomorrow, and that's the only thing I know for sure." he added with a pleasant smile.

"Adam," Darla spoke softly, "tell your Aunt Mary Merry Christmas for me."

"I will and Merry Christmas to all of you." He paused when he saw Walt Delaney step out of the bedroom. "Walt, how's Tom?"

"He'll be fine, I think," Walt stated tiredly, but with confidence. "So Elizabeth's all right?"

"She's fine." Adam smiled. "You folks have a good night." He turned away from the opened door to walk to the hitching post and get back onto his horse.

The Reverend closed the door and sighed with relief. "Thank you, Lord! Oh, thank you, Jesus," he cried out emotionally and hugged Darla tightly again. Then he quickly let her go and reopened the door and stepped outside. "Adam," he called urgently, "what about the men who took her?"

Adam shook his head as he climbed up into the saddle. "They're all dead, except for a young boy. He wasn't much of a threat, I guess." He paused, and then added thoughtfully, "Matt's good at what he does that's for sure. If it was the posse from last night that went up there, I don't think they could have saved her. And who knows if any of them would have come home alive. Anyway, have a good night!"

The Reverend closed the door and looked at Darla. Lettie hurriedly put on her coat and hat. "I have to spread the news," Lettie remarked with excitement. "Everyone needs to know."

"I'm coming with you," Walt said sharing in her excitement.

As their two friends quickly left to spread the news, the Reverend took Darla in his arms lovingly. His lip began to tremble, and he began to cry onto the shoulder of his adored wife.

69

The sunrise revealed clear skies, which promised another beautiful sun-filled day, though it was still quite cold outside with a bitter mountain breeze blowing gently. The small barn was crammed tightly with horses, as Matt looked over his mare, wishing there was something he could feed her. However, the hayloft was as bare as the cabin's kitchen. Matt had stayed up late talking with Charlie and William at the table while Elizabeth went to the back room to sleep. He understood why his relatives came back up to the cabin, but he couldn't honestly say he was glad to see them. He would have liked to talk to Elizabeth for a few more hours while he could because he knew they would never get the chance to talk alone like that again.

The barn door opened and Charlie stepped inside closing the door behind him, carrying his gun belt in his left hand. "We can eat a little breakfast when we get back to town, huh?" Charlie said as he stepped over to his horse. He stroked his mare and looked her over for any sign of injury from the night before.

"Where's William?" Matt asked with a hint of concern in

his voice. William seemed to have a deep desire to tell Gabriel who his father really was. He had brought it up a few times during the night and was displeased with Matt's decision not to tell Gabriel.

"Inside, it's not noon yet. It's a little early for him to venture outside." Charlie tossed a quick grin at Matt. "Don't worry, he won't say anything. He may be a lot of things to everyone else out there, but he's respectful of the family."

"Do you think that's the right decision not to tell him I'm his father, Uncle Charlie?"

Charlie hung his gun belt up on a nail and then rested his arms across his horses back to look at Matt. "I would say it's a fine decision for now anyway, but eventually he'll figure it out."

"Good enough for today, though," Matt stated. "If I'd never come back, I'd never would have known I had a son."

"If you'd never come back, those three," he nodded at the bodies that were lying over the saddles on three tired horses, "would be alive and Elizabeth would be dead. That son of yours and his younger siblings wouldn't have a mother." Charlie raised his eyebrows questioningly. "Are you in love with her again?"

Matt smiled slightly. "I always will love her. But no, I'm not in love with her. We had a good conversation last night that was long overdue. I guess I just miss the way things used to be."

Charlie nodded. "Time moves too fast to not accept the changes. I recommend you wash your hands of the past and start thinking about a future for you. And it doesn't matter if you stick around here or go back to Wyoming, it would just make your aunt Mary happy if she knew you were free of your past and living free. Let the past go, Matt."

Matt nodded but didn't say anything.

Charlie stepped over to the corral that held the three horses with the bodies tied over the saddles. "That boy's going to break down awfully hard when he sees his brother like this. I hate to do that to him."

Matt yawned. "We can send the two boys down the mountain with Elizabeth and we'll follow with those three."

"Well, let's saddle up and get going."

As expected Evan Gray collapsed to his knees and wailed loudly when he saw his brother draped across the back of a horse. Unlike the other two bodies Rodney was covered with a blanket, but they could not hide the fact that Rodney was dead and tied over a saddle. They had tried to keep him out of Evan's sight, but Evan looked for his brother and found him. Elizabeth was quickly on her knees at his side and tried to console the wailing boy, but it did little good.

Evan bent over and vomited what little breakfast he had eaten. Matt looked over at Gabriel, who stood quietly in place holding the reins of the three horses they'd use to ride down the mountain. Elizabeth continued to comfort him while his stomach convulsed to push out what little air was left in it. Matt spoke to her, "You three go ahead and follow the trail down the mountain. We'll wait a bit and follow you down."

Elizabeth looked up at Matt with an intimate desperation in her eyes pleading to him to help her. Her face contorted into a heartbroken grimace as she began to cry. Matt quickly handed the reins of Donovan's horse to Charlie, dismounted, and walked over to Evan. He knelt down and bit his lip searching for the right words to say. "Evan, sit up here," he said softly, while lifting Evan up by his shoulders from the snow. "We need to go, son. I'm sorry, but you need to get on your horse. I know this is hard, but you're going to be all right. I'm sorry, but it's the best we can do."

It took a few minutes for Evan to gather his strength enough to climb into the saddle, but once there he weakly followed Elizabeth, as she led the boys away from the cabin towards home.

The men followed the trail through the snow at a casual pace. They didn't stop until they came to a clearing that gave a broad view of the valley below. In the clearing Elizabeth waited by herself with a smile on her scuffed up face. She greeted the men, "A lady could freeze to death waiting for you guys."

Charlie stopped short and asked, "I thought you were leading the boys down the hill?"

"I was, but they can follow the trail down by themselves. I told them to wait for me at the bottom." She paused, "I wanted to talk to Matthew."

"Oh..." Charlie said sarcastically, "I suppose you want William and me to leave so you can talk privately, am I right?"

She nodded. "Of course you're right, Uncle Charlie."

He smiled. "Well then, how about William and I stay here and look at the view for five or six minutes, while you and Matt move on down the trail? I'm personally in a hurry to get home so I'm gonna be riding up your backsides, if you're lollygagging on the way down. Tie that horse to the other one." He motioned to Matt to tie Donovan's horse to John Birch's.

Elizabeth laughed lightly. "I promise we won't lollygag."

Charlie smiled appreciatively. "Fair enough."

Elizabeth spoke as Matt rode up beside her, "I never expected to see this valley again, you know. I wanted to thank you again for coming for me."

Matt felt his uncle's and cousin's eyes following him as he walked his horse beside Elizabeth's out of the clearing and back into the trees. "It's my pleasure."

"How does it feel to be a hero?" she asked.

"I don't know; I've never been one."

"You've always been one to me, Matt," she said softly.

He nodded sadly. "How's Evan holding up?"

"He's pretty quiet, but he'll be all right I think when we get home and things settle down." She laughed nervously, "If I still have a home."

Matt looked at her caringly. "You must be a little scared about that, huh? You keep mentioning it. I told you last night Tom doesn't care about that right now; all he wants is you back safely."

"For now, but what about later? When the homecoming is over and things are back to normal, don't you think it's once again going to become an issue? I lied to him for fifteen years, Matt. And worse, he just found out his oldest son isn't his. I really don't think my coming home alive is going to make that all disappear. Do you?" she asked sarcastically.

"No," he agreed. "But what it will do is make him realize how important you are to him. No, your coming home isn't going to fix it all, but it does cut a path through his pride and anger to see what is really important. He'll deal with everything else, but he'll love you and Gabriel as much as ever. He doesn't want to lose you."

"How do you think he'll react to Evan moving in?" she asked interestedly.

Matt laughed slightly. "I don't know, Lizzie. That's a tough one."

"You don't smile much, do you?" she questioned. For just a second his smile was nearly childlike, the way she remembered it from many years before.

He frowned and hesitated before answering, "I don't have a lot to smile about. I'm alone most of the time, unless I'm arresting someone. And most of the men I arrest don't really seem to like me too much." He shrugged his shoulders with a slight smile.

"You must get awfully lonely."

"Not so much anymore. I've adapted to being alone pretty well, it's just part of my job."

"Matthew, I always thought you'd become a Reverend or a teacher, but not a..." she stopped wordlessly.

"A what?" Matt asked already knowing what she'd say.

Elizabeth answered slowly, "A deputy marshal. Tom and my father say you are a legal killer, you know an assassin hiding behind a badge."

Matt laughed with disgust. "Why am I not surprised? I've gone after some very dangerous men, Lizzy, and sometimes I can't bring them in alive. Tom and your father may not understand that because they haven't faced the kind of men that I have."

"Believe me, I have first-hand understanding now. But aren't you tired of it? I mean just how much bloodshed can a man stand? It just doesn't sound like you to me," Elizabeth said sincerely.

Matt answered honestly, "I find serving on the side of justice has a favorable contentment within me. I'll answer your question like this; the next town's a little safer because those two men back there, Donovan and the other guy, are riding sidesaddle today. There's a woman in the next town who's just a bit safer today, and... there's a young boy and girl somewhere who can enjoy their day at the swimming hole without those two, the Dobson's or any of the others I've met, riding down and terrorizing them like they did to us." His eyes burned into hers as he finished, "I am a lawman, that's what I do because I believe in what I do. I protect innocent people from predators and when they strike, I track these men down like wolves. Some give up and others want to fight it out. I have been given the ability and tools to defend myself and I won't glamorize it, it is ugly, but they won't hurt anyone else again, because of me. That's why I do it... and that's why I do it well!"

"You do," Elizabeth agreed with a soft voice.

Matt looked at her strangely. "I was kind of expecting you to lecture me like Aunt Mary and everyone else has about putting all of that behind me somehow."

Elizabeth shook her head slowly. "I was there that day, they weren't. They know what happened, but they weren't there, they didn't feel the fear or see the evil in those men's eyes. They weren't being held by one of them or had to listen Joseph's screams. It was just me, you and Tom that did and it's impossible to forget. Tom still has nightmares about it."

Matt nodded. "Me too occasionally. I've always blamed myself for not being able to save Joseph," he said tentatively.

"The only blame belongs to those men," Elizabeth said with great sensitivity. "There was nothing any of us could do about it. You couldn't have saved him if it happened right now today, not being unarmed against five men, you couldn't. So there's no way you could've back then." Her voice rose to a more appreciative tone, "You did save me though! They would have hurt me, Matthew, if it wasn't for you. You've been my hero ever since, twice as much now!" she said with a large grin.

Matt smiled, and he shook his head. "Lizzie, you always could make me smile."

"You know why, don't you?"

"Tell me."

"Because we're friends. We still can be if you move back home."

Matt laughed. "I wish I could, but I have to go back."

Elizabeth stopped her horse and asked Matt seriously, "Then will you do me a favor?"

"What?"

"Will you stop focusing your whole life on what happened on Pearl Creek? If you want to up-hold the law, do it because it's the law, not because some kids might have a terrorizing swimming trip. I love you, Matthew. I always have loved you, and I always will, but what I'd really like for you to do is settle down and find a wonderful woman to fall in love with until you're old and gray. It doesn't matter if that's here or in Cheyenne, but do it for me, please." She took a deep breath and added, "It would be nice if you were a family man when Gabriel learns that you're his father."

Matt looked at her questionably.

She answered before he could speak, "We can't hide it from him forever, Matthew."

"Well, he's a great boy," Matt said awkwardly.

"He's honestly just like his father," she said with a nod to Matt. She kicked her horse. "We'd better keep moving or Charlie's going to ride up our, you know what..." she giggled.

Matt laughed as he rode beside her.

70

Tom stood under the roof of the Reverend's front porch with his left arm in a sling. He wore his brown coat with the bullet hole and blood stain on the shoulder draped over his shoulder and buttoned. Under the brim of his well-worn hat he watched in crazy disbelief as the town's population seemed to triple overnight. The town folks, reporters, photographers and curiosity seekers from Branson and other nearby communities had flooded into the little forgotten town of Willow Falls to see the famed U. S. Deputy Marshal bring Elizabeth home. How the news traveled so fast Tom didn't know, but he couldn't believe the amount of people who chatted, laughed, and enjoyed themselves as they waited on the main street.

"Are all these people here for Mama?" his six-year-old daughter, Rachel asked. She seemed surprised by the size of the crowd as well. She stood at Tom's side holding his right hand.

Tom smiled and nodded. "They sure are sweetheart. It's amazing how many there are, isn't it?"

"Are they all Mama's friends, papa?" Rachel asked.

"I think so. I bet you didn't know she had so many did you?" He noticed Luther Fasana driving his covered wagon into town. On the bench beside him wrapped in warm blanket sat Mary Ziegler. She motioned towards him and Luther pulled the wagon over by Tom and stopped his Mules.

"Tom, how are you feeling?" she asked with a warm expression.

He nodded a little uncomfortably. "I'm all right."

"And your wound?"

"Sore, but I hope it will be okay. The doctor said I was lucky, it's mostly a flesh wound. It could've been a lot worse."

"Amen!" Mary agreed. "It could have been such a worse outcome. Your daughter is so blessed to have her mother and father both come out of this alive. And you know, Thomas, she doesn't even realize how blessed she is, does she?" She continued before Tom could answer, "It's the same with us though, isn't it? The Lord blesses us in ways we can't see and we have no idea how truly blessed we are."

Tom answered sincerely, "I believe that more than ever before."

Mary smiled. "Me too."

Steven Bannister walked over from his blacksmith shop and laughed. "My brother's coming back a hero, and all these reporters are asking me about Matt. But I'm afraid to say anything because if I told some of the stories I know, he'd shoot me for sure!" he laughed.

Tom smiled. "I've got a few of those myself," he chuckled. "We had some good times growing up."

Mary spoke boldly, "You still could, Thomas. The Lord brought Matt home so you and Elizabeth could continue to raise your family. I think it's safe to say you needed Matt to get Elizabeth back alive, but now Matt needs you to forgive him so he can survive." She paused and added purposely, "When you make peace with him, we'll get Matthew back."

Tom looked at Mary skeptically, "How do you figure?"

Mary took a deep breath and answered, "Matthew's afraid of only one man in this whole world, Thomas, and that man is you."

"Me?" Tom asked astonished. "Matt's not afraid of me! He's whipped me at everything we've ever done. Heck, he even threatened to pull me from my horse and beat me to a pulp just yesterday. Trust me, I don't think he's afraid to tangle with me." Tom laughed.

Mary smiled kindly and answered slowly, "Maybe not physically. Matthew's always been a man the principles of right and wrong. He's always been a good and loyal friend, but he betrayed you and he knows it. He loved you like his own brother, Thomas. And I believe it was that guilt which made him leave here and has kept him away for so long. Judas killed himself for betraying Jesus, but Peter ran away, just like Matthew did. And Peter would have kept running if Jesus hadn't tracked him down and forgiven him. Matthew's not afraid of anyone, except you. He wronged you and he can't forgive himself for it, nor does he expect you to. Those kind of spiritual wounds are the most painful wounds of all."

Tom faked ignorance, "He's never wronged me." His lack of skill in the art of lying showed brightly.

Mary's kind eyes saw through him. "You know what I'm talking about."

He seemed momentarily stunned. A moment's worth of tears spread through his eyes and then disappeared as quickly as they had come. "I don't think I do know," he said weakly, again trying to deny any knowledge of being wronged.

Mary shook her head. "Thomas, if he didn't love you, he never would have left. He would have stayed right here and undermined you and your marriage. He left because he couldn't look you in the eyes anymore. There's more to than that of course, but I think ultimately it was facing you that drove him away..."

71

"Mom, look!" Gabriel called loudly. They were about a quarter of a mile outside of Willow Falls and Gabriel was pointing at a large white banner strung up between the first two buildings on the edge of town. It said in big block lettering, "WELCOME HOME" and underneath of it, was a large crowd of people who began to cheer when they saw the riders appear. "Wow!" Gabriel laughed with wonder.

"Well, I'll be," Elizabeth gasped at the large crowd that came to greet her. "Look Matthew, its..." she stopped in mid-sentence and simply stared in amazement with a smile.

Matt nodded towards town with a soft grin. "It's for you," he said, while watching her face shine in the sunlight. "I'll bet there are three little ones over there waiting for you right now." Elizabeth looked at him with large tears growing in her eyes. "Get going! They're waiting for you," he urged her to go. The crowd cheered while waving them in.

"Thank you," she whispered.

Matt smiled. "Go."

Elizabeth laughed. "Come on, boys, let's go home!"

"Wait," Matt spoke seriously, "Evan will be safer riding

beside me into that group. We'll meet you there."

"Evan, I'll see you in town, okay?" she asked quickly, not noticing the worried expression on his face. "Well," she laughed, "come on, Gabriel, I'll race you!" She kicked her horse and giggled her way past Gabriel. He kicked his horse and followed her quickly.

Matt couldn't help but to smile as he watched her race towards her family. Elizabeth pulled her horse to a stop and jumped out of the saddle and ran to meet Tom and her children. Tom and Elizabeth wrapped in a long and loving embrace.

Matt's eyes were misting slightly when he noticed Evan staring at him. "Are you nervous about going to your new home?" Matt asked to make conversation.

Evan shrugged. His wide blue eyes seemed lost in a puddle of anxious tears.

"Yeah, well, you'll do all right," Matt said awkwardly.

"Why are we waiting for those men?" Evan asked in a trembling voice. His voice grew weak and his face twisted painfully as he said, "I don't want to see Rodney like that."

Matt nodded quietly. "I want you to keep in mind that your brother is in heaven. He's in the presence of God Almighty now, Evan, not on that horse. Okay?"

Evan nodded sorrowfully.

Matt continued gently, "I need to talk to my cousin before riding into that crowd. I do apologize for forcing this on you, but for your own safety you need to ride beside me. Just don't look back," Matt gave his best advice.

Before long Charlie and William rode up beside them. William smiled when he saw the crowd. There was a loud cheer that arose for the riders bringing the dead. He looked over at Evan and said, "It looks like a party. It might be a hanging party!"

"William," Matt said shaking his head with a slight smile. "I haven't slept much in two nights and I'm tired. I'd appreciate it if you'd keep the newsmen away from me."

William grinned with pleasure. "I have a feeling they'll be playing cards and taking turns buying me drinks. You know my theory: if they want to get a story from me, they'd better be buying for me first!"

Matt looked at him sternly. "Don't say anything to the newsmen about Gabriel, William," Matt warned. "If you do, I'll tell them that you were too afraid to go after Donovan Moskin to begin with because he kicked your hide down south once before."

"What?" William scoffed. "That's not true and you know it!"

Matt smirked. "I know, but if I went to the papers they'd believe me and print it. Don't mention Gabriel at all, I mean it!" he warned.

"Matt, what the..."

Charlie broke in, "Boys, let's go home."

THE CROWD WAS like a thick wall of smiling faces clapping their hands and cheering for the man that saved the helpless lady. Evan rode between Matt and William as the four men entered town. None smiled, although William seemed to sit straighter.

A man with a badge stood in front of the crowd with his two deputies, each deputy held a shotgun in their hands. The lawman held up a hand to stop the tired riders and spoke proudly, "I'm Sheriff Tim Wright and I'm filling in for Sheriff Smith while he recuperates. I'll take the prisoner for you, the rest have their own picture stands right over there." He pointed at three empty wooden caskets leaning against the front of the livery stable. He continued, "It's an honor to welcome you home, Marshal." He stepped forward to take the reins of Evan's horse. Evan leaned towards Matt.

"Who are you?" Matt asked curtly.

"My name's Tim Wright, I'm the Branson Sheriff," he spoke louder with a friendly tone to be heard by the reporters in particular.

Matt wasn't smiling even though he felt the eyes of everyone on him. "There are no charges against this boy. He's free to go."

"What?" Tim asked loudly and then laughed uncomfortably. "From what I understand there's horse theft, breaking out of jail while kidnapping an innocent woman and three counts of murder. Those are some serious charges against him, I'd say."

"The men responsible for all of that are dead. This boy and his brother were victims as well."

"Well," Sheriff Wright said, beginning to sound nervous, "just the same, I'd better take him into custody until Judge Jacoby acquits him." Again he attempted to take the reins.

"Sheriff Wright," Matt stated, hardening his tone, "I told you there are..." he stopped to watch Elizabeth quickly moving forward through the crowd while holding her little daughter's hand. She was followed by Tom and the rest of her family. "Sheriff, he's not going to jail, he's coming home with me."

"What?" Tom stammered from behind her.

"What?" Sheriff Wright echoed Tom almost simultaneously.

"He's an orphan and I'm taking him in," Elizabeth explained.

Tom shook his head dumbfounded. "Whoa! What are

you talking about? He can't live with us. What are you thinking, Elizabeth?"

"I'm taking in Evan," Elizabeth answered Tom.

Matt interrupted after a yawn, "I'll take Evan out to the Big Z for now..."

Elizabeth turned toward Matt. "He's coming home with me, you know that! His home's with me."

"Lizzy," Matt said gently, "you are married: you both need to agree on that decision. Don't discuss it like this, not in front of this crowd. Go home and talk to Tom about it tonight, but don't do it here. Evan will be fine out at the Big Z." He nodded at Tom and then put his attention back on Sheriff Wright. "Sheriff, you can take the bodies, but if I hear that the boy's casket was left open for public display, I will personally come looking for you. I don't care what you do with the two men, but the boy's casket you'd better cover and cover it right now!" Matt finished with a stern voice.

Sheriff Wright nodded understandably. "What about the charges?"

"Charge the two dead men if you want to," he said simply and nudged his horse ahead through the crowd. He ignored all the people who patted his legs and asked dozens of questions. He led Evan's horse by the reins and rode silently through the crowd. He saw his family at the blacksmith shop patiently waiting for him and he made his way towards them.

"Marshal, aren't you going to tell us what happened?"

"How'd you get the best of the Moskin Gang?"

"Who's the boy?"

"Oh, they should have known better than to run from you, huh Marshal?"

"Hey, Matt, aren't you going to say anything?"

Matt looked at that reporter and answered, "No." It left

the reporter speechless enough to hear William call from the saloon door. "Anyone who wants to hear the story of how Matt and I saved the woman, come inside." The reporter from the Branson Gazette and the others, went to hear the story and seek out any details that they could gather to write an article upon.

Matt shook his head with a slight chuckle as he stopped his mare in front of the blacksmith shop. His Aunt Mary stood up from her chair. "Aunt Mary, this is Evan. He needs a place to stay for a few days..." he said with a yawn. "Now, if you don't mind, I'd like to go home."

As he rode beside Evan through town he noticed Reverend Ash and his wife, Darla, standing alone on their front porch waiting for him. As he neared, they stepped carefully down onto the packed snow-covered street to meet him. Matt stopped his horse and nodded at Missus Ash with a soft smile, she smiled pleasantly.

Reverend Ash looked up at Matt with watery eyes. "Matthew, I can't thank you enough for bringing my baby home. Matthew, will you come to the church service tomorrow? Please."

Matt looked over at the white church that was next door to the house and exhaled a deep breath. "I was kicked out of there, Reverend."

"Please," The Reverend repeated while he placed his hand on Matt's leg. He had the longing expression of a pleading child. "Promise me that you'll come tomorrow, please."

Matt nodded slightly. "I'll come," he sounded more skeptical than convinced.

"Thank you," Reverend Ash whispered. He watched as Matt led the rest of their family out of town, except for William, who was hosting a growing party in the saloon.

72

Matt yawned quietly as he sat in the back pew closest to the door between his Aunt Mary and sister Annie. Across the aisle Steven's family and Albert's family crowded together to fit into the pew. Other members of the family were mixed in with the rest of the congregation as Reverend Ash took his place in front of the wooden lectern.

Annie nudged his arm and whispered, "If you fall asleep in church, Aunt Mary's going to smack you silly!" She nodded with a smile.

Mary whispered across Matt to Annie, "And if you don't stop talking in church, I'll smack you!"

Matt laughed quietly. He looked at Annie with a wide smile to rub it in a little more.

Reverend Ash, from his lectern, was relieved to see Matt in attendance with his family. Though it was normally a disrespectful offense to him, he was glad to see Matt fooling around with his sister in the back pew. He smiled comfortingly to his wife, Darla, who was in her usual place in the front pew beside Elizabeth, with Tom and their children.

Reverend Ash opened his Bible and took a deep breath

before speaking. His voice was low and purposeful, "I've been working on this sermon for two weeks." He held up three pieces of paper filled with notes, then laid them down on the lectern. "It's about the Lord's grace and the many ways we don't appreciate it. I'm not giving that sermon today. It is far too inadequate for what the Lord has done for us in the past few days. Quite frankly, I don't have a sermon today, but what I do have is..." he paused to take a breath. He squeezed his lips together tightly before continuing, "What I do have is a lifetime of experiences, good ones and bad, but in the last few days, I've learned more about myself than I've ever wanted to know. Especially about my faults and the Lord has revealed many. If you'll bear with me, I'm going to share some of those with you."

He took a deep breath and exhaled before continuing, "Husbands, honor your wives. Treat her like the dove she is, gentlemen. Don't be harsh in word or by hand, but rather come along beside her and listen to what she has to say. Appreciate her, because, gentlemen, she is the heart and soul of your homes. She is the one who pours her heart into making your home shine from the inside out. If your home's not shining, then maybe you need put more effort into making her fire burn a little brighter, because gentlemen, we have a lot to do with how hot or cold that fire in our wife burns. We can build it up to a roaring blaze or we can put it out completely by how we treat her. A good place to start is don't ever profane her name in public or in private. She is your wife and should be treated as such, with respect, faithfulness and love. She is supposed to be your friend and partner in this life, and I hope she is your best friend. Men honor your wives."

He looked at his wife, Darla, momentarily. "I've been married for a long time, but I didn't honor my wife the way I should have. I've hurt her unknowingly, and yes, at times, uncaringly... and even deliberately. It is to my shame that I didn't love and appreciate her the way I do now that I am getting old. It's getting late into my seasons and I now understand how deeply I love and depend on Darla. And it really is to my shame that I didn't realize that years ago when I was younger. Men, now's your chance, honor your wives; never let her fear you in any way and always forgive her. Remember husbands, Jesus wrote the sins of the adulteress in the dust." He paused as he looked out over the congregation and then compassionately at Tom. "He didn't carve her sins, mistakes, or errors into stone, nor should we. Gentlemen, always be gentle with your wives."

He paused effectively. "Wives, honor your husbands. Encourage him with the strength of Samson, but correct him with the meekness of a fawn. Wives, honor your husbands; stand behind him as a pillar of strength that he can rely upon. Never discourage or undermine his God-given authority over your home, but rather strive to be the encourager, the listener, the friend, the faithful mate. It's been said that behind every great man is a greater woman. Ladies..." he spoke purposely, "you have the sensitive position of building up or tearing down your husband's ambition. I invite you to decide to build up your husband's character and pursuit of his dreams for your family."

He paused to look at his beloved wife before continuing, "Like my wife has done for me all these years. Thank you, Darla, for being all that you've been to me. I truly wouldn't be here today if it wasn't for you," he said with a sincere smile.

"Fathers, honor your children." He swallowed and bit his bottom lip tightly. "I raised my only God-given daughter with a strict hand. I did what I thought was best, and I did not spare the rod of discipline, but I did not discipline in love either." His tears grew thick in his eyes. "When Elizabeth was little, we had a service out on Pearl Creek. Elizabeth and some other kids disappeared and we all frantically went looking for them. When we found them, Elizabeth had ruined her white church dress and when we got home I gave her a beating." He took a deep breath and added softly, "Late that night as I sat in my den reading, Elizabeth entered my study and handed me this rock," his voice cracked as he held up the heart shaped rock. "'It's a heart,' she said..." he gasped. His voice grew high pitched as he tried not to sob, "I got it for you, Daddy, because I love you."

The Reverend struggled emotionally to continue, "I never gave her the opportunity to explain why she got her dress muddy, nor did I care. I was angry and punished my only baby for that reason alone, I was angry. I did exactly what the Bible says not to do; I embittered my child. I never said the words she needed to hear the most, Elizabeth, I love you." He looked into his daughter's eyes. "I've kept this rock on my desk ever since that day to remind me of that. These past few days I've held on to this rock with one hand and my faith in Jesus, my rock, in my other."

"Amen!" some of the congregation shouted joyfully.

"Fathers," the Reverend continued, "Honor your children. Every child longs to be loved by their father so tell your children that you love them. Gentlemen, you only have one chance to raise your child in a world that does not care about them. Take your responsibility seriously because God does! Teach your children what's right and wrong, hold them accountable for their actions and teach them to be responsible adults. Fathers, honor your children, discipline them, but do it in love. I urge you to spend time with them, play with them, listen to them, teach them, and let them know you love them because, believe me, when they're grown you'll wish you had! I do."

He wiped his eyes. "I've been the Reverend of this church for a long time. To my knowledge, I've always been regarded as a good man, hopefully, a Godly man." His eyes filled with moisture as he continued, "But I was a bad husband to my wife and a bad father to my daughter. I am so sorry, Darla. I'm sorry, Elizabeth," he said sincerely.

He wiped his eyes and focused back on the congregation and spoke frankly, "I have been a Reverend for almost forty years now. I entered the ministry because I felt led by the Lord to do so and I have never taken that responsibility lightly. The book of James makes it clear that teachers of the Lord's word will be held to a stricter judgment. Therefore, I have made it my life's mission to teach the truth, just as the Bible says it. As your shepherd I have given you Biblically sound doctrine to the best of my ability and I will continue to do so even when it's uncomfortable and unpopular. That being said, there's another part to being a Reverend of a congregation and that's the responsibility of a shepherd is to watch over his flock. I've had the privilege of serving the Willow Falls Christian Church for thirty-four years. I have been woken up in the middle of the night numerous times to help the people of this town when they needed me. I have chased after and brought back the lost sheep and I have snuffed out the dissention of gossip before it fractured our church in two. I have been aggressive in protecting our little church from certain kinds of people who would want to compromise my teachings for the surface of the Gospel, not the depth of Christian living. I have dedicated my life to being a good shepherd."

He looked down at the lectern and looked back up at the congregation. "In all of the years that I've been in the ministry, I've been needed a lot. But some years ago one young man in particular needed me more than anyone ever has and I abandoned him. I won't go into the details, but when he came knocking on my doorstep I rejected him. I chased him out of our flock into the wilderness where quite frankly, I didn't care what happened to him. If I ever hated someone... it was Matt Bannister." He stopped to look at the congregation, they were listening intently. Matt stared down at the floor without any expression on his face.

The Reverend's breathing grew heavy. "The Lord has made some things very clear to me lately. One of them is that I punished a young man who had gone through enough. I shunned him and encouraged the church to reject him as well, which is... wrong. The book of James talks about the power of the tongue and the untold damage it can cause when it's not controlled. The book of James also says that God is the judge, not me. I had no right to slander you, Matt, but I did." His lips pressed together tightly as he took another deep breath and said with a higher pitched voice, "Matthew, I was wrong; and I hope you can forgive me. I have no excuse for my actions, except that I was a self-right-eous fool. The damage is done, I know, and there's nothing I can do about that now, but I do need you to know that I am truly sorry," he said with a tear rolling down his cheek.

The Reverend wiped his eyes and continued, "Open your Bibles to First Samuel, chapter 16, verse 7. In the middle of the verse it says,

'The Lord does not look at the things man looks at. Man looks at the outward appearance, but the Lord looks at the heart.'"

He looked up at the congregation. "We all know that don't we? Well, that also applies to situations too. What we see and gossip about is casting judgment on someone for something that just might be part of Gods plan for that person. Take Joseph for an example, he was sold into slavery and eventually thrown into prison, some would say he must have deserved it, but he did not. He was an innocent and Godly man. Job lost everything, his finances, his family and his health, and his friends condemned him for it. We know Job had done nothing wrong to deserve what was happening, in fact he was a righteous man. So righteous in fact that God pointed that out to Satan."

He paused. "I condemned a young man for doing something that I couldn't understand and didn't agree with. I cast judgment upon him because of what I *could see* and then true to the book of James, I cursed him to others with my tongue. Do you see how it all ties together? I was looking at the outside, and what I saw I didn't like, so I bluntly condemned it! But the Lord saw his heart! And thank God He did because Matt Bannister is a Godly man no matter what I have told you all in the past." Another tear slid down his cheek as he spoke softly, "This is precisely what it means in First Samuel when it says, *Man looks at the outward appearance, but the Lord looks at the heart.* Might I suggest we leave the judging to Jesus and start saying instead, 'that's between them and God' rather than tearing people down and condemning them for something we may not know everything about. I dare say it, we Christians tend to gossip foolishly, and foolish gossip tears people, friendships, relationships and churches apart. The tongue... yes, even our own tongue can destroy another person's faith, hope, or life. Let us not be guilty of that from this point forward, and strive to encourage others no matter how a situation may appear, because it could be God's plan for them and have nothing to do with their conduct or heart. Let us not condemn, but love and encourage them."

He paused to address Matt. "Matthew, I ask you to

forgive me. I don't know how many lives you have saved since you left here. I do know that you saved Elizabeth's life and I thank God for bringing you home this Christmas. I'm under the heavy conviction that the Lord's placed you in your position and given you all of your experiences, so you could save the life of our daughter, and I thank you for that. I owe you more than I could ever repay and I just hope you will accept my apology and feel welcome to come back to our community and our church. God bless you."

The congregation stood up in unison and applauded while turning to face him in the back row. Matt stood awkwardly and waved shyly while stepping out into the aisle and towards the door. Aunt Mary reached over quickly and tugged at his coat-tail, "Where are you going?"

Matt leaned down and spoke softly, "I need to go. I'll be back at the ranch later." His eyes were slightly moist, and he seemed eager to leave.

"I'll come with you," Annie stated.

"No, I want to be alone," he said and cast one last glance at Reverend Ash before walking towards the door.

"Matthew," Reverend Ash's deep voice called out, stopping him at the door. "If I've offended you, I didn't mean to. I was hoping for a new beginning."

Matt shook his head slowly. "You didn't offend me, Reverend. I'm just... I have to go," he said quickly and walked out before the Reverend could respond. The congregation stood in an awkward silence looking towards the door.

Reverend Ash revealed the disappointment in his voice, "Let's pray." He hoped Matt would forgive him some day and once again take a welcomed seat as a member of his congregation.

73

Tom Smith had a pretty fair idea of where Matt had gone when he saw the direction of his horse tracks. Unable to ride horseback himself, he asked Darius to drive him out to Pearl Creek on his wagon. As Tom had guessed, Matt's horse, was tied to a tree, atop the brushy bank of the swimming hole where Joseph was killed. Darius remained on the wagon while Tom slowly and carefully walked down the trail to the river. Matt leaned against a fallen tree in Lee's dark suit with his hands in his pockets. He stared at the big old willow tree that Joseph had been hung from. A new rope was tied to the same branch for a younger generation to swing off of.

"You look like a banker, standing there," Tom stated, trying to sound friendly. "I thought I might find you here."

Matt nodded wordlessly. He asked pointedly with a nod at the tree, "It hasn't changed much, has it?"

"No. In the summer it all looks exactly the same as it did. Kids swing out over the water and have a great time just like we used to."

"You'd never know something so wicked happened here,

would you?" Matt asked while staring at the big thick branch that went out over the water.

"No."

"So what'd you come out here for?" Matt asked in a distant voice that was neither friendly nor unfriendly.

Tom sounded unsure of himself as he answered, "I guess, I wanted to talk to you."

"About?"

"I wanted to thank you for bringing Elizabeth home. I couldn't have done it, no matter how much I wanted to," he admitted.

"You're welcome," Matt answered quickly. He looked at Tom for the first time. "Are you taking Evan in?"

Tom took a deep breath. "I guess. I don't know how it will all work out, but Elizabeth's persistent that he's moving in." He paused, "I knew she wanted to take both of those boys home the first time she laid eyes on them. So, who knows, maybe it will be fine, we'll see."

"He's a good kid, and he needs a family. He doesn't have anyone anymore."

"I know," was all Tom said.

There was an awkward silence that seemed to create more tension with each uncomfortable passing second. "What's on your mind?" Matt asked, knowing there was something more Tom wanted to say.

"Well," Tom began, "what are your plans?"

Matt shook his head slowly. "I don't make many plans Tom, I haven't in a long time."

"Are you going back to Wyoming?" Tom asked pointedly.

Matt took a deep breath and sighed irritably. "Yeah, I'm going back after New Year's, I already told you that. You didn't have to come all the way out here to ask me again." He looked at Tom scornfully and added, "I'll try not to kill anyone in the meantime."

Tom laughed to himself as he shook his head. "Matt, I didn't come here to run you out of town. We both know even if I tried, I couldn't do it, anyway. I came here to clear the slate between us. You know three days ago I was losing my family because of you. Learning that Gabriel was your son and not mine is pretty... hard." Tom's tone changed to one of emotional effort, "I guess, I always knew it, but I never believed it until Elizabeth... admitted it."

Matt's body seemed to sag heavily against the fallen tree as he looked down at the ground shamefully.

Tom continued, "You betrayed me, Matt, and you know it. Even though we weren't necessarily friends at the time, I was still her husband, and you both betrayed me."

Matt nodded agreeing.

"Three days ago, I swore I'd never forgive her or you. But when those men took her... Elizabeth, and I stayed up all night talking and... I forgave her. I love her too much not to forgive her. Gabriel will always be my son, nothing's going to change that, he's my son, he's my boy. But, I have to forgive you too. If I don't, I will get bitter and that bitterness will drive a wedge into my family and I won't allow that to happen. So, for what it's worth, Matt, I forgive you for betraying me. From this point on, I won't bring it up again. I forgive you, Matt," Tom finished softly.

Matt wiped his eyes and looked at Tom with a tight-lipped effort not to weep, his tears were thick and heavy in his eyes.

Tom stepped forward holding out his right hand. "Friends?"

Matt took his hand in a firm grip and shook it. As he

wiped his eyes again he laughed slightly. "I must've got something in my eyes."

Tom let go of Matt's hand and nodded. "Sometimes I get something in my eyes down here too." He looked around at the swimming hole and spoke, "You know Matt, we just need to let the past go right here where it started. We need to leave this place free from the garbage we've both carried with us for all these years. Don't you think? Maybe we can both sleep better at night if we just let it go."

Matt looked at the rope hanging from the limb and then looked at Tom seriously. "Thank you, Tom. I think that's a good idea."

Tom shrugged slightly and then grimaced with pain from his shoulder. "Let's get out of here and talk about a new beginning. Branson's growing like a weed and worse and worse people are coming farther West. We could use you to help keep the peace around here."

Matt chuckled. "I don't know how content I'd be, being the Willow Falls deputy," Matt said half-heartedly.

Tom laughed. "Well if another Donovan Moskin comes through town and takes someone else, we're going to need you, and that's the truth."

Matt searched Tom's eyes questionably. "You want me to stay around here?"

"No, I need you to stay here. The county needs you to stay here, and I came to ask you to stay here."

Matt frowned. "I..."

Tom interrupted, "How'd you like the sermon today?" he asked changing the subject quickly.

Matt shook his head. "It was nice... I never expected to hear it."

"The Lord works in wonderful ways, Matt. I never

dreamed I'd hear it either. Nor did I ever think I'd invite you to come home with me, but Elizabeth's making a big lunch and is expecting me to bring you home." Tom paused to let the words sink in, then he added, "My little ones and Gabriel all want to thank you in person. Will you come home with me?"

Matt smiled and his eyes grew moist again. "Yeah, that sounds nice... real nice."

74

Business was always good for Marcus Swindall, but this Christmas season was better than most. The kidnapping and rescue over in Willow Falls had been huge news and sparked new interest in his book, *"The Biography of Matt Bannister"*. Marcus had sold at least two-dozen copies of the book since then, but it had now been two weeks since the rescue and the excitement was dying down. Marcus, like everyone else, read the papers and one reporter in particular made the observation that Willow Falls was a bad resting place for outlaws. On that idea, Marcus decided to rewrite his biography of Matt Bannister.

Of course, he'd have to keep some of the stories of the marshal's life the same, but he could offer a tidbit of new information that recently came to light about the famous Pearl Creek gunfight. Perhaps, he could liven up the romance a little by portraying the kids half nude as they swam unsupervised or he could portray that Joseph kid as deaf and dumb perhaps, and Matt as the long arm of justice. The ideas flowed, but he wanted to hurry and get the finished work in print before the excitement of the most recent story died completely.

Matt Bannister was a sellable market in Branson. His roots were here and being a local boy, everyone took an interest in the famous lawman. Marcus had sold his book locally in his store, but when his new and improved edition was completed, he hoped to sell it nation-wide. It would be a unique biography in the fact that it was written by, as he put it, "a hometown friend who watched Matt grow up." It wasn't exactly true, but who would know the difference in New York City or Dallas, Texas. It was a book meant to feed an action-starved public and at sixty-five cents a copy for the new hard-cover, expanded edition, Marcus Swindall would soon be living next door to Lee Bannister. He could wave good morning to Lee, while wearing his own suit and riding in his own black buggy with a hired driver, or at least, he dreamed to be.

"There you go, Hank. Tell the missus hello for me," Marcus said as a customer finished paying for a few dry items for his wife. Two ladies were in line behind the parting gentleman, one of them set an item on the counter to purchase. She asked, "Mister Swindall, when will you be getting more of that gray flannel? Jim desperately needs a new shirt."

"Soon. I ordered it two weeks ago and I'm expecting it soon. When it arrives, I'll save the first cutting for you," he replied cheerfully. Business was good.

"I'd so thank you," she said.

"It's my pleasure." He cast his eyes at the gentleman who'd been slowly shopping. He was dressed in a long buffalo hide coat with a thick wide hood that covered his head. He was now looking at blankets. Marcus had to watch people, especially strangers, because not everyone was honest and this man acted suspicious. He kept his back to the shopkeeper for the most part and appeared to be a down on his luck old buffalo hunter by the look of his heavy coat. He probably trying to steal something and needed to be watched. As Marcus looked, he noticed that the stranger wore leather moccasins on his feet and he sighed inwardly. "You ladies have a wonderful day," he said to the departing women. His attention went to the displaced Indian who probably didn't have a dime to his name. "Can I help you find something?" he asked tartly.

The stranger turned to face Marcus. He pulled his hood back with his left hand, revealing his face while his right hand slipped inside his coat and pulled out his Colt revolver. The motions were quick, too quick! All Marcus saw was a glimpse of fluid motion and then he stood staring at the barrel of a pistol. Behind it was a set of hard and dangerous brown eyes.

Marcus froze in immediate terror. "Please don't shoot! Look, you can have the money... you can have it all... just please don't shoot!" he begged.

Matt asked harshly, "Are you Marcus Swindle?"

"Swindall. Yes, I am, sir," he admitted carefully after correcting the pronunciation of his name.

"I have the right man then," Matt remarked and pulled the hammer back on his Colt with his thumb. The hammer clicked loudly. It remained pointed at Marcus.

"Please! Take anything you want, I won't say a word, please just don't kill me," Marcus begged. He raised his hands in surrendering fashion to the gunman.

"Did you write those books?" Matt demanded as he pointed his finger at a display rack of "Biography of Matt Bannister" books that were on the counter to the right of Marcus.

"Yes... yes I did," Marcus admitted. "Why?" he added as a second thought.

Quickly, Matt's pistol left Marcus and aimed at the rack of books and fired. The rack of books exploded off the counter. Marcus screamed in terror and looked at the shredded books as they scattered across the floor. He looked back at the stranger who again had his gun pointed at him. Marcus was too petrified to move although his body trembled when he began to weep and beg for his life.

Matt pulled his coat back with his left hand and revealed his silver star pinned to his shirt lapel. With his revolver still leveled at Marcus, he said, "I'm Matt Bannister. Mister Swindle, if I ever read my name in one of your books again, it'll be you I shoot! I can't stand people like you who write lies and twisted truths! And just so you know it, Joseph was my friend, my best friend! Remember what I said, because I'm not going anywhere and I'll be around!" He holstered his revolver and walked to the door, and then looked back at Marcus, who stared at him with a horrified expression. "Have a good day, Mister Swindall," Matt said with a smile before stepping outside into a growing crowd of curious and frightened onlookers. Matt climbed onto his mare and spoke to the crowd of concerned citizens, "Marcus Swindall is out of the book writing business," he explained.

He gave a friendly nod and then rode away as they ran into the store to check on Mister Swindall. Matt smiled a very free and contented smile, one he hadn't known in years.... A bit more than fifteen, to be exact.

A LOOK AT: SWEETHOME (MATT BANNISTER WESTERN 2)

Welcome to Sweethome, a town owned by the cruel Thacker family.

This sweeping western novel exposes town corruption to religious persecution. From the world of professional boxing to the farthest northern logging camps and the human suffering and tragedies in between, Sweethome is written to answer the age old question: Can any good come out of tragedy?

There is hope for those who believe.

COMING SOON from Ken Pratt and CKN Christian Publishing

ABOUT THE AUTHOR

Ken Pratt and his wife, Cathy, have been married for 22 years and are blessed with five children and six grandchildren. They live on the Oregon Coast where they are raising the youngest of their children. Though the Pratts have had many trials over the years, in 2012 Cathy, a prospering realtor at the time, was diagnosed with Early Onset Alzheimer's at the age of 45. Kenneth, otherwise known as "Ken" says, "We just take it one day at a time and enjoy the time we have with her. I believe that's why people can connect with the characters I write about. We all go through hard times and wonder if life will ever get any better when everything appears to be so dark. I have seen the providence of God work in my life many times. It is my greatest desire to write stories that bring hope to the reader, no matter what they are going through. Life can get tough, but hope is always available if we learn to trust Jesus, and wait on Him."

Ken Pratt grew up in the small farming community of Dayton, Oregon. He worked through his school years on a farm and ventured to Petersburg, Alaska at the age of sixteen to work in a salmon cannery. It was a summer job he would keep for the next four years. He has worked as a gas station attendant, at a fertilizer plant, cheese factory, a warehouseman, a high school wrestling coach, manufacturing equipment, underground construction, steel mill, funeral director/embalmer, retirement community, and building maintenance.

Ken worked to make a living, but his passion has always been writing. Having a busy family, the only "free" time he had to write was late at night getting no more than five hours of sleep a night. He has penned several novels that are being published along with several children stories as well. Ken Pratt says, "If you want something bad enough, you'll sacrifice something else to get it. I sacrifice sleep. I do not write to be a best seller or for wealth, I write to bring hope into the lives of the hopeless and encourage the disheartened through the lives of the characters and God's providence in my stories. There is always 'Hope' and that is the purpose of my books."

Find Ken Pratt at:
http://christiankindlenews.com/our-authors/ken-pratt/

Made in the USA
Coppell, TX
01 November 2021